NO IVY LEAGUE

HAZEL NEWLEVANT

ROAR™

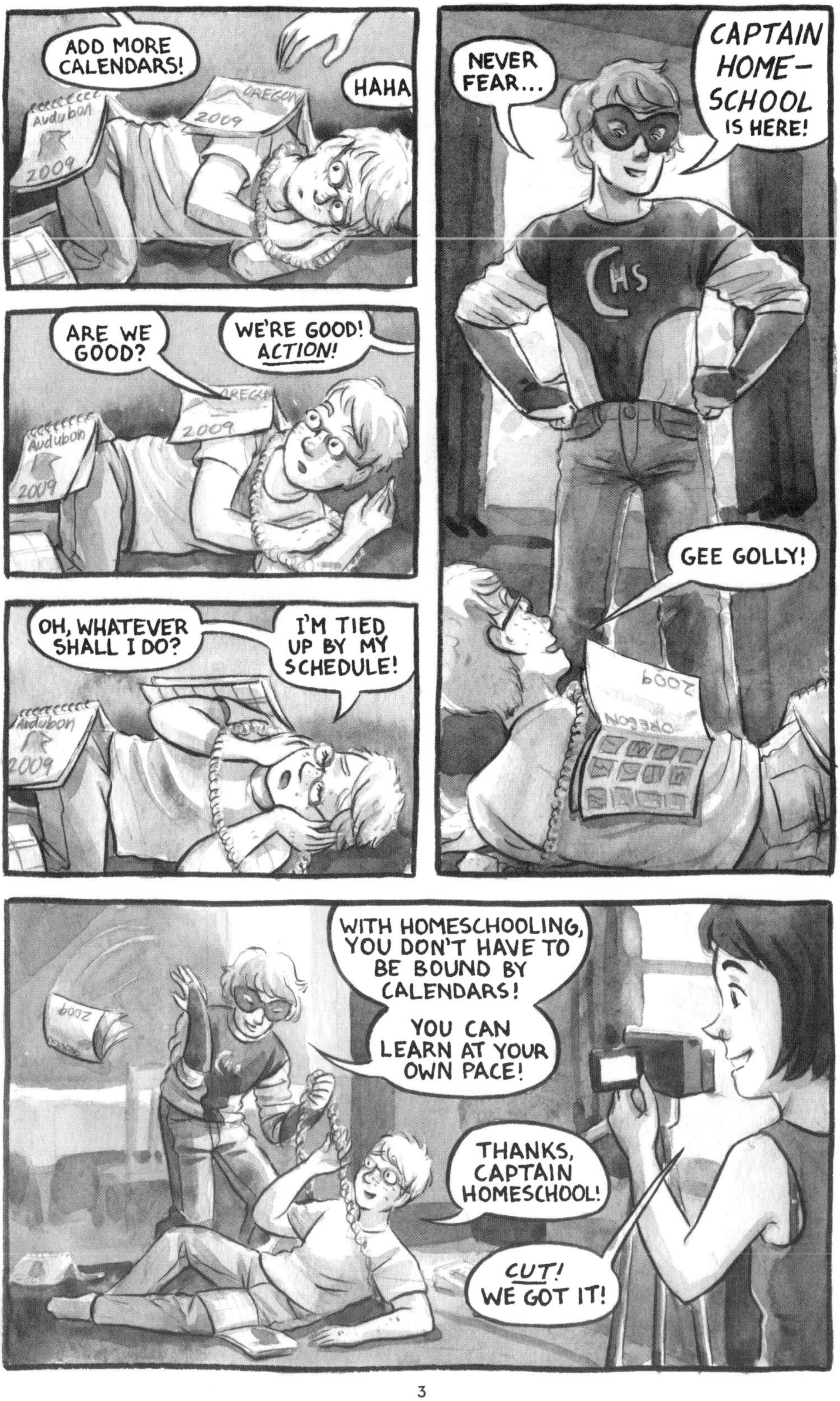
ADD MORE CALENDARS!
HAHA
Audubon 2009
OREGON 2009
NEVER FEAR...
CAPTAIN HOME-SCHOOL IS HERE!
CHS
ARE WE GOOD?
WE'RE GOOD! ACTION!
OH, WHATEVER SHALL I DO?
I'M TIED UP BY MY SCHEDULE!
GEE GOLLY!
WITH HOMESCHOOLING, YOU DON'T HAVE TO BE BOUND BY CALENDARS!
YOU CAN LEARN AT YOUR OWN PACE!
THANKS, CAPTAIN HOMESCHOOL!
CUT! WE GOT IT!

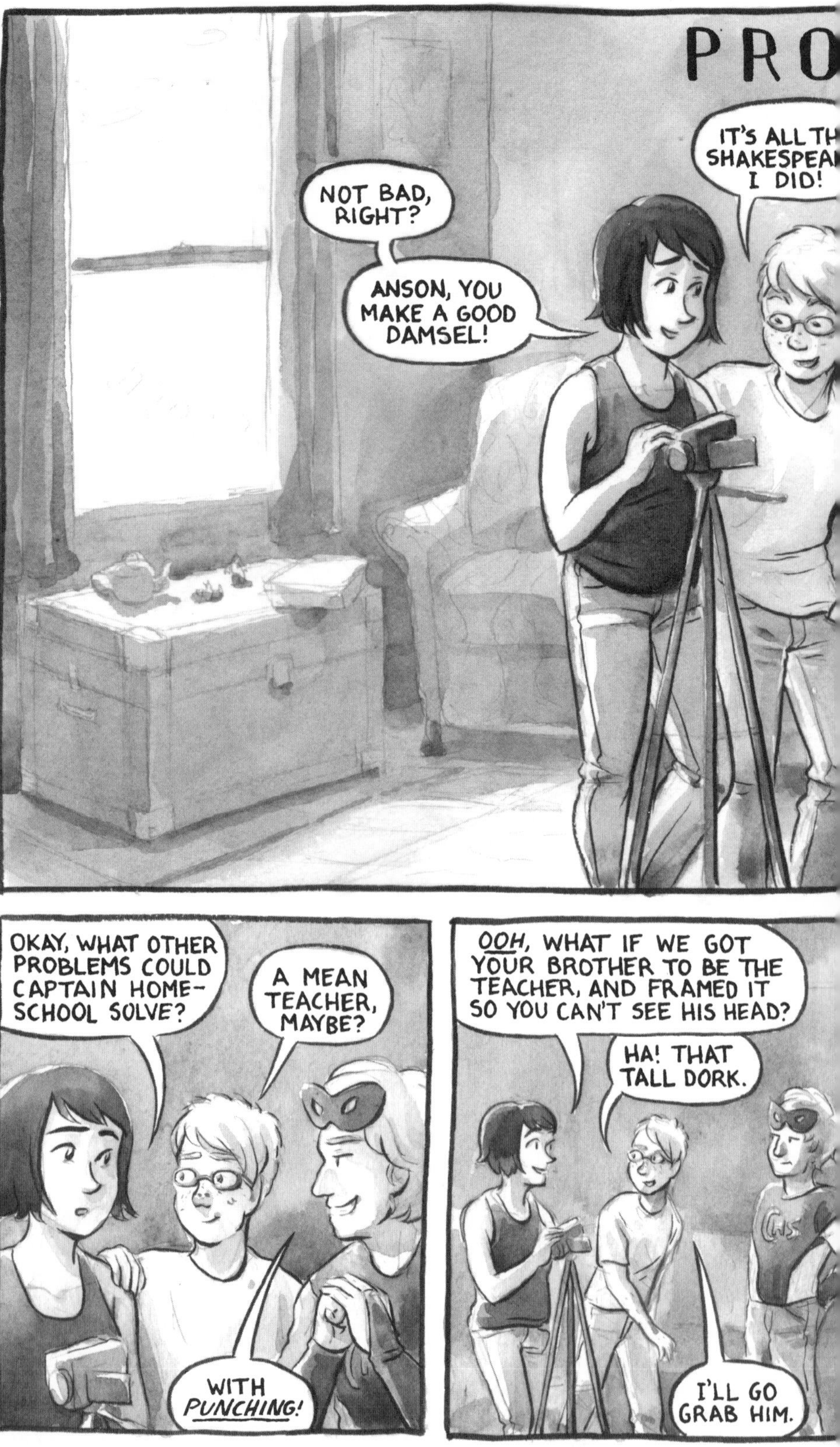
PRO
NOT BAD, RIGHT?
ANSON, YOU MAKE A GOOD DAMSEL!
IT'S ALL TH
SHAKESPEA
I DID!
OKAY, WHAT OTHER PROBLEMS COULD CAPTAIN HOME-SCHOOL SOLVE?
A MEAN TEACHER, MAYBE?
WITH PUNCHING!
OOH, WHAT IF WE GOT YOUR BROTHER TO BE THE TEACHER, AND FRAMED IT SO YOU CAN'T SEE HIS HEAD?
HA! THAT TALL DORK.
I'LL GO GRAB HIM.

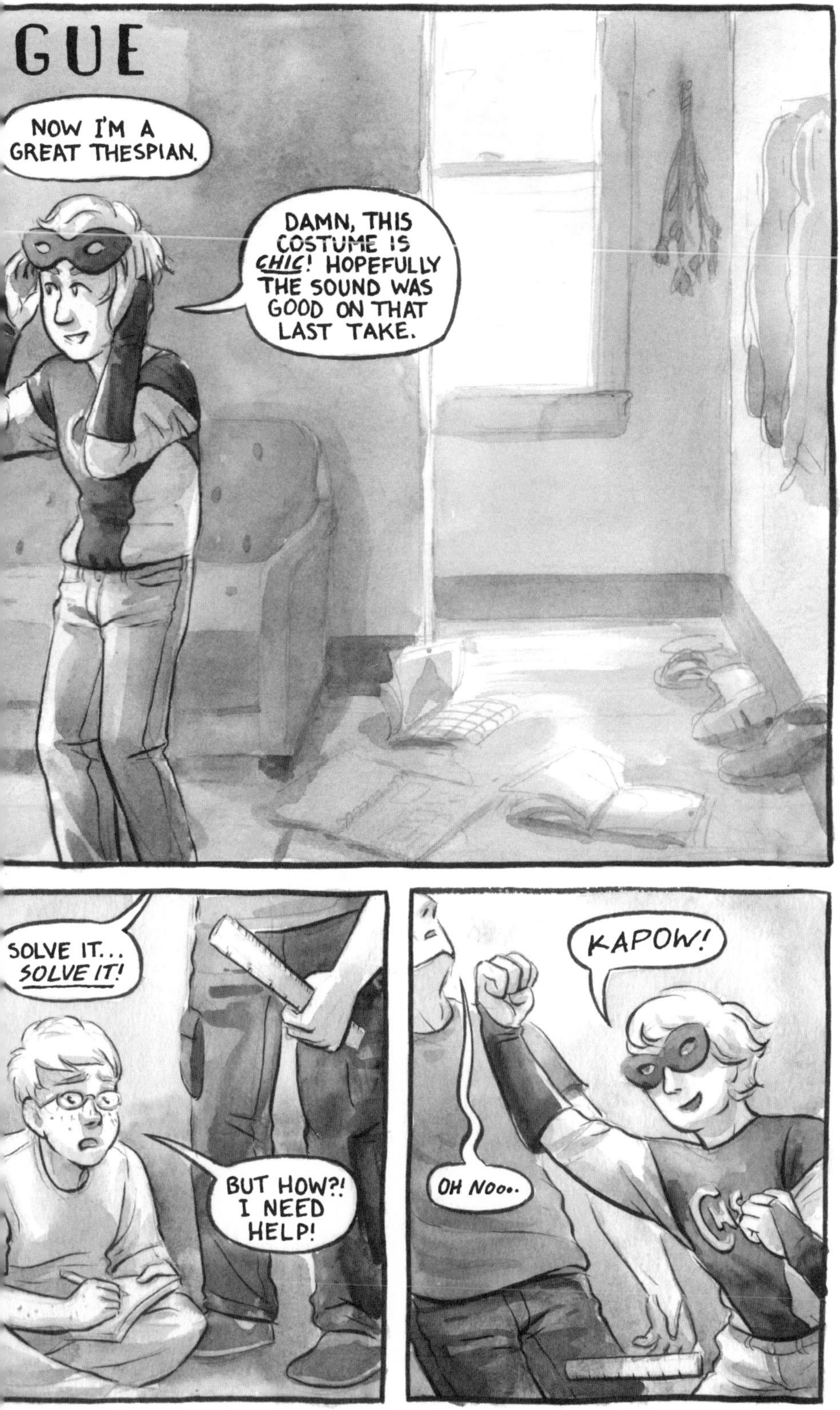
GUE
NOW I'M A GREAT THESPIAN.
DAMN, THIS COSTUME IS CHIC! HOPEFULLY THE SOUND WAS GOOD ON THAT LAST TAKE.
SOLVE IT... SOLVE IT!
BUT HOW?! I NEED HELP!
KAPOW!
OH Noo..

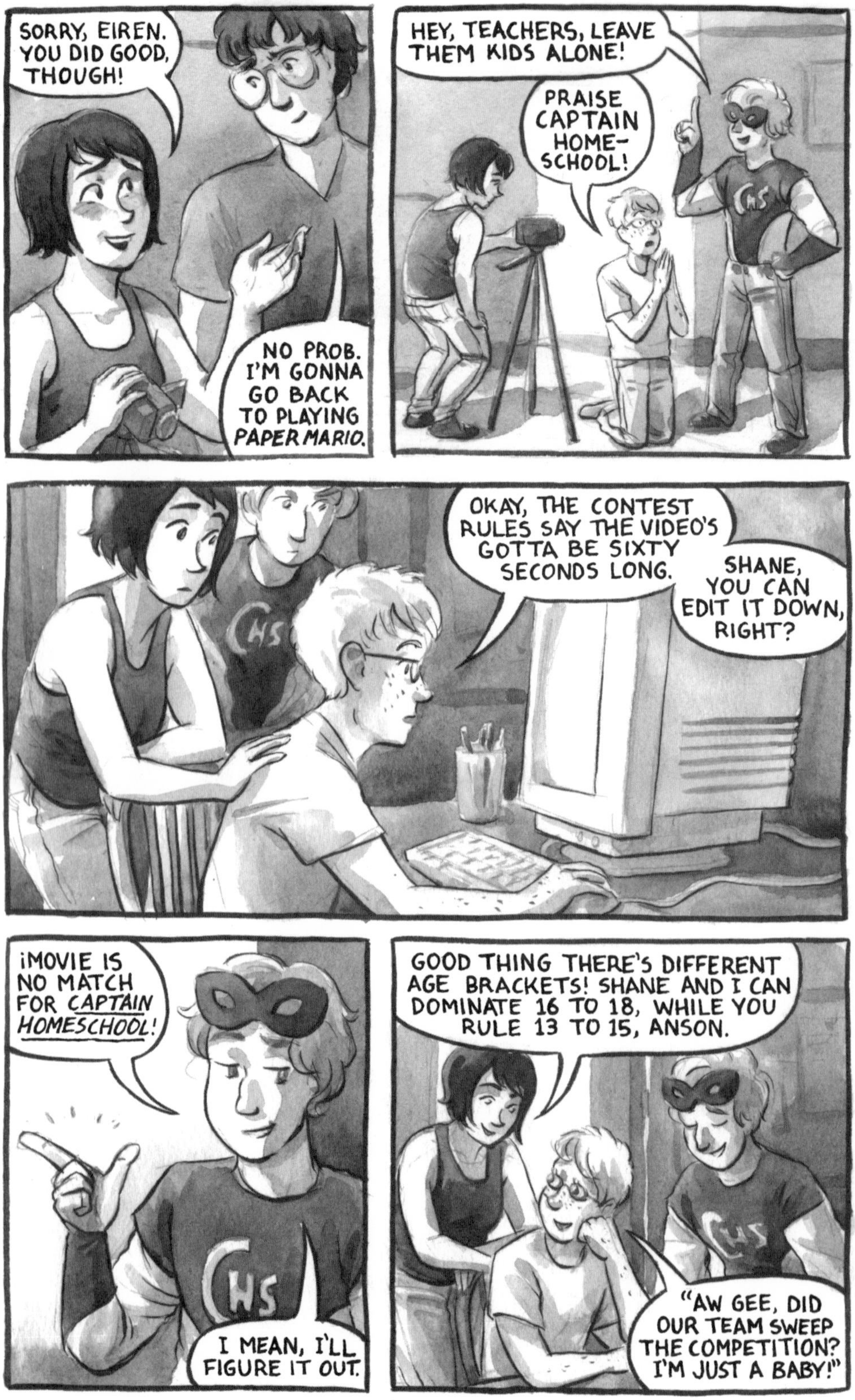
SORRY, EIREN. YOU DID GOOD, THOUGH!
NO PROB. I'M GONNA GO BACK TO PLAYING *PAPER MARIO.*
HEY, TEACHERS, LEAVE THEM KIDS ALONE!
PRAISE CAPTAIN HOME-SCHOOL!
OKAY, THE CONTEST RULES SAY THE VIDEO'S GOTTA BE SIXTY SECONDS LONG.
SHANE, YOU CAN EDIT IT DOWN, RIGHT?
¡MOVIE IS NO MATCH FOR *CAPTAIN HOMESCHOOL*!
I MEAN, I'LL FIGURE IT OUT.
GOOD THING THERE'S DIFFERENT AGE BRACKETS! SHANE AND I CAN DOMINATE 16 TO 18, WHILE YOU RULE 13 TO 15, ANSON.
"AW GEE, DID OUR TEAM SWEEP THE COMPETITION? I'M JUST A BABY!"

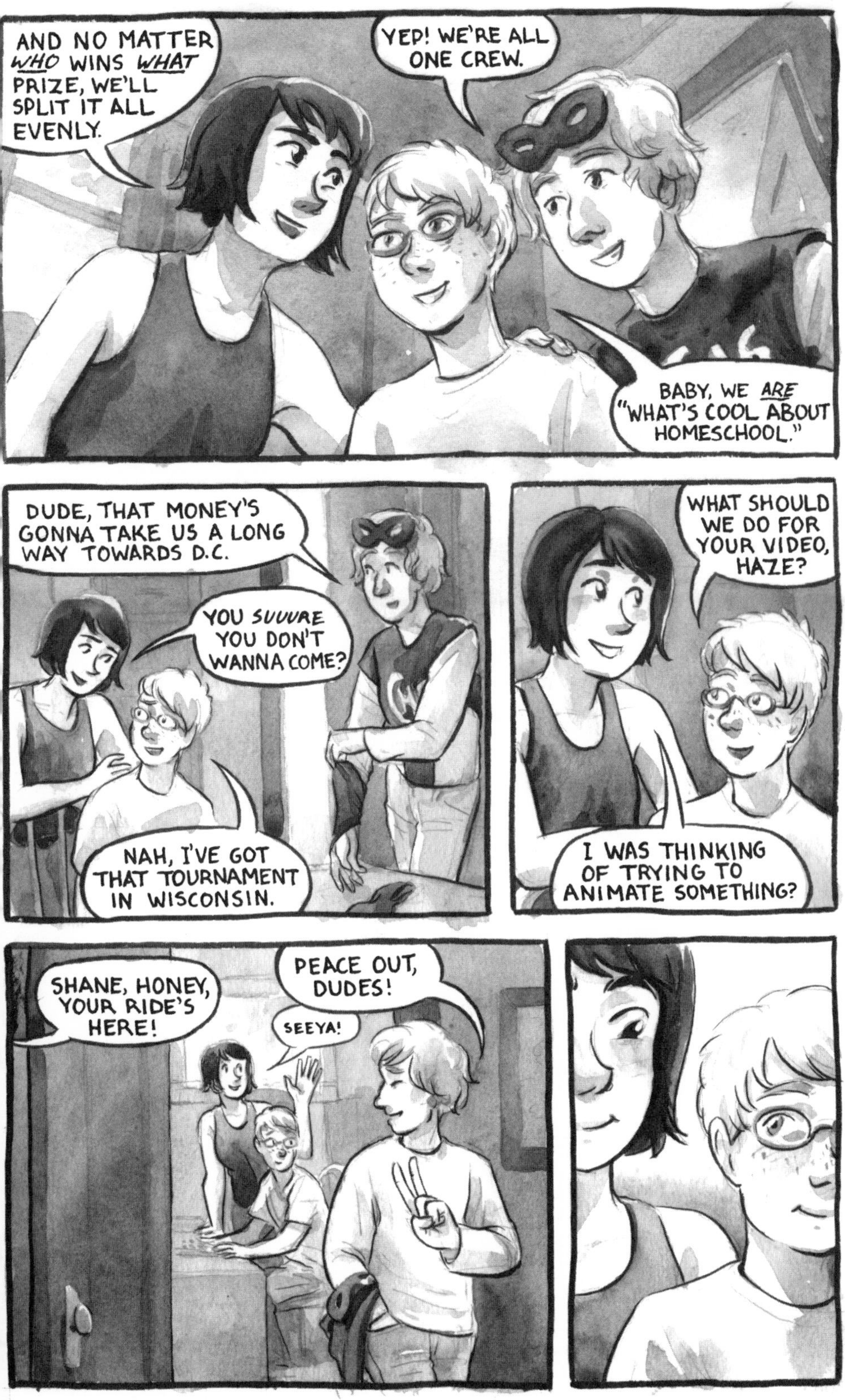

AND NO MATTER WHO WINS WHAT PRIZE, WE'LL SPLIT IT ALL EVENLY.
YEP! WE'RE ALL ONE CREW.
BABY, WE ARE "WHAT'S COOL ABOUT HOMESCHOOL."
DUDE, THAT MONEY'S GONNA TAKE US A LONG WAY TOWARDS D.C.
YOU SUUURE YOU DON'T WANNA COME?
NAH, I'VE GOT THAT TOURNAMENT IN WISCONSIN.
WHAT SHOULD WE DO FOR YOUR VIDEO, HAZE?
I WAS THINKING OF TRYING TO ANIMATE SOMETHING?
SHANE, HONEY, YOUR RIDE'S HERE!
PEACE OUT, DUDES!
SEEYA!

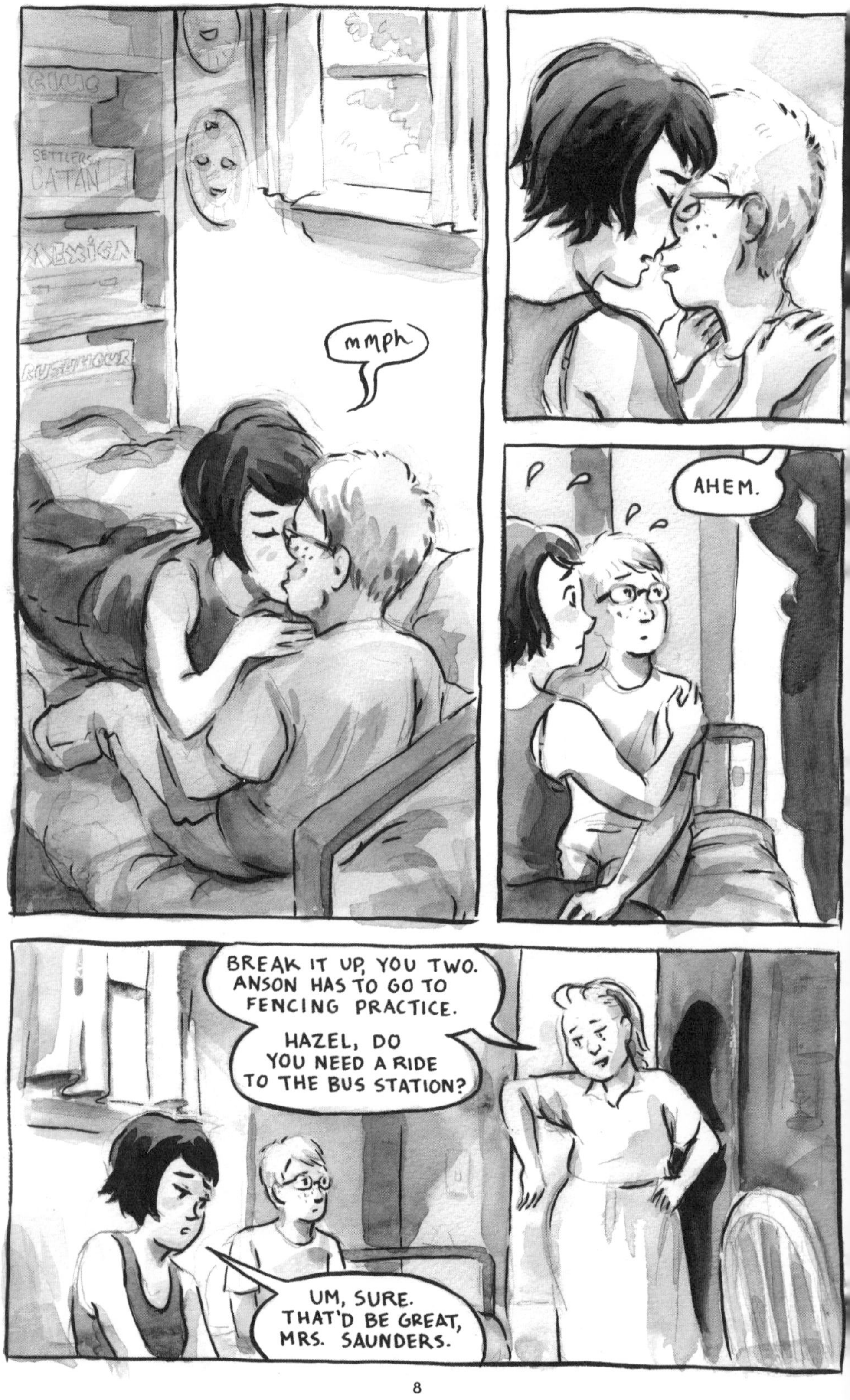
mmph
AHEM.
BREAK IT UP, YOU TWO. ANSON HAS TO GO TO FENCING PRACTICE.
HAZEL, DO YOU NEED A RIDE TO THE BUS STATION?
UM, SURE. THAT'D BE GREAT, MRS. SAUNDERS.

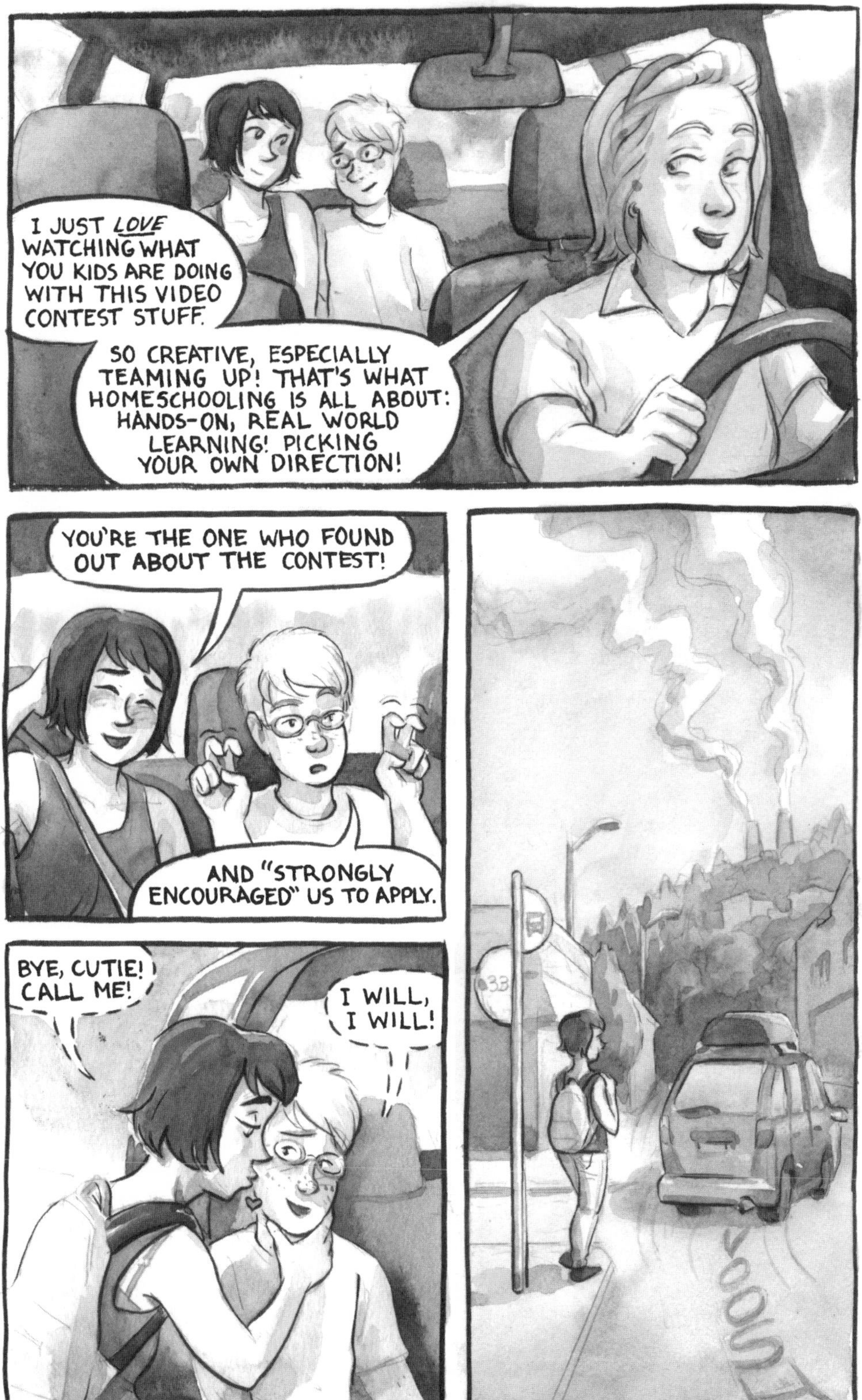
I JUST LOVE WATCHING WHAT YOU KIDS ARE DOING WITH THIS VIDEO CONTEST STUFF.
SO CREATIVE, ESPECIALLY TEAMING UP! THAT'S WHAT HOMESCHOOLING IS ALL ABOUT: HANDS-ON, REAL WORLD LEARNING! PICKING YOUR OWN DIRECTION!
YOU'RE THE ONE WHO FOUND OUT ABOUT THE CONTEST!
AND "STRONGLY ENCOURAGED" US TO APPLY.
BYE, CUTIE! CALL ME!
I WILL, I WILL!
33

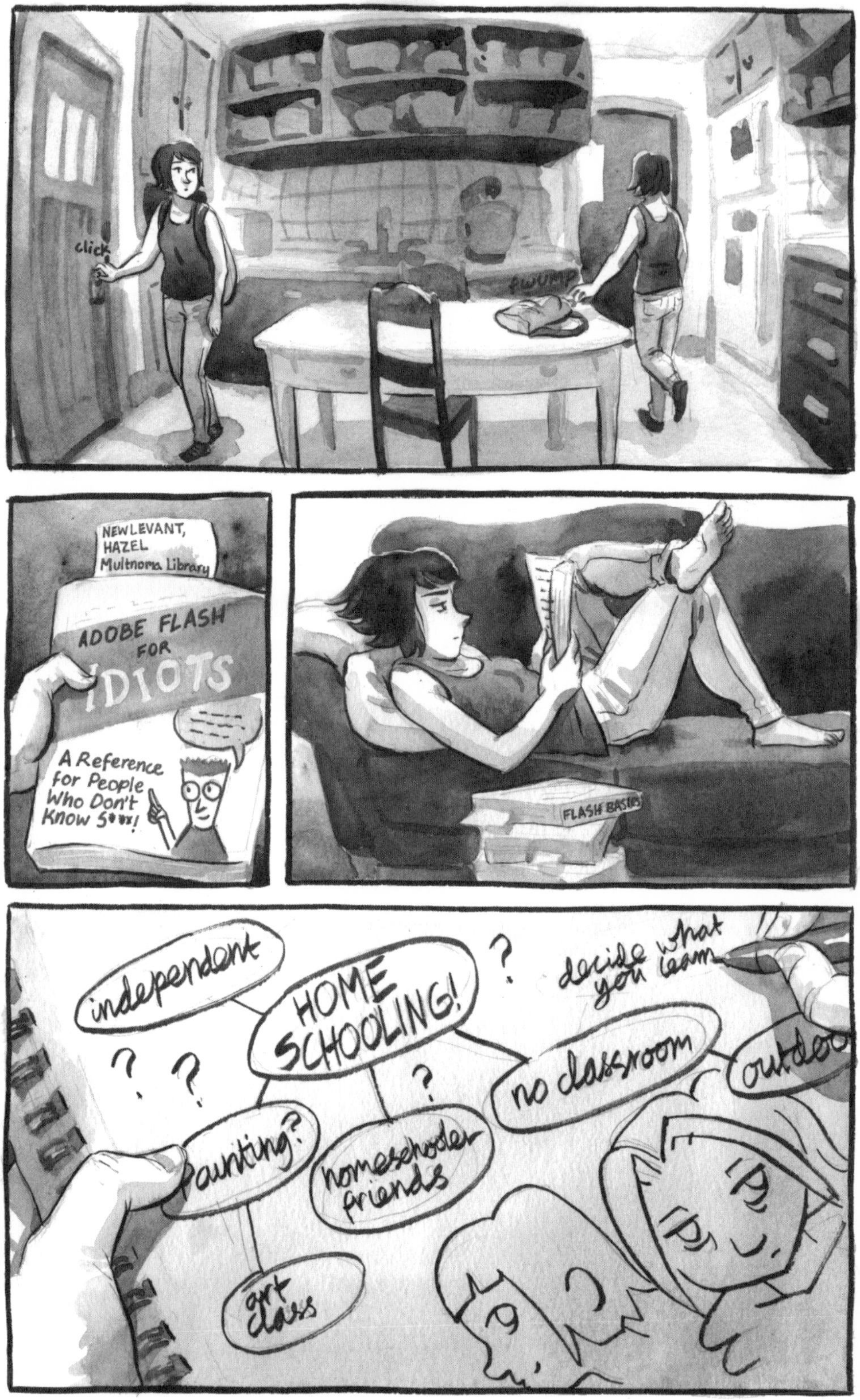
click
fwump
NEWLEVANT, HAZEL
Multnoma Library
ADOBE FLASH FOR IDIOTS
A Reference for People Who Don't Know S**x!
FLASH BASICS
HOME SCHOOLING!
independent
decide what you learn
no classroom
outdoo
painting?
homeschooler friends
art class

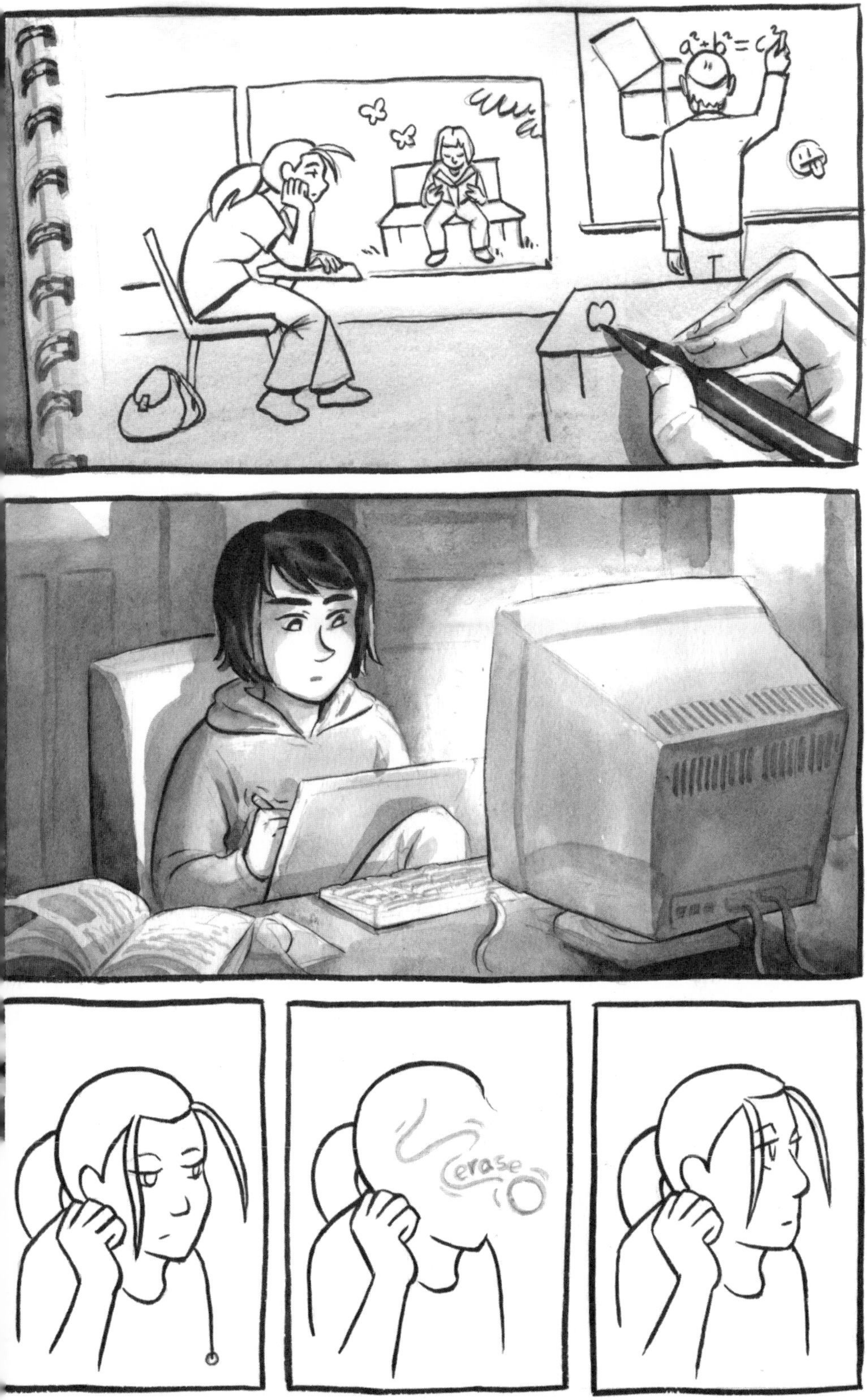

$a^2+b^2=c^2$
erase

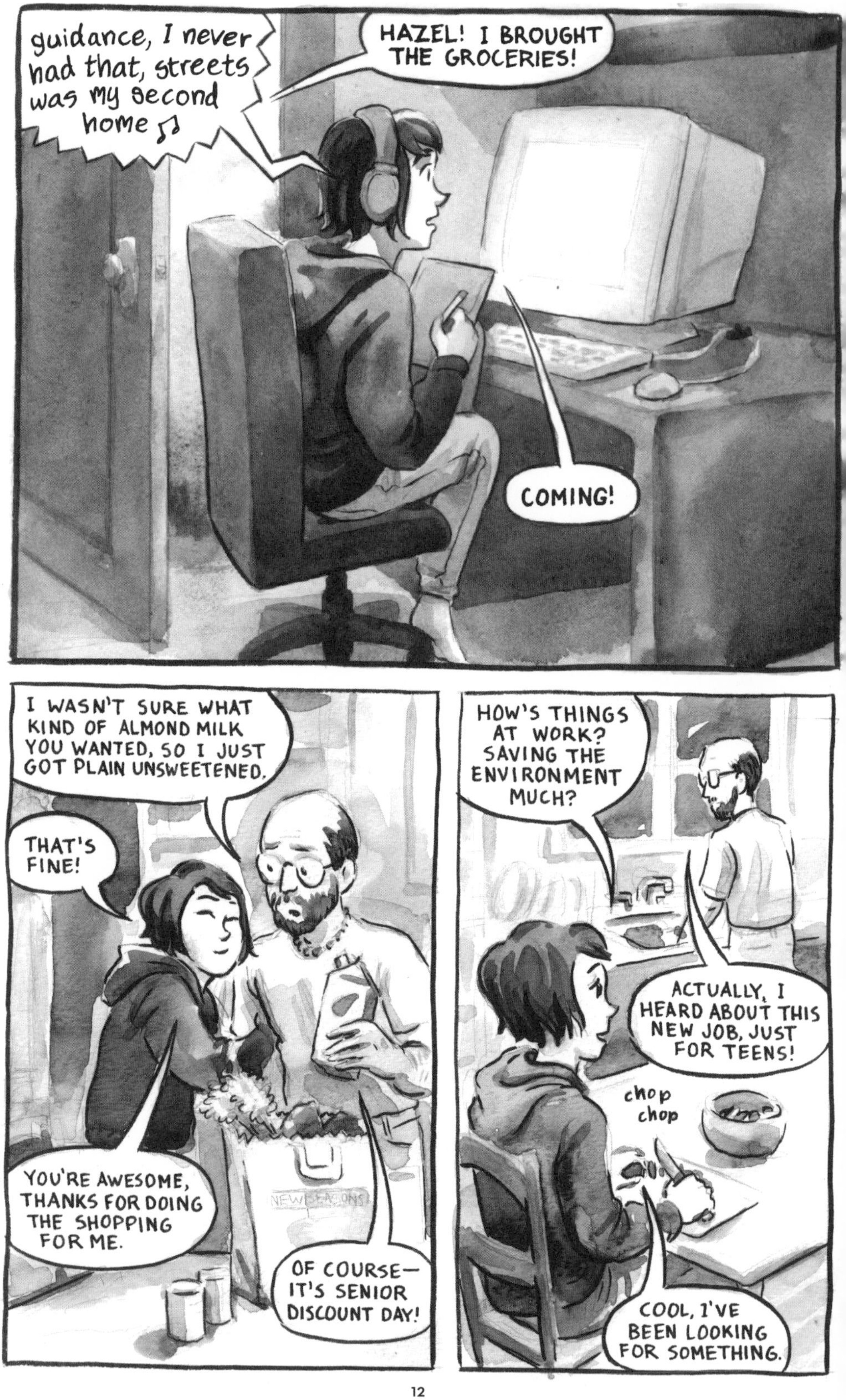
guidance, I never had that, streets was my second home ♫
HAZEL! I BROUGHT THE GROCERIES!
COMING!
I WASN'T SURE WHAT KIND OF ALMOND MILK YOU WANTED, SO I JUST GOT PLAIN UNSWEETENED.
THAT'S FINE!
YOU'RE AWESOME, THANKS FOR DOING THE SHOPPING FOR ME.
NEW SEASONS
OF COURSE— IT'S SENIOR DISCOUNT DAY!
HOW'S THINGS AT WORK? SAVING THE ENVIRONMENT MUCH?
ACTUALLY, I HEARD ABOUT THIS NEW JOB, JUST FOR TEENS!
chop chop
COOL, I'VE BEEN LOOKING FOR SOMETHING.

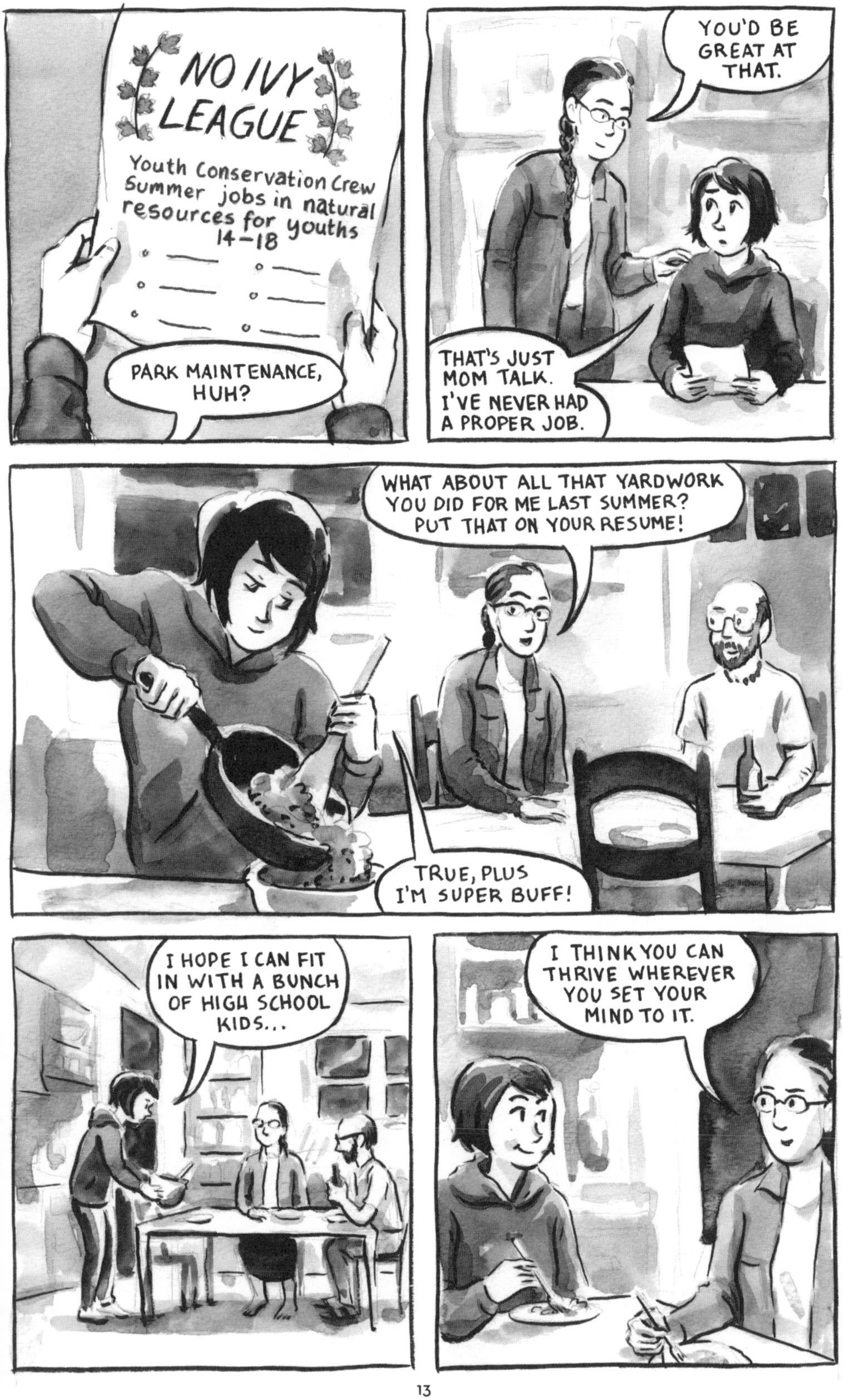
NO IVY LEAGUE
Youth Conservation Crew Summer jobs in natural resources for youths 14–18
PARK MAINTENANCE, HUH?
YOU'D BE GREAT AT THAT.
THAT'S JUST MOM TALK. I'VE NEVER HAD A PROPER JOB.
WHAT ABOUT ALL THAT YARDWORK YOU DID FOR ME LAST SUMMER? PUT THAT ON YOUR RESUME!
TRUE, PLUS I'M SUPER BUFF!
I HOPE I CAN FIT IN WITH A BUNCH OF HIGH SCHOOL KIDS...
I THINK YOU CAN THRIVE WHEREVER YOU SET YOUR MIND TO IT.

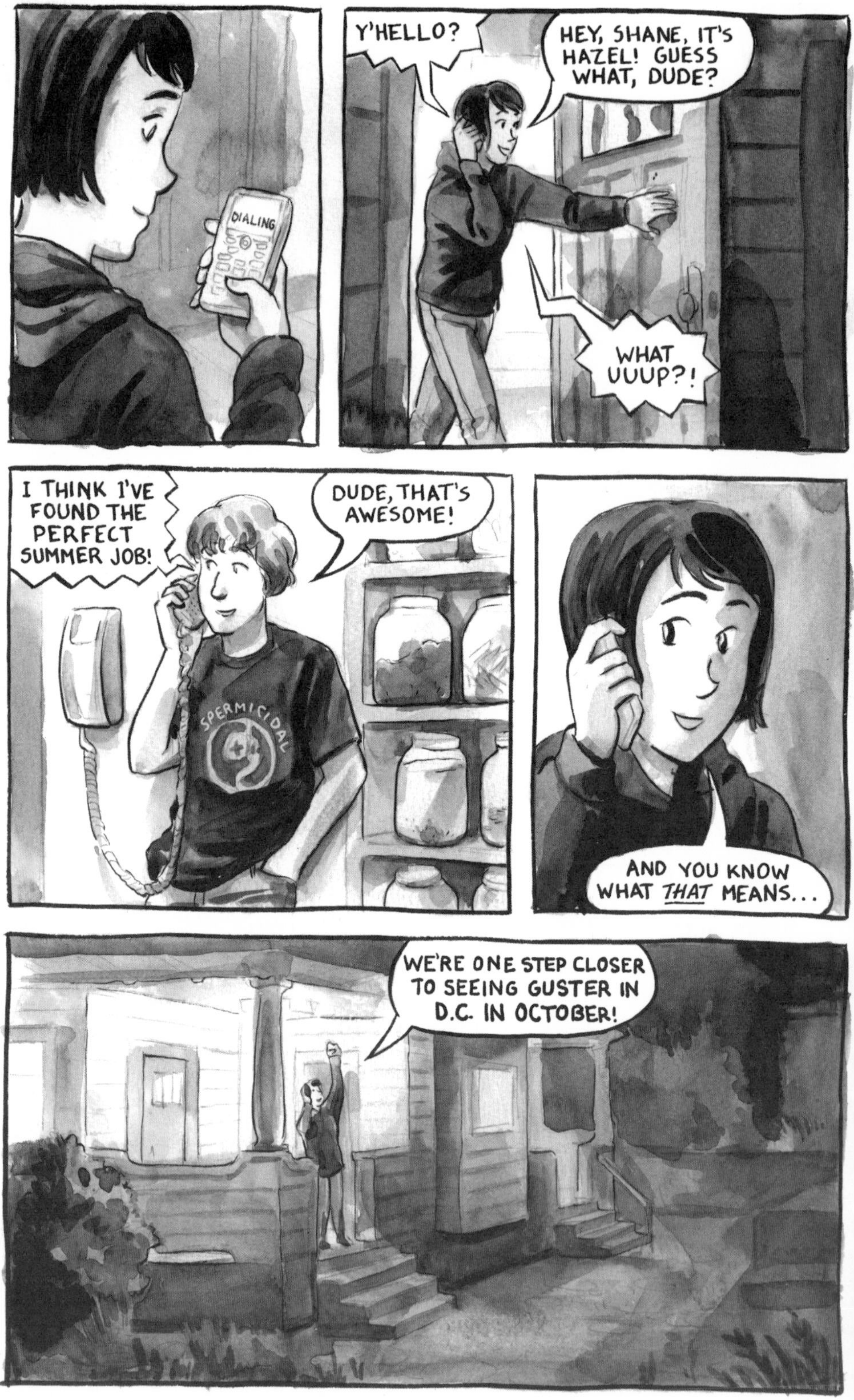
DIALING
Y'HELLO?
HEY, SHANE, IT'S HAZEL! GUESS WHAT, DUDE?
WHAT UUUP?!
I THINK I'VE FOUND THE PERFECT SUMMER JOB!
DUDE, THAT'S AWESOME!
SPERMICIDAL
AND YOU KNOW WHAT THAT MEANS...
WE'RE ONE STEP CLOSER TO SEEING GUSTER IN D.C. IN OCTOBER!

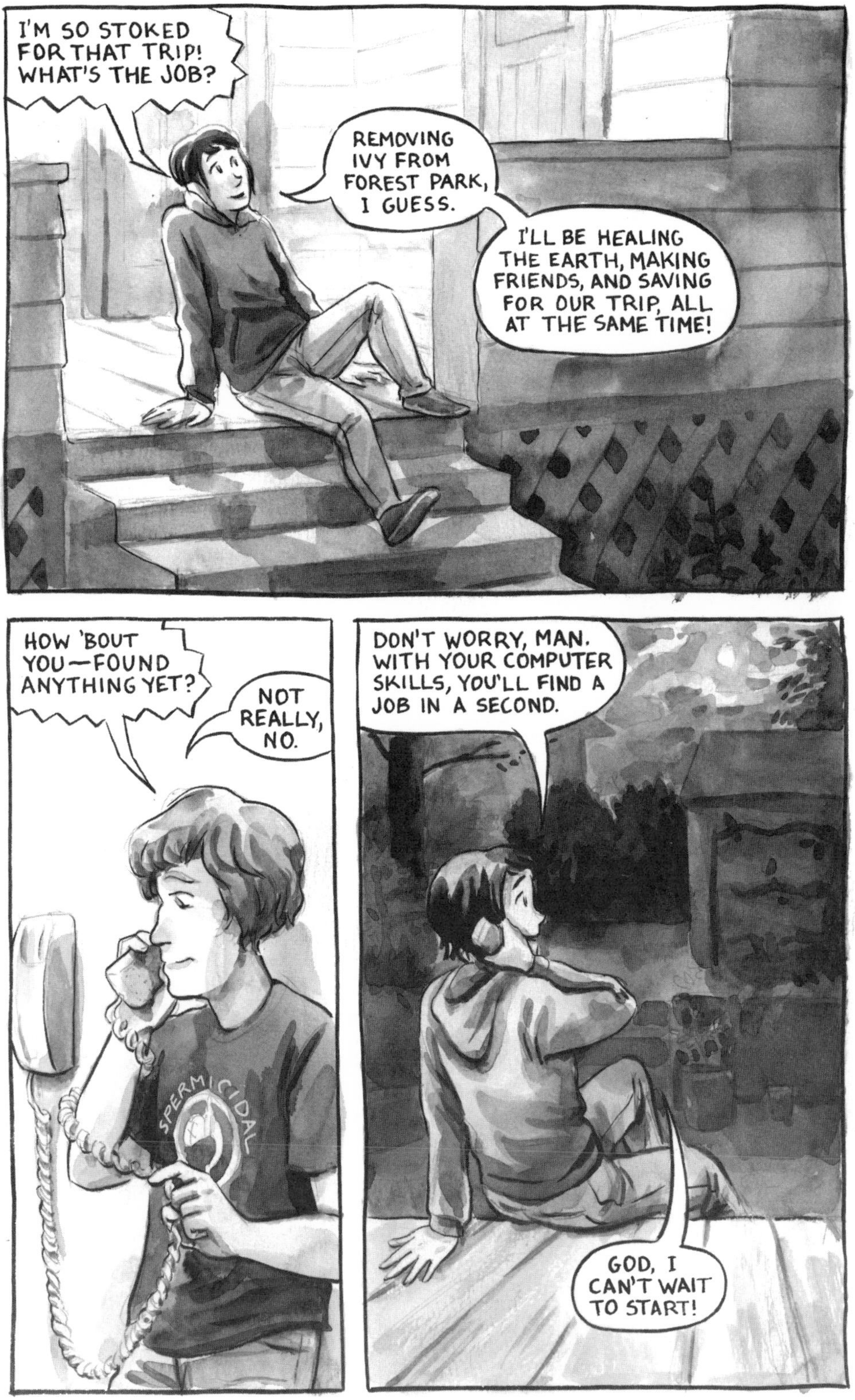
I'M SO STOKED FOR THAT TRIP! WHAT'S THE JOB?
REMOVING IVY FROM FOREST PARK, I GUESS.
I'LL BE HEALING THE EARTH, MAKING FRIENDS, AND SAVING FOR OUR TRIP, ALL AT THE SAME TIME!
HOW 'BOUT YOU—FOUND ANYTHING YET?
NOT REALLY, NO.
SPERMICIDAL
DON'T WORRY, MAN. WITH YOUR COMPUTER SKILLS, YOU'LL FIND A JOB IN A SECOND.
GOD, I CAN'T WAIT TO START!

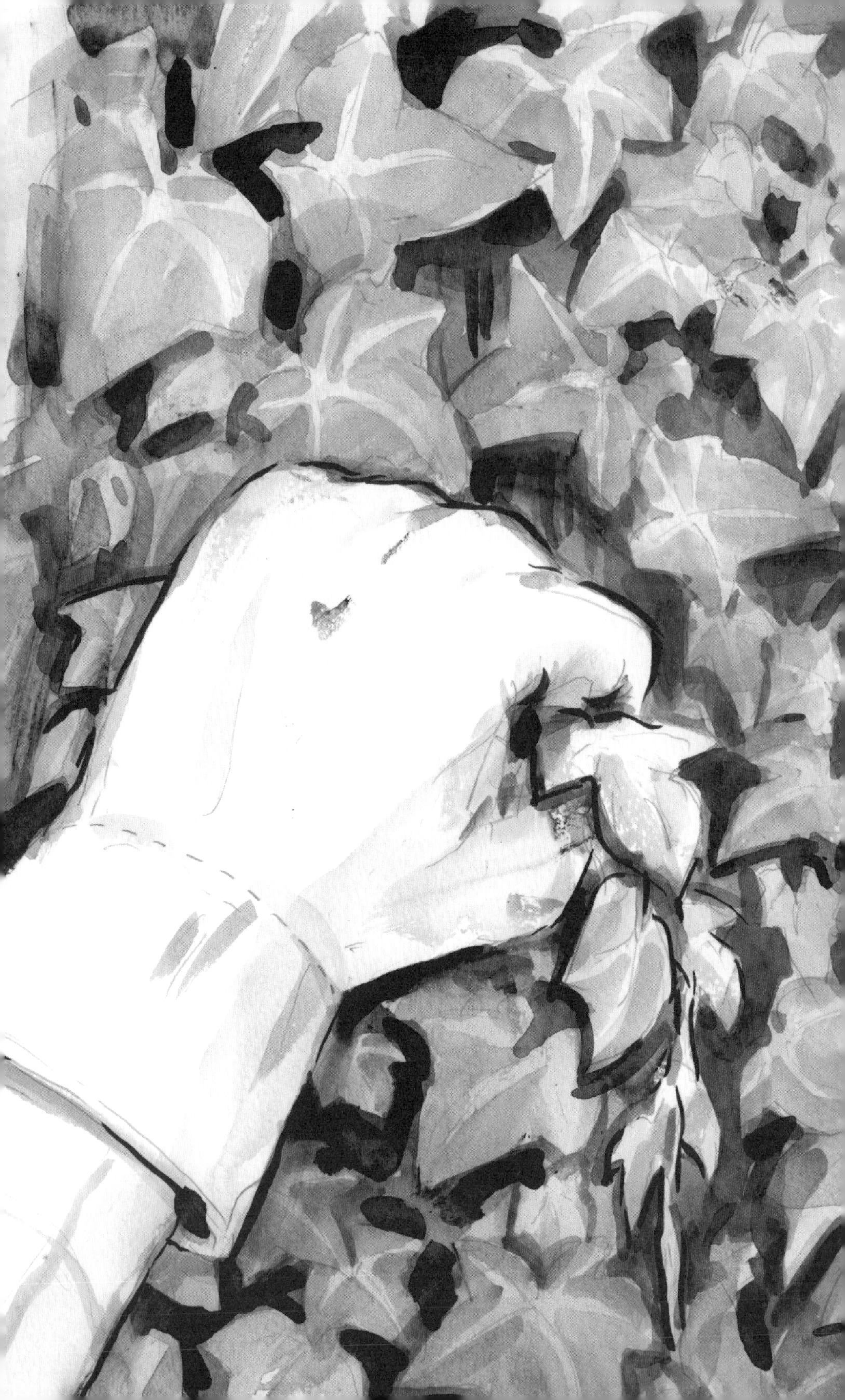

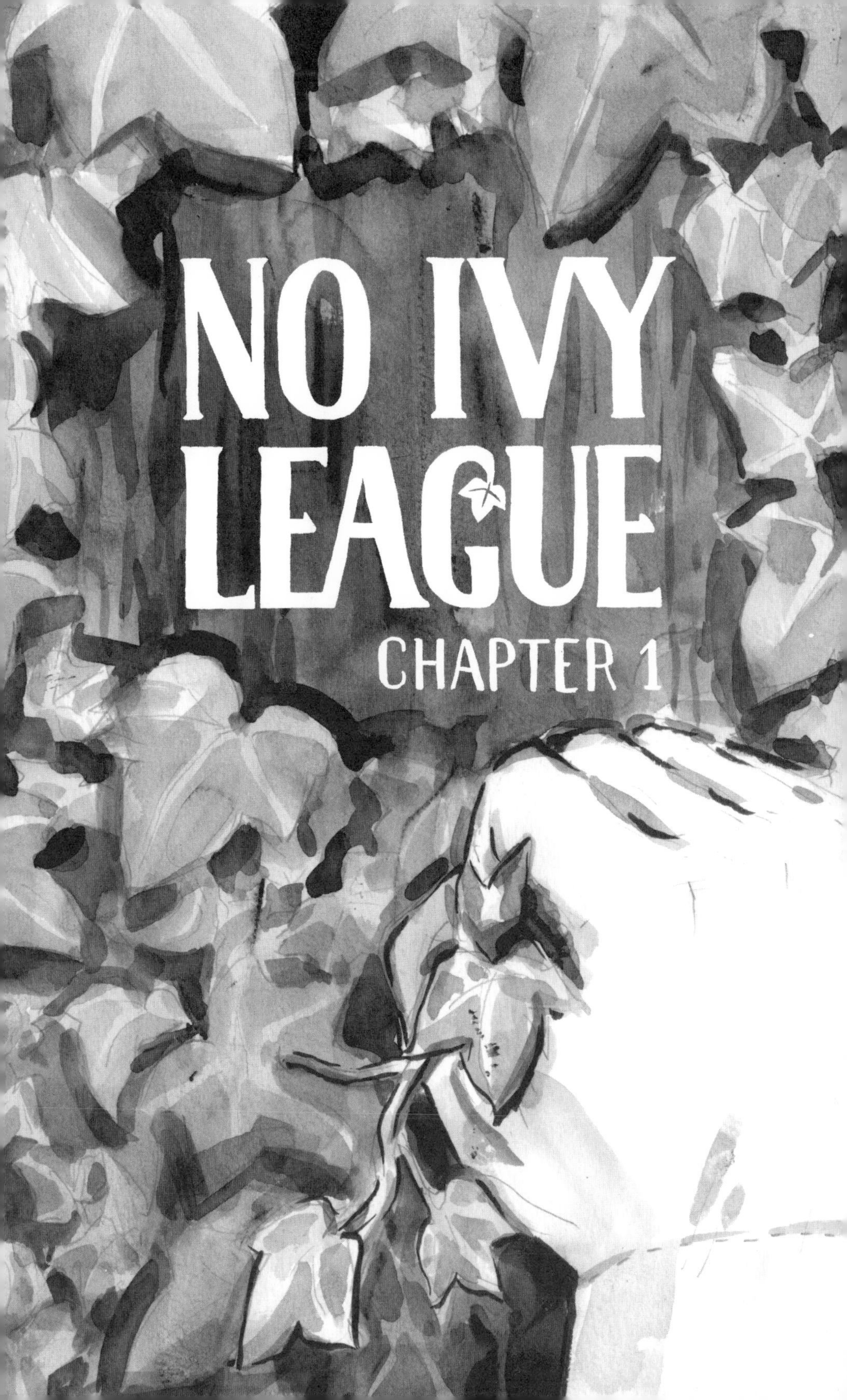
NO IVY LEAGUE
CHAPTER 1

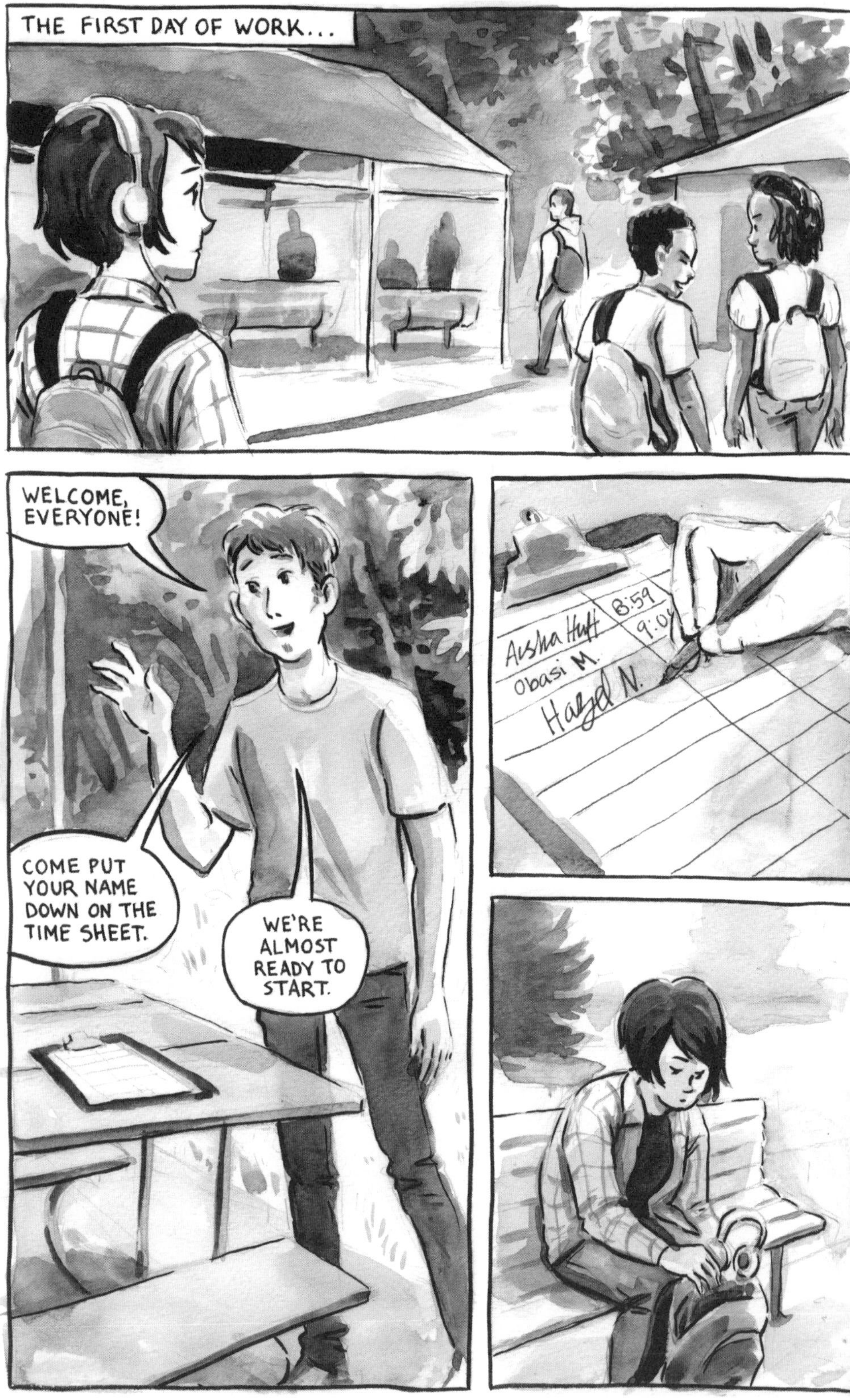
THE FIRST DAY OF WORK...
WELCOME, EVERYONE!
COME PUT YOUR NAME DOWN ON THE TIME SHEET.
WE'RE ALMOST READY TO START.
Aisha Huff
8:59
Obasi M.
Hazel N.

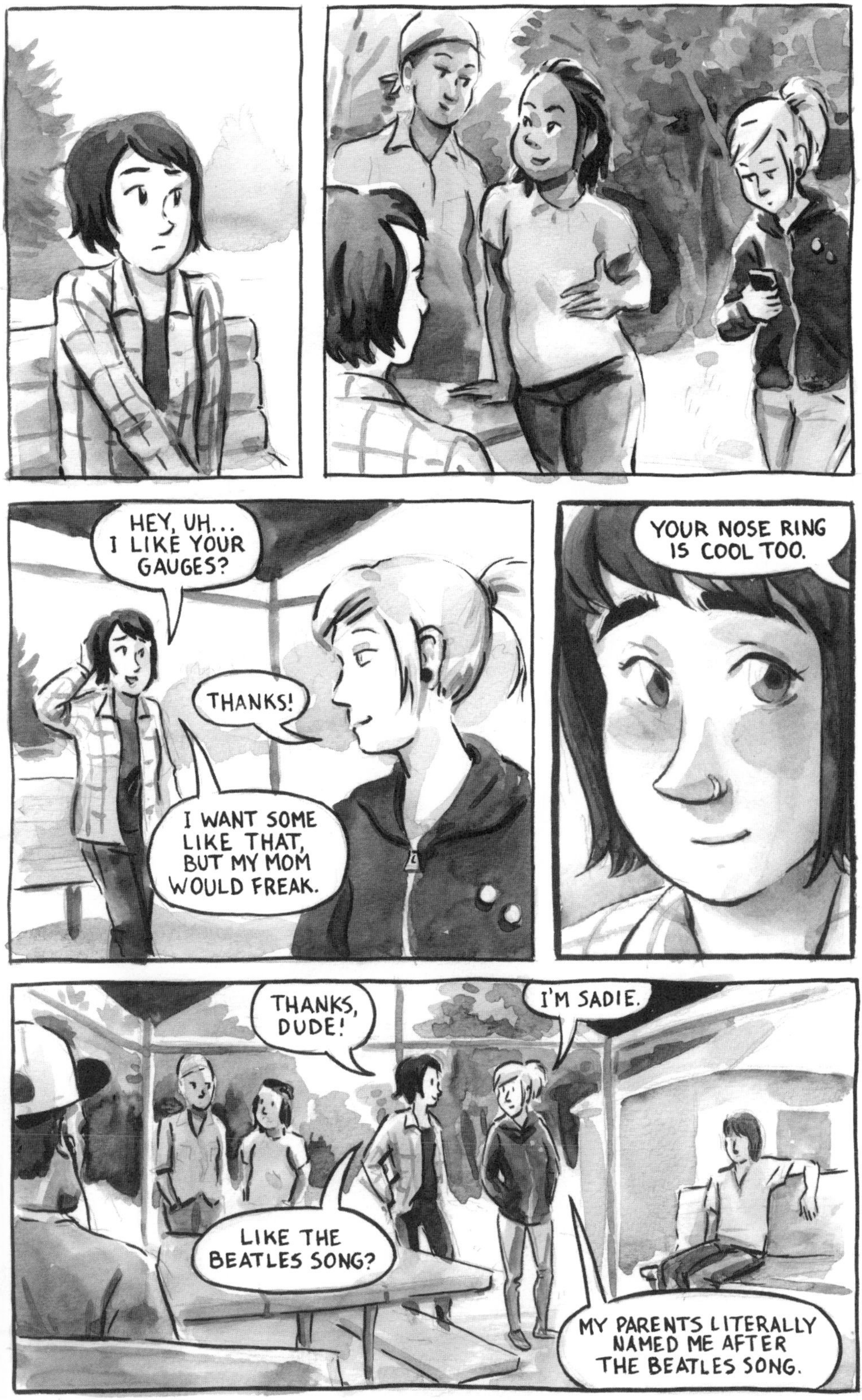
HEY, UH...
I LIKE YOUR GAUGES?
THANKS!
I WANT SOME LIKE THAT, BUT MY MOM WOULD FREAK.
YOUR NOSE RING IS COOL TOO.
THANKS, DUDE!
I'M SADIE.
LIKE THE BEATLES SONG?
MY PARENTS LITERALLY NAMED ME AFTER THE BEATLES SONG.

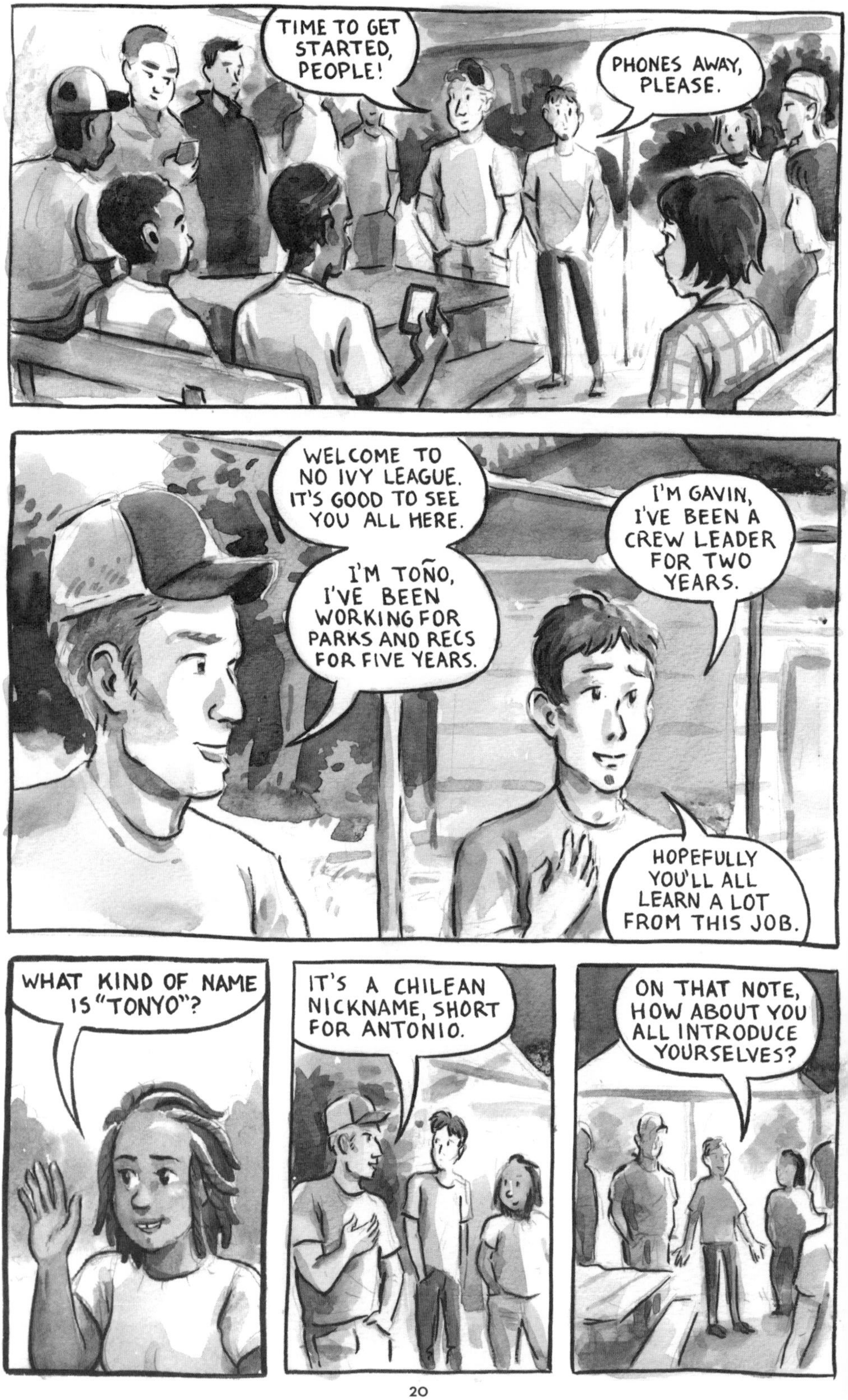
TIME TO GET STARTED, PEOPLE!
PHONES AWAY, PLEASE.
WELCOME TO NO IVY LEAGUE. IT'S GOOD TO SEE YOU ALL HERE.
I'M TOÑO, I'VE BEEN WORKING FOR PARKS AND RECS FOR FIVE YEARS.
I'M GAVIN, I'VE BEEN A CREW LEADER FOR TWO YEARS.
HOPEFULLY YOU'LL ALL LEARN A LOT FROM THIS JOB.
WHAT KIND OF NAME IS "TONYO"?
IT'S A CHILEAN NICKNAME, SHORT FOR ANTONIO.
ON THAT NOTE, HOW ABOUT YOU ALL INTRODUCE YOURSELVES?

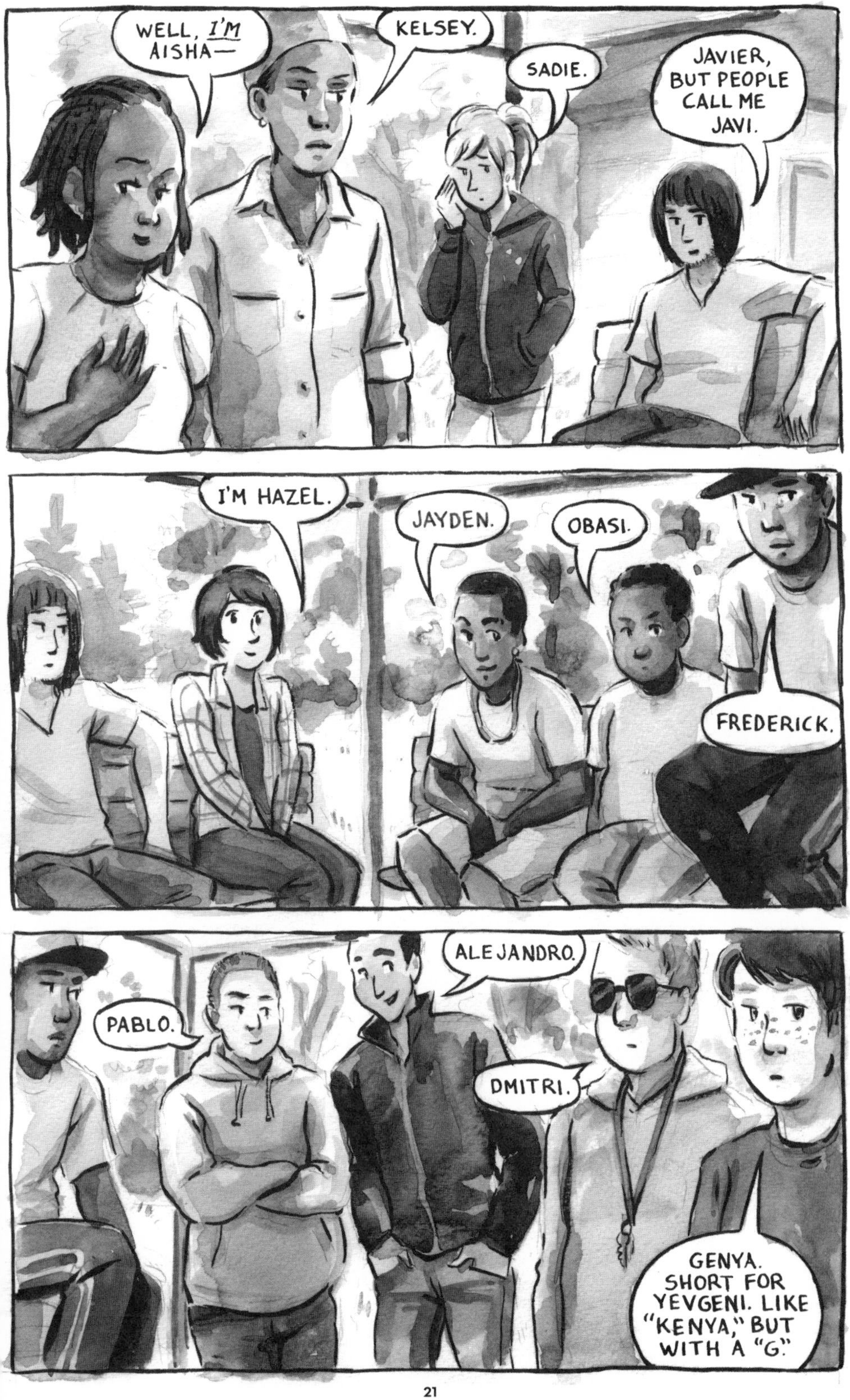
WELL, I'M AISHA—
KELSEY.
SADIE.
JAVIER, BUT PEOPLE CALL ME JAVI.
I'M HAZEL.
JAYDEN.
OBASI.
FREDERICK.
PABLO.
ALEJANDRO.
DMITRI.
GENYA. SHORT FOR YEVGENI. LIKE "KENYA," BUT WITH A "G."

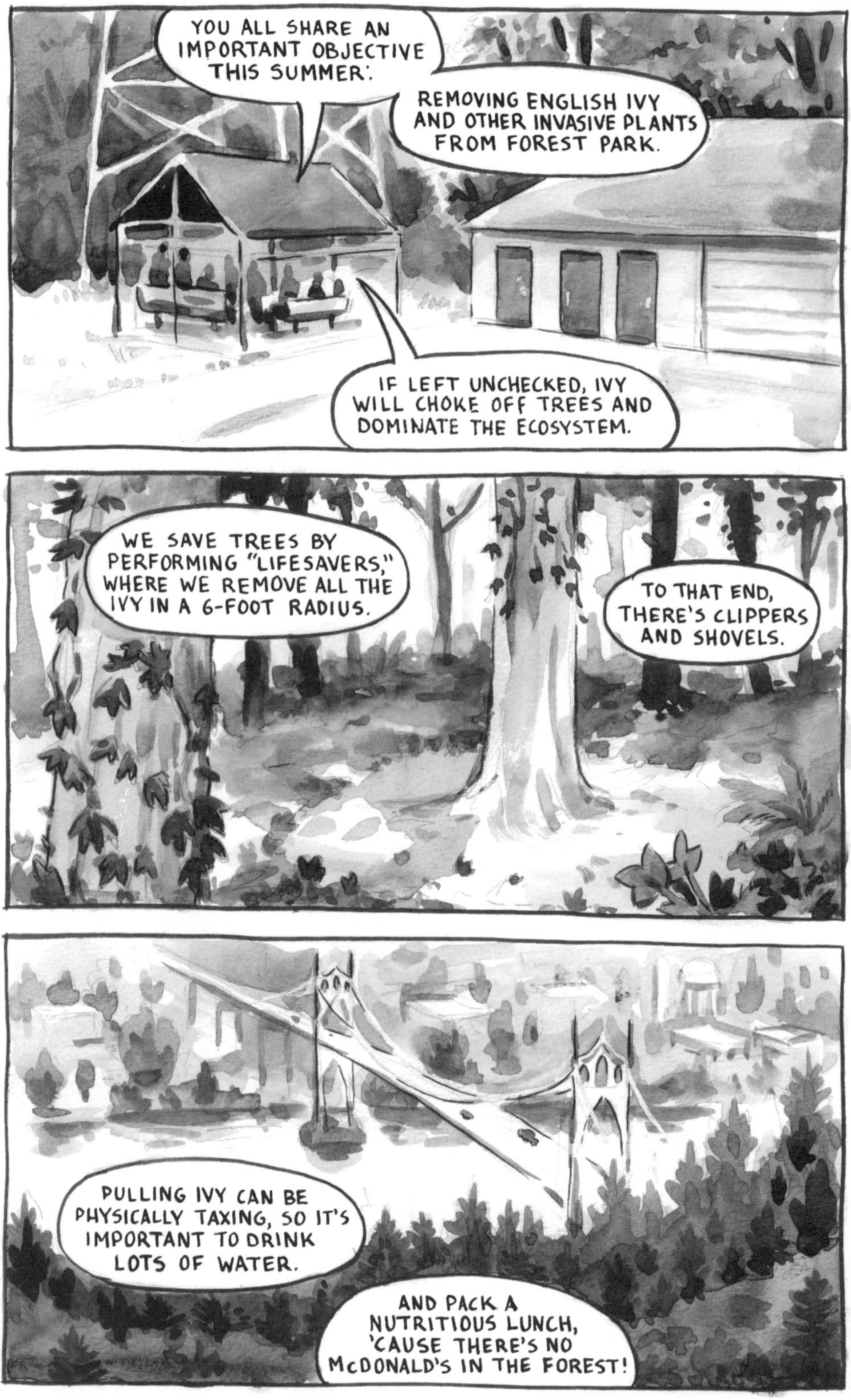
YOU ALL SHARE AN IMPORTANT OBJECTIVE THIS SUMMER:
REMOVING ENGLISH IVY AND OTHER INVASIVE PLANTS FROM FOREST PARK.
IF LEFT UNCHECKED, IVY WILL CHOKE OFF TREES AND DOMINATE THE ECOSYSTEM.
WE SAVE TREES BY PERFORMING "LIFESAVERS," WHERE WE REMOVE ALL THE IVY IN A 6-FOOT RADIUS.
TO THAT END, THERE'S CLIPPERS AND SHOVELS.
PULLING IVY CAN BE PHYSICALLY TAXING, SO IT'S IMPORTANT TO DRINK LOTS OF WATER.
AND PACK A NUTRITIOUS LUNCH, 'CAUSE THERE'S NO McDONALD'S IN THE FOREST!

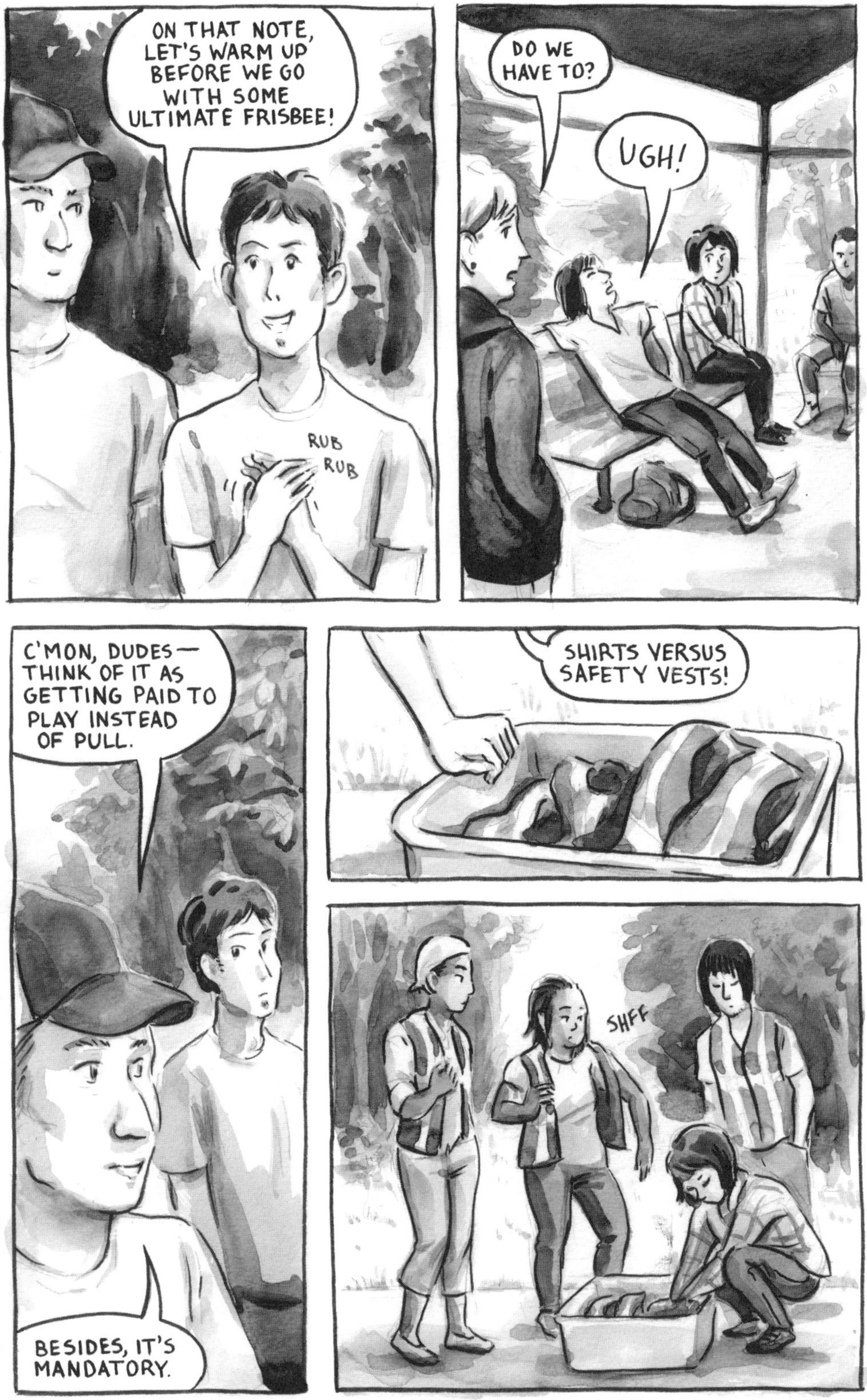
ON THAT NOTE, LET'S WARM UP BEFORE WE GO WITH SOME ULTIMATE FRISBEE!
RUB RUB
DO WE HAVE TO?
UGH!
C'MON, DUDES— THINK OF IT AS GETTING PAID TO PLAY INSTEAD OF PULL.
BESIDES, IT'S MANDATORY.
SHIRTS VERSUS SAFETY VESTS!
SHFF

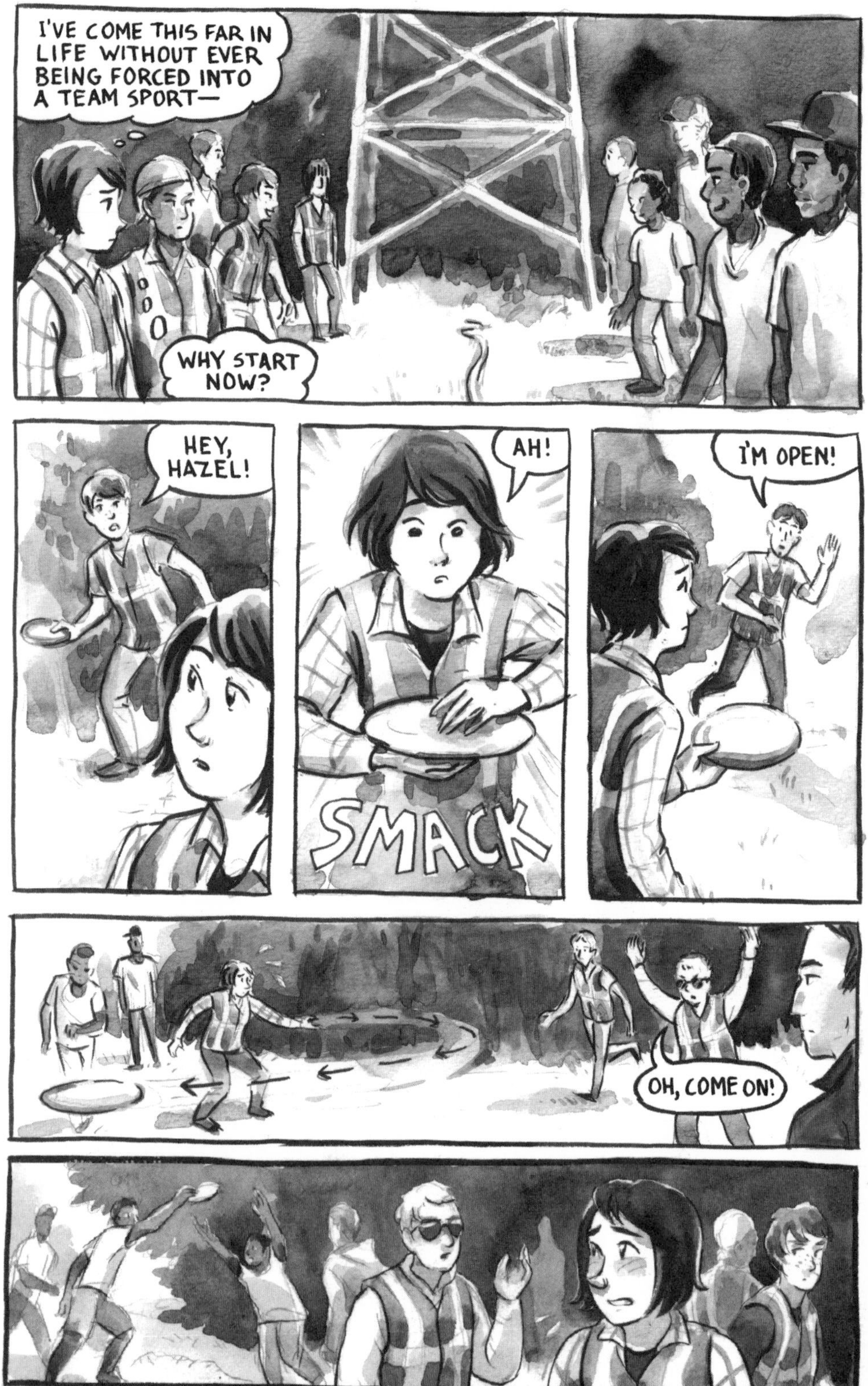
I'VE COME THIS FAR IN LIFE WITHOUT EVER BEING FORCED INTO A TEAM SPORT—
WHY START NOW?
HEY, HAZEL!
AH!
SMACK
I'M OPEN!
OH, COME ON!

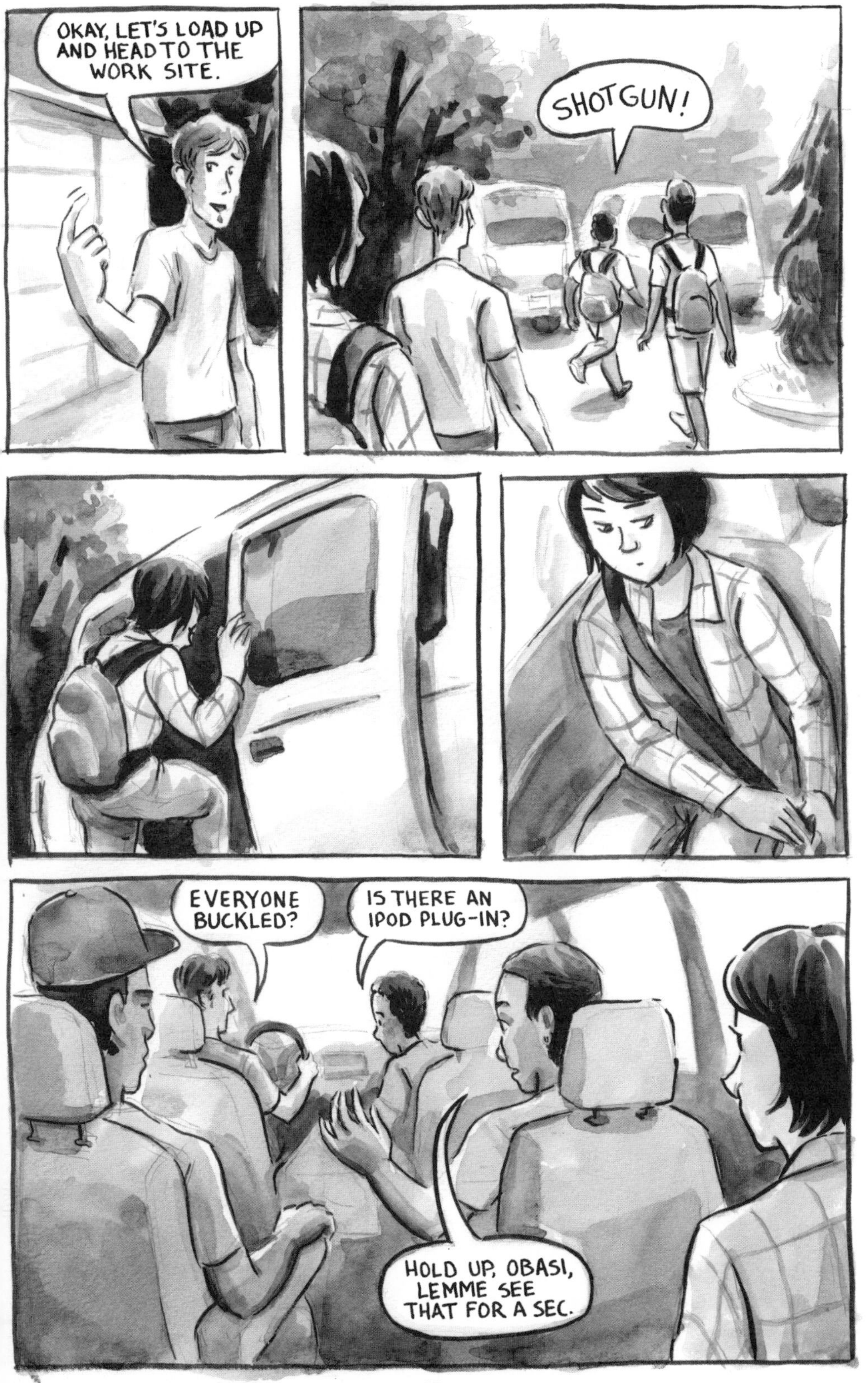
OKAY, LET'S LOAD UP AND HEAD TO THE WORK SITE.
SHOTGUN!
EVERYONE BUCKLED?
IS THERE AN IPOD PLUG-IN?
HOLD UP, OBASI, LEMME SEE THAT FOR A SEC.

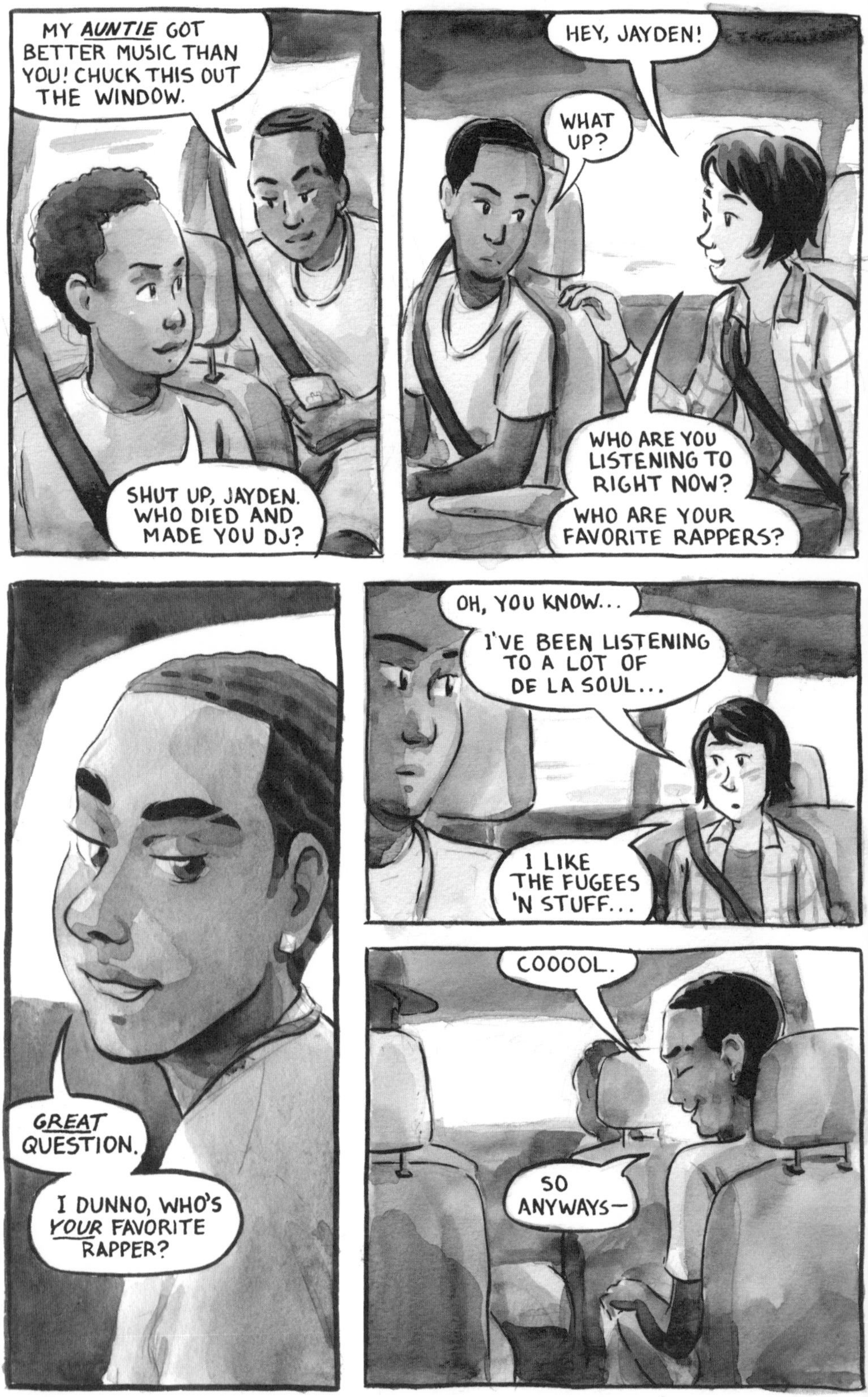
MY AUNTIE GOT BETTER MUSIC THAN YOU! CHUCK THIS OUT THE WINDOW.
SHUT UP, JAYDEN. WHO DIED AND MADE YOU DJ?
HEY, JAYDEN!
WHAT UP?
WHO ARE YOU LISTENING TO RIGHT NOW?
WHO ARE YOUR FAVORITE RAPPERS?
GREAT QUESTION.
I DUNNO, WHO'S YOUR FAVORITE RAPPER?
OH, YOU KNOW...
I'VE BEEN LISTENING TO A LOT OF DE LA SOUL...
I LIKE THE FUGEES 'N STUFF...
COOOOL.
SO ANYWAYS—

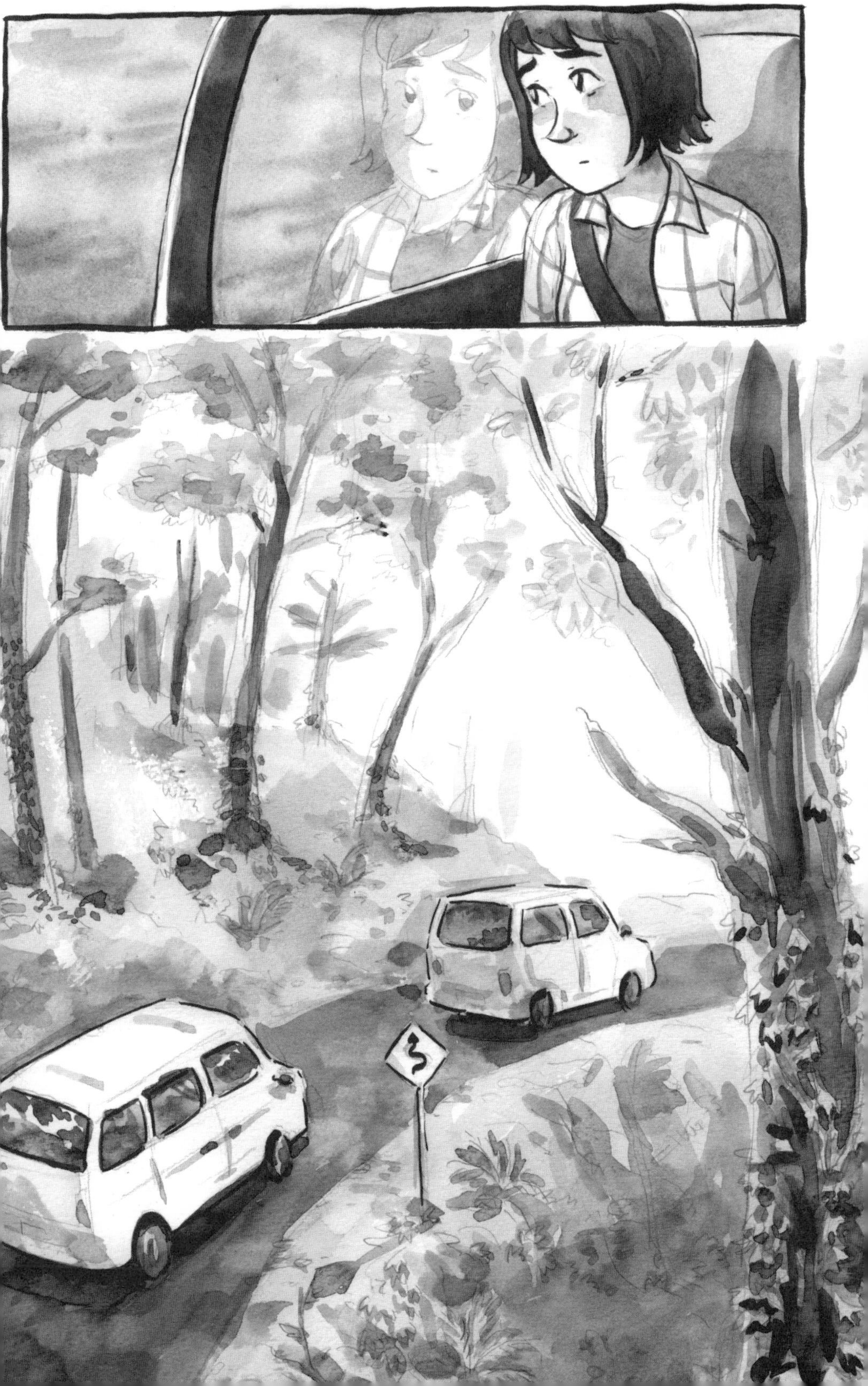

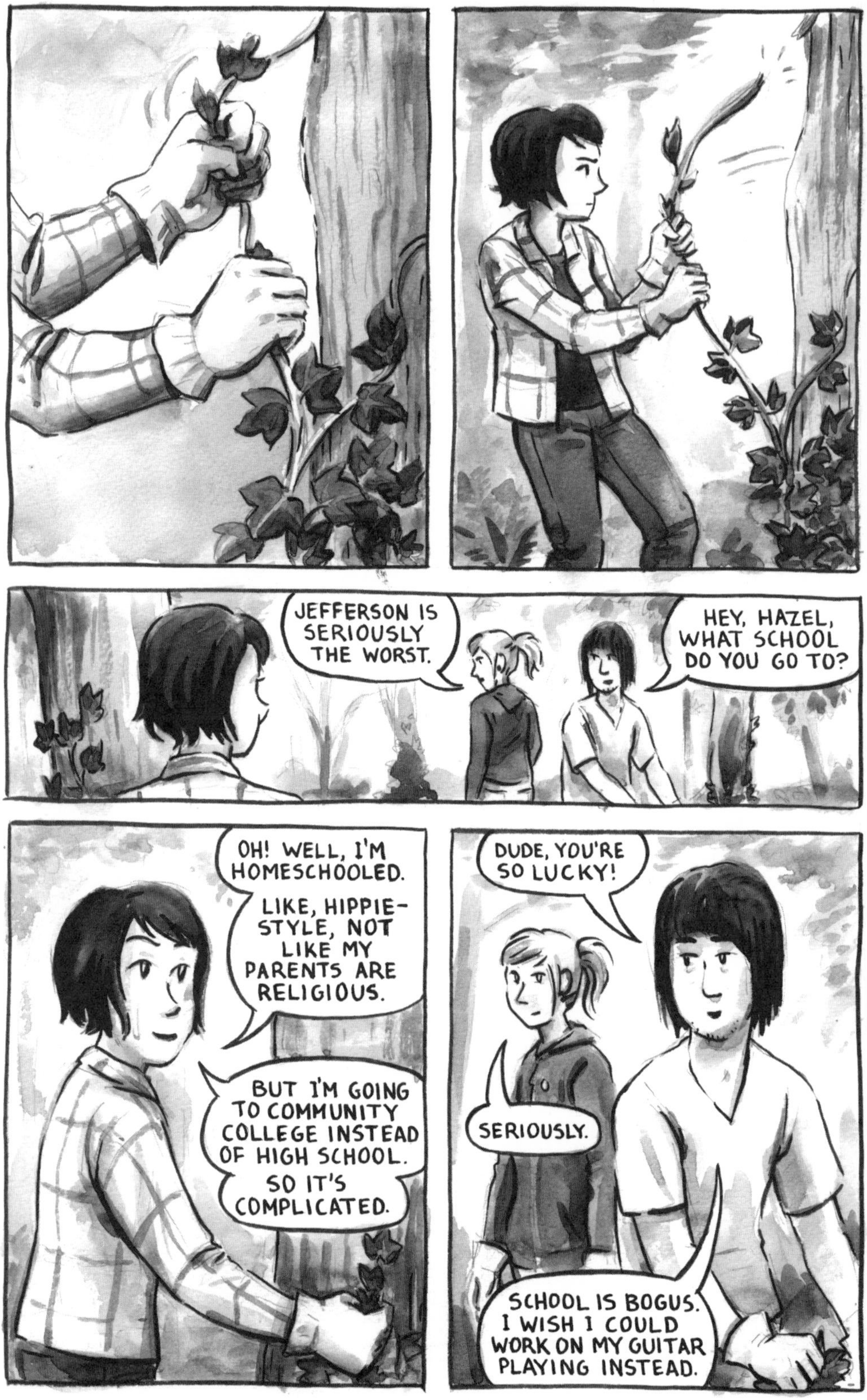
JEFFERSON IS SERIOUSLY THE WORST.
HEY, HAZEL, WHAT SCHOOL DO YOU GO TO?
OH! WELL, I'M HOMESCHOOLED.
LIKE, HIPPIE-STYLE, NOT LIKE MY PARENTS ARE RELIGIOUS.
BUT I'M GOING TO COMMUNITY COLLEGE INSTEAD OF HIGH SCHOOL.
SO IT'S COMPLICATED.
DUDE, YOU'RE SO LUCKY!
SERIOUSLY.
SCHOOL IS BOGUS. I WISH I COULD WORK ON MY GUITAR PLAYING INSTEAD.

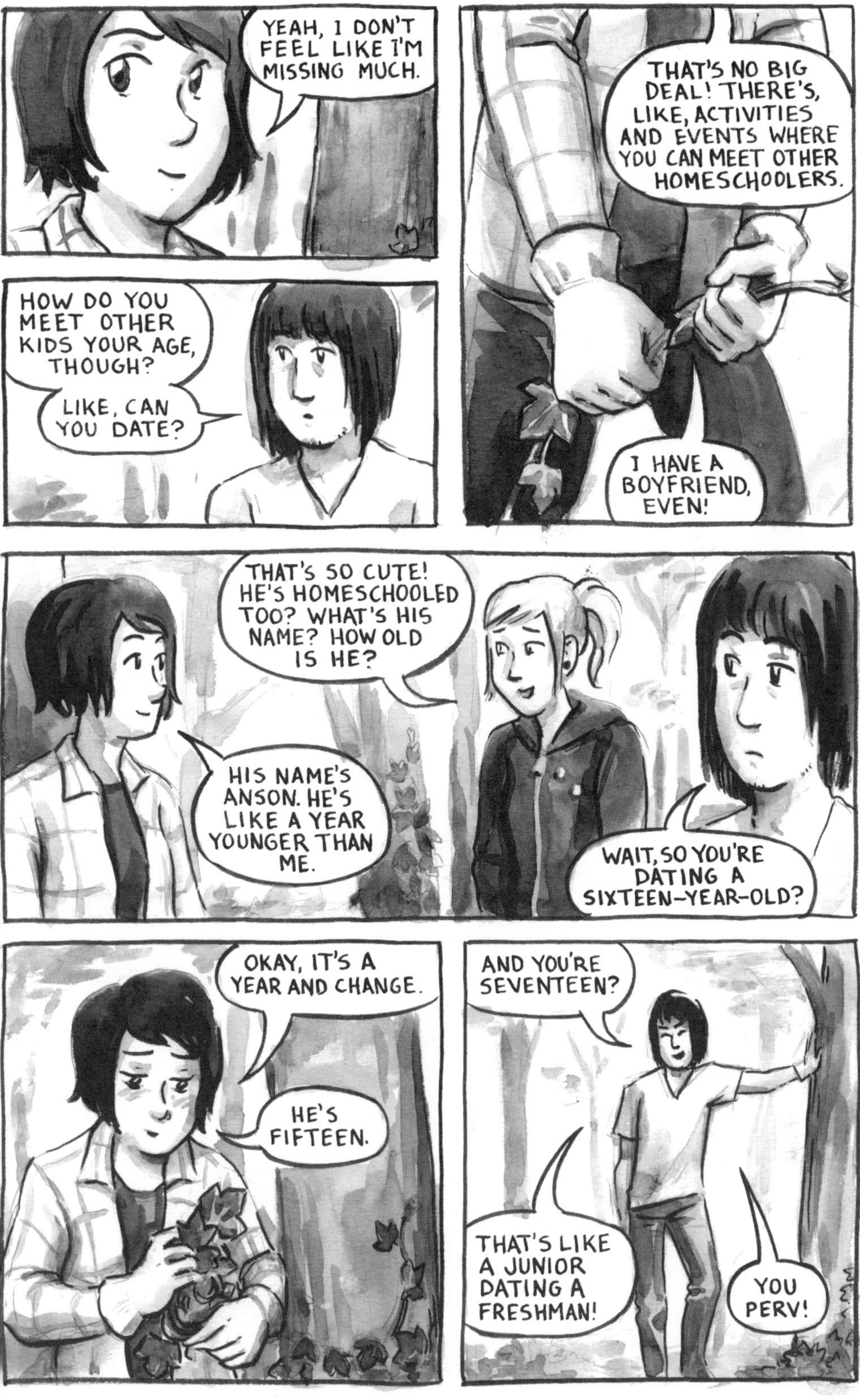
YEAH, I DON'T FEEL LIKE I'M MISSING MUCH.
HOW DO YOU MEET OTHER KIDS YOUR AGE, THOUGH?
LIKE, CAN YOU DATE?
THAT'S NO BIG DEAL! THERE'S, LIKE, ACTIVITIES AND EVENTS WHERE YOU CAN MEET OTHER HOMESCHOOLERS.
I HAVE A BOYFRIEND, EVEN!
THAT'S SO CUTE! HE'S HOMESCHOOLED TOO? WHAT'S HIS NAME? HOW OLD IS HE?
HIS NAME'S ANSON. HE'S LIKE A YEAR YOUNGER THAN ME.
WAIT, SO YOU'RE DATING A SIXTEEN-YEAR-OLD?
OKAY, IT'S A YEAR AND CHANGE.
HE'S FIFTEEN.
AND YOU'RE SEVENTEEN?
THAT'S LIKE A JUNIOR DATING A FRESHMAN!
YOU PERV!

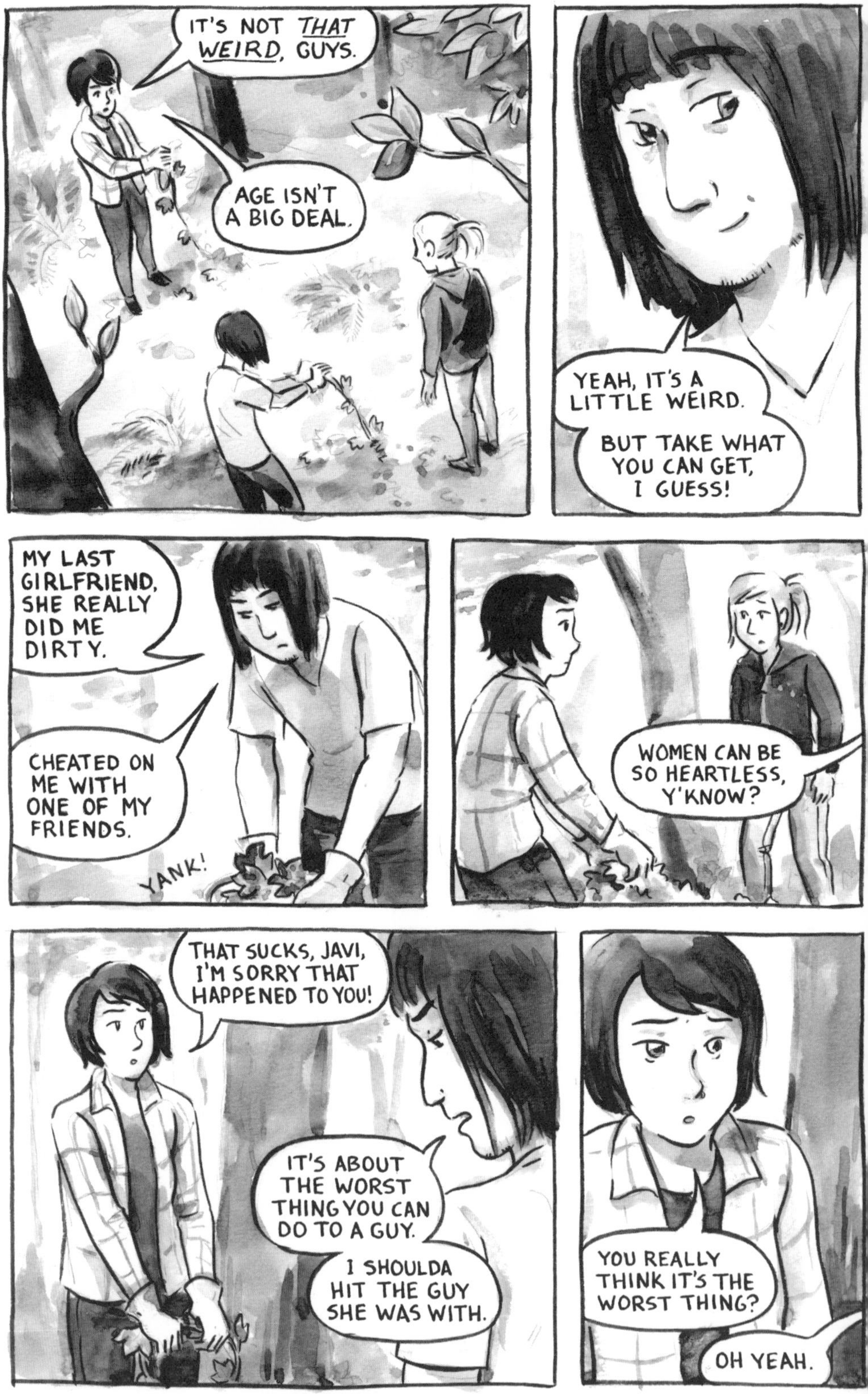
IT'S NOT THAT WEIRD, GUYS.
AGE ISN'T A BIG DEAL.
YEAH, IT'S A LITTLE WEIRD.
BUT TAKE WHAT YOU CAN GET, I GUESS!
MY LAST GIRLFRIEND, SHE REALLY DID ME DIRTY.
CHEATED ON ME WITH ONE OF MY FRIENDS.
YANK!
WOMEN CAN BE SO HEARTLESS, Y'KNOW?
THAT SUCKS, JAVI, I'M SORRY THAT HAPPENED TO YOU!
IT'S ABOUT THE WORST THING YOU CAN DO TO A GUY.
I SHOULDA HIT THE GUY SHE WAS WITH.
YOU REALLY THINK IT'S THE WORST THING?
OH YEAH.

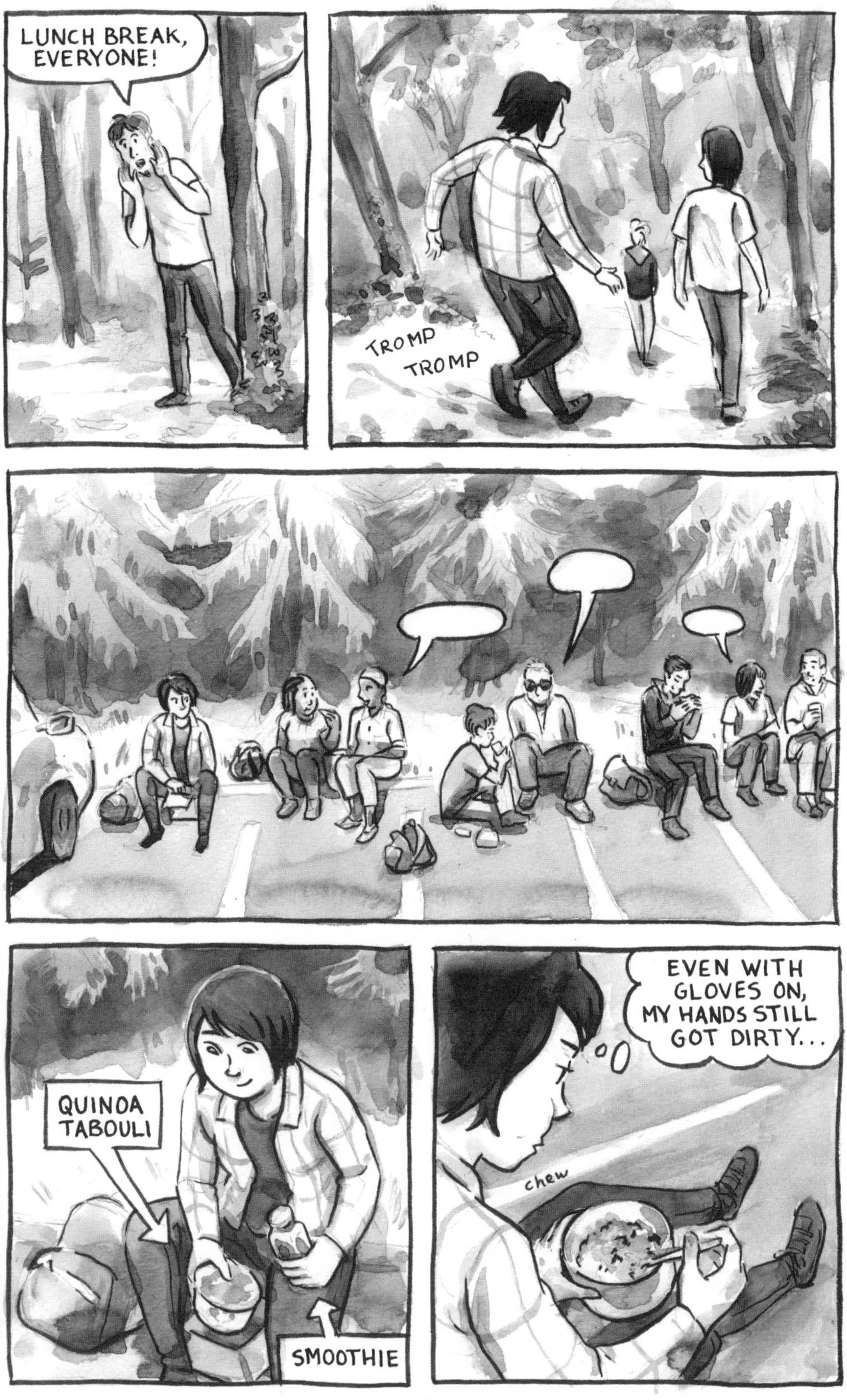
LUNCH BREAK, EVERYONE!
TROMP
TROMP
QUINOA TABOULI
SMOOTHIE
EVEN WITH GLOVES ON, MY HANDS STILL GOT DIRTY...
chew

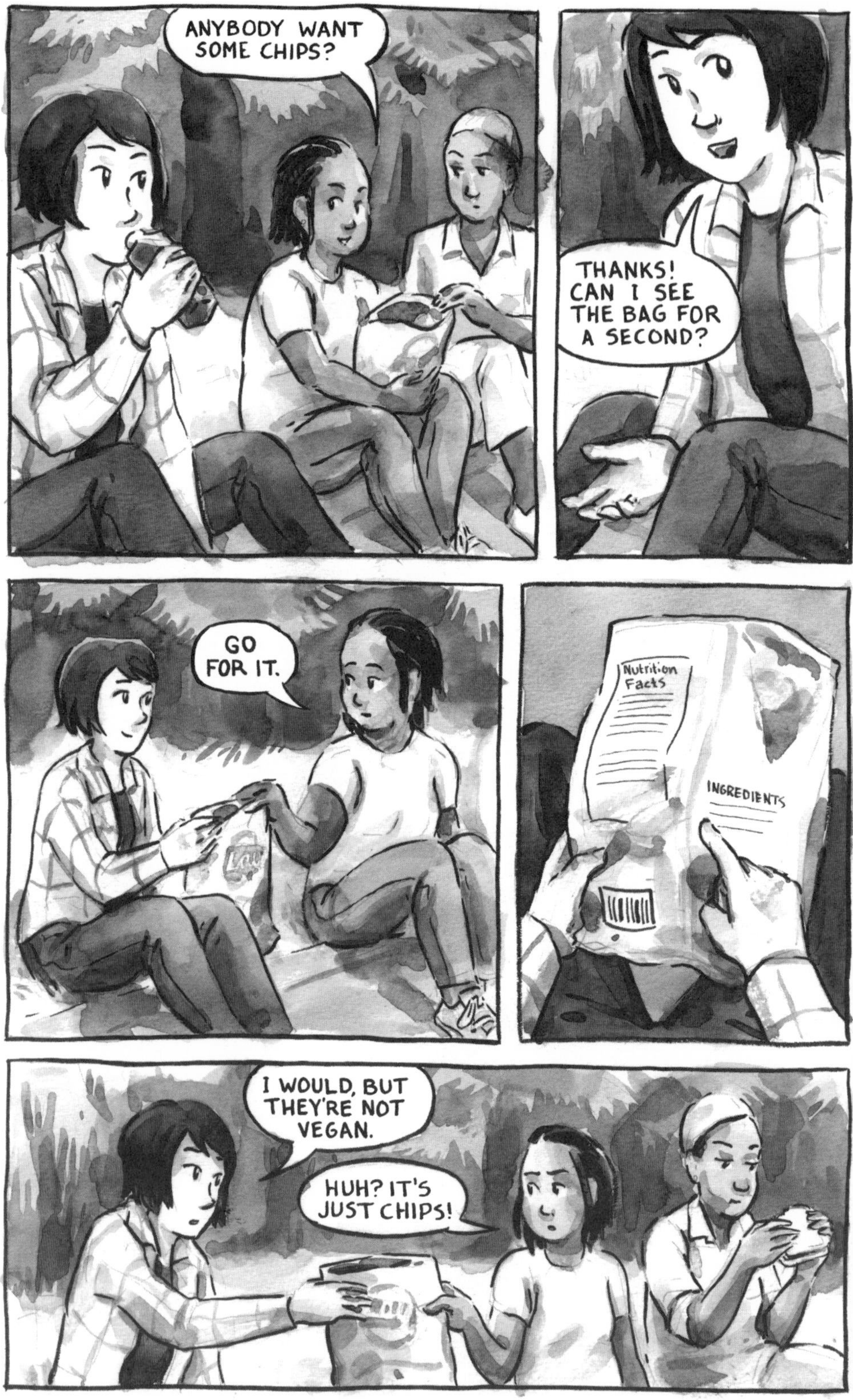
ANYBODY WANT SOME CHIPS?
THANKS! CAN I SEE THE BAG FOR A SECOND?
GO FOR IT.
Nutrition Facts
INGREDIENTS
I WOULD, BUT THEY'RE NOT VEGAN.
HUH? IT'S JUST CHIPS!

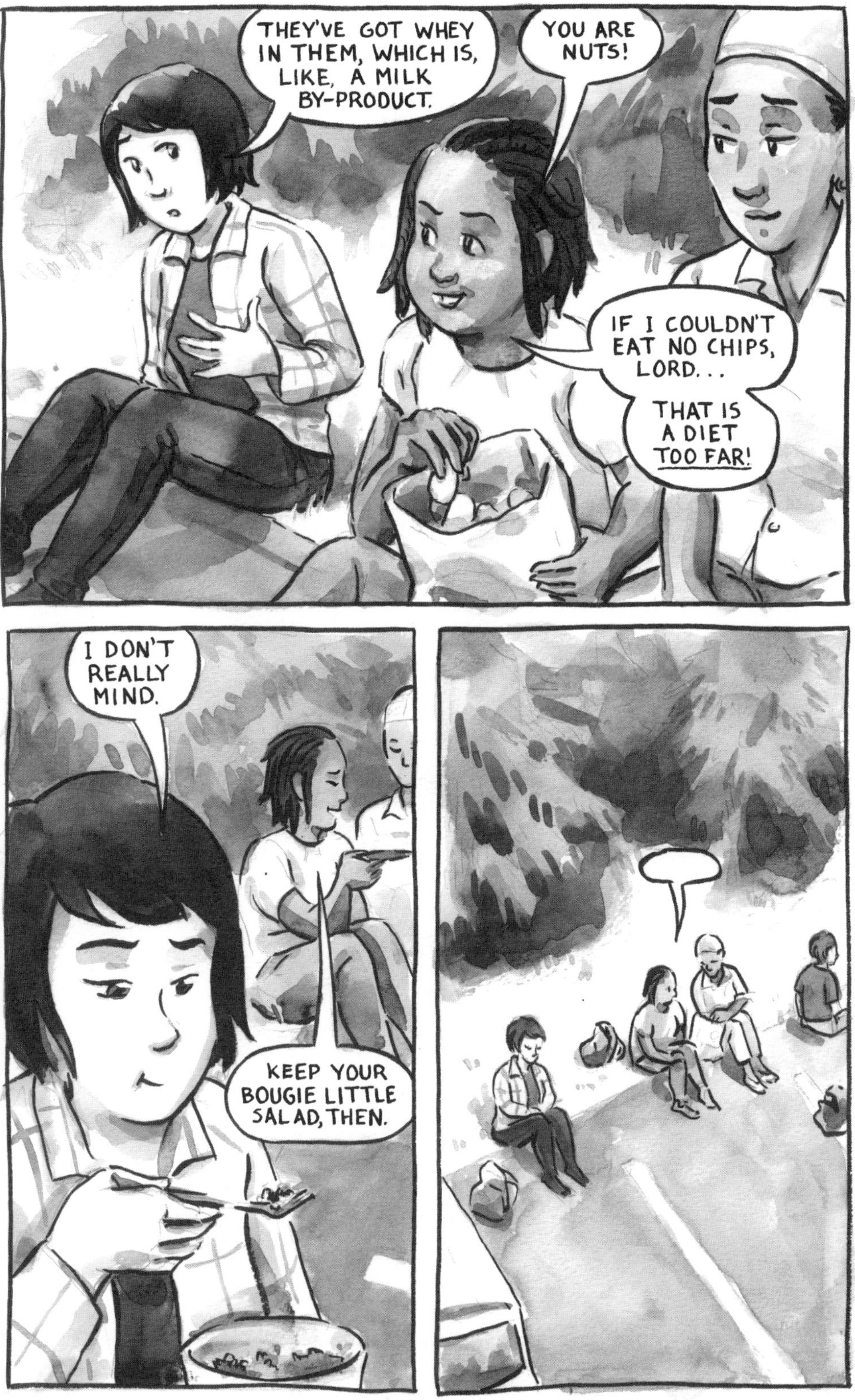
THEY'VE GOT WHEY IN THEM, WHICH IS, LIKE, A MILK BY-PRODUCT.
YOU ARE NUTS!
IF I COULDN'T EAT NO CHIPS, LORD. . .
THAT IS A DIET TOO FAR!
I DON'T REALLY MIND.
KEEP YOUR BOUGIE LITTLE SALAD, THEN.

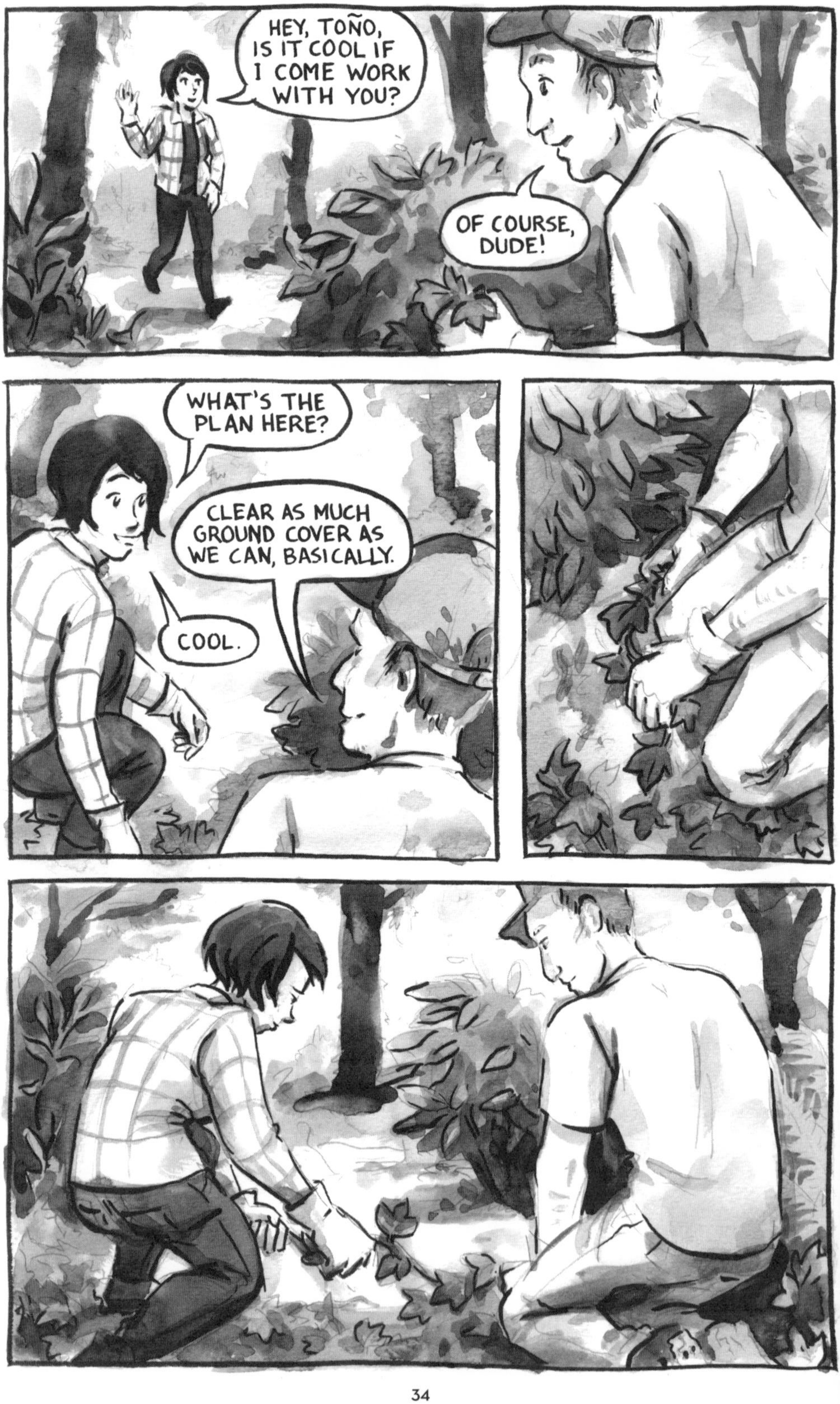
HEY, TOÑO, IS IT COOL IF I COME WORK WITH YOU?
OF COURSE, DUDE!
WHAT'S THE PLAN HERE?
CLEAR AS MUCH GROUND COVER AS WE CAN, BASICALLY.
COOL.

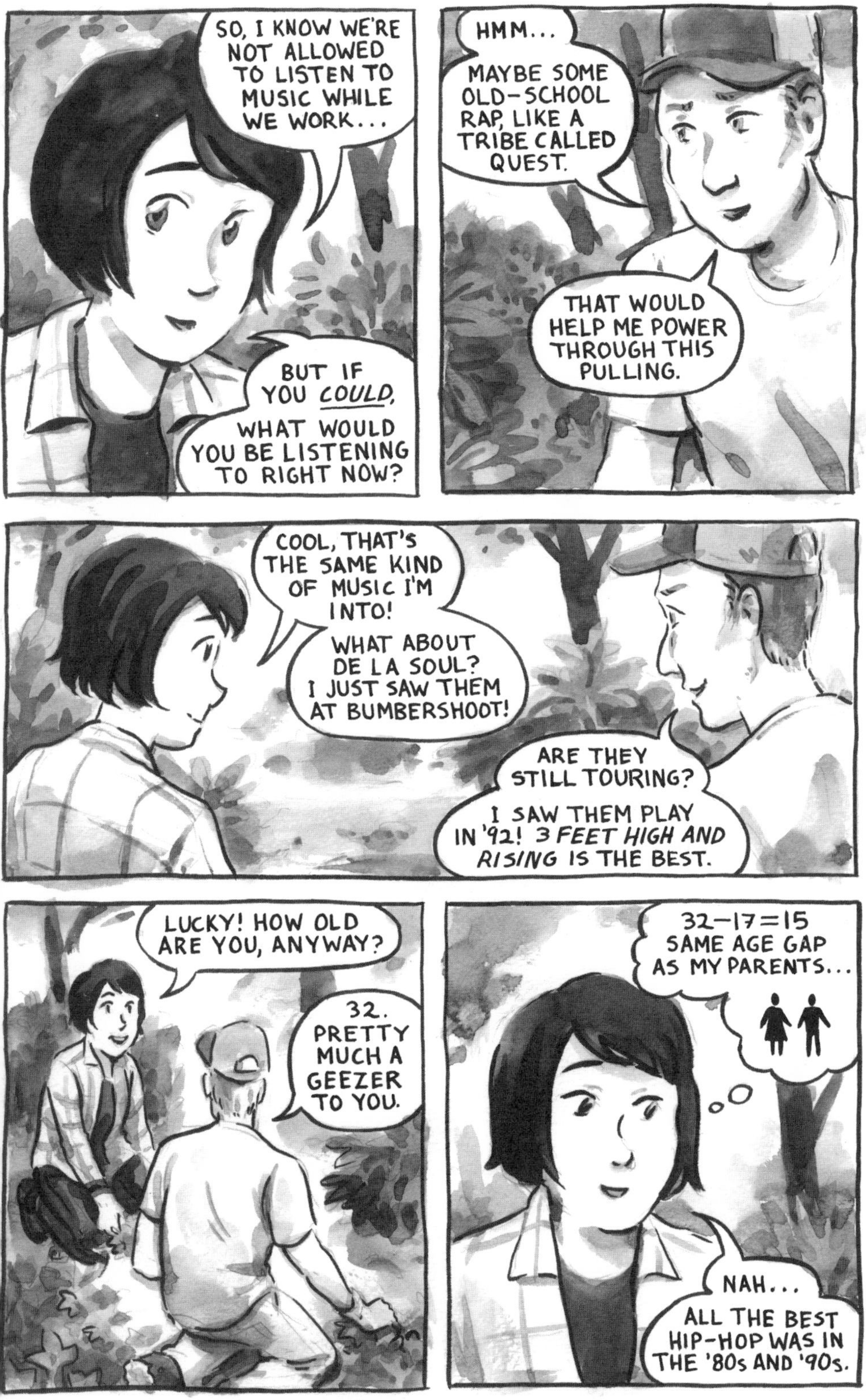
SO, I KNOW WE'RE NOT ALLOWED TO LISTEN TO MUSIC WHILE WE WORK...
BUT IF YOU COULD,
WHAT WOULD YOU BE LISTENING TO RIGHT NOW?
HMM...
MAYBE SOME OLD-SCHOOL RAP, LIKE A TRIBE CALLED QUEST.
THAT WOULD HELP ME POWER THROUGH THIS PULLING.
COOL, THAT'S THE SAME KIND OF MUSIC I'M INTO!
WHAT ABOUT DE LA SOUL? I JUST SAW THEM AT BUMBERSHOOT!
ARE THEY STILL TOURING?
I SAW THEM PLAY IN '92! 3 FEET HIGH AND RISING IS THE BEST.
LUCKY! HOW OLD ARE YOU, ANYWAY?
32. PRETTY MUCH A GEEZER TO YOU.
32−17=15
SAME AGE GAP AS MY PARENTS...
NAH...
ALL THE BEST HIP-HOP WAS IN THE '80s AND '90s.

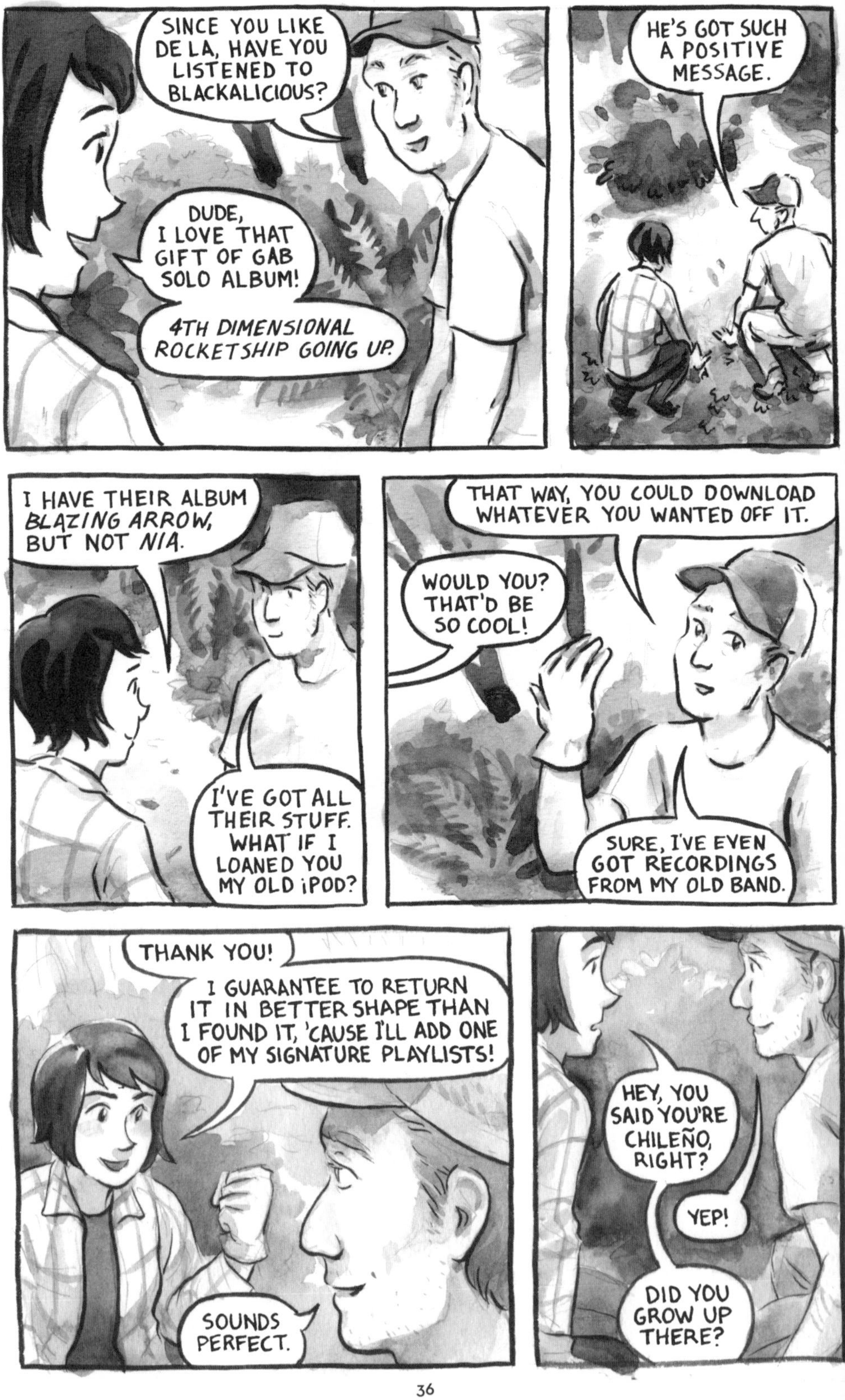
SINCE YOU LIKE DE LA, HAVE YOU LISTENED TO BLACKALICIOUS?
DUDE, I LOVE THAT GIFT OF GAB SOLO ALBUM!
4TH DIMENSIONAL ROCKETSHIP GOING UP.
HE'S GOT SUCH A POSITIVE MESSAGE.
I HAVE THEIR ALBUM *BLAZING ARROW*, BUT NOT *NIA*.
I'VE GOT ALL THEIR STUFF. WHAT IF I LOANED YOU MY OLD iPOD?
THAT WAY, YOU COULD DOWNLOAD WHATEVER YOU WANTED OFF IT.
WOULD YOU? THAT'D BE SO COOL!
SURE, I'VE EVEN GOT RECORDINGS FROM MY OLD BAND.
THANK YOU!
I GUARANTEE TO RETURN IT IN BETTER SHAPE THAN I FOUND IT, 'CAUSE I'LL ADD ONE OF MY SIGNATURE PLAYLISTS!
SOUNDS PERFECT.
HEY, YOU SAID YOU'RE CHILEÑO, RIGHT?
YEP!
DID YOU GROW UP THERE?

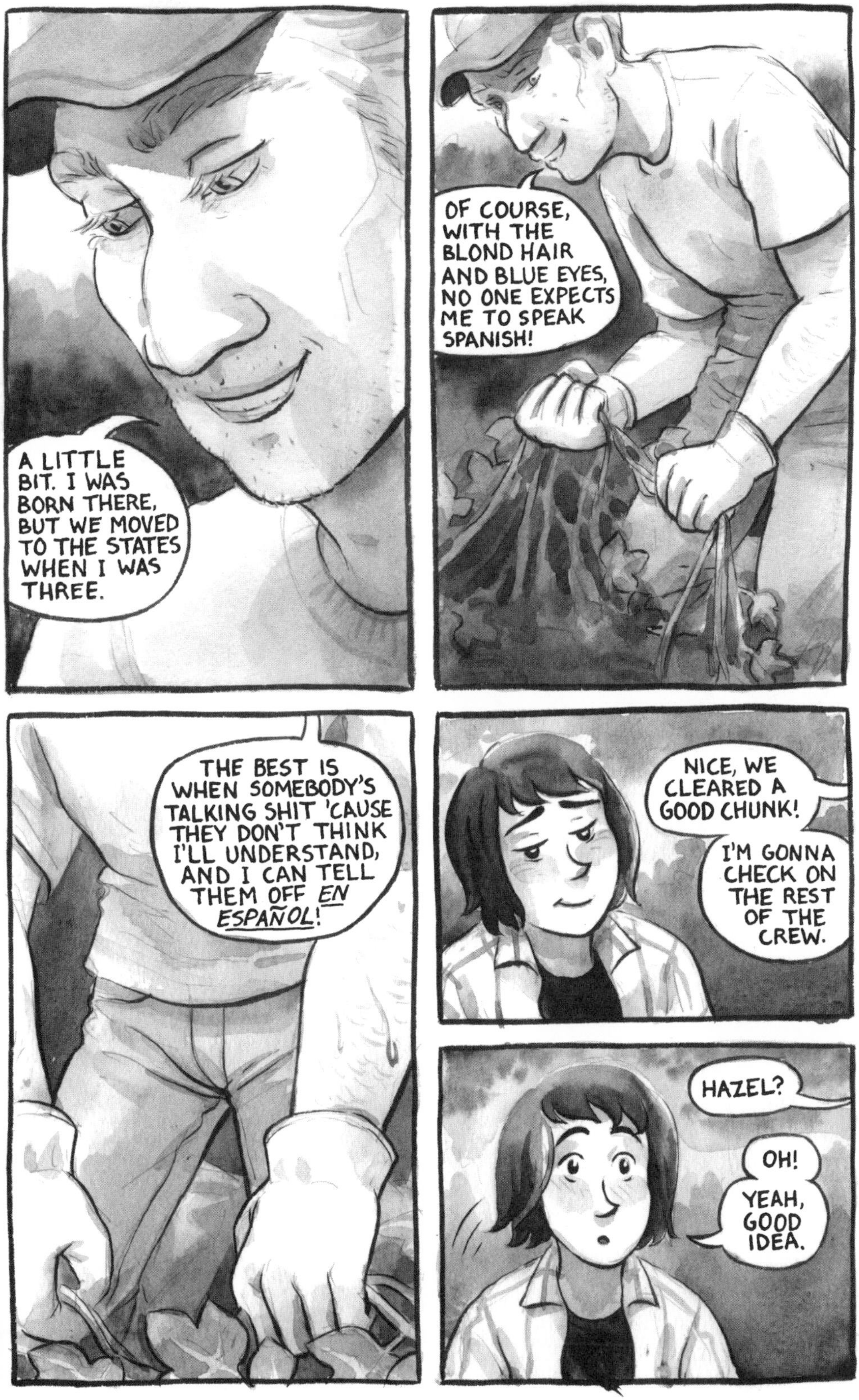
A LITTLE BIT. I WAS BORN THERE, BUT WE MOVED TO THE STATES WHEN I WAS THREE.
OF COURSE, WITH THE BLOND HAIR AND BLUE EYES, NO ONE EXPECTS ME TO SPEAK SPANISH!
THE BEST IS WHEN SOMEBODY'S TALKING SHIT 'CAUSE THEY DON'T THINK I'LL UNDERSTAND, AND I CAN TELL THEM OFF EN ESPAÑOL!
NICE, WE CLEARED A GOOD CHUNK!
I'M GONNA CHECK ON THE REST OF THE CREW.
HAZEL?
OH!
YEAH, GOOD IDEA.

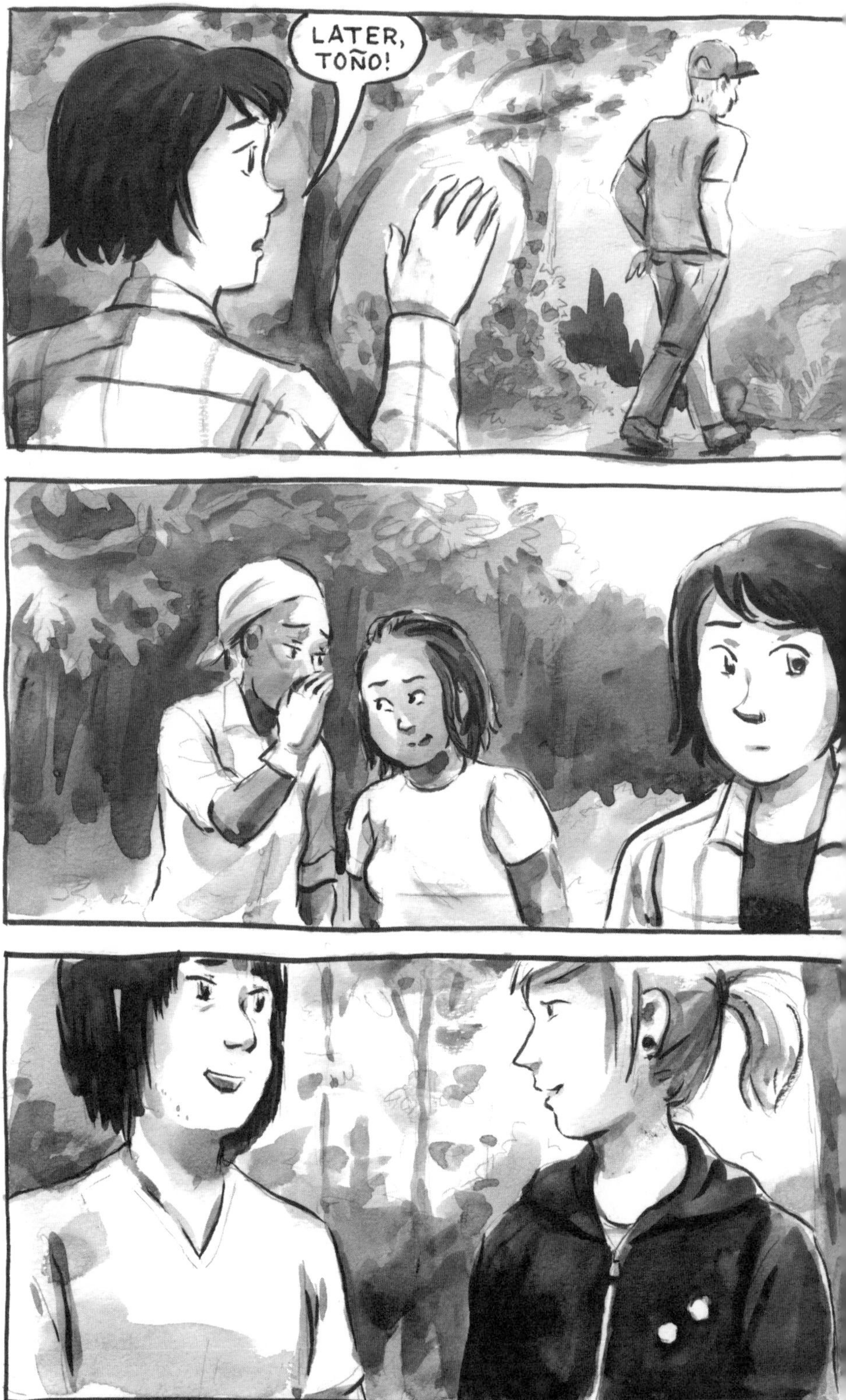
LATER, TOÑO!

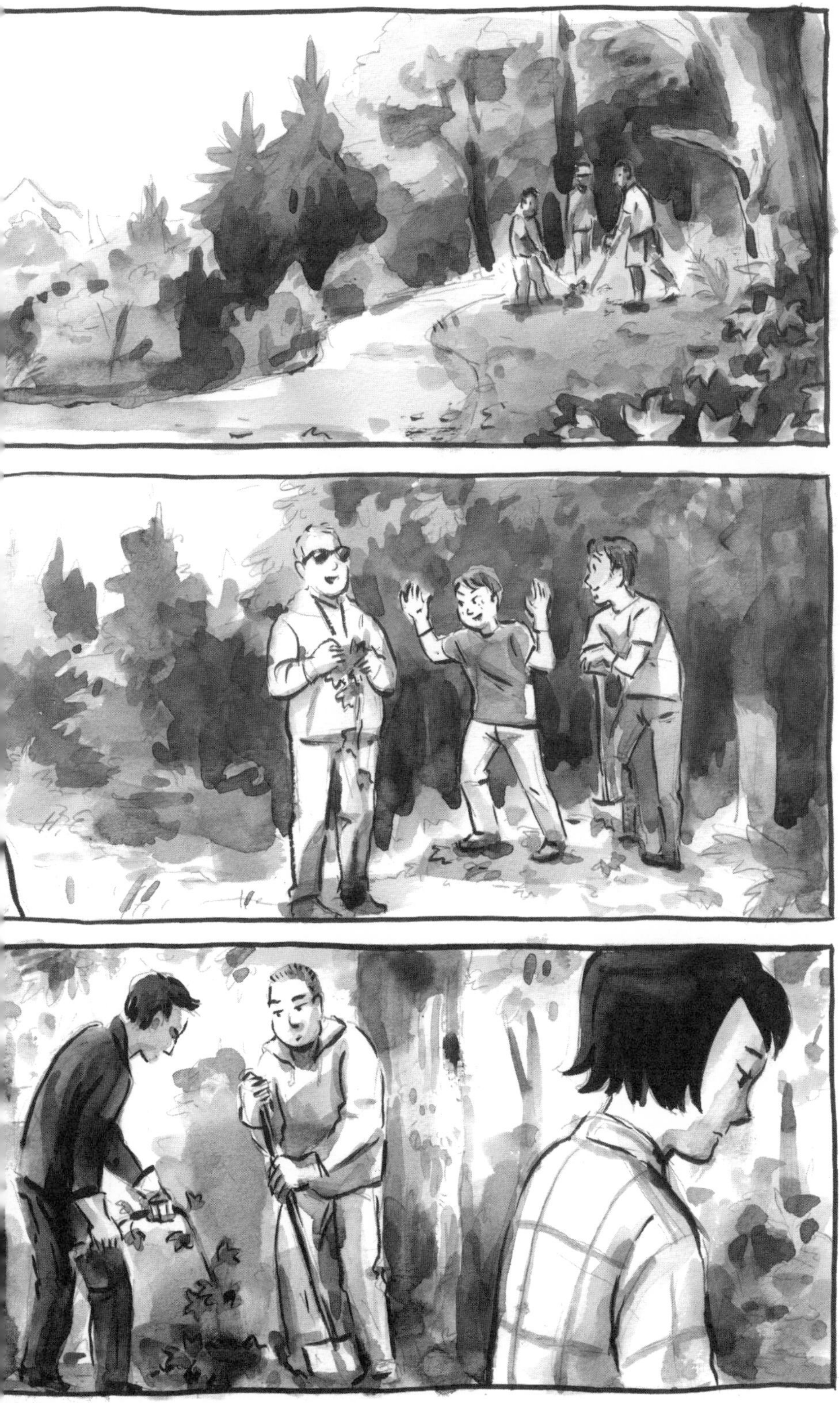

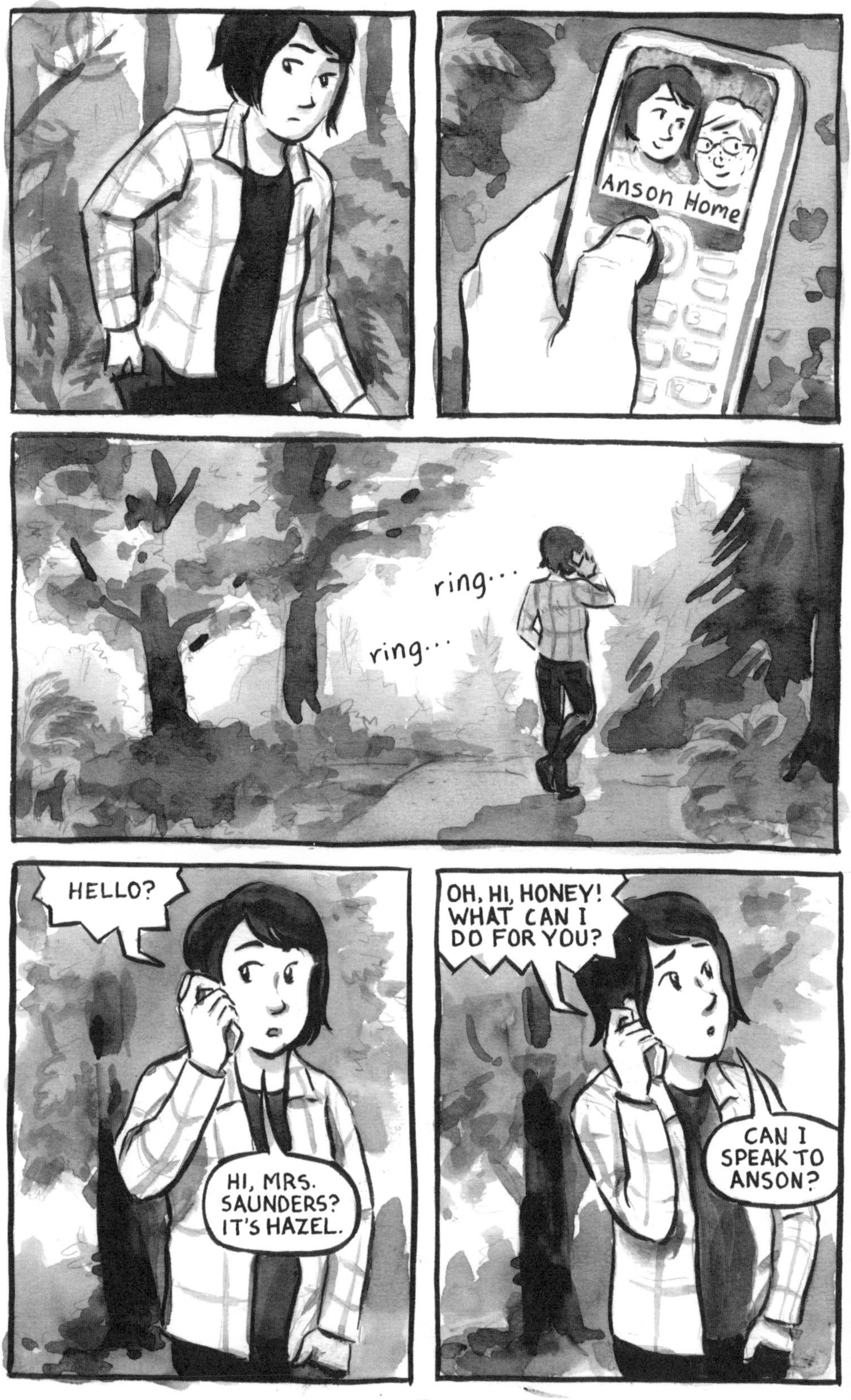
Anson Home
ring...
ring...
HELLO?
HI, MRS. SAUNDERS? IT'S HAZEL.
OH, HI, HONEY! WHAT CAN I DO FOR YOU?
CAN I SPEAK TO ANSON?

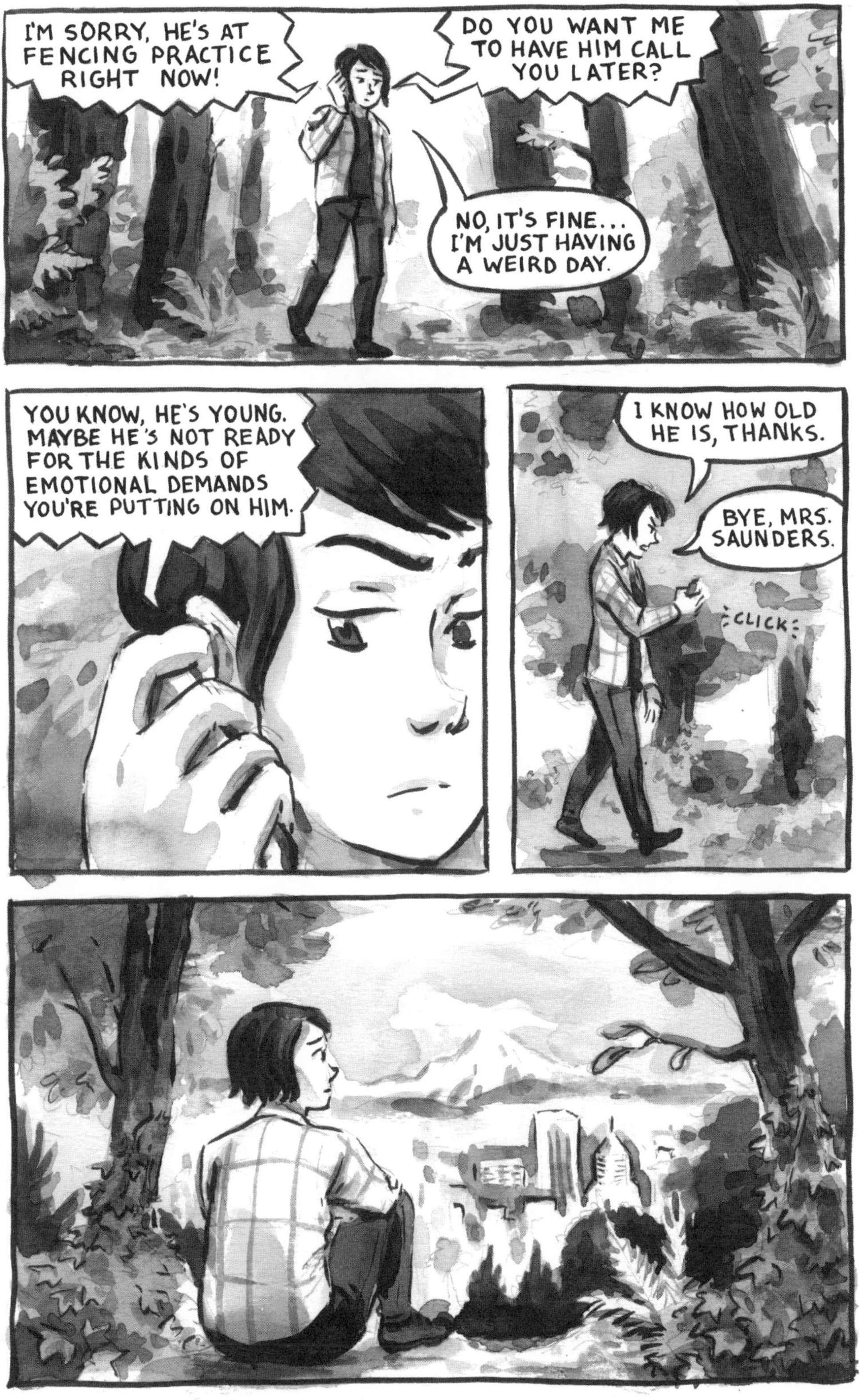
I'M SORRY, HE'S AT FENCING PRACTICE RIGHT NOW!
DO YOU WANT ME TO HAVE HIM CALL YOU LATER?
NO, IT'S FINE... I'M JUST HAVING A WEIRD DAY.
YOU KNOW, HE'S YOUNG. MAYBE HE'S NOT READY FOR THE KINDS OF EMOTIONAL DEMANDS YOU'RE PUTTING ON HIM.
I KNOW HOW OLD HE IS, THANKS.
BYE, MRS. SAUNDERS.
CLICK

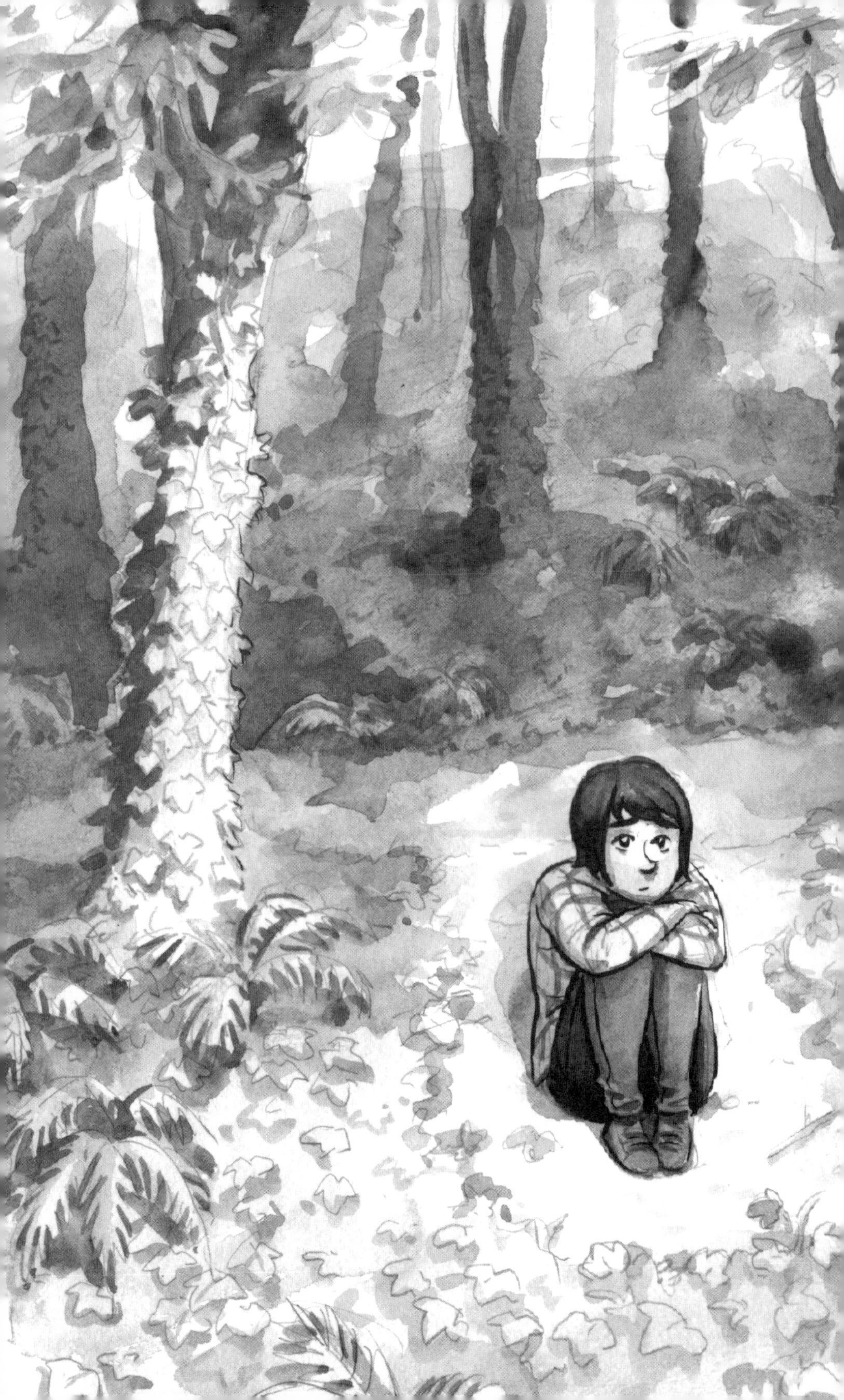

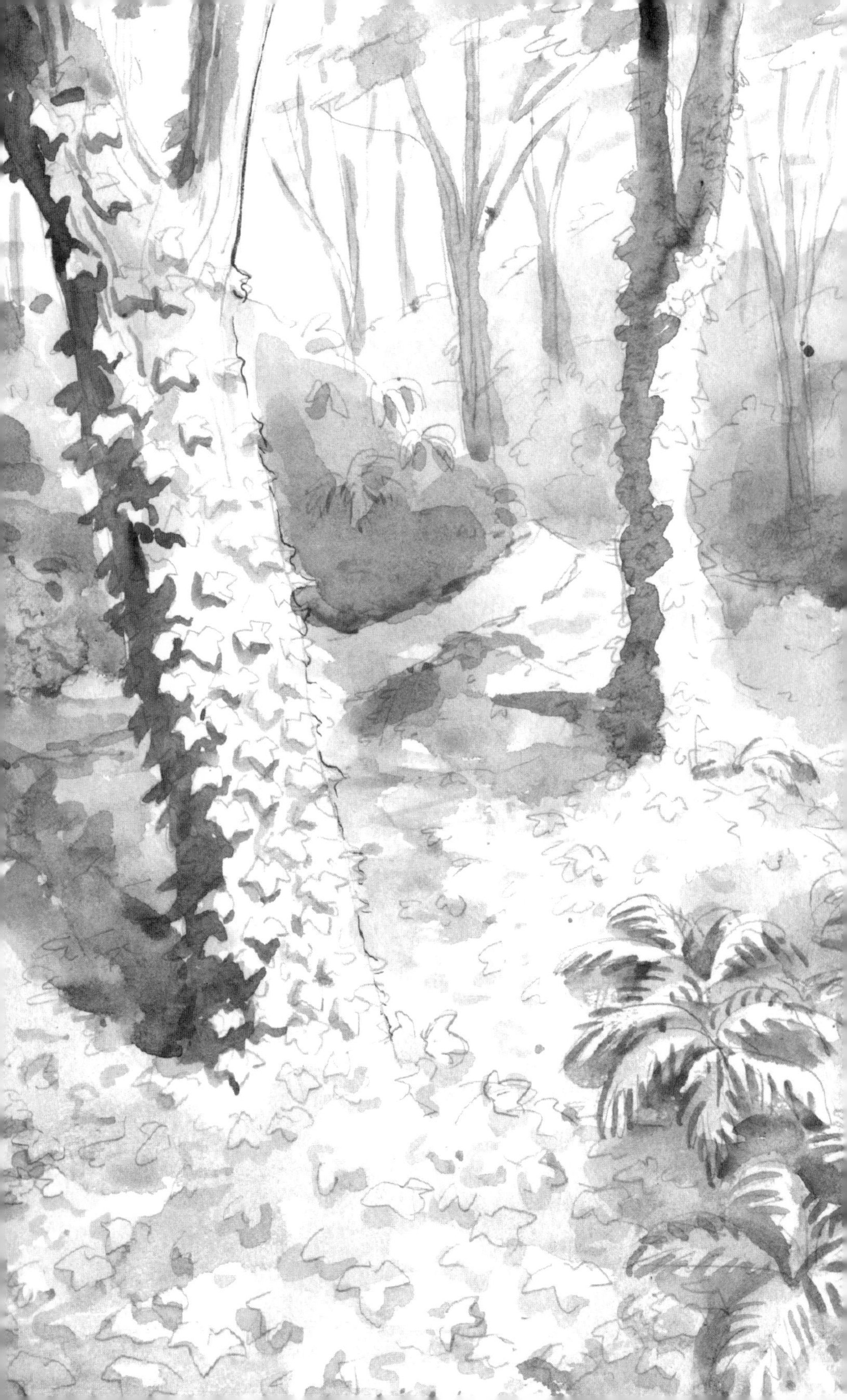

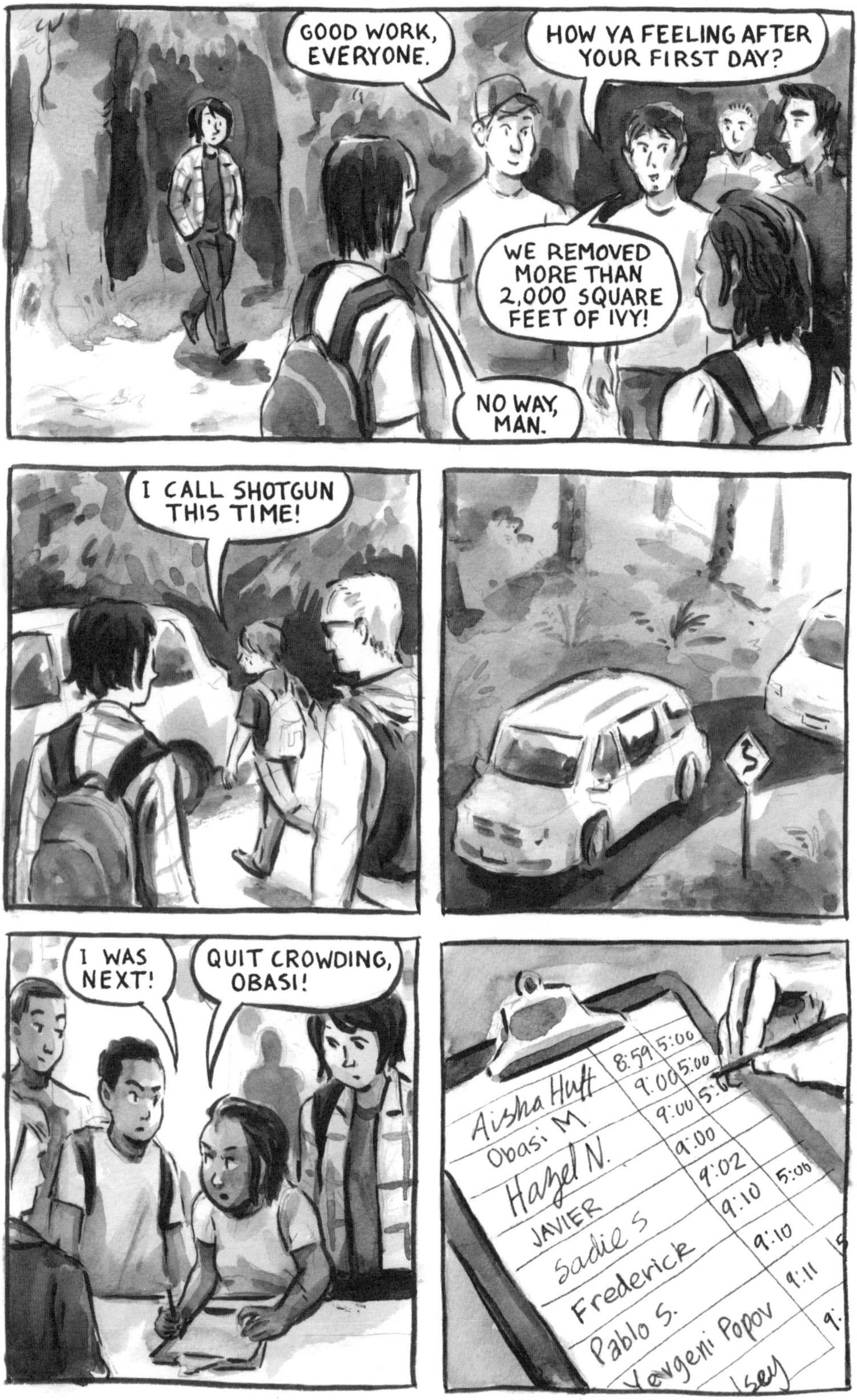
GOOD WORK, EVERYONE.
HOW YA FEELING AFTER YOUR FIRST DAY?
WE REMOVED MORE THAN 2,000 SQUARE FEET OF IVY!
NO WAY, MAN.
I CALL SHOTGUN THIS TIME!
I WAS NEXT!
QUIT CROWDING, OBASI!
Aisha Huft 8:59 5:00
Obasi M 9:00 5:00
Hazel N. 9:00
JAVIER 9:00
Sadie S 9:02 5:00
Frederick 9:10
Pablo S. 9:10
Yevgeni Popov 9:11

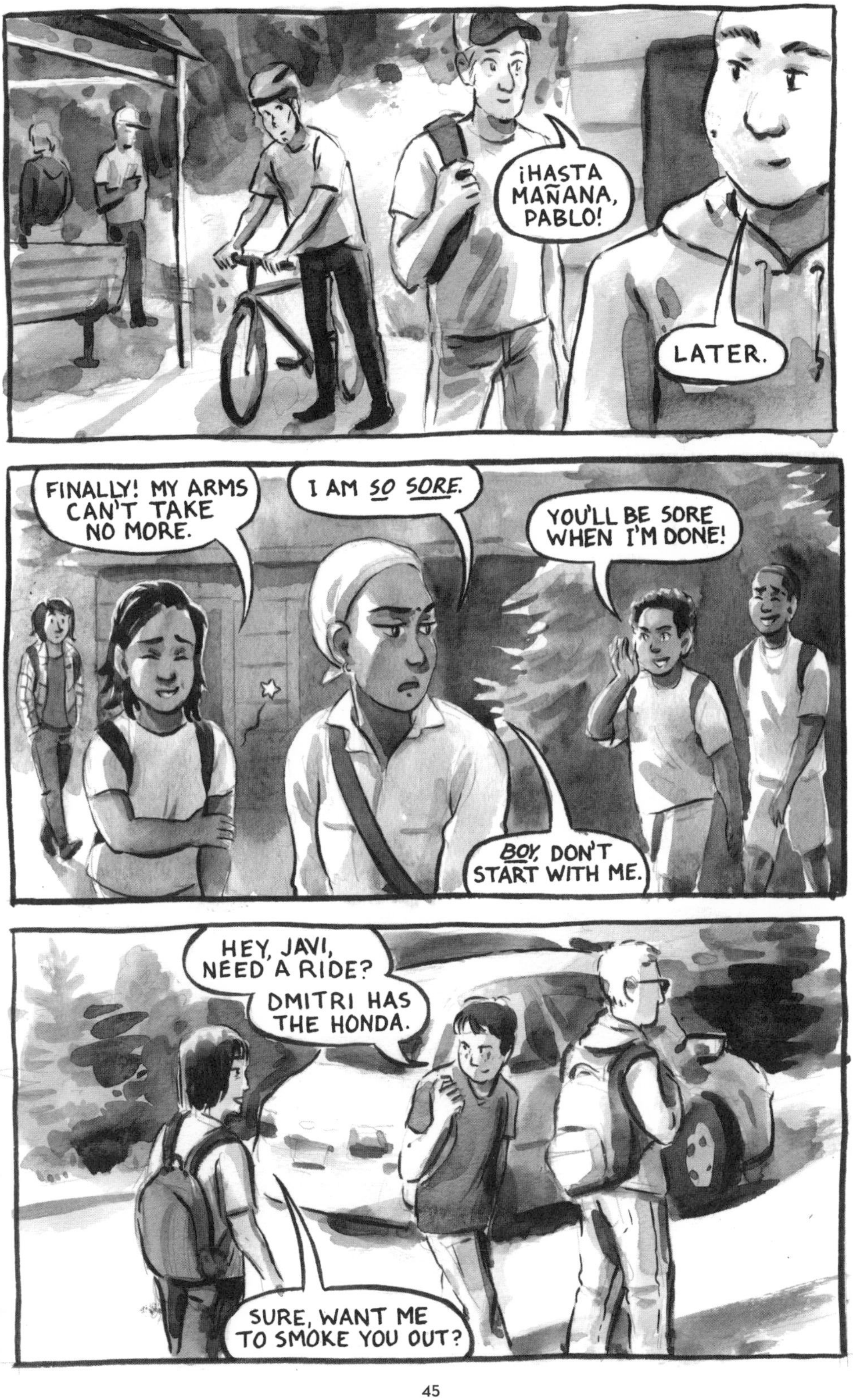
¡HASTA MAÑANA, PABLO!
LATER.
FINALLY! MY ARMS CAN'T TAKE NO MORE.
I AM SO SORE.
YOU'LL BE SORE WHEN I'M DONE!
BOY, DON'T START WITH ME.
HEY, JAVI, NEED A RIDE?
DMITRI HAS THE HONDA.
SURE, WANT ME TO SMOKE YOU OUT?

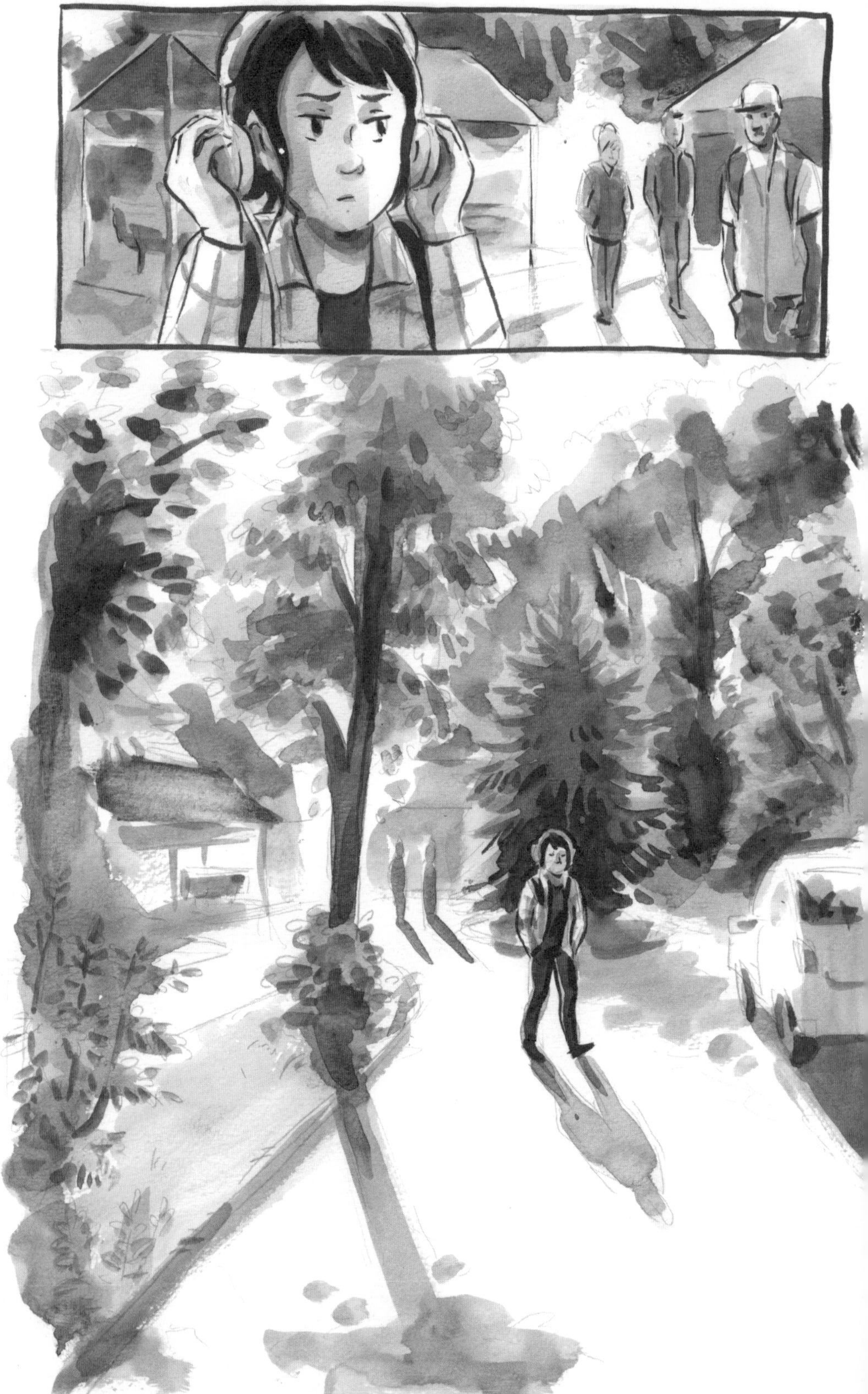

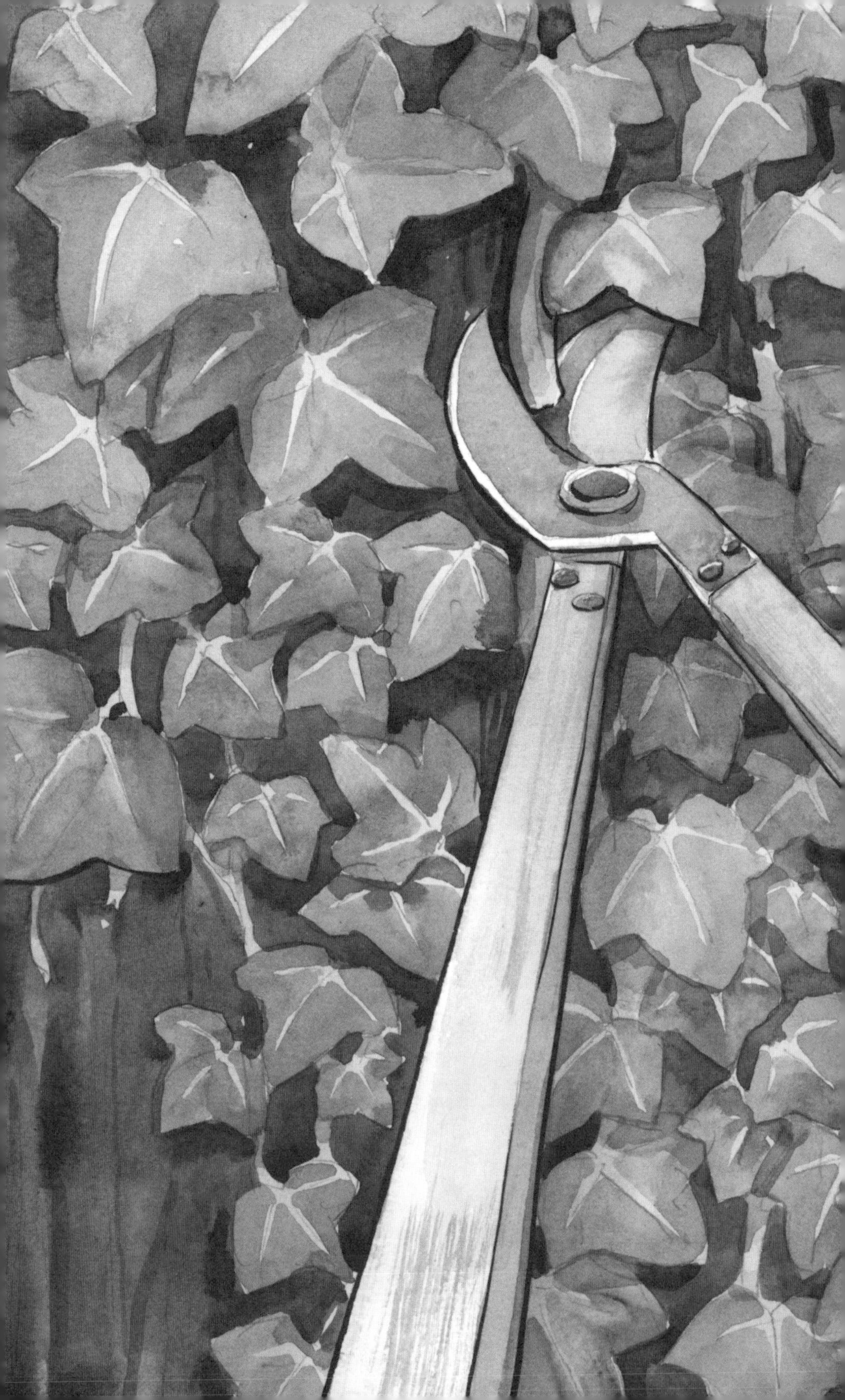

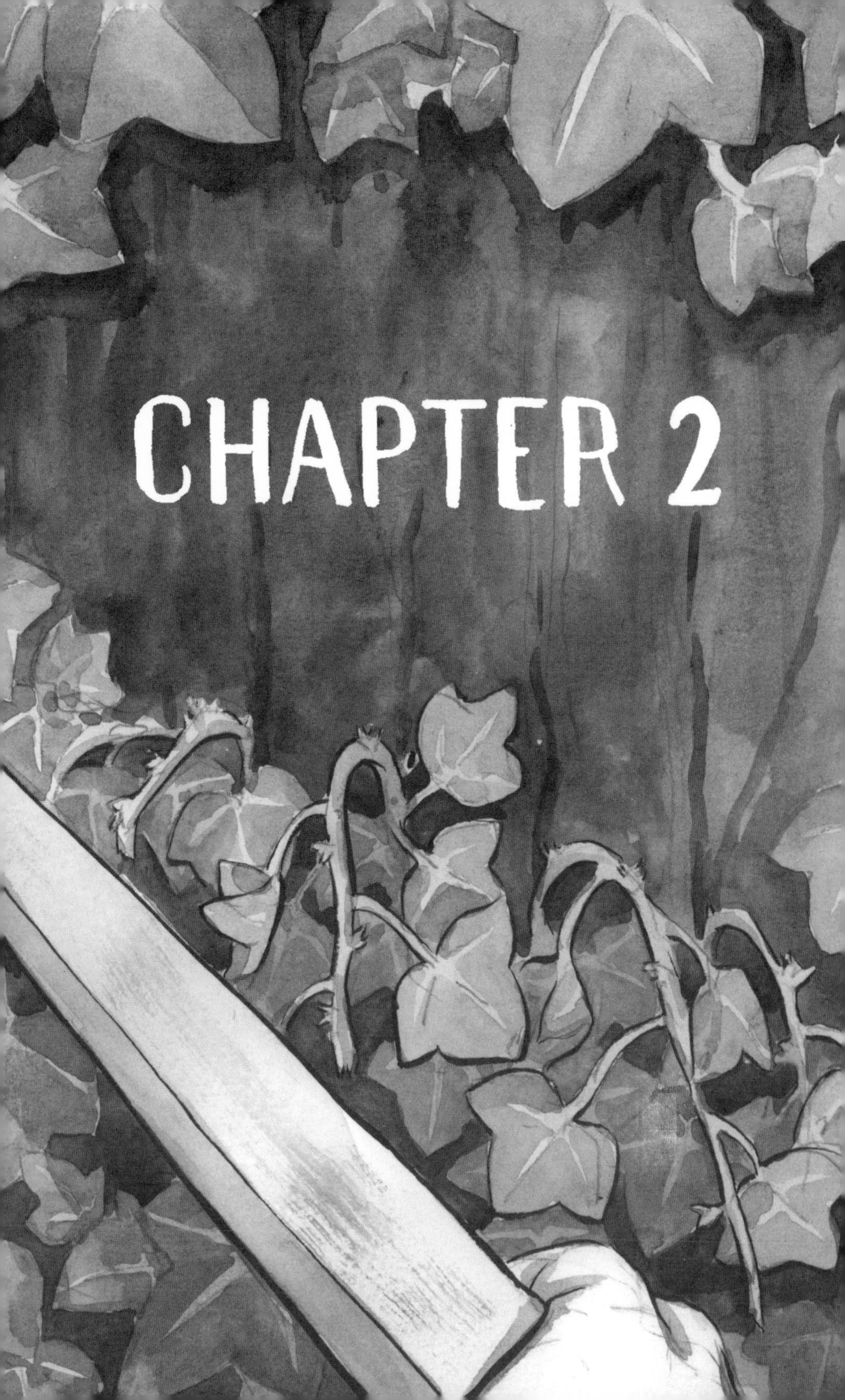
CHAPTER 2

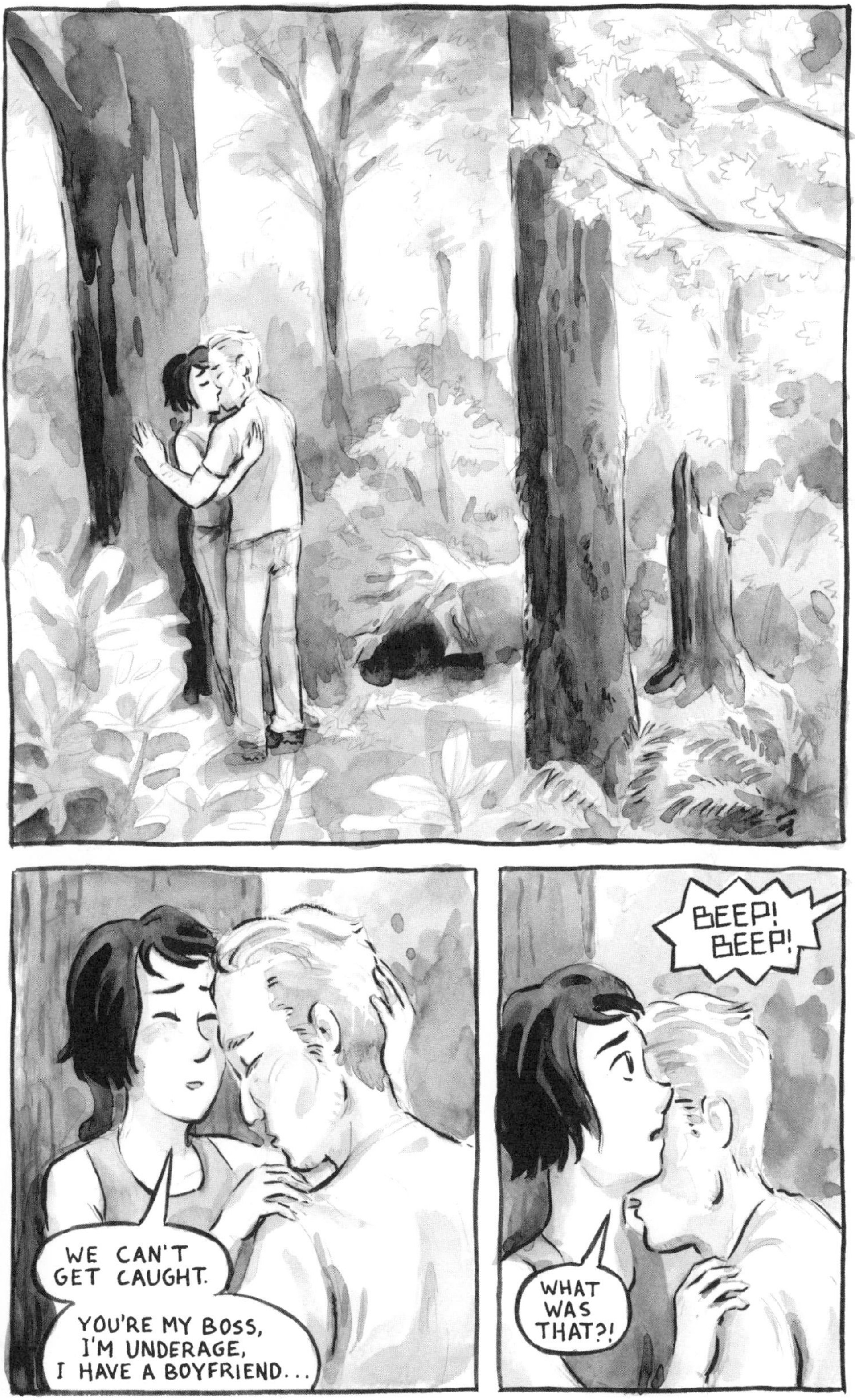
WE CAN'T GET CAUGHT.
YOU'RE MY BOSS, I'M UNDERAGE, I HAVE A BOYFRIEND...
BEEP! BEEP!
WHAT WAS THAT?!

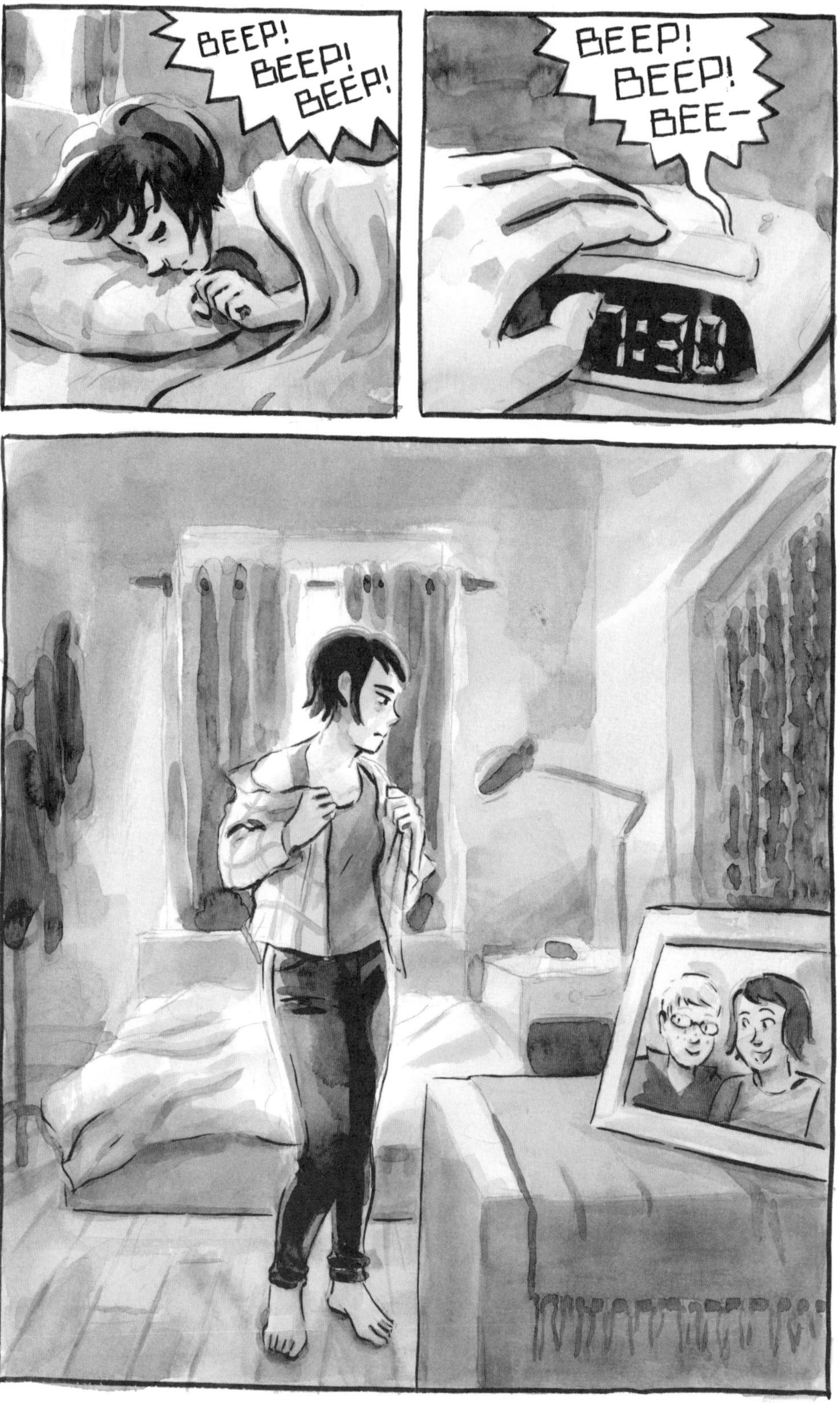
BEEP! BEEP! BEEP!
BEEP! BEEP! BEE-

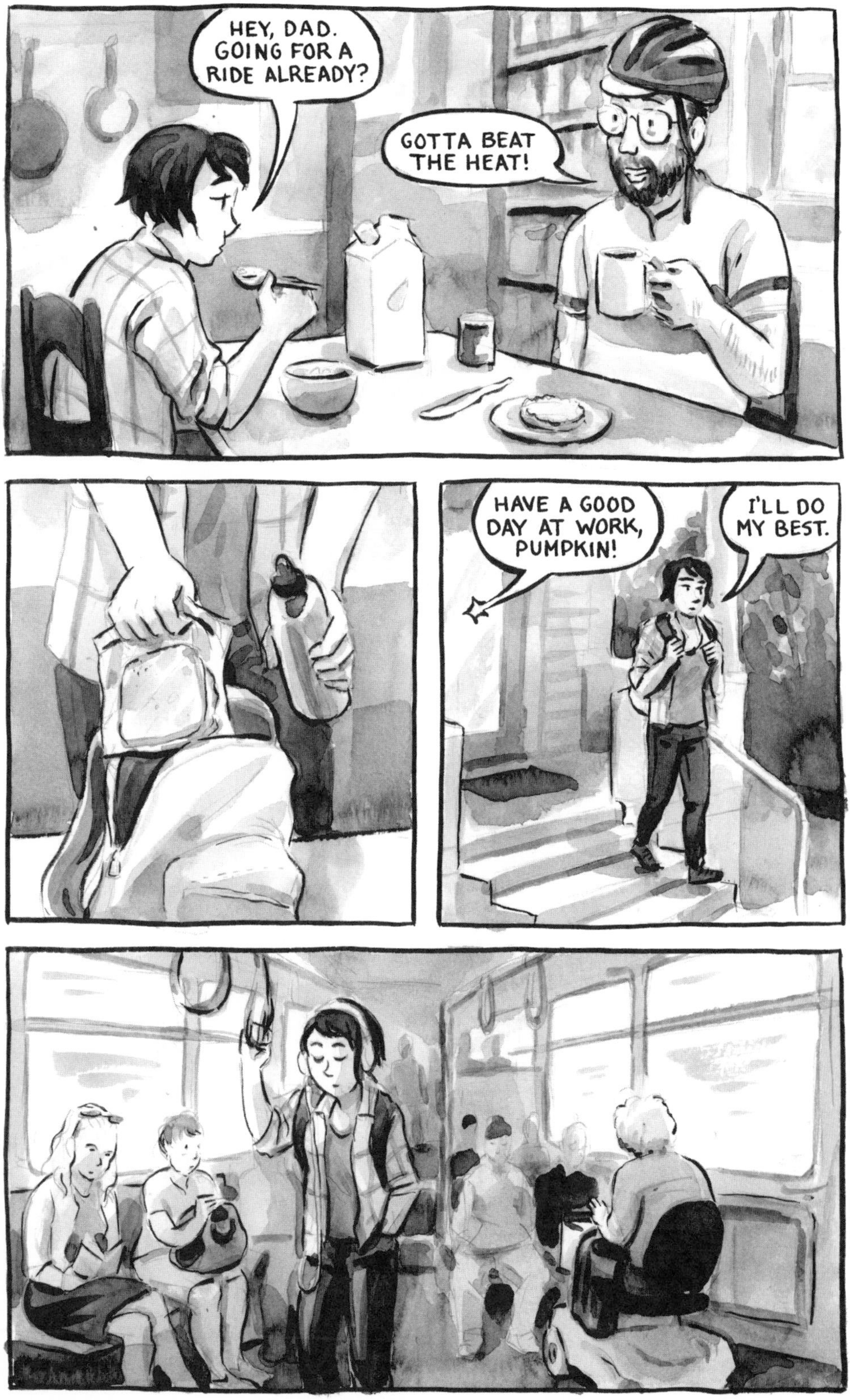
HEY, DAD. GOING FOR A RIDE ALREADY?
GOTTA BEAT THE HEAT!
HAVE A GOOD DAY AT WORK, PUMPKIN!
I'LL DO MY BEST.

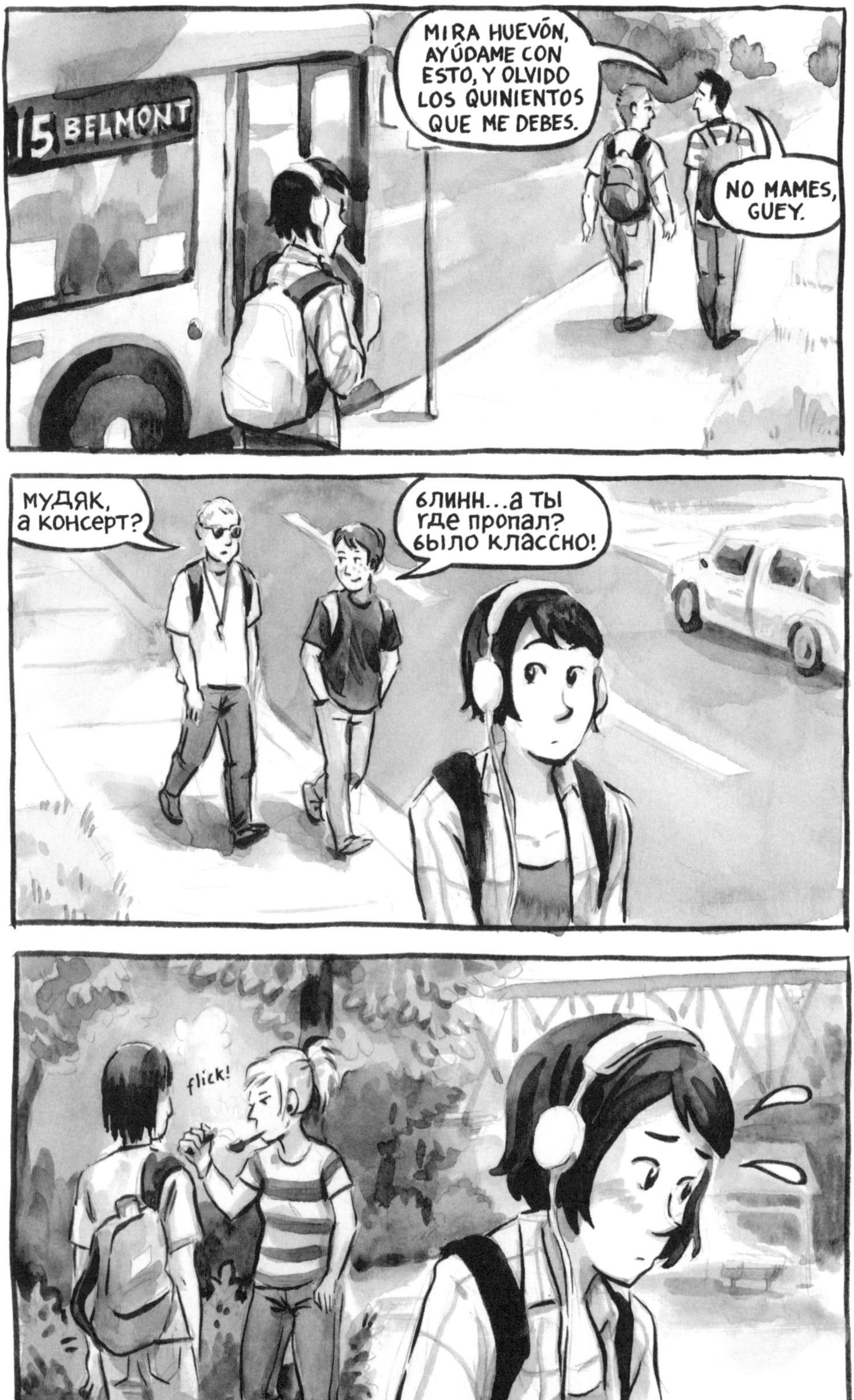
15 BELMONT
MIRA HUEVÓN, AYÚDAME CON ESTO, Y OLVIDO LOS QUINIENTOS QUE ME DEBES.
NO MAMES, GUEY.
мудяк, а консерт?
блинн...а ты где пропал? было классно!
flick!

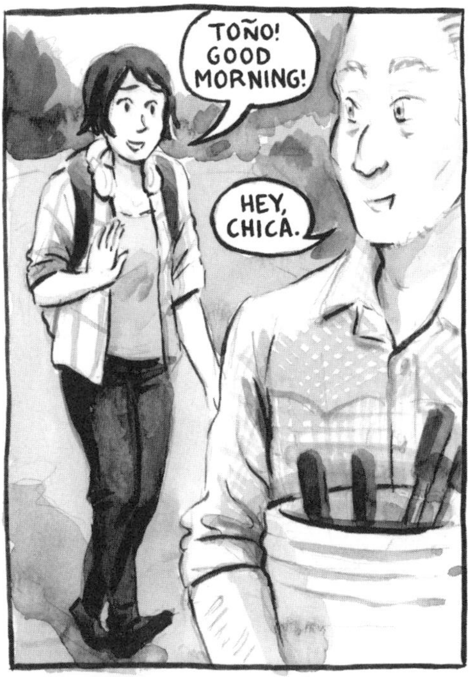
TOÑO! GOOD MORNING!
HEY, CHICA.

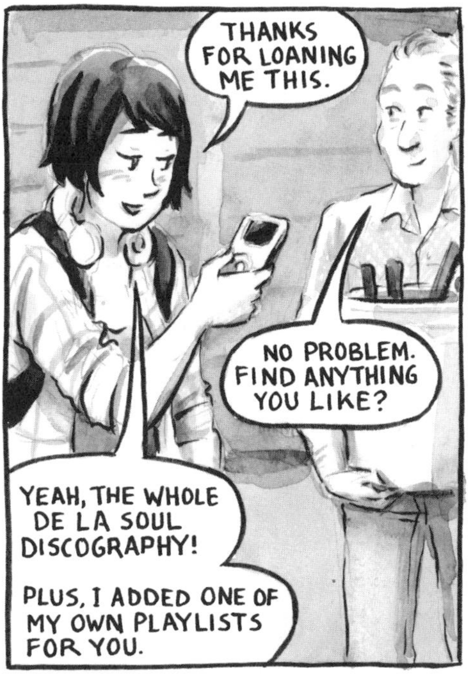
THANKS FOR LOANING ME THIS.
NO PROBLEM. FIND ANYTHING YOU LIKE?
YEAH, THE WHOLE DE LA SOUL DISCOGRAPHY!
PLUS, I ADDED ONE OF MY OWN PLAYLISTS FOR YOU.

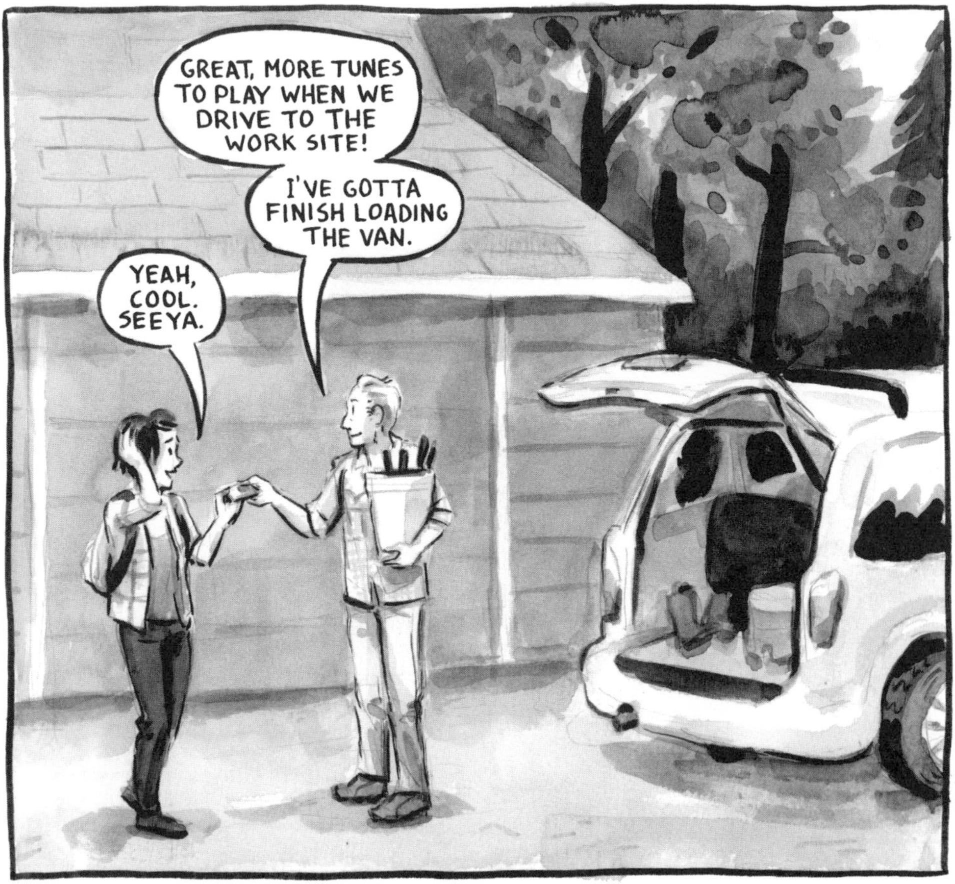
GREAT, MORE TUNES TO PLAY WHEN WE DRIVE TO THE WORK SITE!
I'VE GOTTA FINISH LOADING THE VAN.
YEAH, COOL. SEEYA.

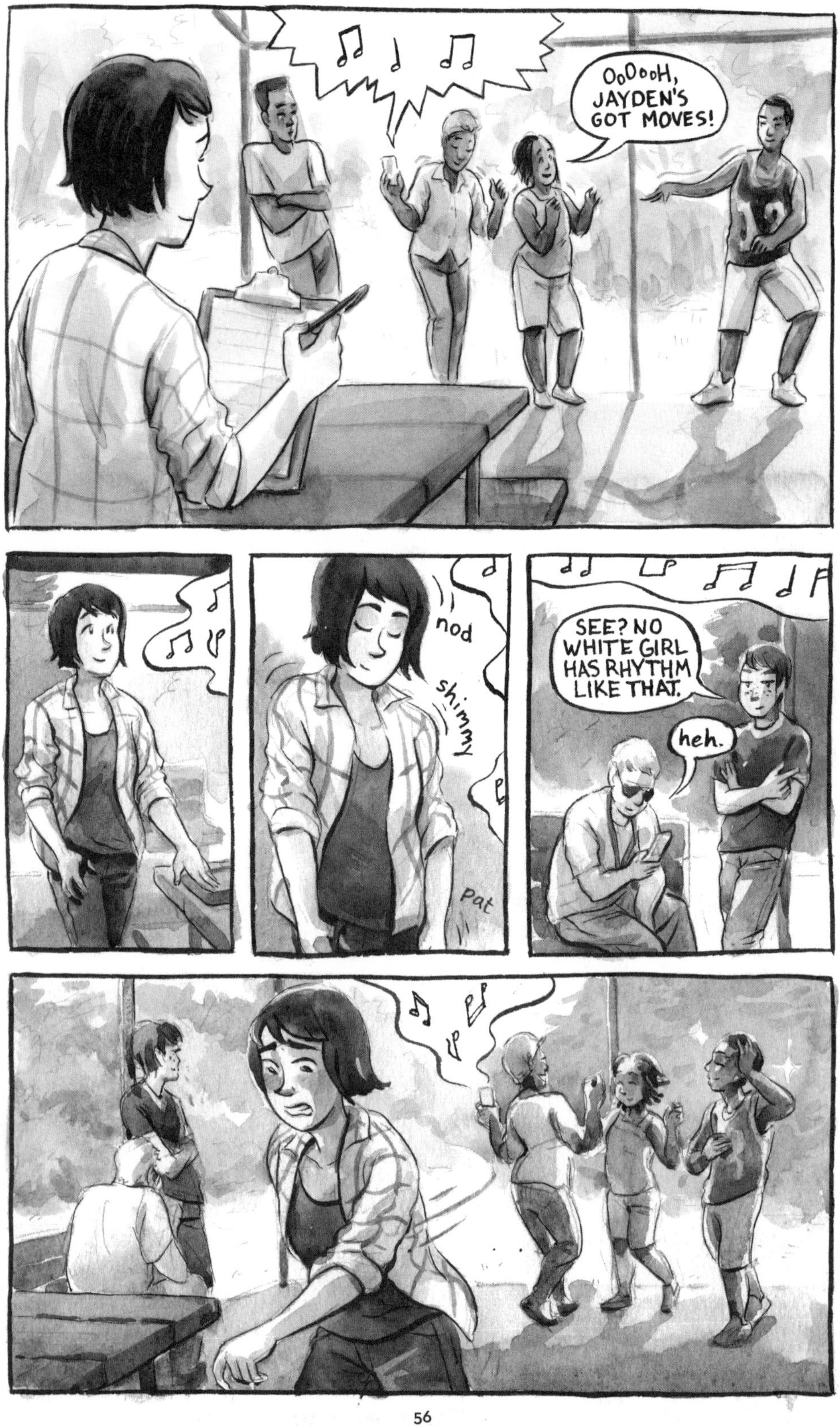
OoOooH, JAYDEN'S GOT MOVES!
nod
shimmy
pat
SEE? NO WHITE GIRL HAS RHYTHM LIKE THAT.
heh.

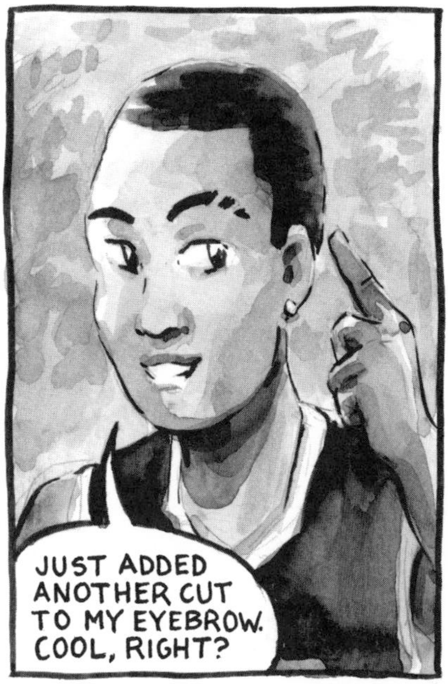
JUST ADDED ANOTHER CUT TO MY EYEBROW. COOL, RIGHT?

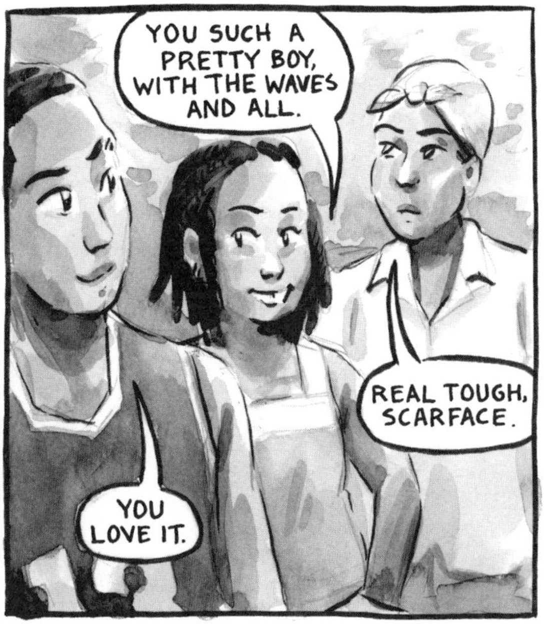
YOU SUCH A PRETTY BOY, WITH THE WAVES AND ALL.
REAL TOUGH, SCARFACE.
YOU LOVE IT.

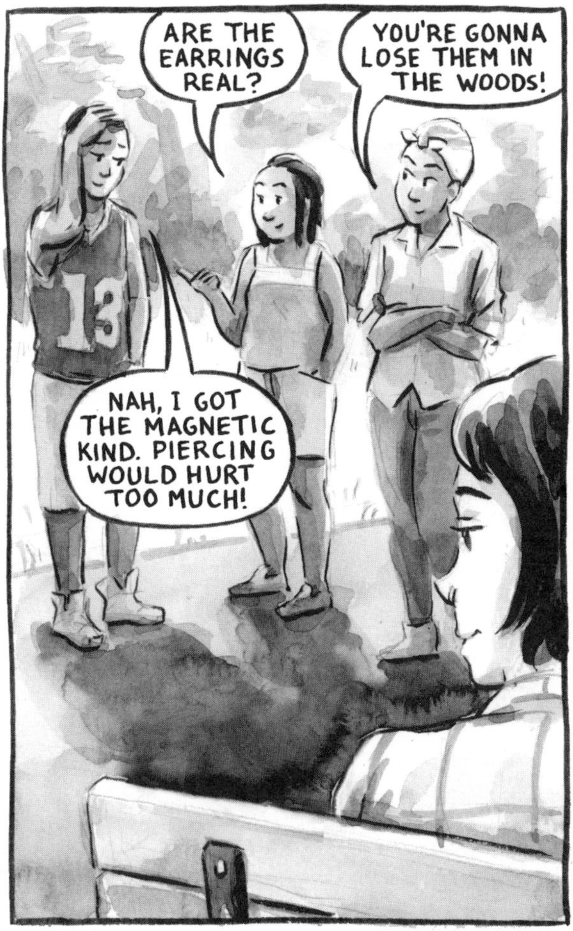
ARE THE EARRINGS REAL?
YOU'RE GONNA LOSE THEM IN THE WOODS!
NAH, I GOT THE MAGNETIC KIND. PIERCING WOULD HURT TOO MUCH!

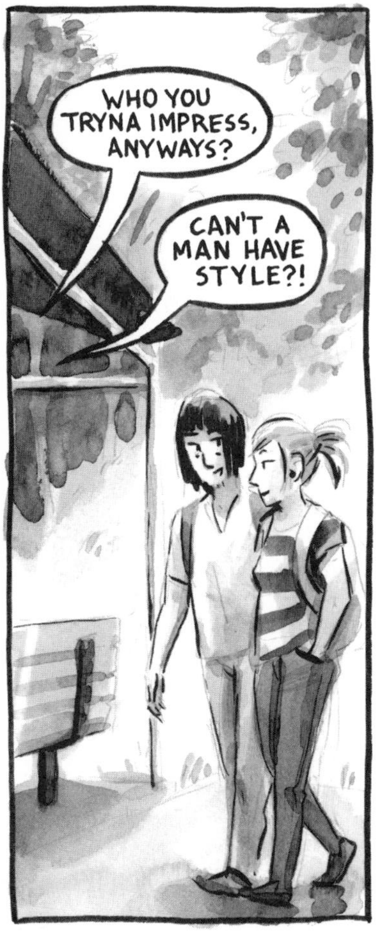
WHO YOU TRYNA IMPRESS, ANYWAYS?
CAN'T A MAN HAVE STYLE?!

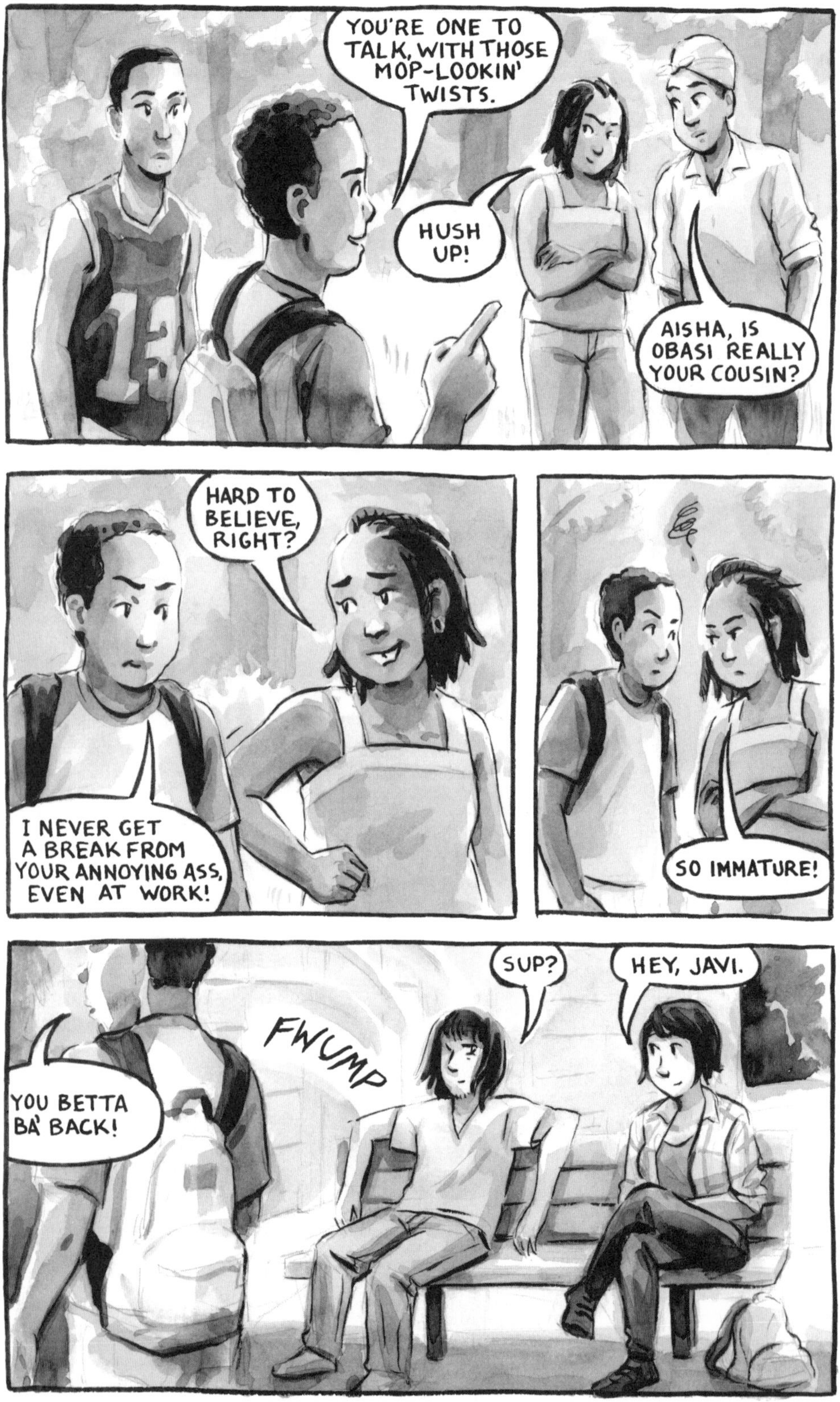
YOU'RE ONE TO TALK, WITH THOSE MOP-LOOKIN' TWISTS.
HUSH UP!
AISHA, IS OBASI REALLY YOUR COUSIN?
HARD TO BELIEVE, RIGHT?
I NEVER GET A BREAK FROM YOUR ANNOYING ASS, EVEN AT WORK!
SO IMMATURE!
YOU BETTA BA' BACK!
FWUMP
SUP?
HEY, JAVI.

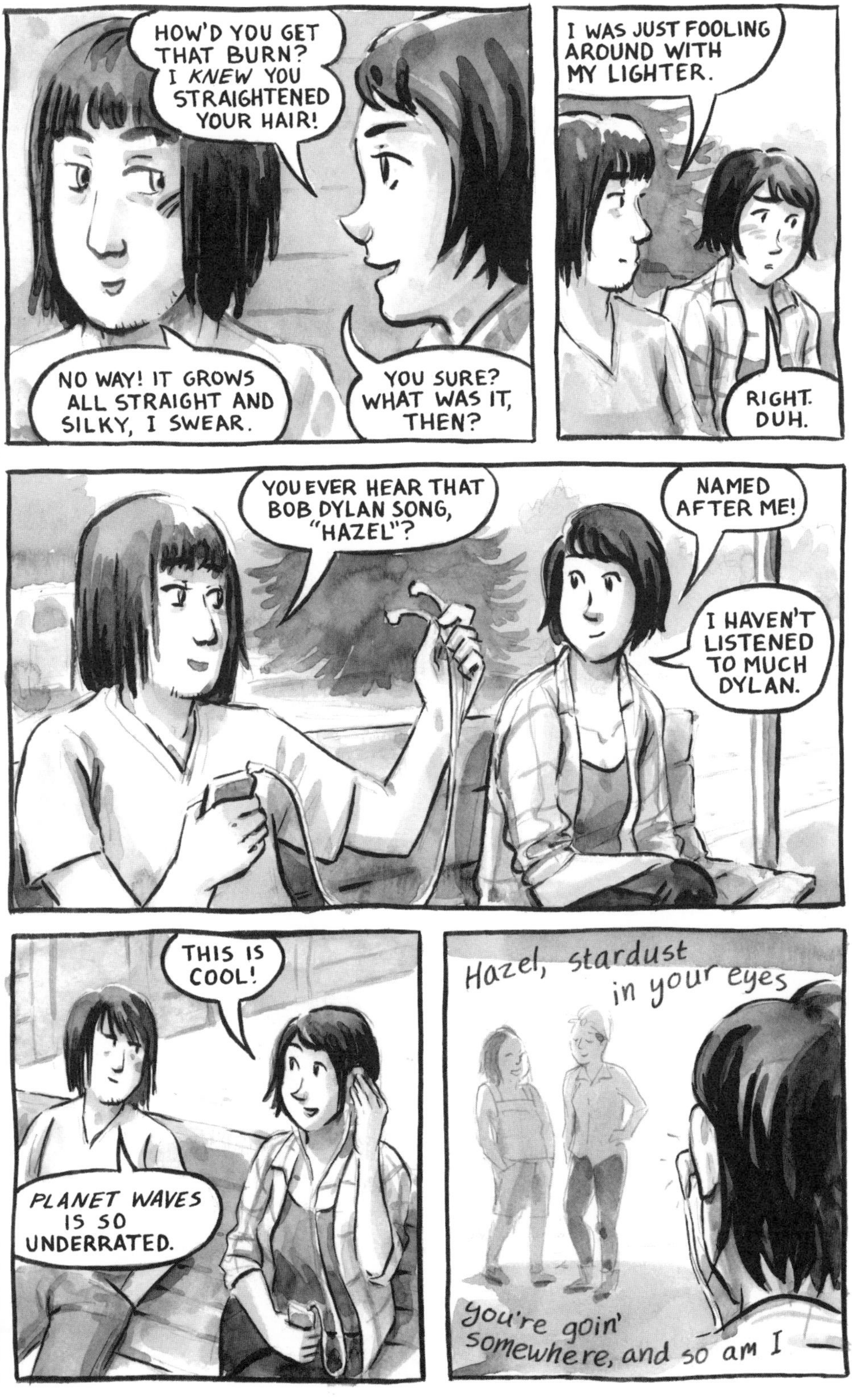
HOW'D YOU GET THAT BURN? I *KNEW* YOU STRAIGHTENED YOUR HAIR!
NO WAY! IT GROWS ALL STRAIGHT AND SILKY, I SWEAR.
YOU SURE? WHAT WAS IT, THEN?
I WAS JUST FOOLING AROUND WITH MY LIGHTER.
RIGHT. DUH.
YOU EVER HEAR THAT BOB DYLAN SONG, "HAZEL"?
NAMED AFTER ME!
I HAVEN'T LISTENED TO MUCH DYLAN.
THIS IS COOL!
PLANET WAVES IS SO UNDERRATED.
Hazel, stardust in your eyes
you're goin' somewhere, and so am I

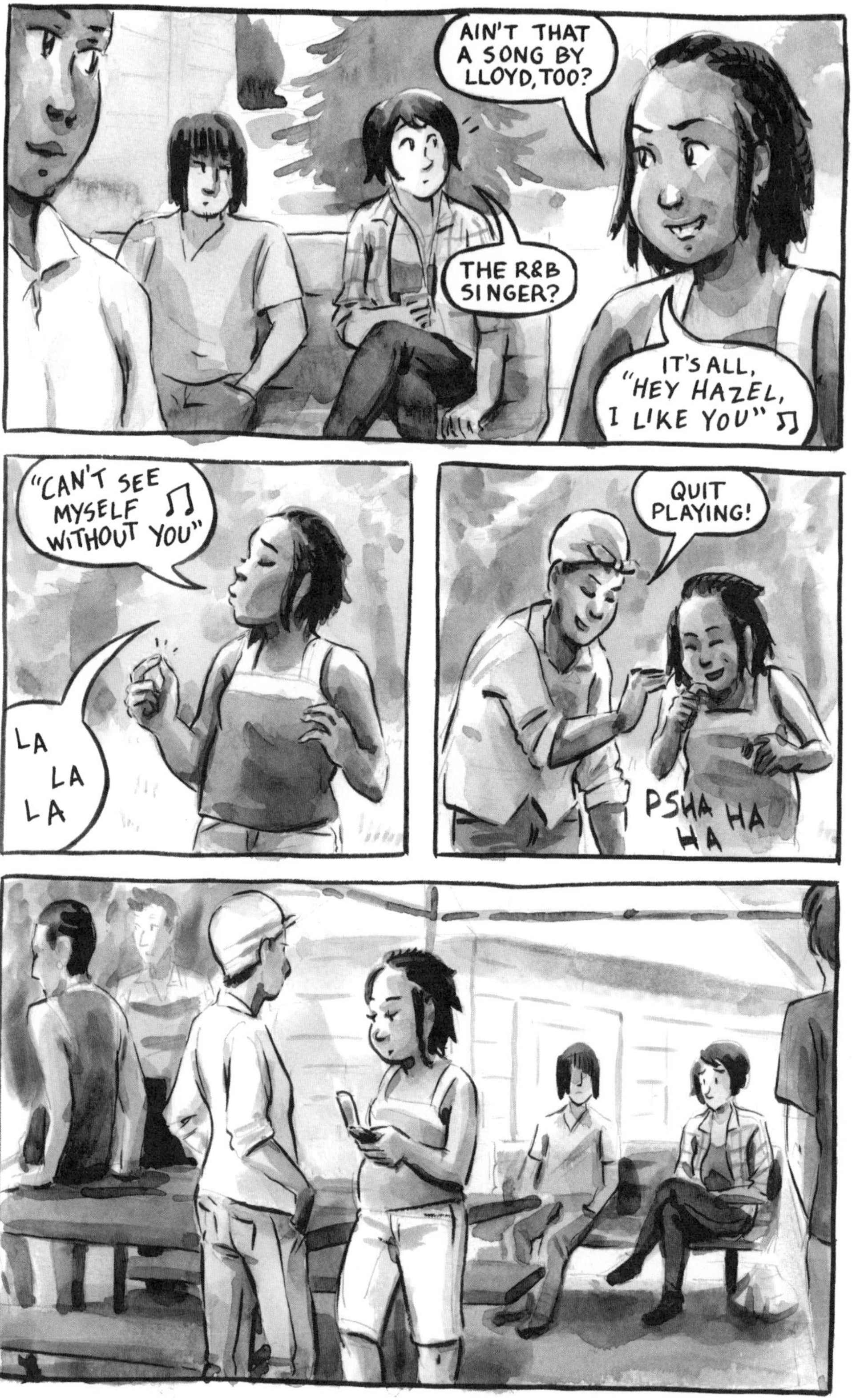
AIN'T THAT A SONG BY LLOYD, TOO?
THE R&B SINGER?
IT'S ALL, "HEY HAZEL, I LIKE YOU" ♫
"CAN'T SEE MYSELF ♫ WITHOUT YOU"
LA LA LA
QUIT PLAYING!
PSHA HA HA HA

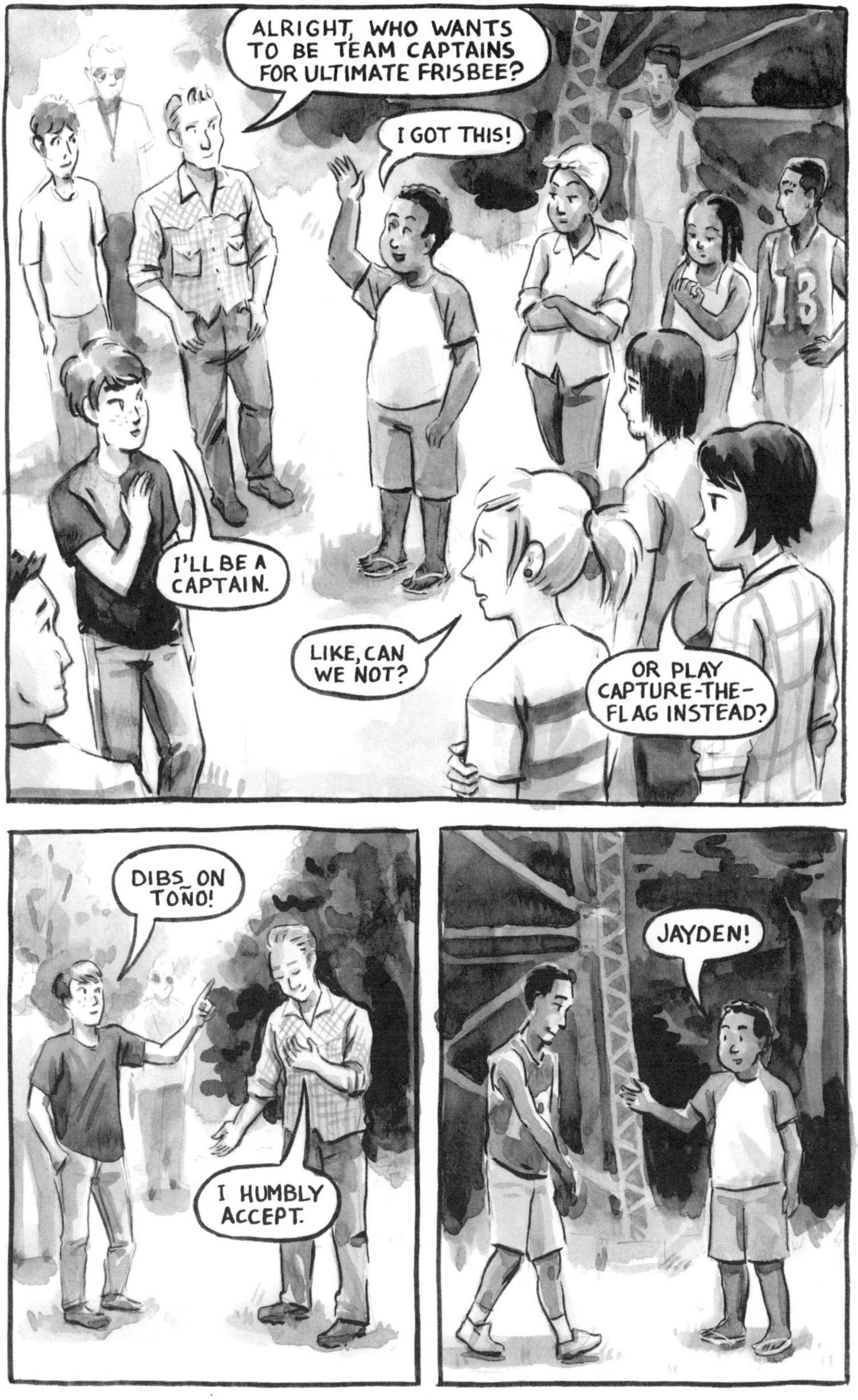
ALRIGHT, WHO WANTS TO BE TEAM CAPTAINS FOR ULTIMATE FRISBEE?
I GOT THIS!
I'LL BE A CAPTAIN.
LIKE, CAN WE NOT?
OR PLAY CAPTURE-THE-FLAG INSTEAD?
DIBS ON TOÑO!
I HUMBLY ACCEPT.
JAYDEN!

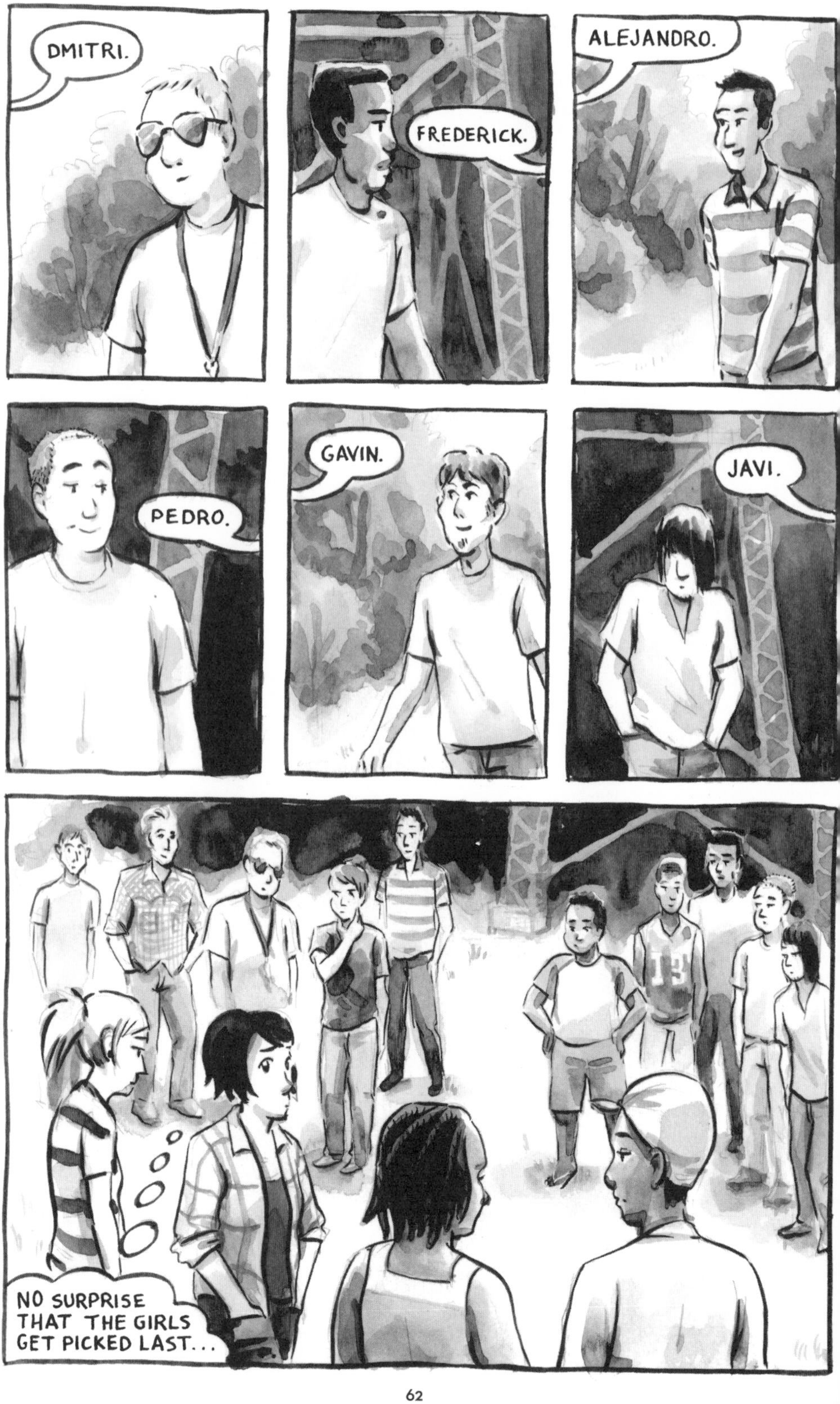
DMITRI.
FREDERICK.
ALEJANDRO.
PEDRO.
GAVIN.
JAVI.
NO SURPRISE THAT THE GIRLS GET PICKED LAST...

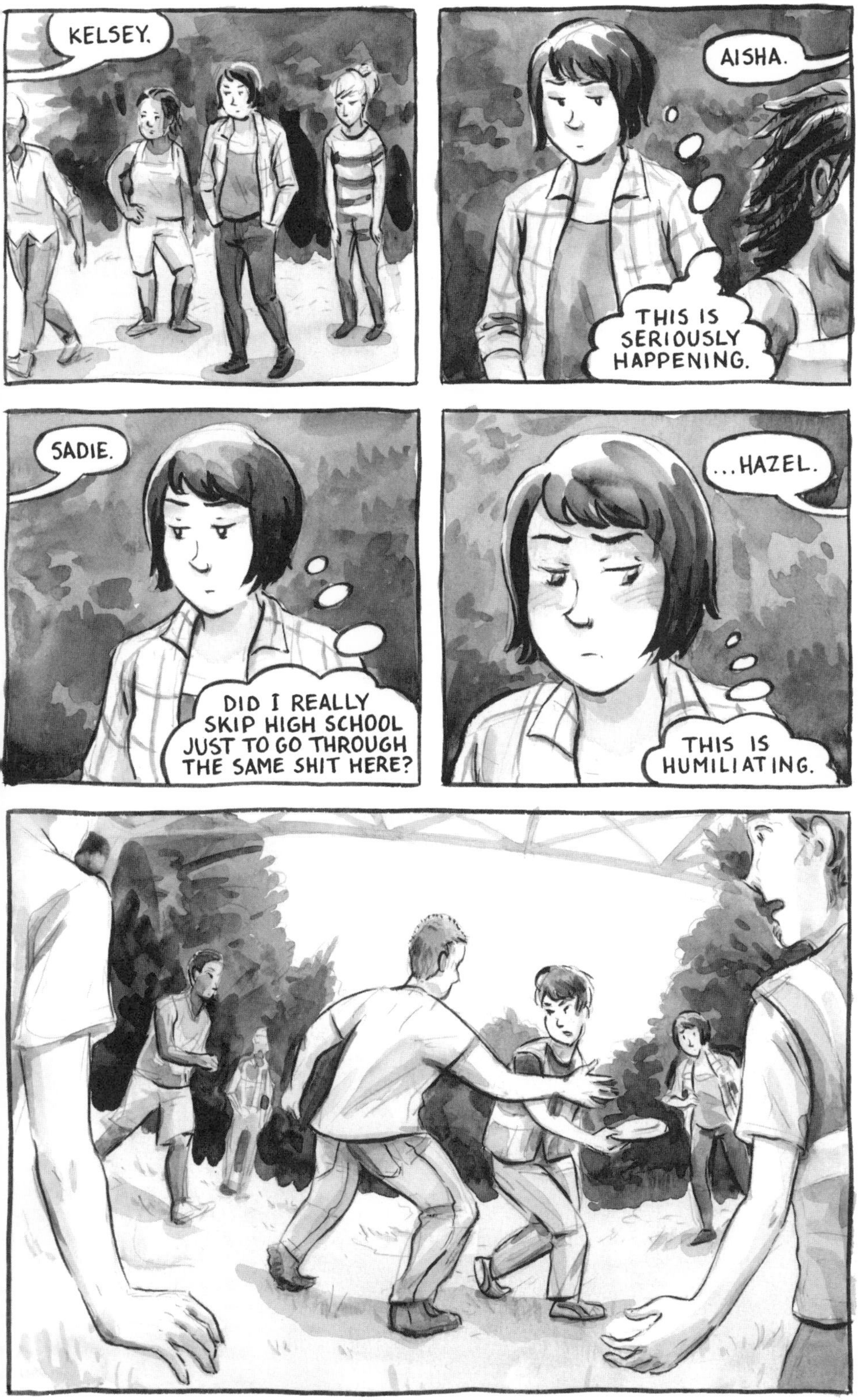
KELSEY.
AISHA.
THIS IS SERIOUSLY HAPPENING.
SADIE.
DID I REALLY SKIP HIGH SCHOOL JUST TO GO THROUGH THE SAME SHIT HERE?
...HAZEL.
THIS IS HUMILIATING.

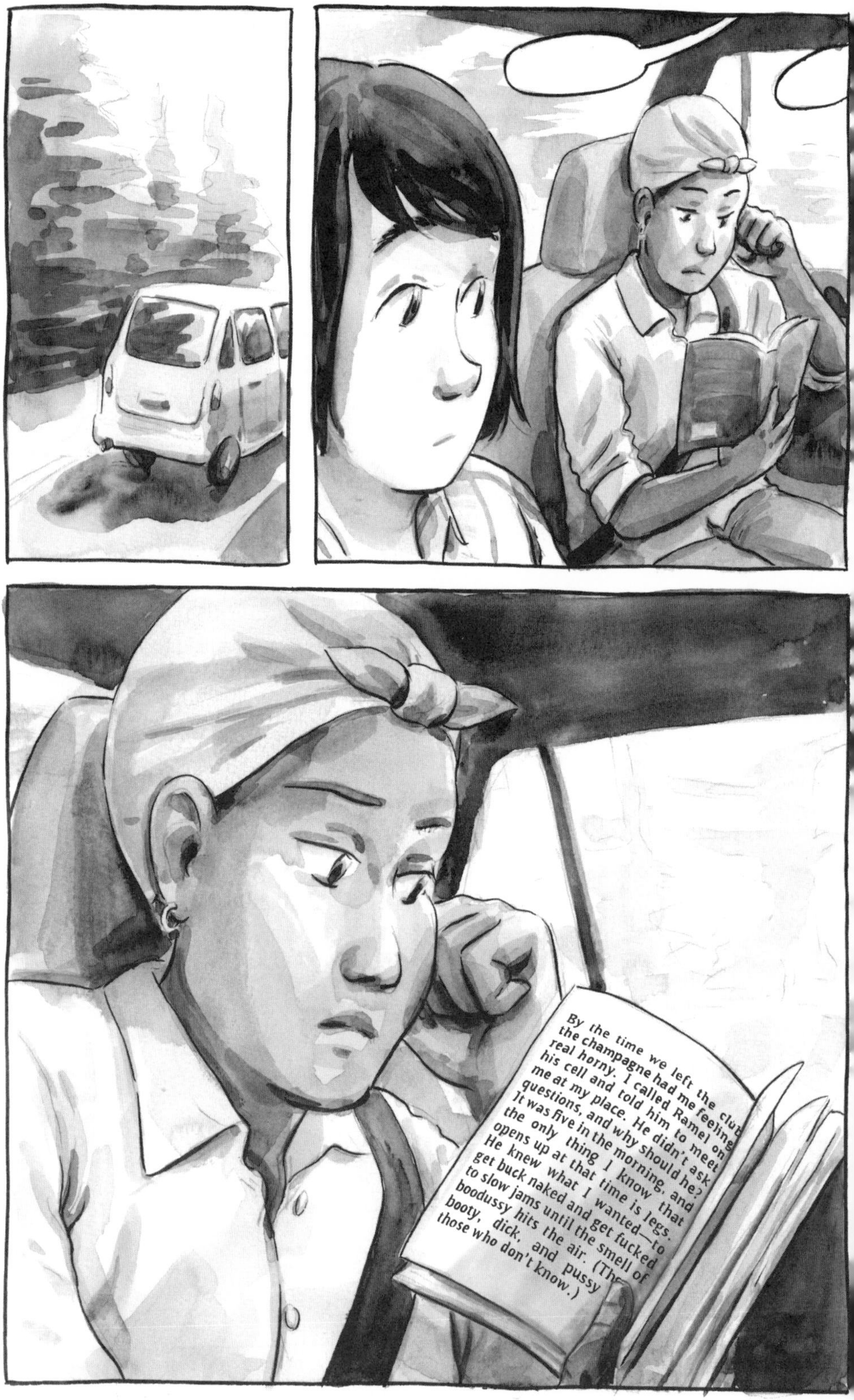
By the time we left the clu
the champagne had me feeling
real horny. I called Ramel on
his cell and told him to meet
me at my place. He didn't ask
questions, and why should he?
It was five in the morning, and
the only thing I know that
opens up at that time is legs.
He knew what I wanted—to
get buck naked and get fucked
to slow jams until the smell of
boodussy hits the air. (Th
booty, dick, and pussy
those who don't know.)

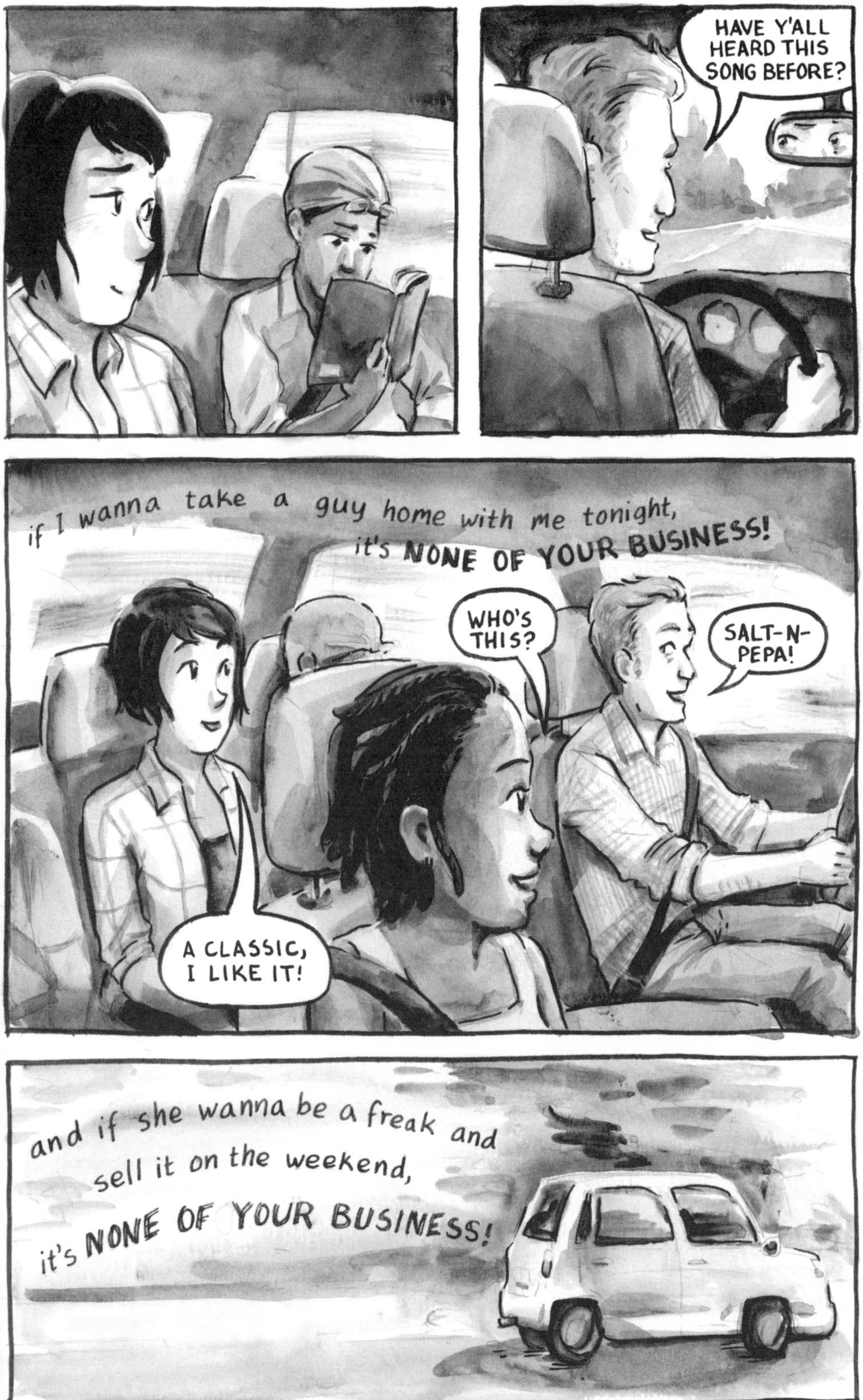
HAVE Y'ALL HEARD THIS SONG BEFORE?
if I wanna take a guy home with me tonight, it's NONE OF YOUR BUSINESS!
WHO'S THIS?
SALT-N-PEPA!
A CLASSIC, I LIKE IT!
and if she wanna be a freak and sell it on the weekend, it's NONE OF YOUR BUSINESS!

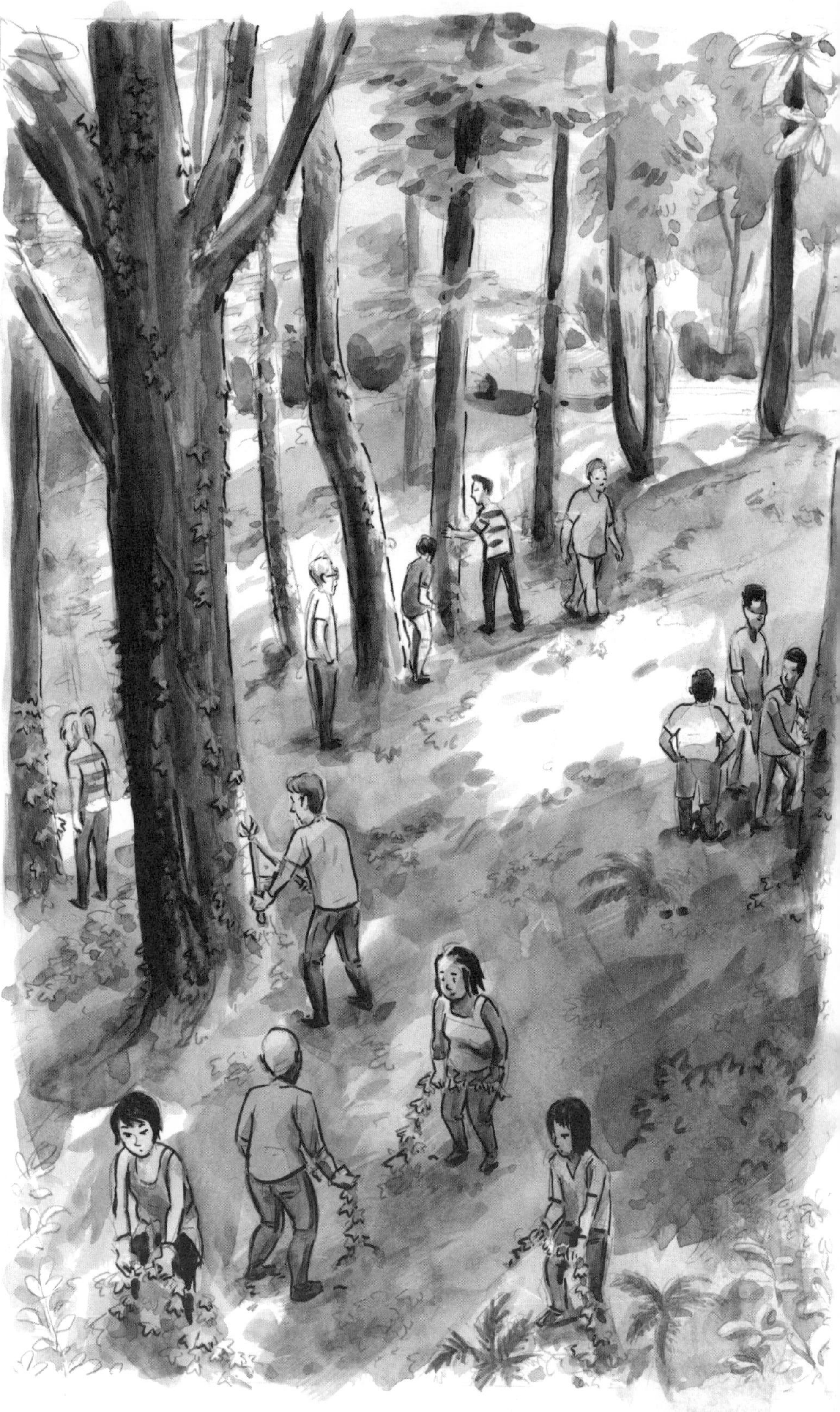

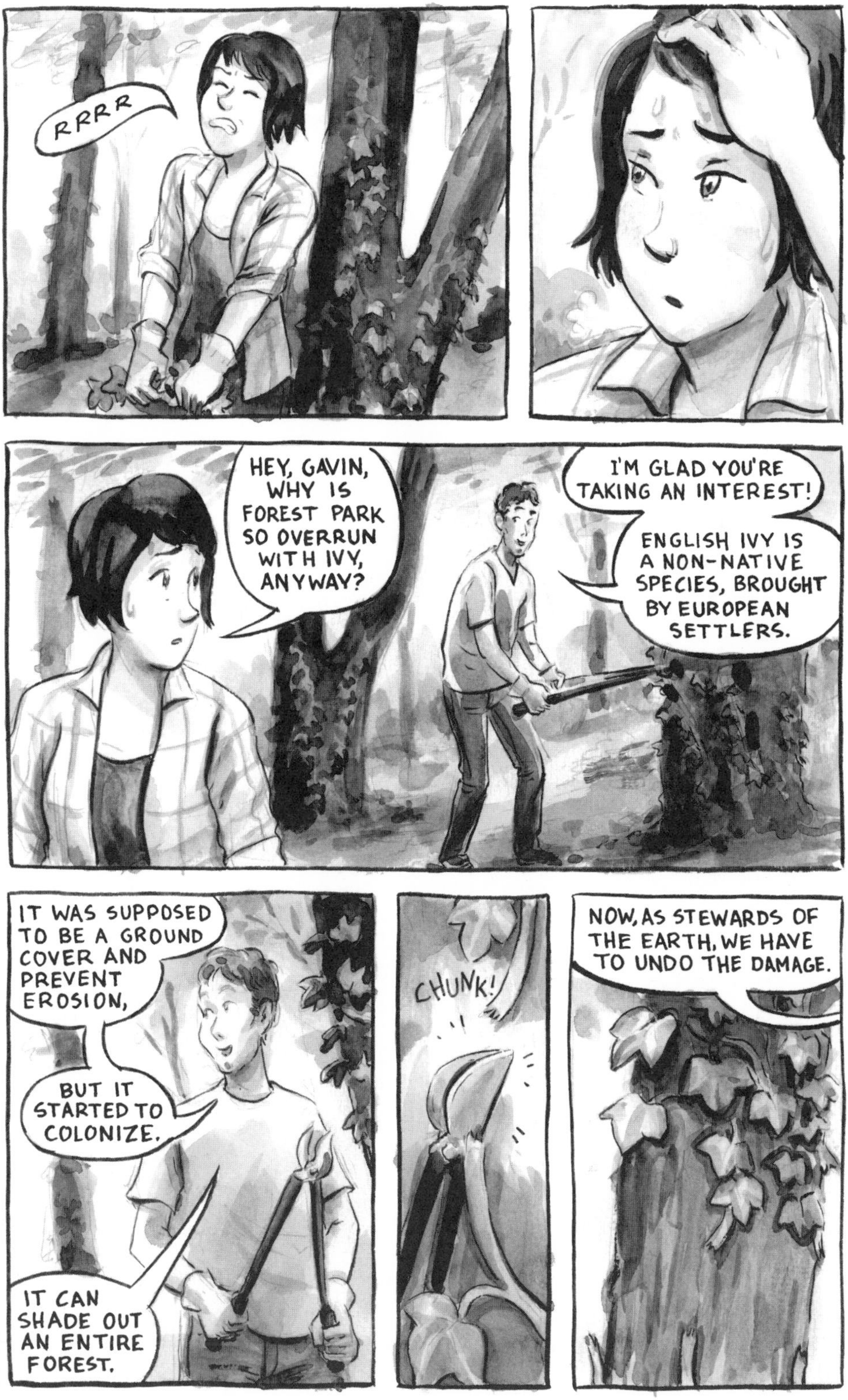
RRRR
HEY, GAVIN, WHY IS FOREST PARK SO OVERRUN WITH IVY, ANYWAY?
I'M GLAD YOU'RE TAKING AN INTEREST!
ENGLISH IVY IS A NON-NATIVE SPECIES, BROUGHT BY EUROPEAN SETTLERS.
IT WAS SUPPOSED TO BE A GROUND COVER AND PREVENT EROSION,
BUT IT STARTED TO COLONIZE.
IT CAN SHADE OUT AN ENTIRE FOREST.
CHUNK!
NOW, AS STEWARDS OF THE EARTH, WE HAVE TO UNDO THE DAMAGE.

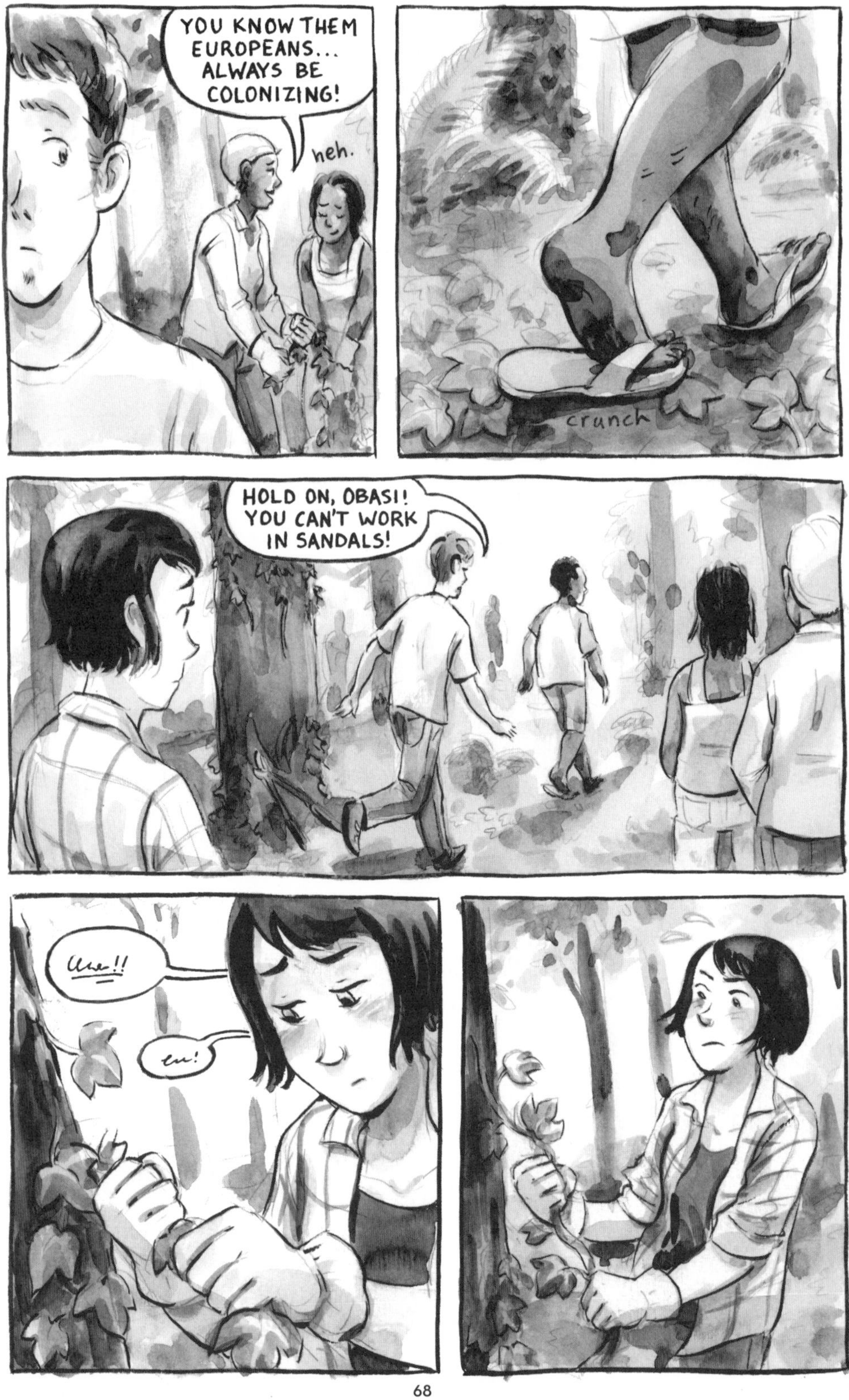
YOU KNOW THEM EUROPEANS... ALWAYS BE COLONIZING!
heh.
crunch
HOLD ON, OBASI! YOU CAN'T WORK IN SANDALS!

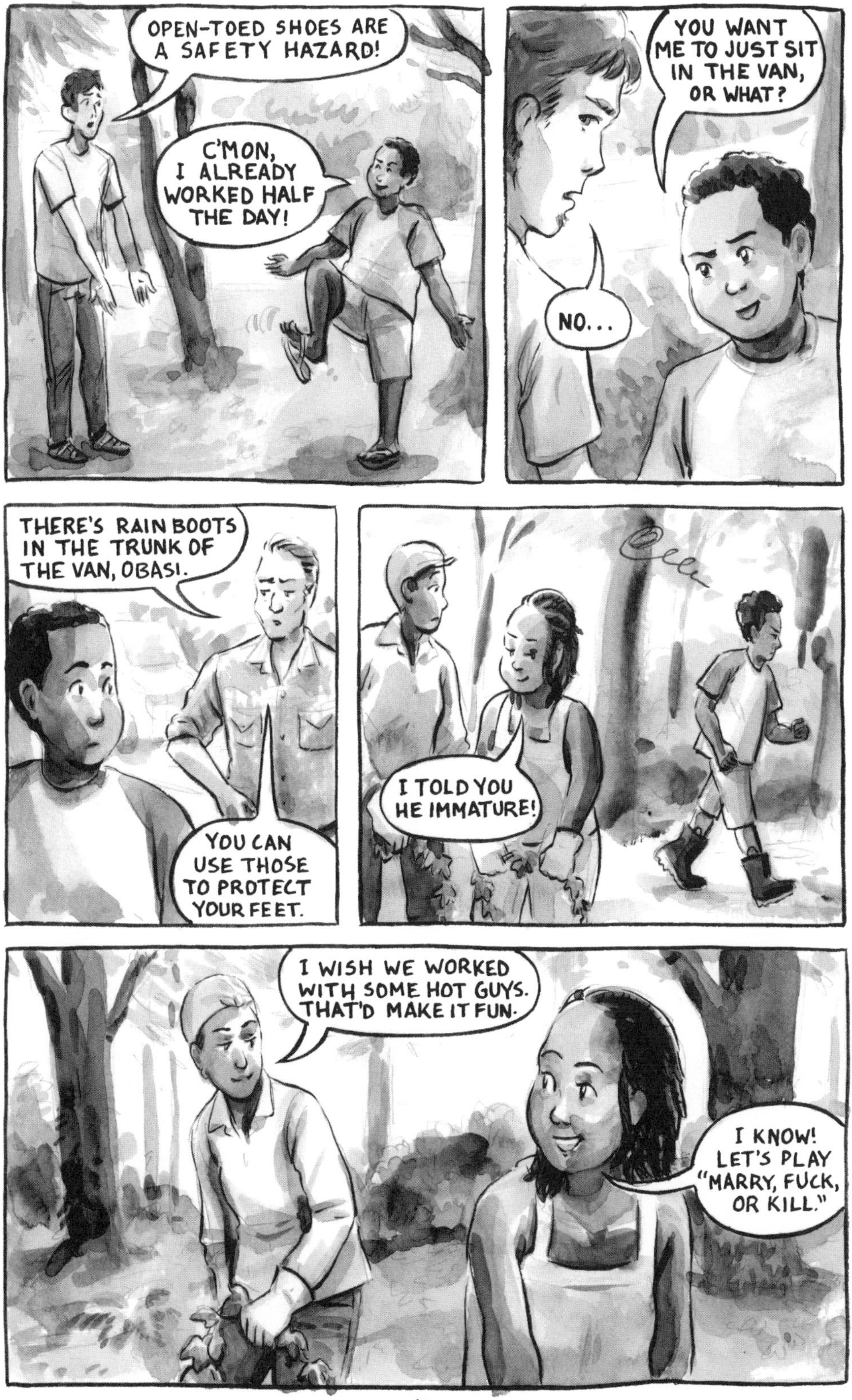
OPEN-TOED SHOES ARE A SAFETY HAZARD!
C'MON, I ALREADY WORKED HALF THE DAY!
YOU WANT ME TO JUST SIT IN THE VAN, OR WHAT?
NO...
THERE'S RAIN BOOTS IN THE TRUNK OF THE VAN, OBASI.
YOU CAN USE THOSE TO PROTECT YOUR FEET.
I TOLD YOU HE IMMATURE!
I WISH WE WORKED WITH SOME HOT GUYS. THAT'D MAKE IT FUN.
I KNOW! LET'S PLAY "MARRY, FUCK, OR KILL."

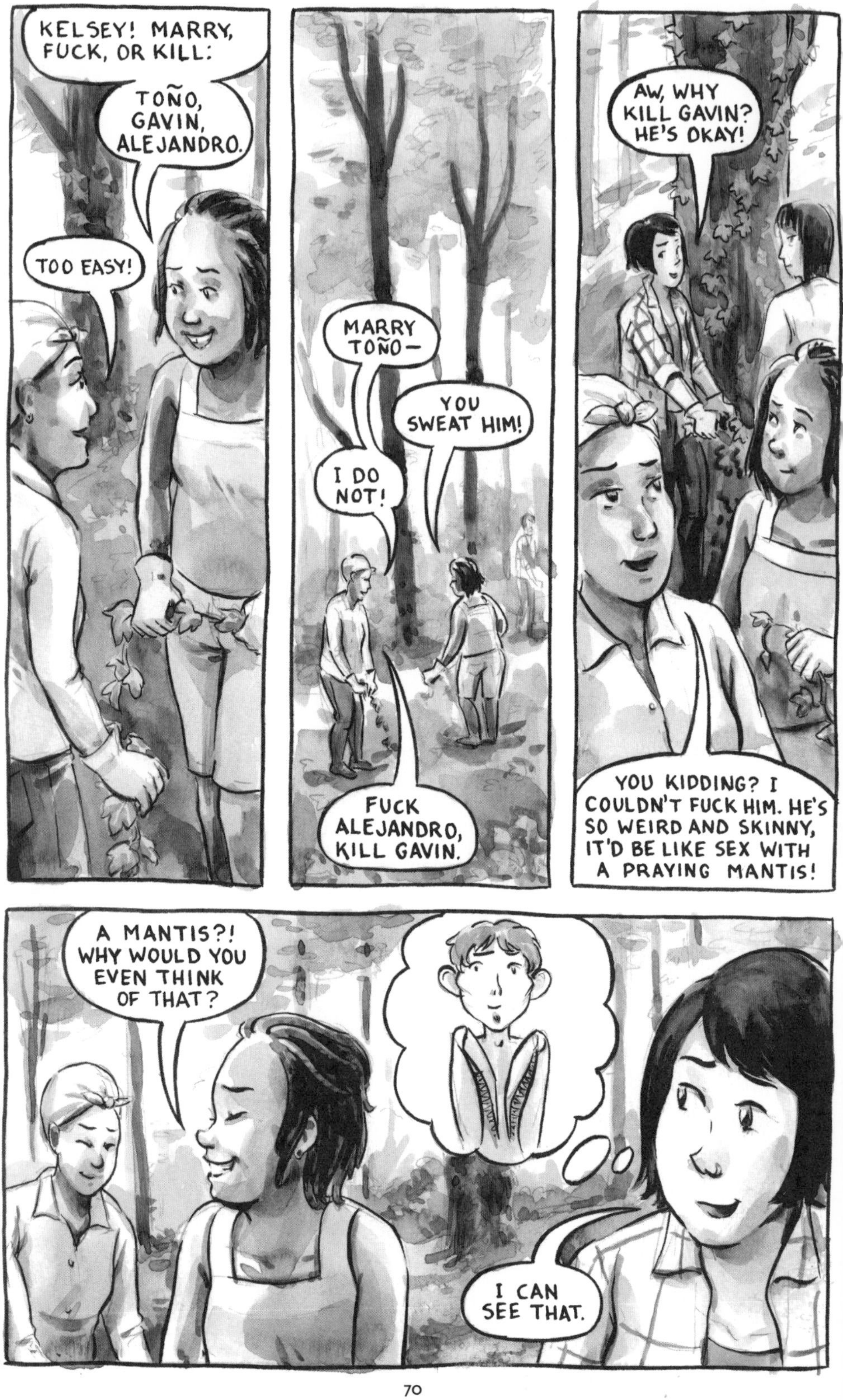
KELSEY! MARRY, FUCK, OR KILL:
TOÑO, GAVIN, ALEJANDRO.
TOO EASY!
MARRY TOÑO—
YOU SWEAT HIM!
I DO NOT!
FUCK ALEJANDRO, KILL GAVIN.
AW, WHY KILL GAVIN? HE'S OKAY!
YOU KIDDING? I COULDN'T FUCK HIM. HE'S SO WEIRD AND SKINNY, IT'D BE LIKE SEX WITH A PRAYING MANTIS!
A MANTIS?! WHY WOULD YOU EVEN THINK OF THAT?
I CAN SEE THAT.

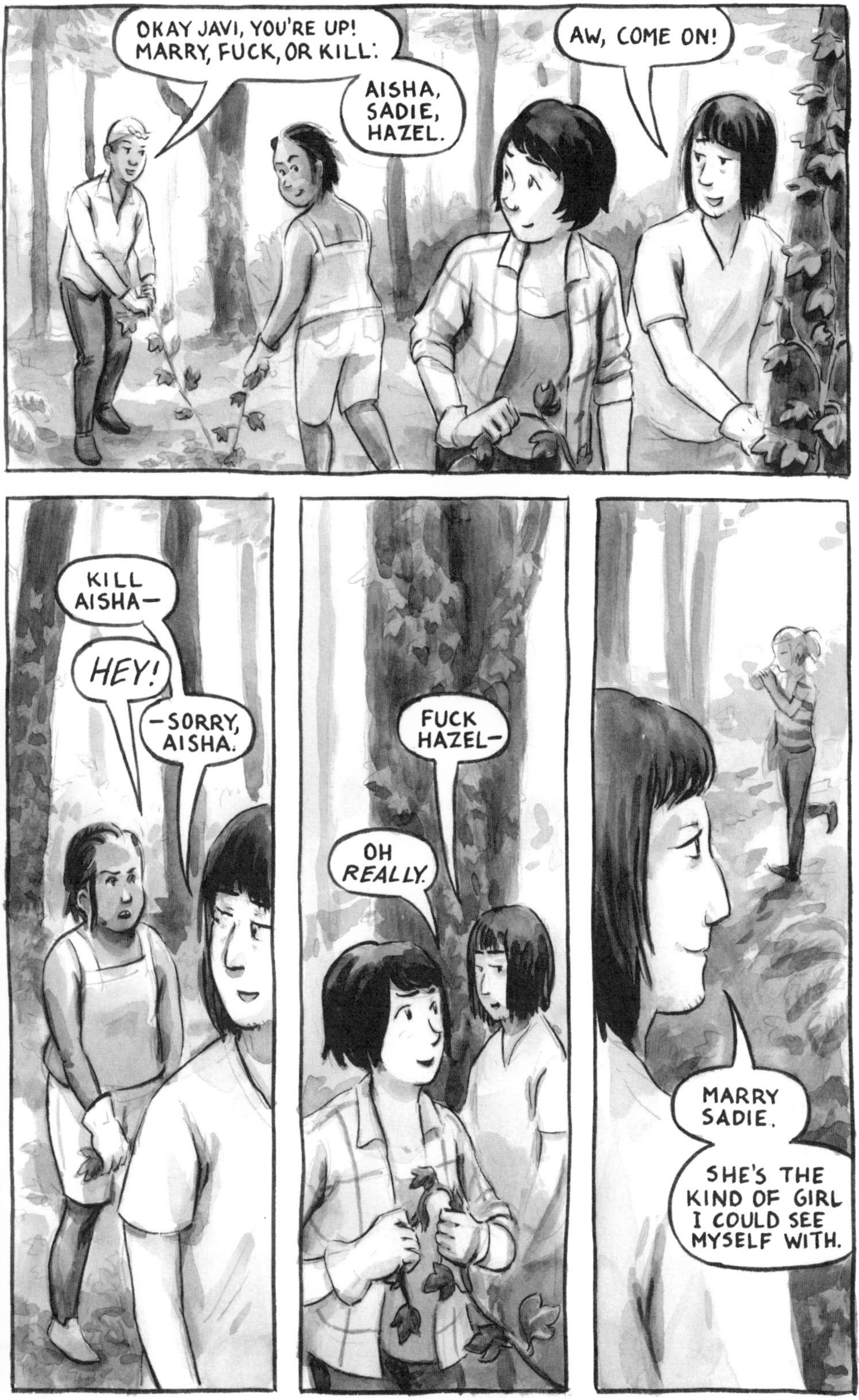
OKAY JAVI, YOU'RE UP! MARRY, FUCK, OR KILL:
AISHA, SADIE, HAZEL.
AW, COME ON!
KILL AISHA—
HEY!
—SORRY, AISHA.
FUCK HAZEL—
OH REALLY.
MARRY SADIE.
SHE'S THE KIND OF GIRL I COULD SEE MYSELF WITH.

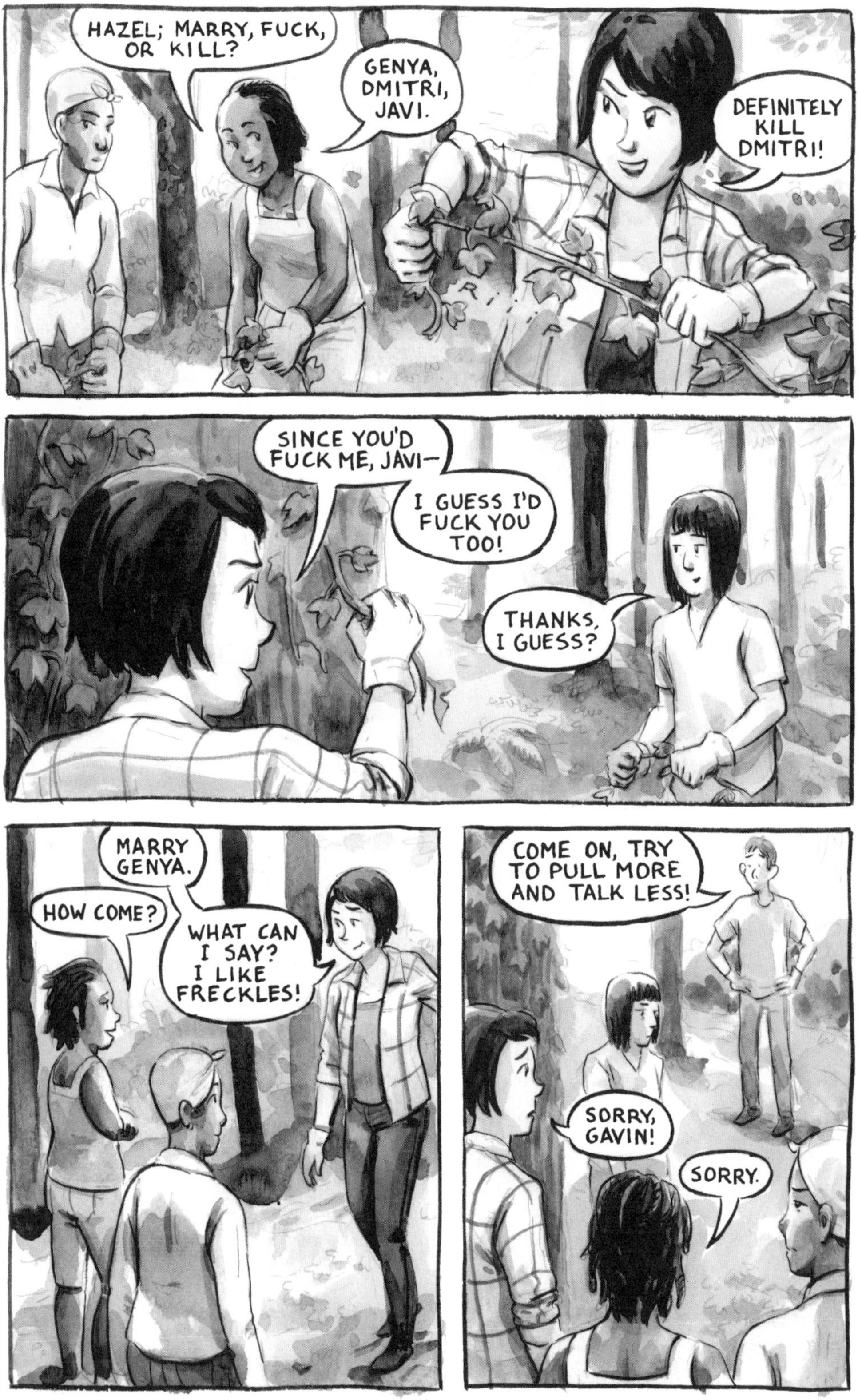
HAZEL; MARRY, FUCK, OR KILL?
GENYA, DMITRI, JAVI.
DEFINITELY KILL DMITRI!
SINCE YOU'D FUCK ME, JAVI—
I GUESS I'D FUCK YOU TOO!
THANKS, I GUESS?
MARRY GENYA.
HOW COME?
WHAT CAN I SAY? I LIKE FRECKLES!
COME ON, TRY TO PULL MORE AND TALK LESS!
SORRY, GAVIN!
SORRY.

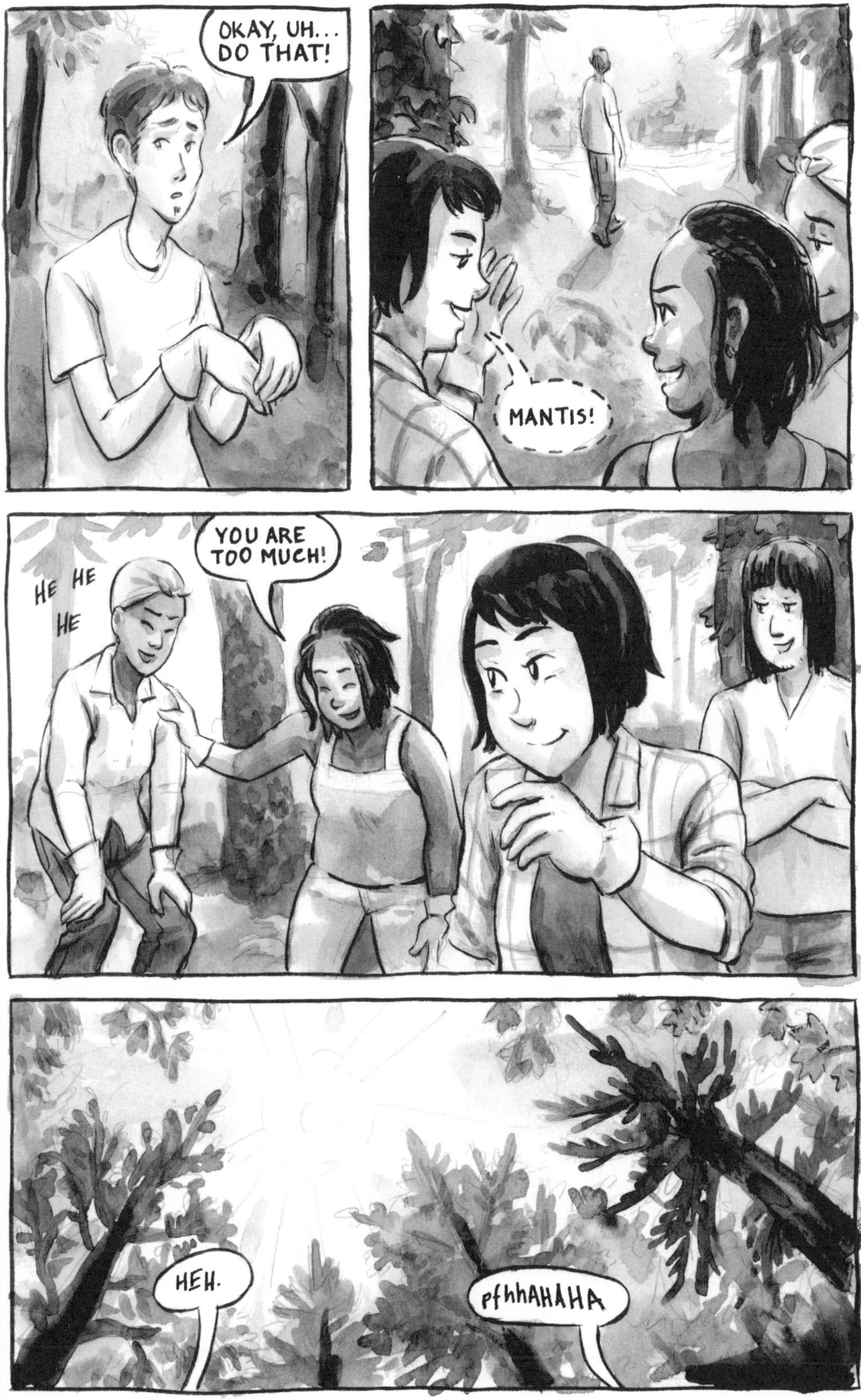
OKAY, UH... DO THAT!
MANTIS!
HE HE HE
YOU ARE TOO MUCH!
HEH.
pfhhAHAHA

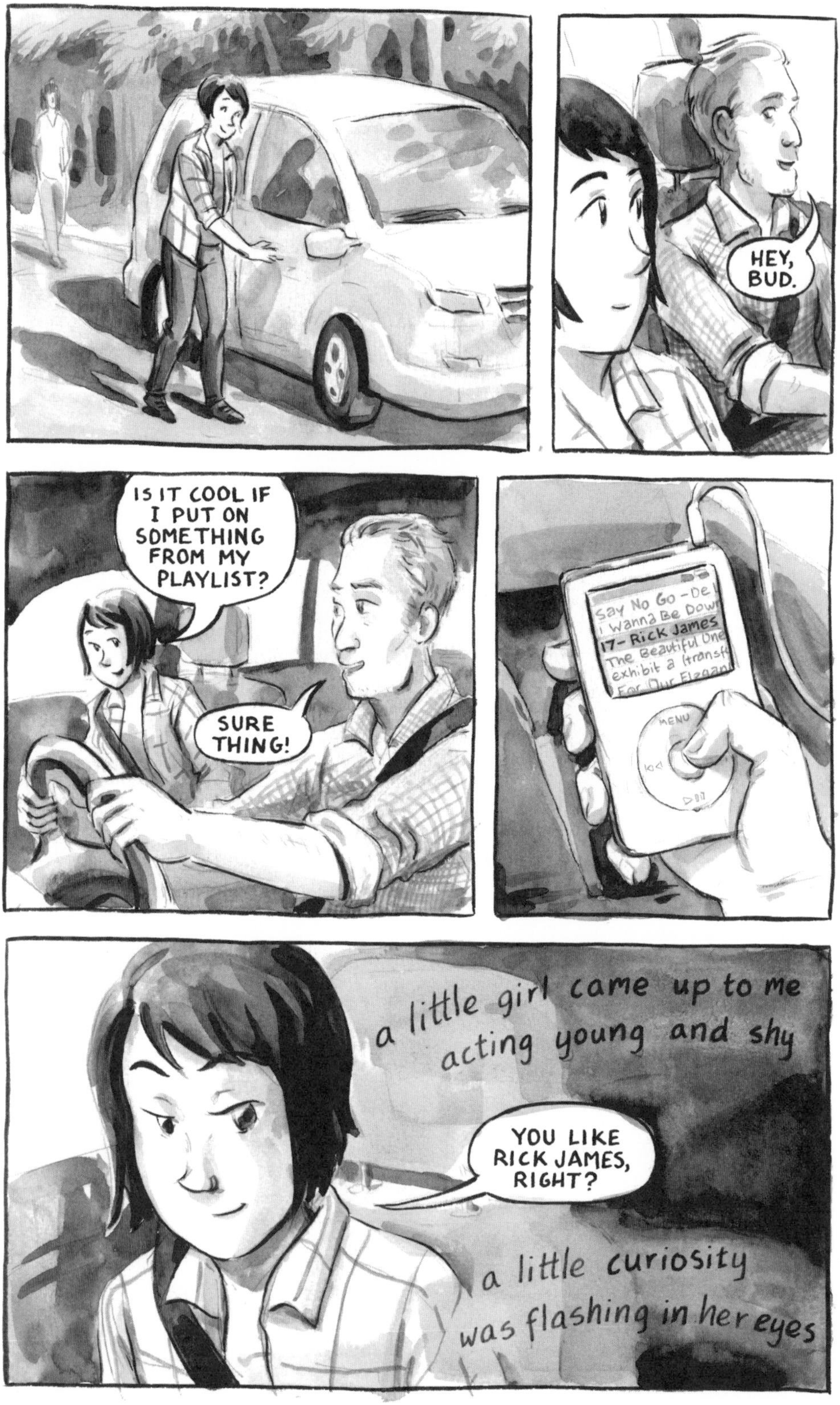
HEY, BUD.
IS IT COOL IF I PUT ON SOMETHING FROM MY PLAYLIST?
SURE THING!
17- Rick James
MENU
a little girl came up to me
acting young and shy
YOU LIKE RICK JAMES, RIGHT?
a little curiosity
was flashing in her eyes

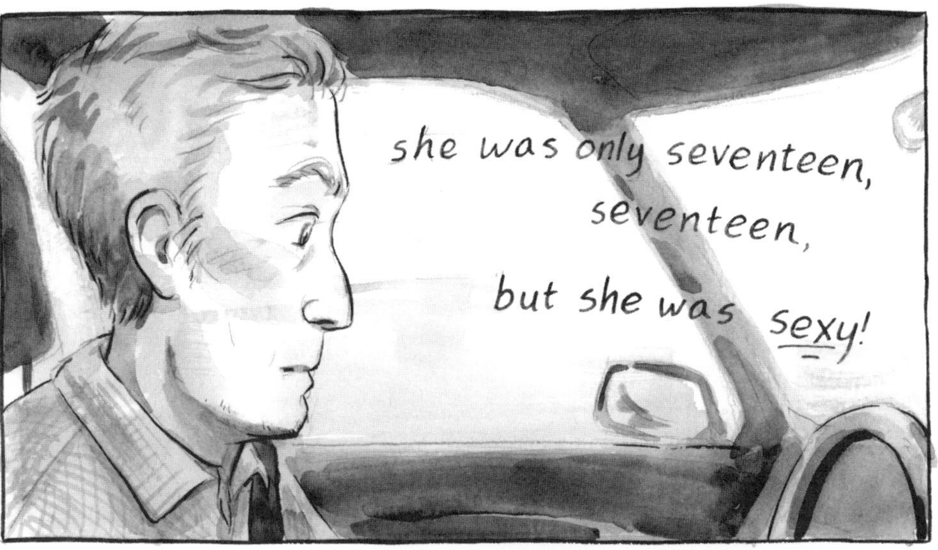
she was only seventeen,
seventeen,
but she was sexy!

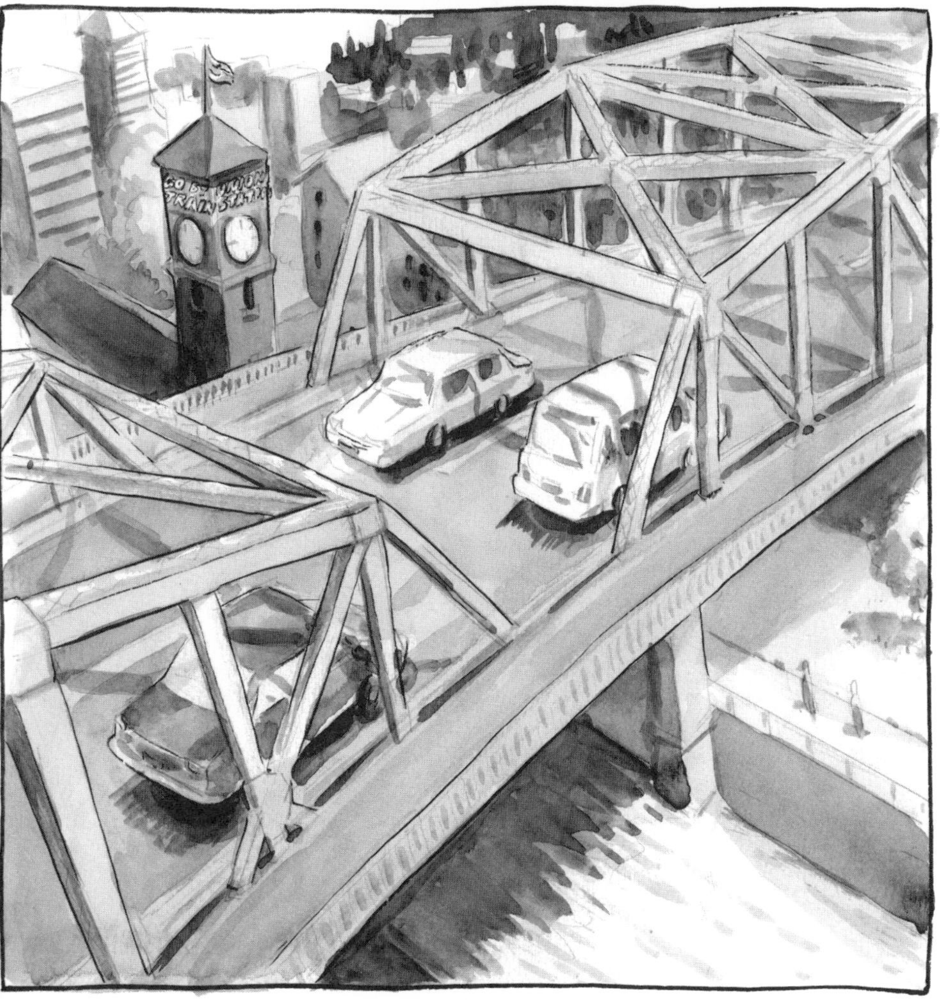

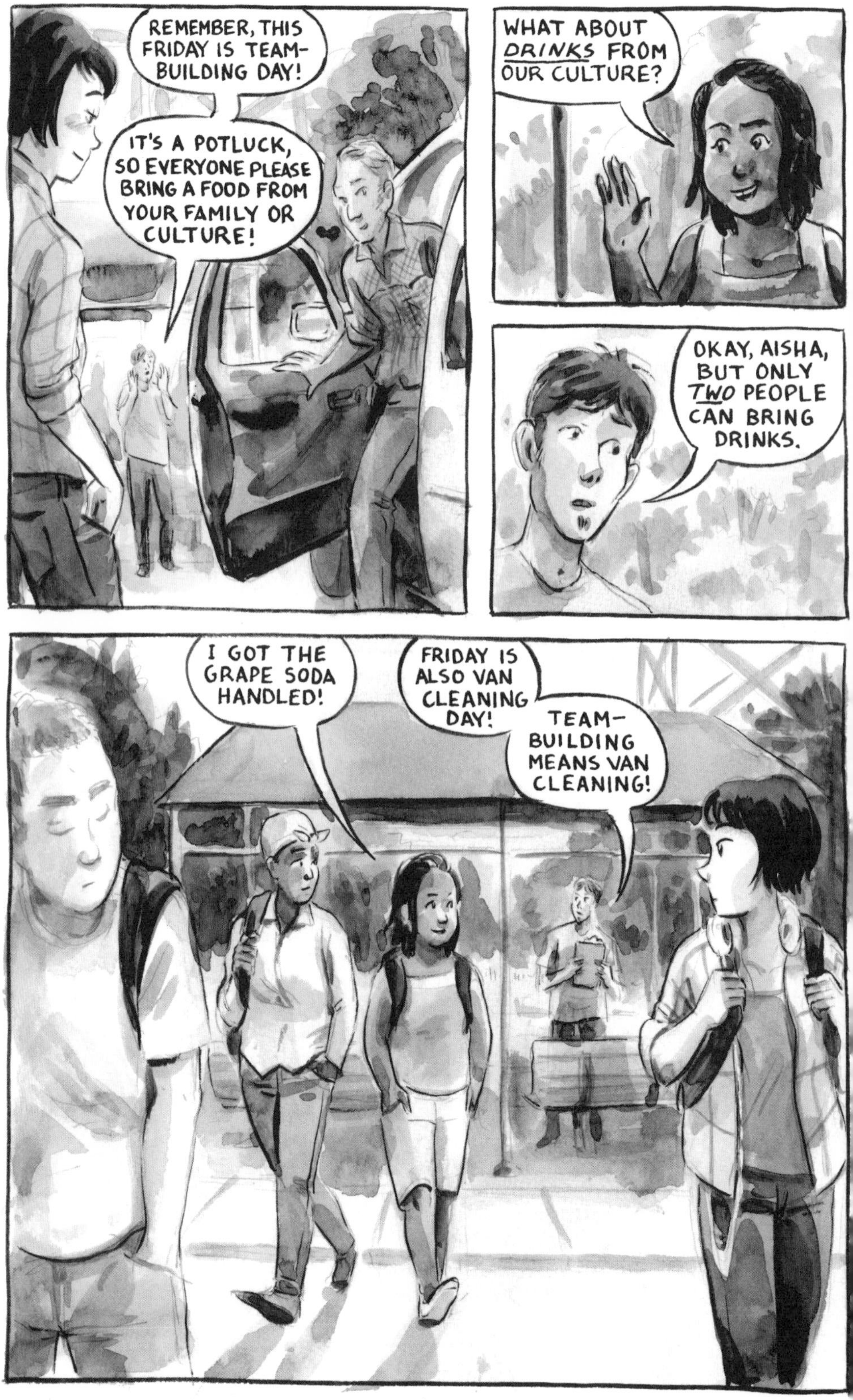
REMEMBER, THIS FRIDAY IS TEAM-BUILDING DAY!
IT'S A POTLUCK, SO EVERYONE PLEASE BRING A FOOD FROM YOUR FAMILY OR CULTURE!
WHAT ABOUT DRINKS FROM OUR CULTURE?
OKAY, AISHA, BUT ONLY TWO PEOPLE CAN BRING DRINKS.
I GOT THE GRAPE SODA HANDLED!
FRIDAY IS ALSO VAN CLEANING DAY!
TEAM-BUILDING MEANS VAN CLEANING!

$$a^2 + b^2 \sqrt{\ } \; \pi \; 3$$

TIMELINE | MOTION EDITOR

50 55 60 65 70 75 80 85 90 95 100 105

▶🗀 face closeup
▼🗀 Teacher
   🚩 upper arm
   🚩 hand 1
   🚩 forearm
   ◀▶ mask
      🗎 chalkboard

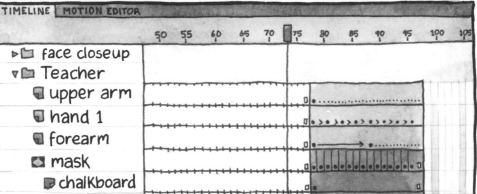

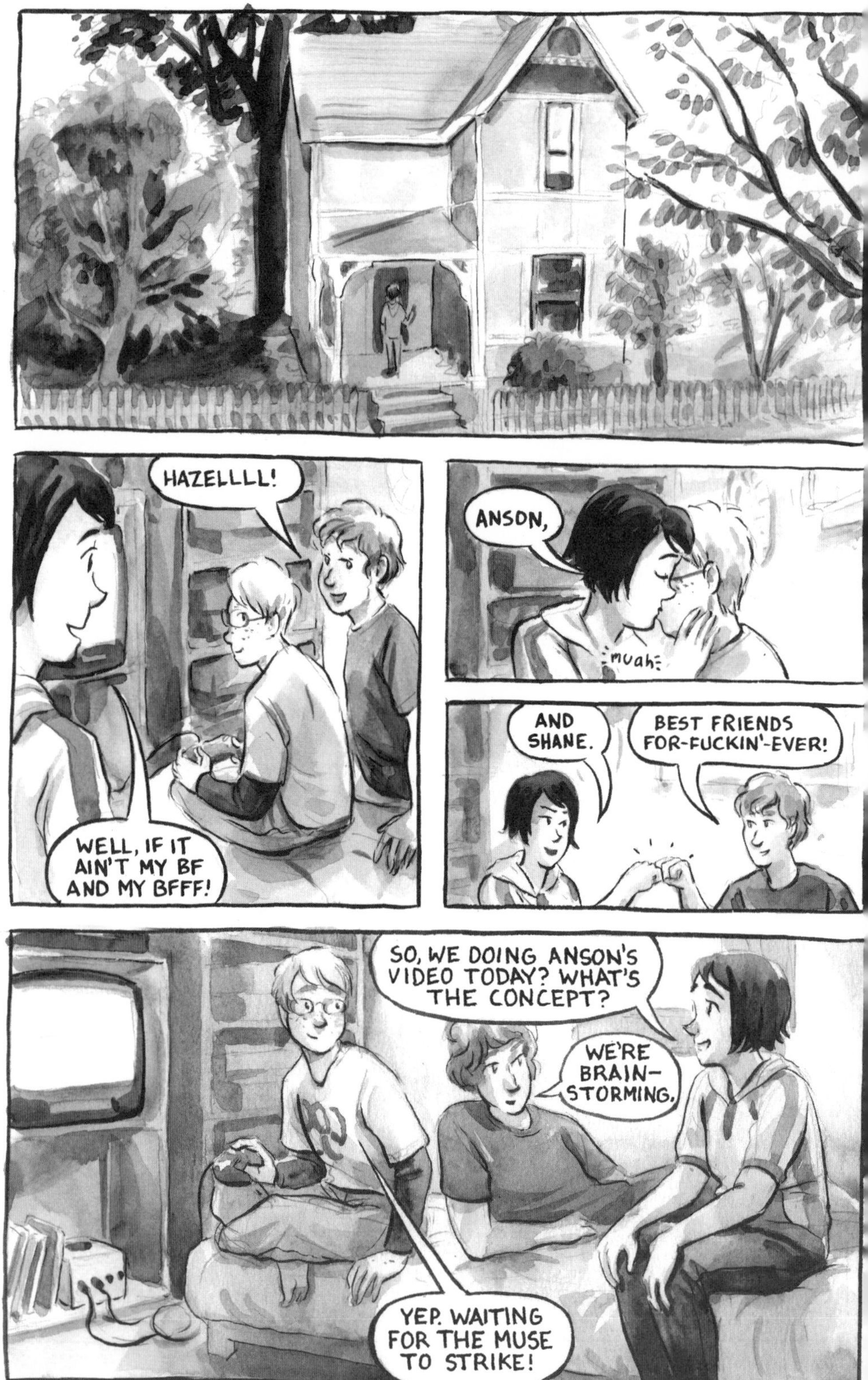
HAZELLLL!
WELL, IF IT AIN'T MY BF AND MY BFFF!
ANSON,
muah
AND SHANE.
BEST FRIENDS FOR-FUCKIN'-EVER!
SO, WE DOING ANSON'S VIDEO TODAY? WHAT'S THE CONCEPT?
WE'RE BRAIN-STORMING.
YEP. WAITING FOR THE MUSE TO STRIKE!

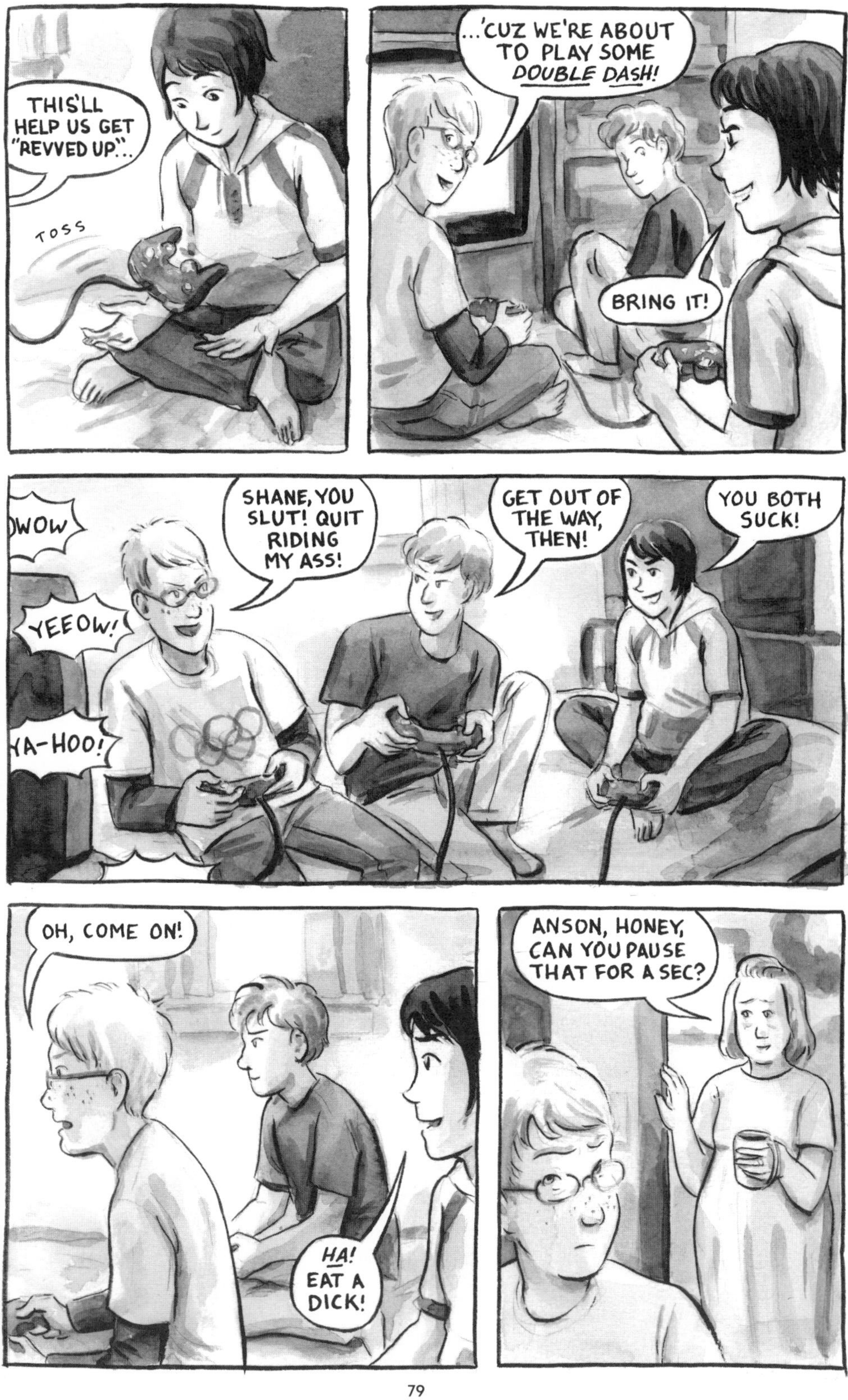
THIS'LL HELP US GET "REVVED UP"...
TOSS
...'CUZ WE'RE ABOUT TO PLAY SOME DOUBLE DASH!
BRING IT!
WOW
YEEOW!
YA-HOO!
SHANE, YOU SLUT! QUIT RIDING MY ASS!
GET OUT OF THE WAY, THEN!
YOU BOTH SUCK!
OH, COME ON!
HA! EAT A DICK!
ANSON, HONEY, CAN YOU PAUSE THAT FOR A SEC?

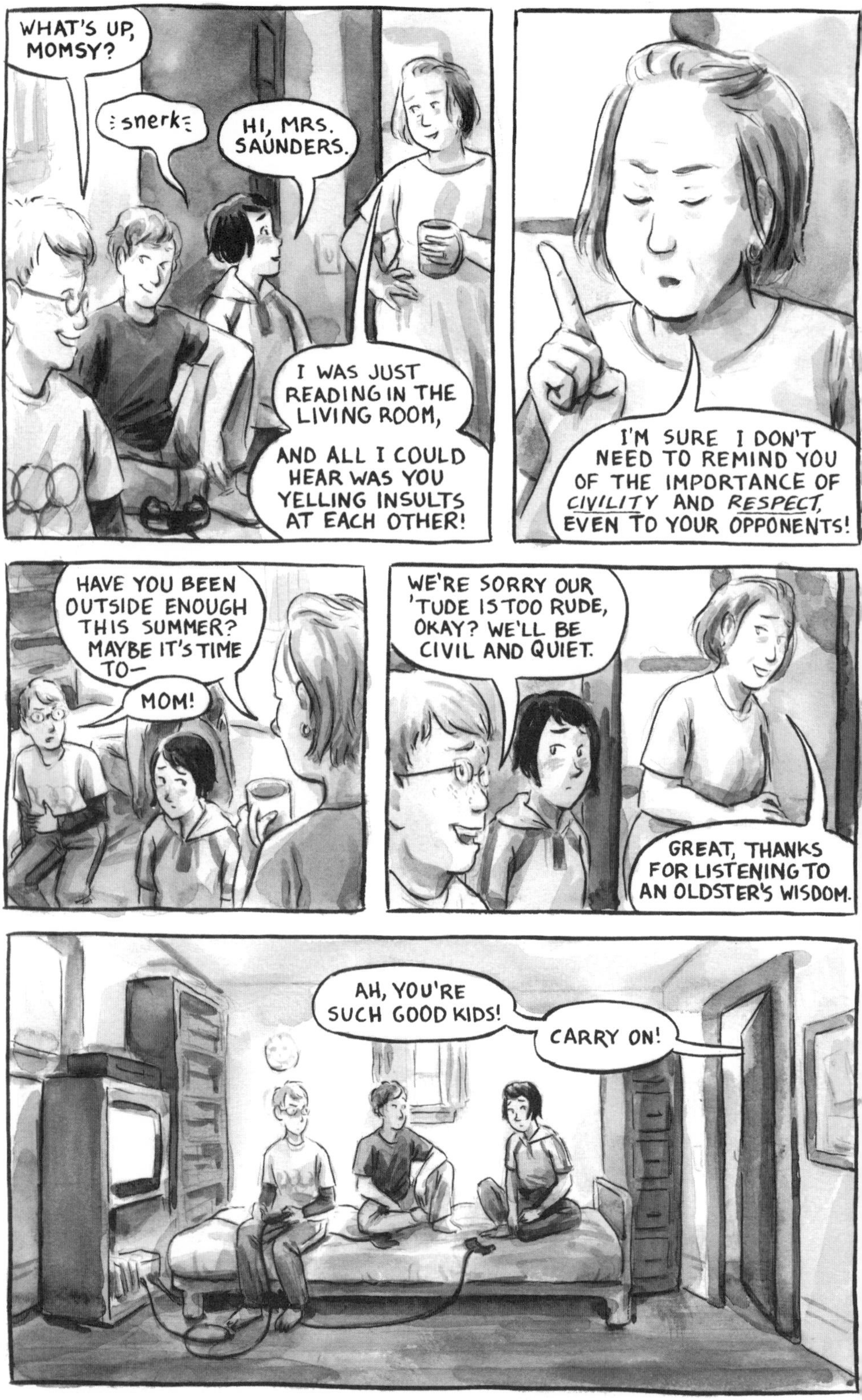
WHAT'S UP, MOMSY?
snerk
HI, MRS. SAUNDERS.
I WAS JUST READING IN THE LIVING ROOM,
AND ALL I COULD HEAR WAS YOU YELLING INSULTS AT EACH OTHER!
I'M SURE I DON'T NEED TO REMIND YOU OF THE IMPORTANCE OF CIVILITY AND RESPECT, EVEN TO YOUR OPPONENTS!
HAVE YOU BEEN OUTSIDE ENOUGH THIS SUMMER? MAYBE IT'S TIME TO—
MOM!
WE'RE SORRY OUR 'TUDE IS TOO RUDE, OKAY? WE'LL BE CIVIL AND QUIET.
GREAT, THANKS FOR LISTENING TO AN OLDSTER'S WISDOM.
AH, YOU'RE SUCH GOOD KIDS!
CARRY ON!

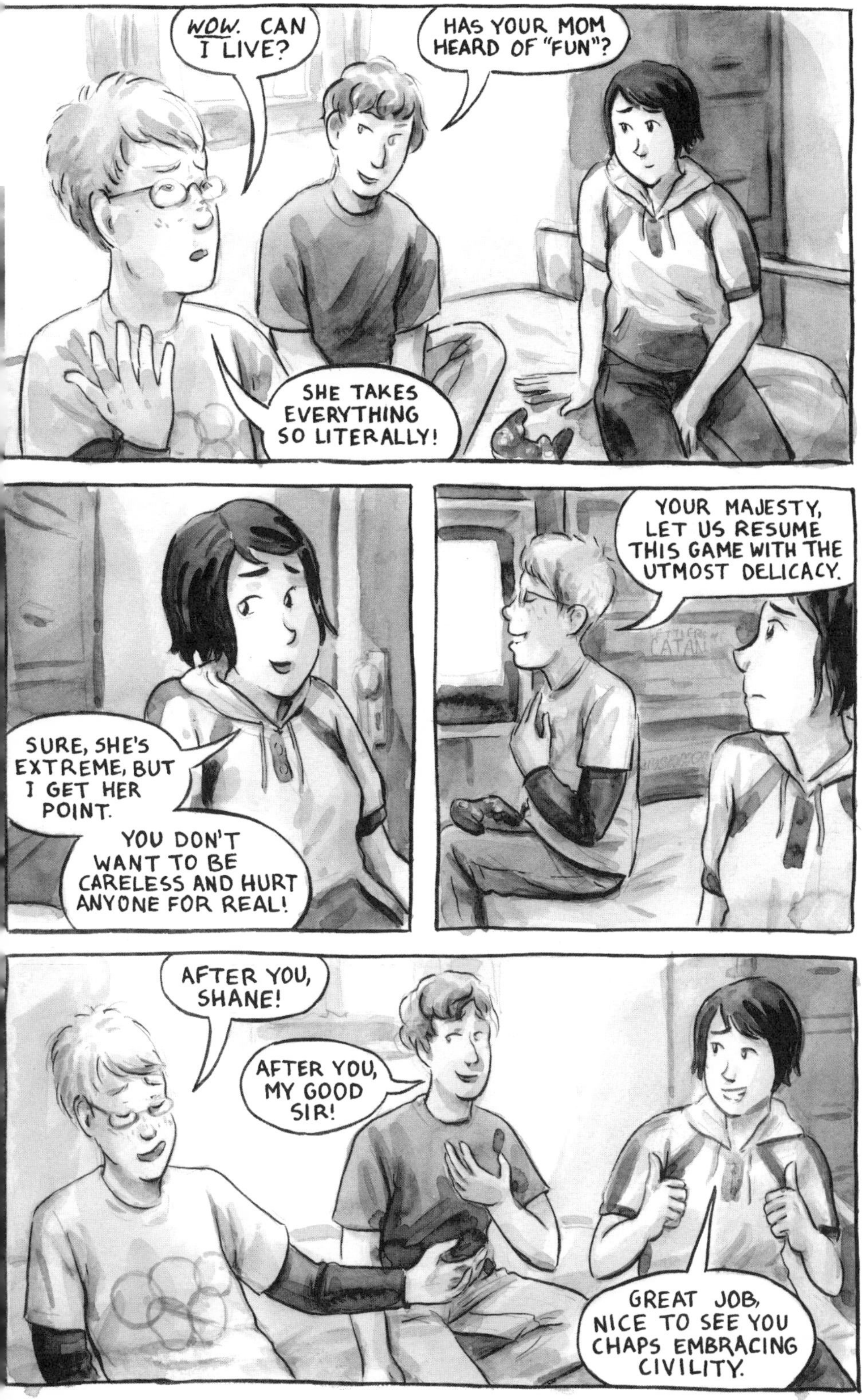
WOW. CAN I LIVE?
HAS YOUR MOM HEARD OF "FUN"?
SHE TAKES EVERYTHING SO LITERALLY!
SURE, SHE'S EXTREME, BUT I GET HER POINT.
YOU DON'T WANT TO BE CARELESS AND HURT ANYONE FOR REAL!
YOUR MAJESTY, LET US RESUME THIS GAME WITH THE UTMOST DELICACY.
AFTER YOU, SHANE!
AFTER YOU, MY GOOD SIR!
GREAT JOB, NICE TO SEE YOU CHAPS EMBRACING CIVILITY.

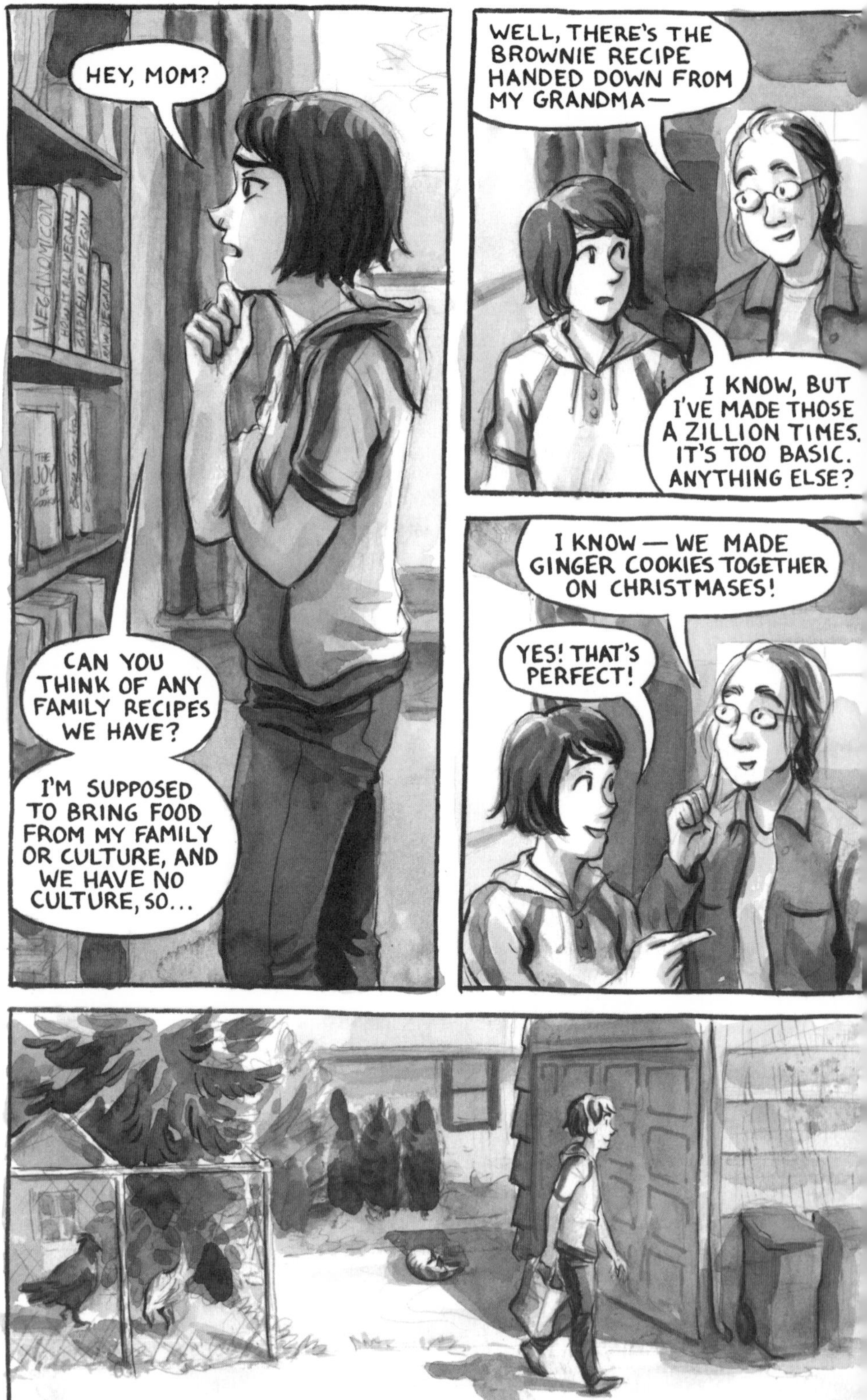
HEY, MOM?
CAN YOU THINK OF ANY FAMILY RECIPES WE HAVE?
I'M SUPPOSED TO BRING FOOD FROM MY FAMILY OR CULTURE, AND WE HAVE NO CULTURE, SO...
VEGANOMICON
HOW IT ALL VEGAN
GARDEN OF VEGAN
RAW VEGAN
THE JOY OF COOKING
WELL, THERE'S THE BROWNIE RECIPE HANDED DOWN FROM MY GRANDMA—
I KNOW, BUT I'VE MADE THOSE A ZILLION TIMES. IT'S TOO BASIC. ANYTHING ELSE?
I KNOW — WE MADE GINGER COOKIES TOGETHER ON CHRISTMASES!
YES! THAT'S PERFECT!

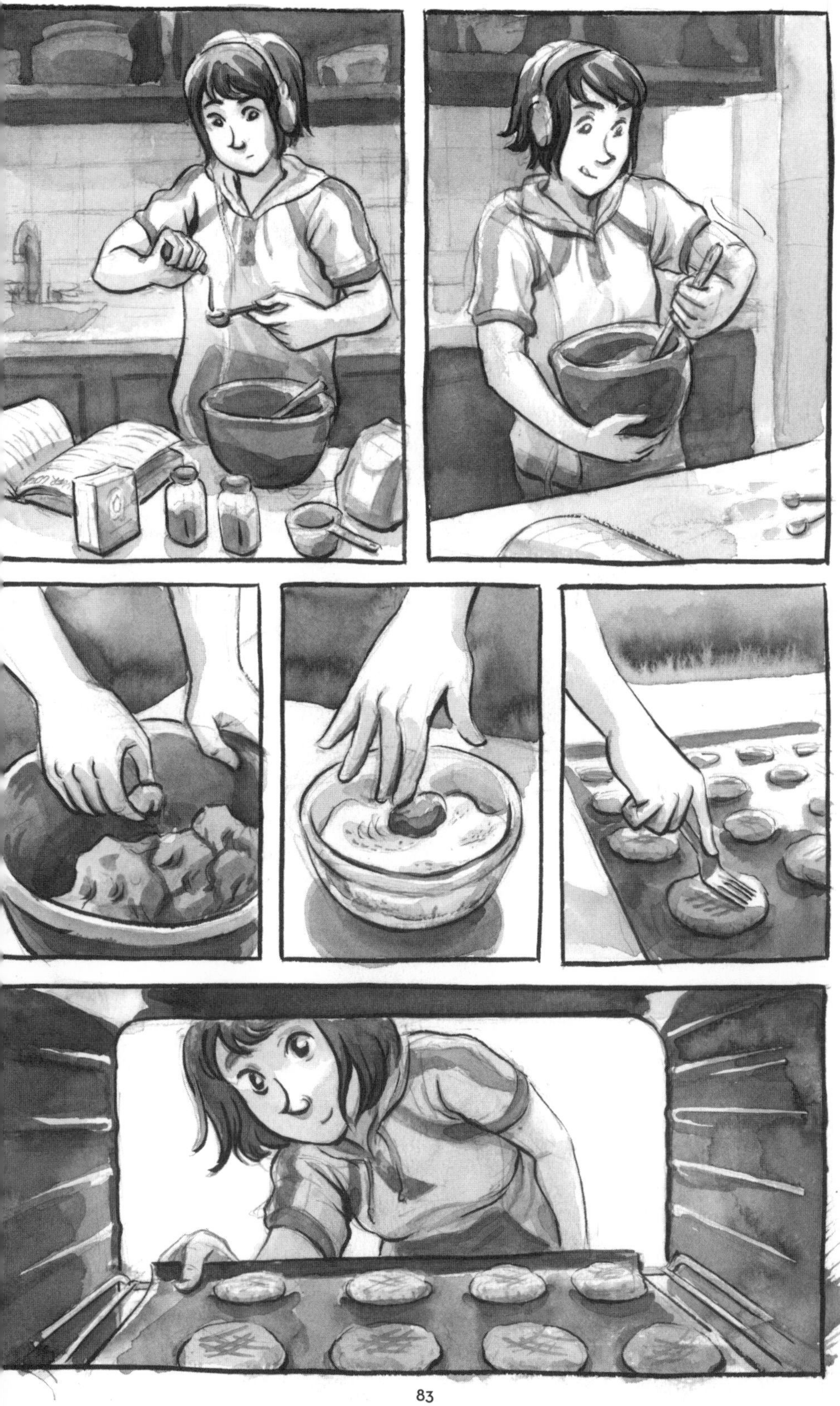

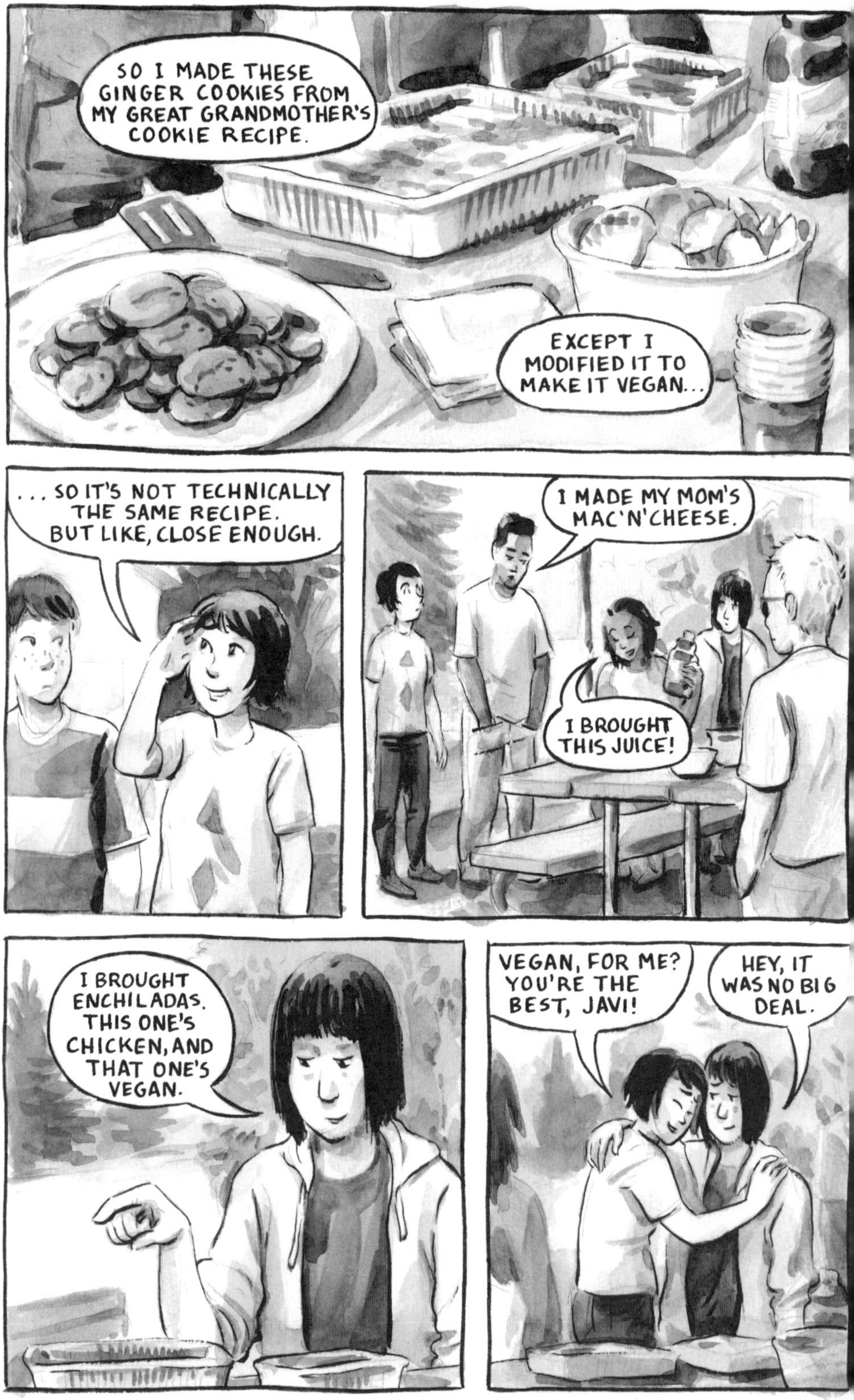
SO I MADE THESE GINGER COOKIES FROM MY GREAT GRANDMOTHER'S COOKIE RECIPE.
EXCEPT I MODIFIED IT TO MAKE IT VEGAN...
... SO IT'S NOT TECHNICALLY THE SAME RECIPE. BUT LIKE, CLOSE ENOUGH.
I MADE MY MOM'S MAC'N'CHEESE.
I BROUGHT THIS JUICE!
I BROUGHT ENCHILADAS. THIS ONE'S CHICKEN, AND THAT ONE'S VEGAN.
VEGAN, FOR ME? YOU'RE THE BEST, JAVI!
HEY, IT WAS NO BIG DEAL.

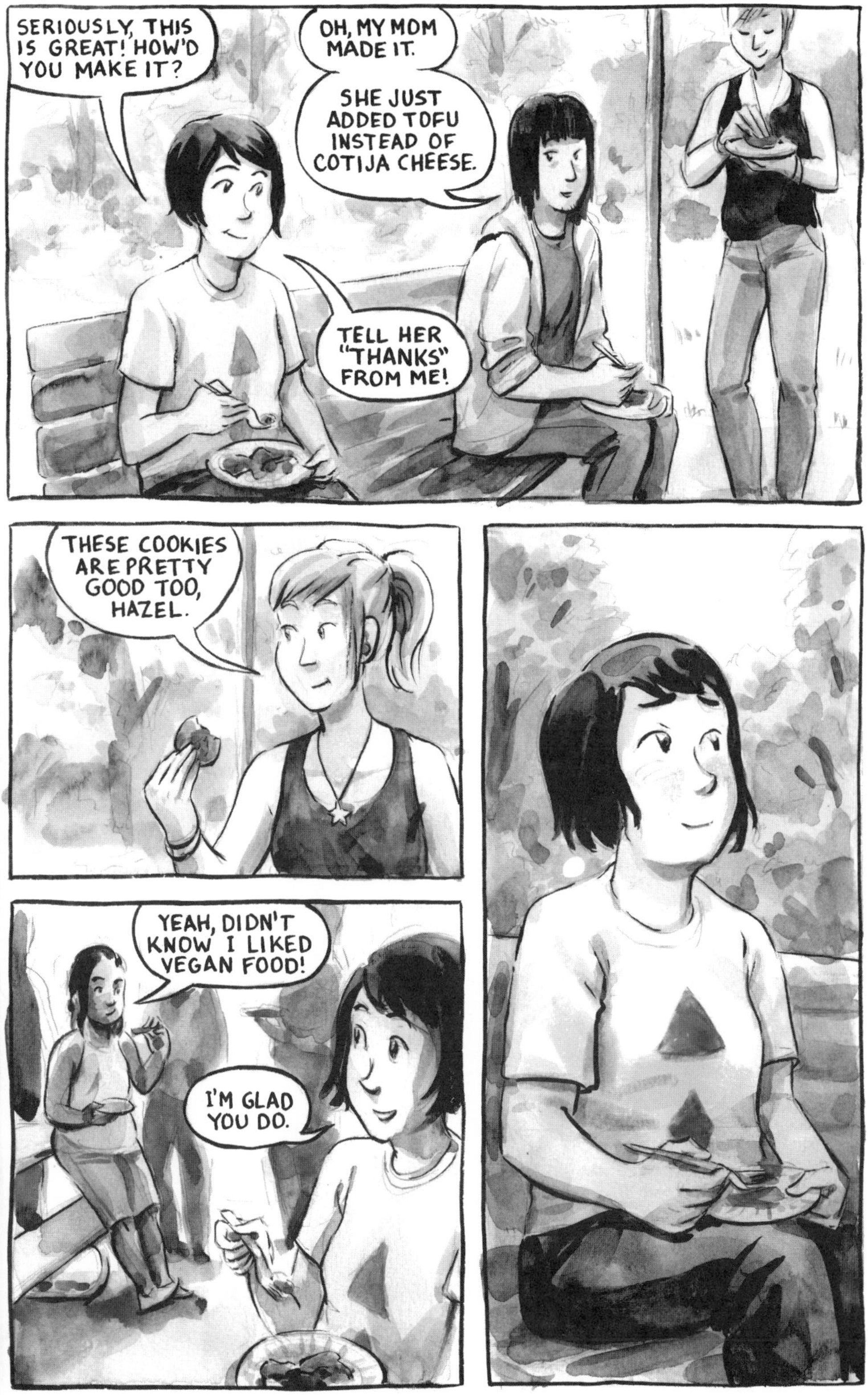
SERIOUSLY, THIS IS GREAT! HOW'D YOU MAKE IT?
OH, MY MOM MADE IT.
SHE JUST ADDED TOFU INSTEAD OF COTIJA CHEESE.
TELL HER "THANKS" FROM ME!
THESE COOKIES ARE PRETTY GOOD TOO, HAZEL.
YEAH, DIDN'T KNOW I LIKED VEGAN FOOD!
I'M GLAD YOU DO.

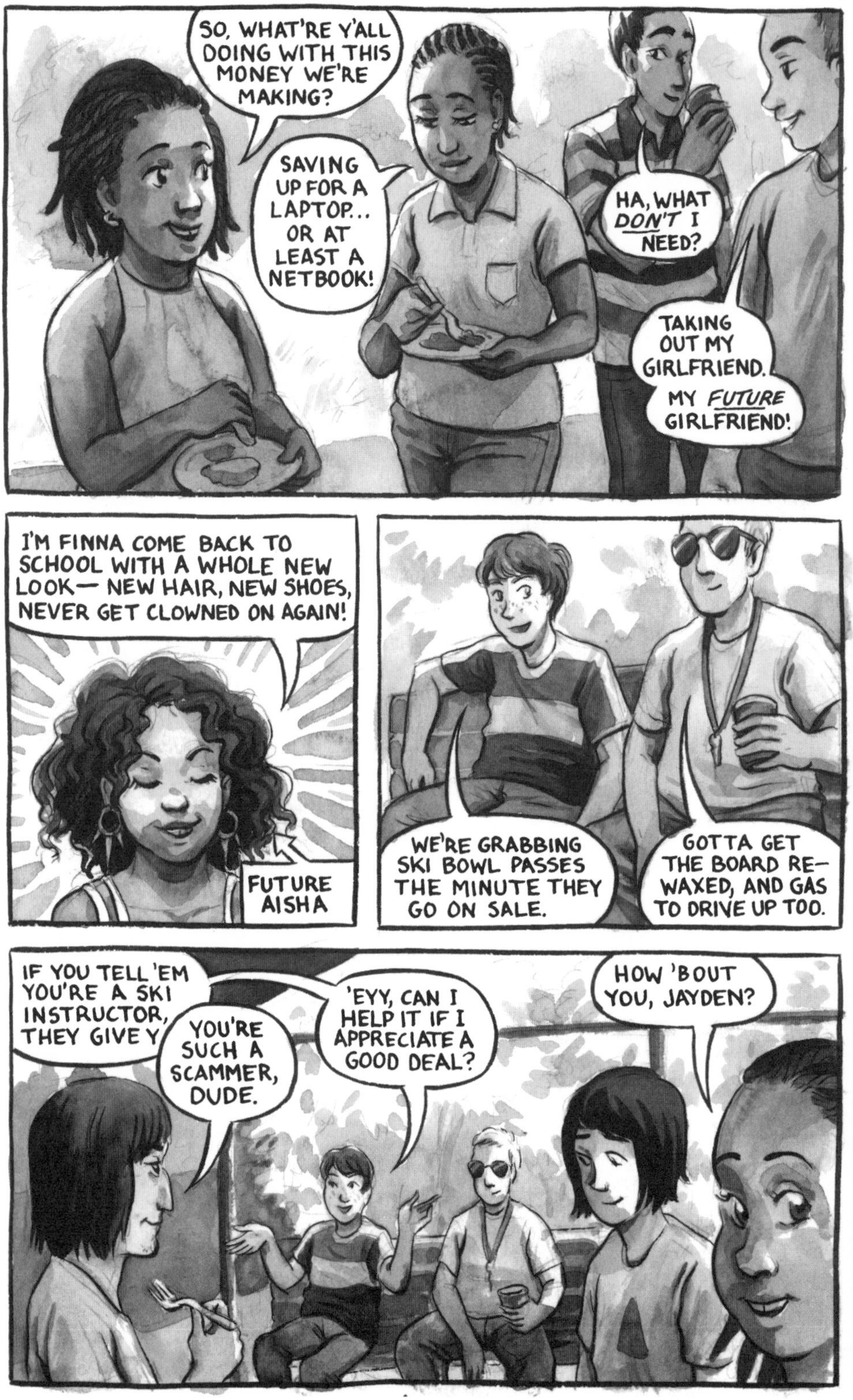
SO, WHAT'RE Y'ALL DOING WITH THIS MONEY WE'RE MAKING?
SAVING UP FOR A LAPTOP... OR AT LEAST A NETBOOK!
HA, WHAT *DON'T* I NEED?
TAKING OUT MY GIRLFRIEND.
MY *FUTURE* GIRLFRIEND!
I'M FINNA COME BACK TO SCHOOL WITH A WHOLE NEW LOOK— NEW HAIR, NEW SHOES, NEVER GET CLOWNED ON AGAIN!
FUTURE AISHA
WE'RE GRABBING SKI BOWL PASSES THE MINUTE THEY GO ON SALE.
GOTTA GET THE BOARD RE-WAXED, AND GAS TO DRIVE UP TOO.
IF YOU TELL 'EM YOU'RE A SKI INSTRUCTOR, THEY GIVE Y
YOU'RE SUCH A SCAMMER, DUDE.
'EYY, CAN I HELP IT IF I APPRECIATE A GOOD DEAL?
HOW 'BOUT YOU, JAYDEN?

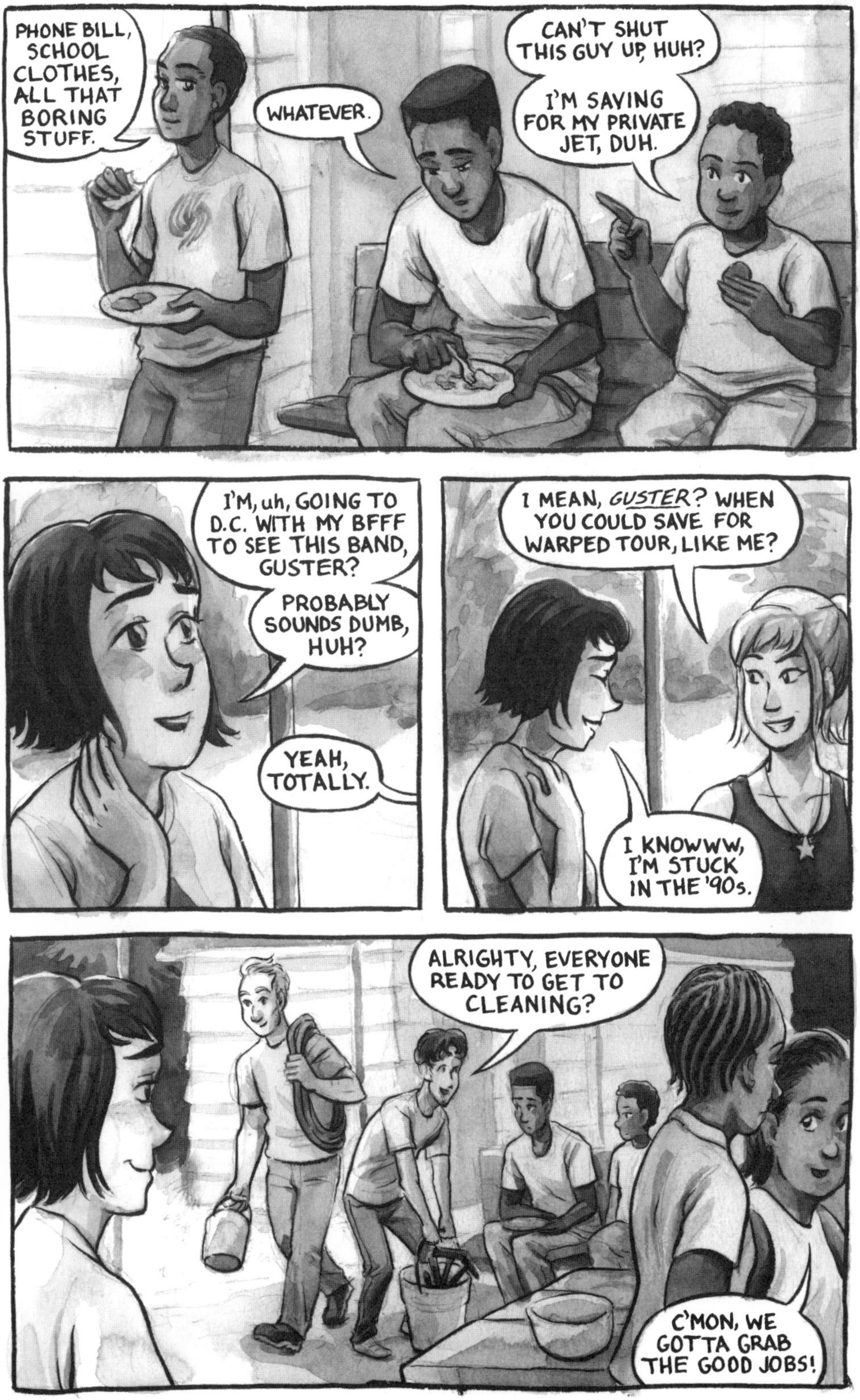
PHONE BILL, SCHOOL CLOTHES, ALL THAT BORING STUFF.
WHATEVER.
CAN'T SHUT THIS GUY UP, HUH?
I'M SAVING FOR MY PRIVATE JET, DUH.
I'M, uh, GOING TO D.C. WITH MY BFFF TO SEE THIS BAND, GUSTER?
PROBABLY SOUNDS DUMB, HUH?
YEAH, TOTALLY.
I MEAN, GUSTER? WHEN YOU COULD SAVE FOR WARPED TOUR, LIKE ME?
I KNOWWW, I'M STUCK IN THE '90s.
ALRIGHTY, EVERYONE READY TO GET TO CLEANING?
C'MON, WE GOTTA GRAB THE GOOD JOBS!

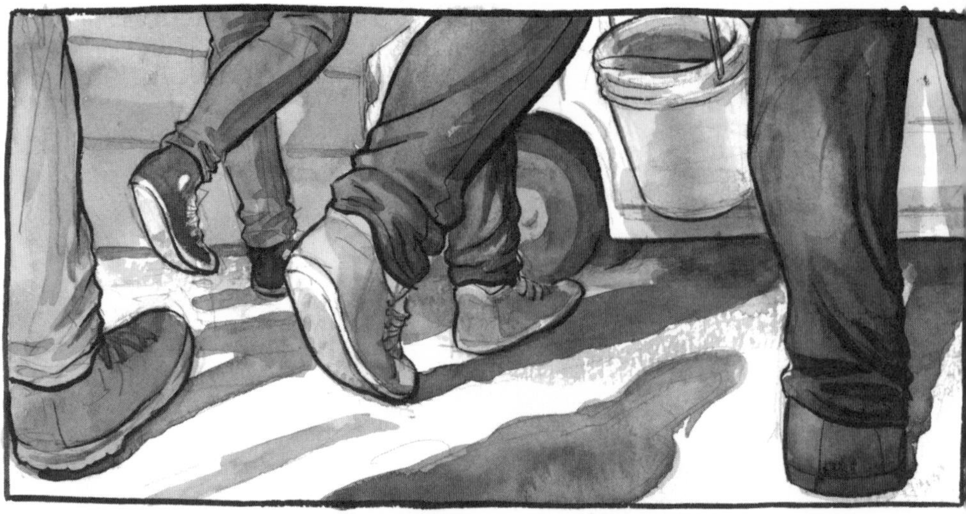

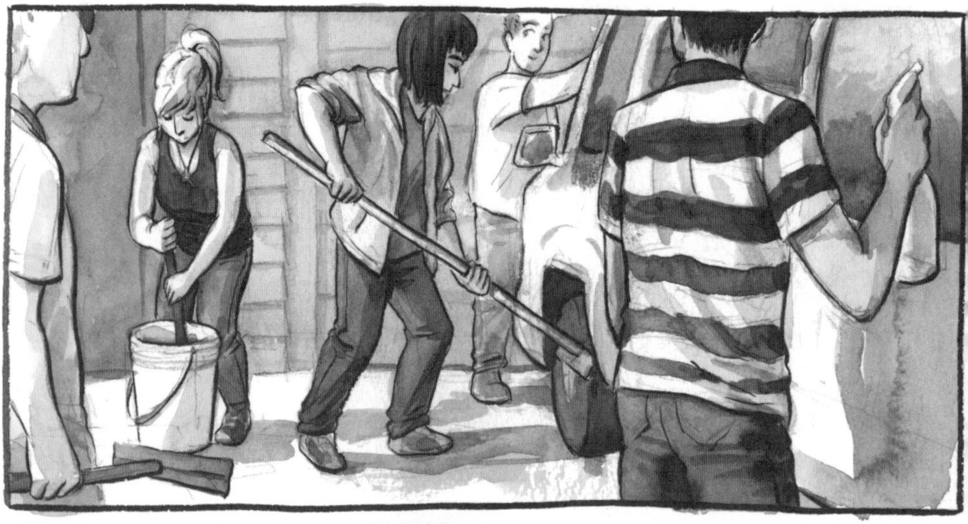

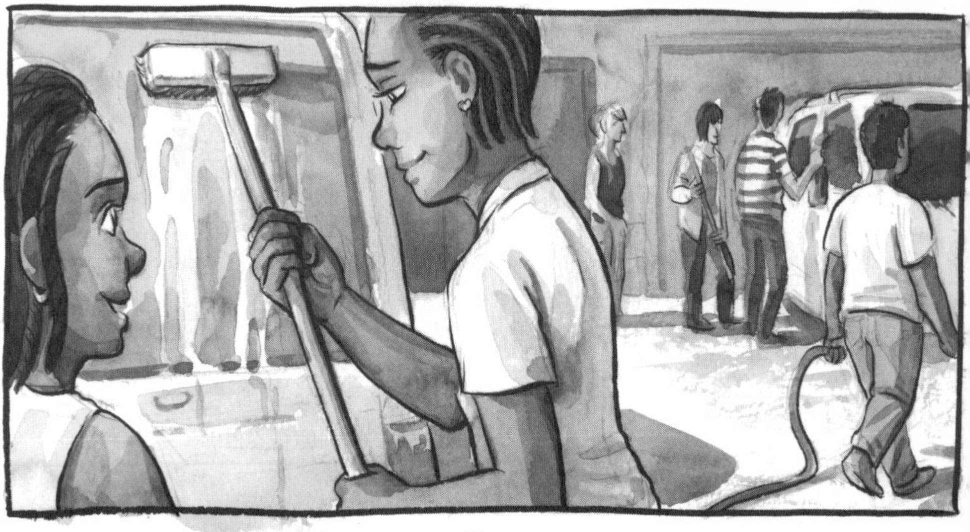

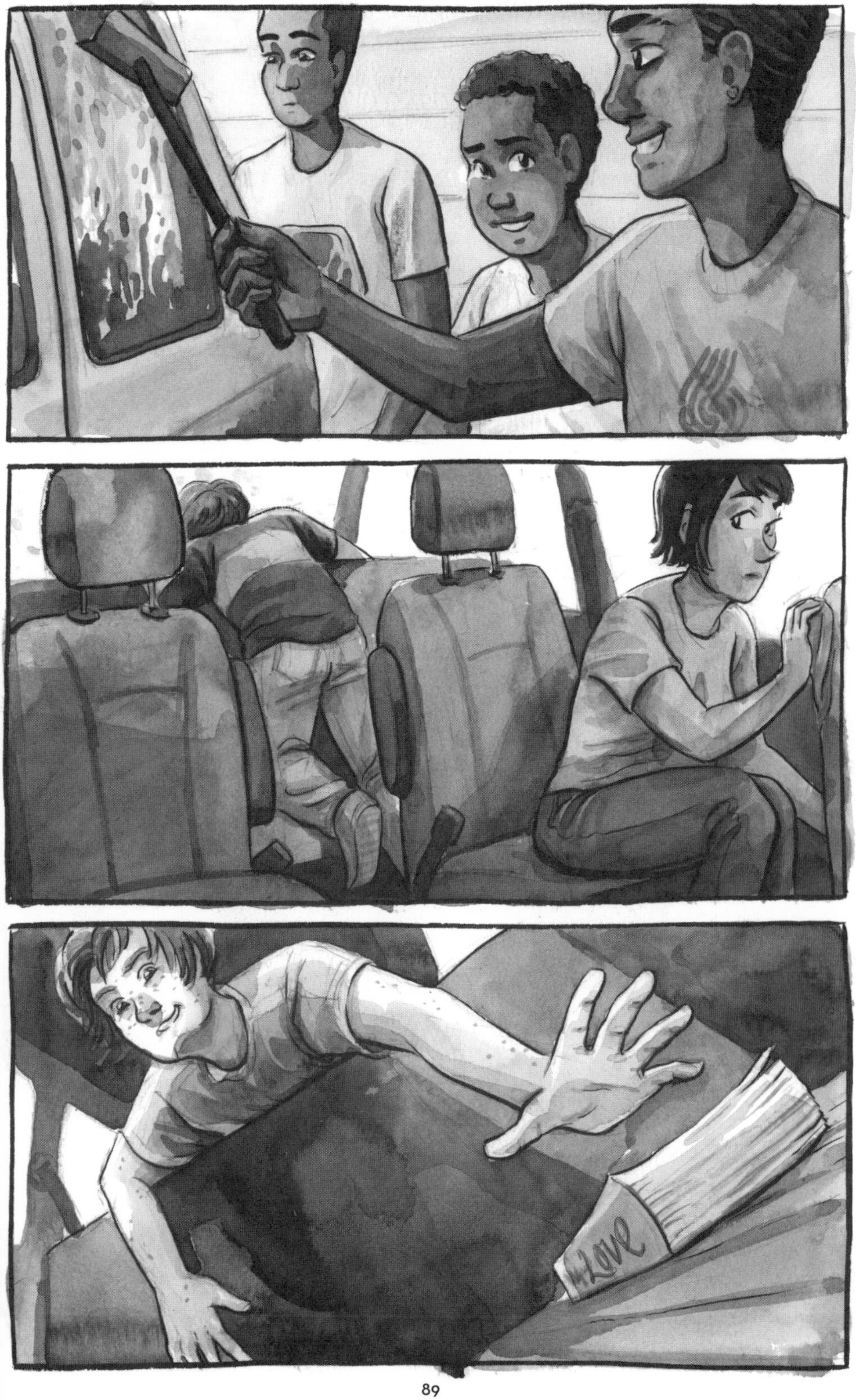
Love

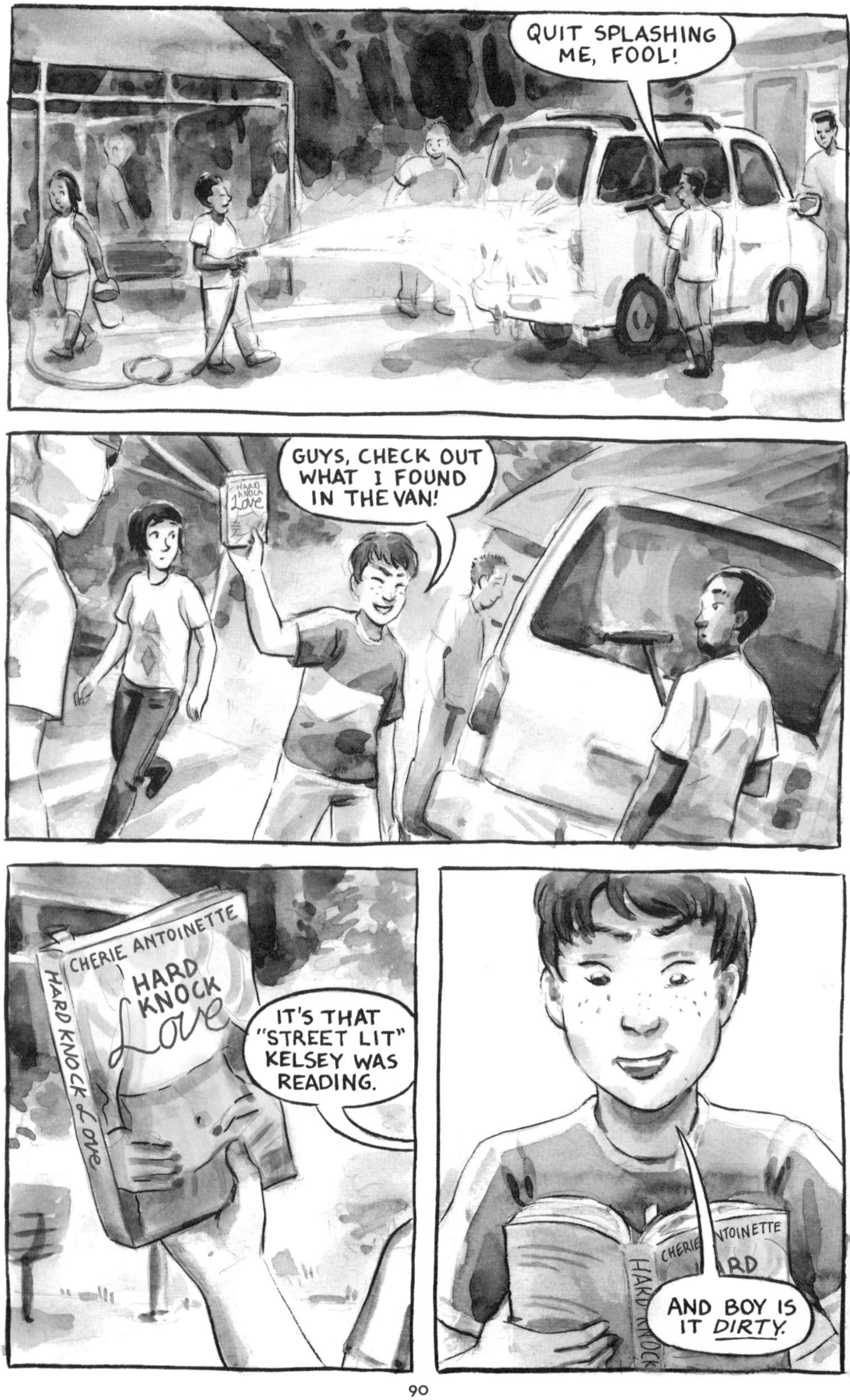
QUIT SPLASHING ME, FOOL!
GUYS, CHECK OUT WHAT I FOUND IN THE VAN!
CHERIE ANTOINETTE HARD KNOCK Love
IT'S THAT "STREET LIT" KELSEY WAS READING.
AND BOY IS IT DIRTY.

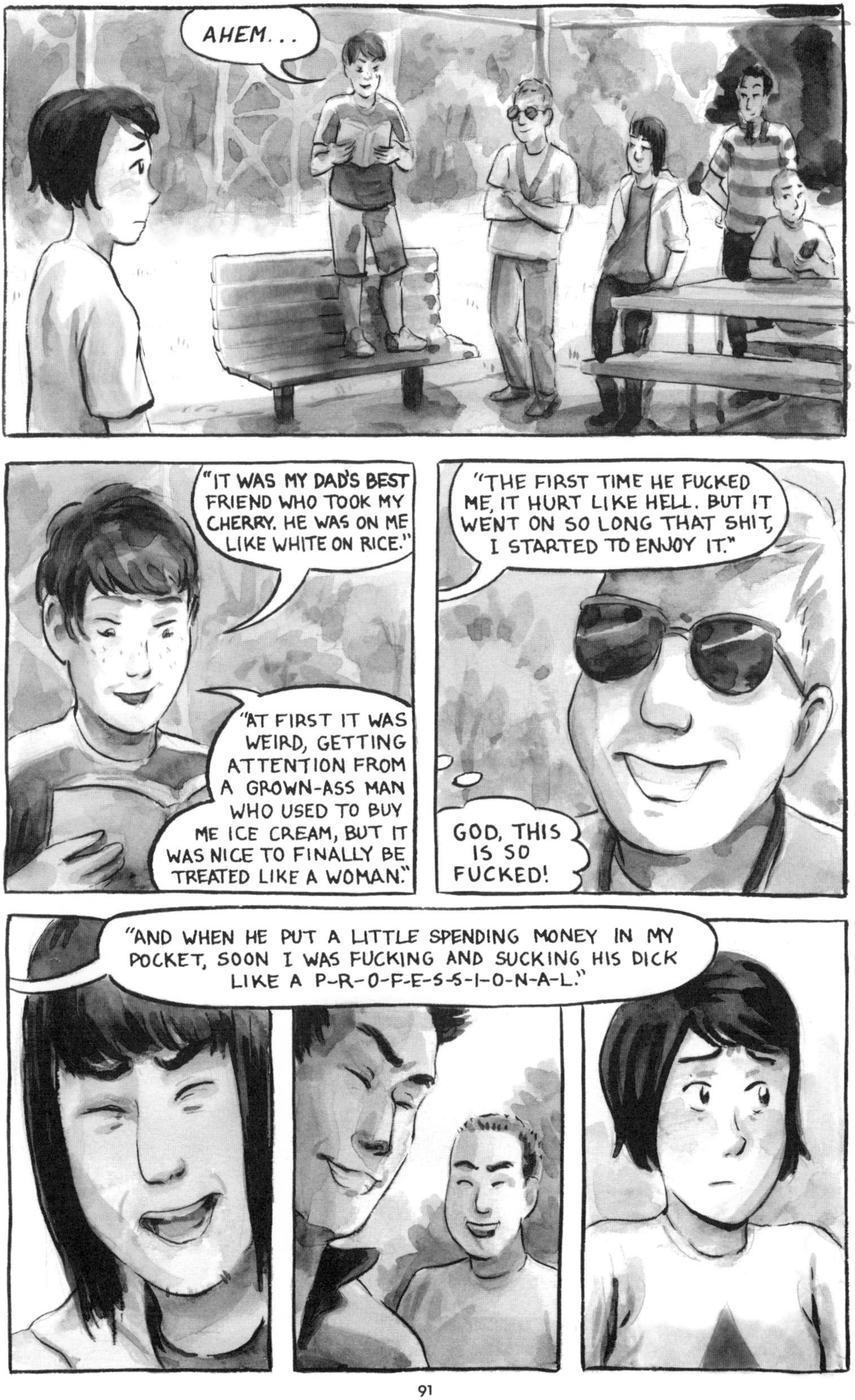
AHEM...
"IT WAS MY DAD'S BEST FRIEND WHO TOOK MY CHERRY. HE WAS ON ME LIKE WHITE ON RICE."
"AT FIRST IT WAS WEIRD, GETTING ATTENTION FROM A GROWN-ASS MAN WHO USED TO BUY ME ICE CREAM, BUT IT WAS NICE TO FINALLY BE TREATED LIKE A WOMAN."
"THE FIRST TIME HE FUCKED ME, IT HURT LIKE HELL. BUT IT WENT ON SO LONG THAT SHIT, I STARTED TO ENJOY IT."
GOD, THIS IS SO FUCKED!
"AND WHEN HE PUT A LITTLE SPENDING MONEY IN MY POCKET, SOON I WAS FUCKING AND SUCKING HIS DICK LIKE A P-R-O-F-E-S-S-I-O-N-A-L."

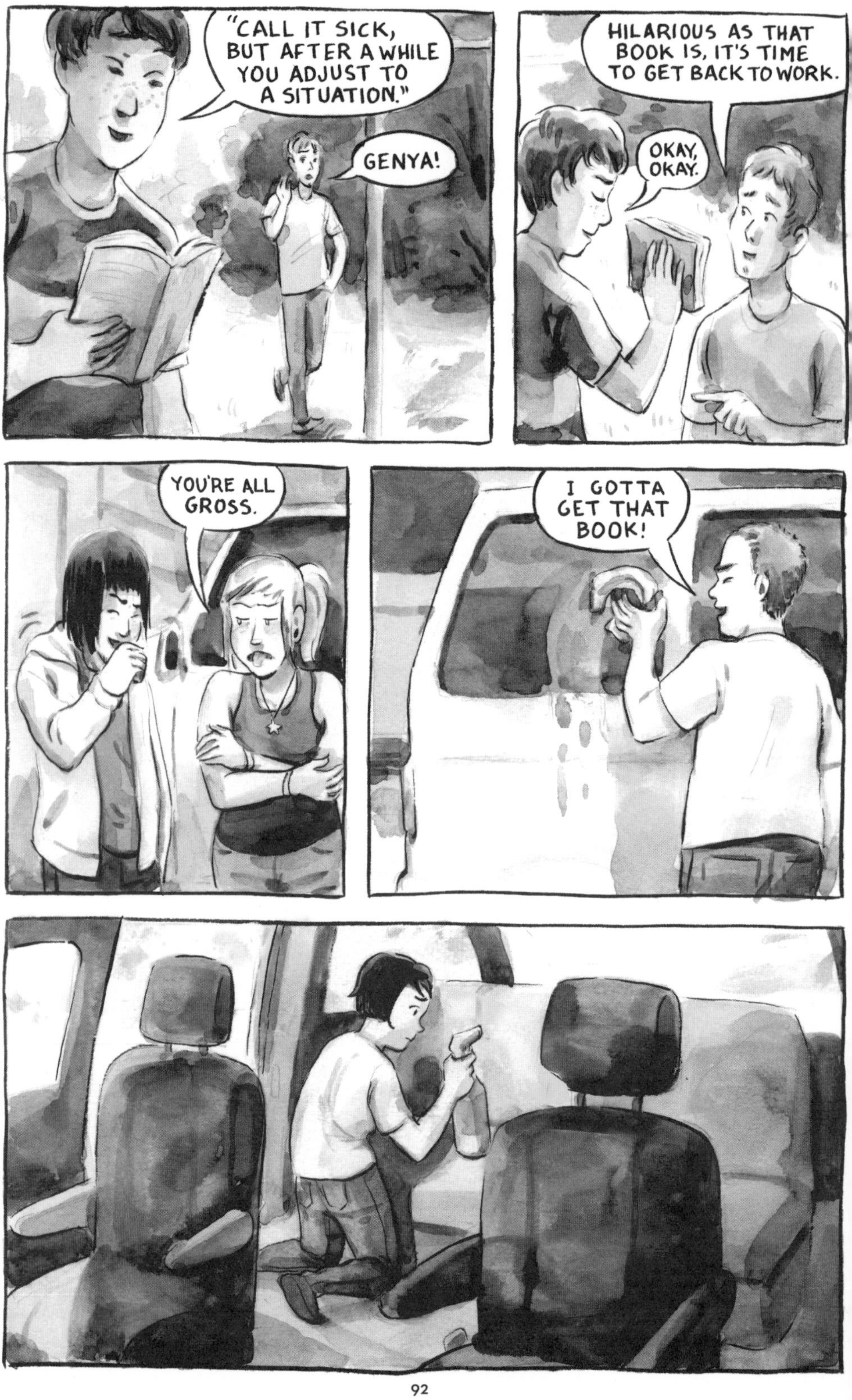
"CALL IT SICK, BUT AFTER A WHILE YOU ADJUST TO A SITUATION."
GENYA!
HILARIOUS AS THAT BOOK IS, IT'S TIME TO GET BACK TO WORK.
OKAY, OKAY.
YOU'RE ALL GROSS.
I GOTTA GET THAT BOOK!

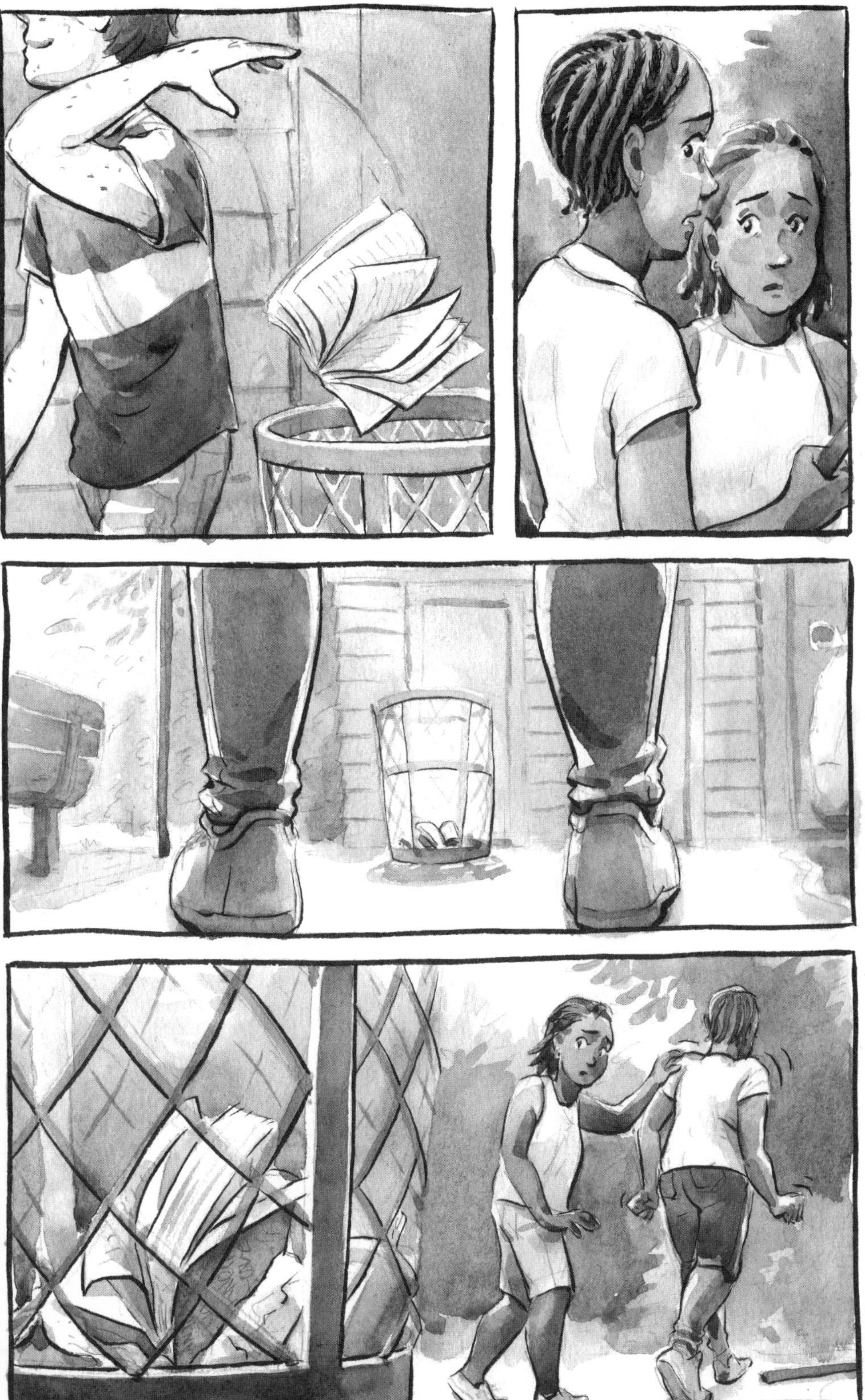

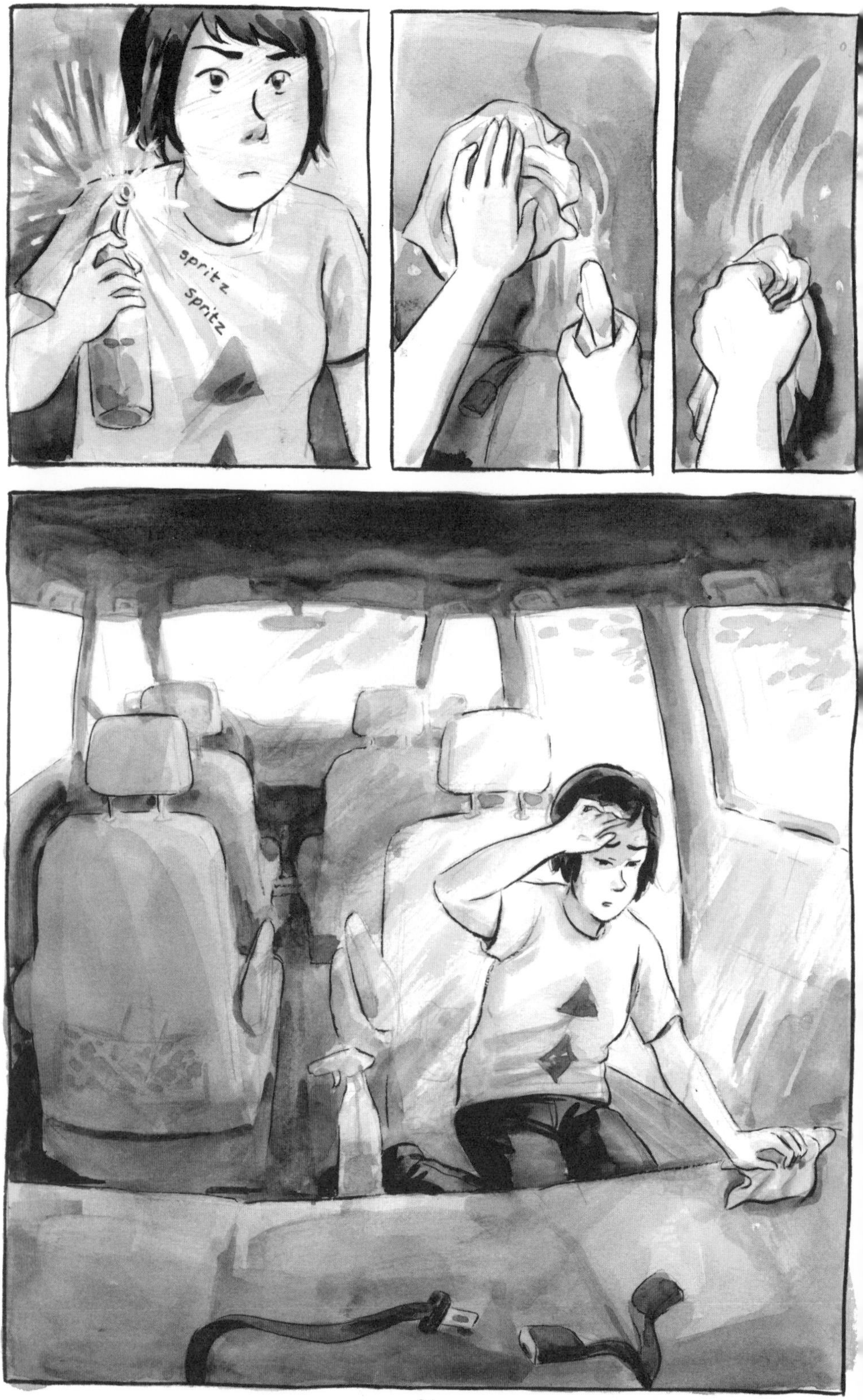
spritz
spritz

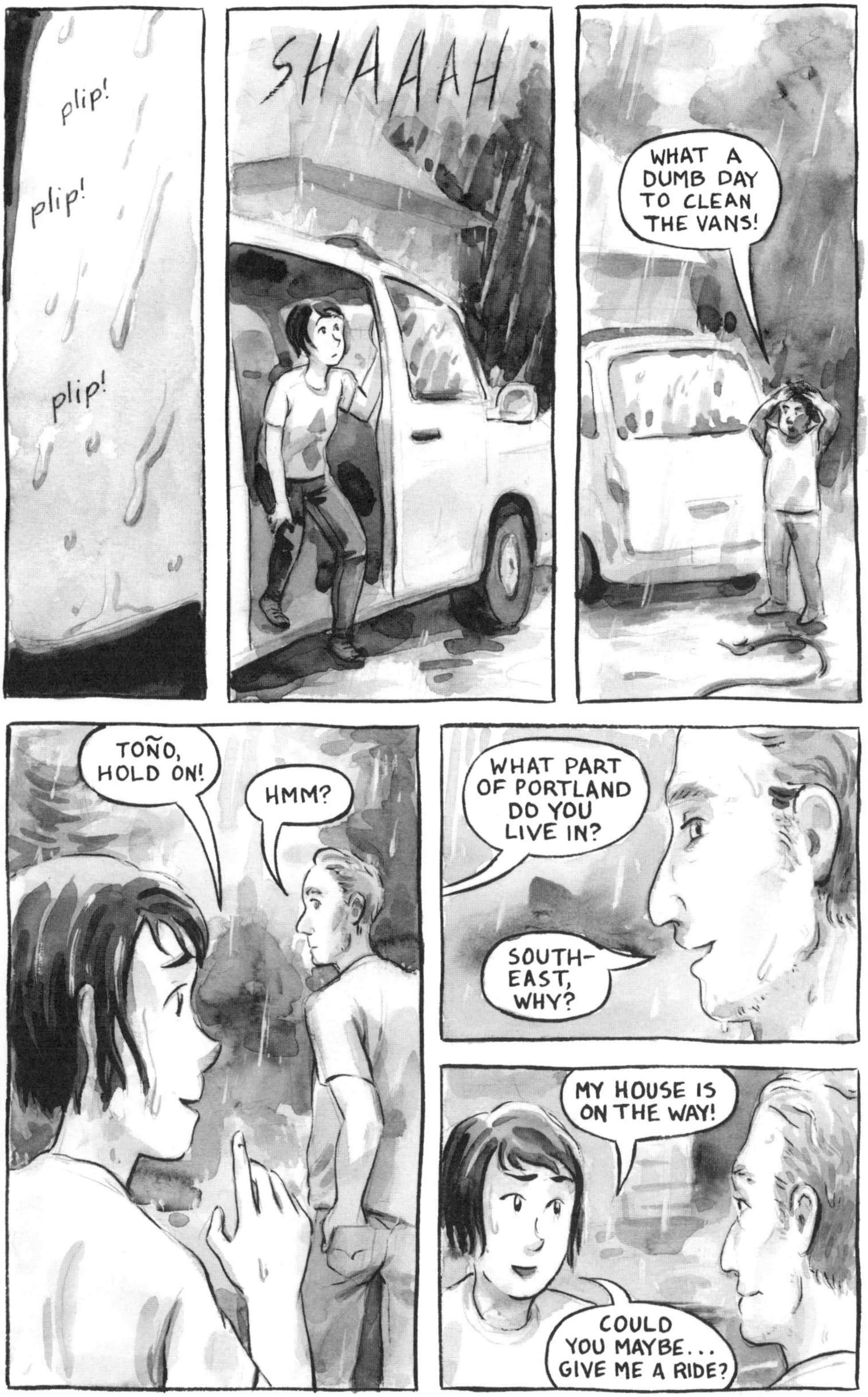
plip!
plip!
plip!
SHAAAH
WHAT A DUMB DAY TO CLEAN THE VANS!
TOÑO, HOLD ON!
HMM?
WHAT PART OF PORTLAND DO YOU LIVE IN?
SOUTH-EAST, WHY?
MY HOUSE IS ON THE WAY!
COULD YOU MAYBE... GIVE ME A RIDE?

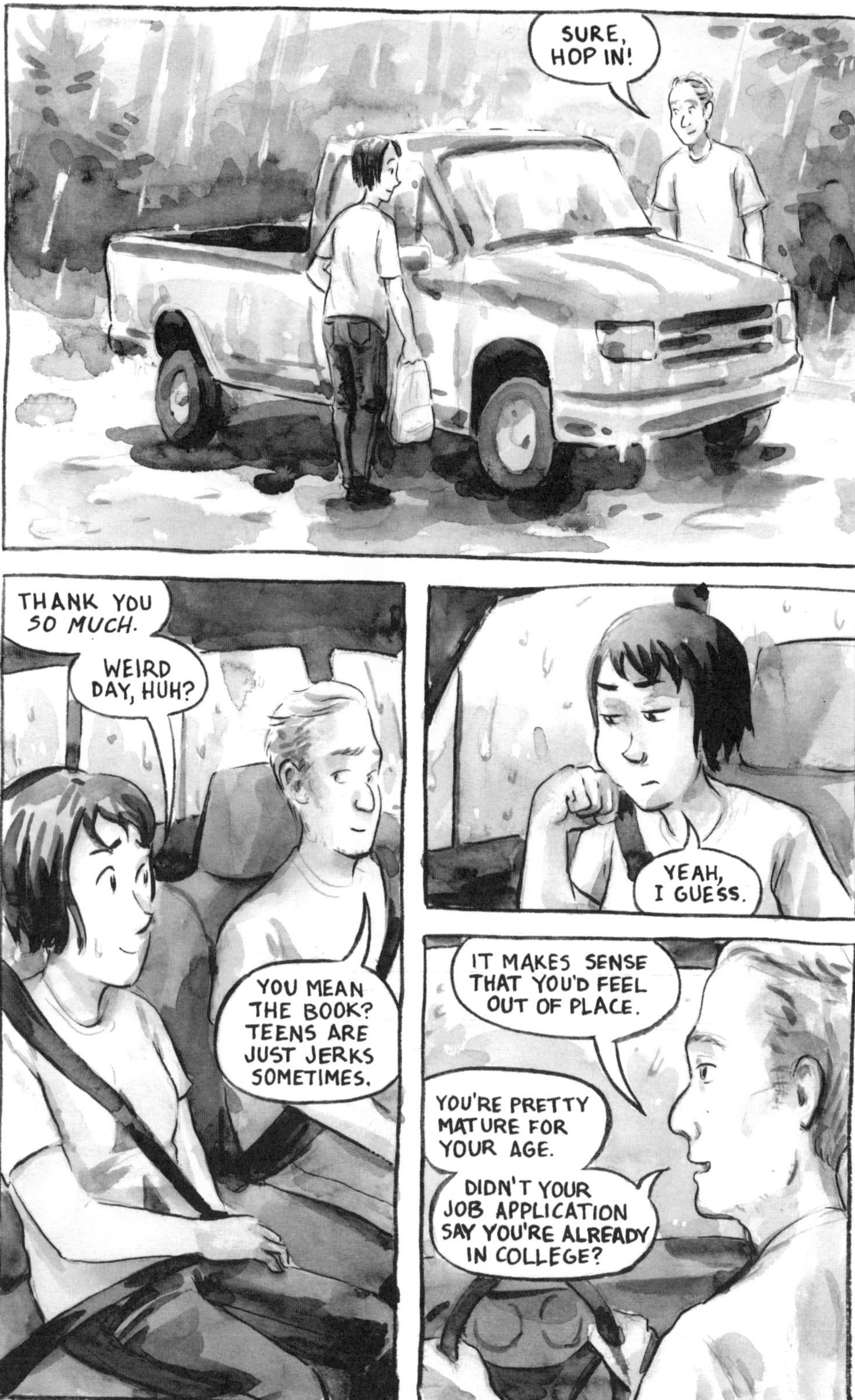
SURE, HOP IN!
THANK YOU SO MUCH.
WEIRD DAY, HUH?
YOU MEAN THE BOOK? TEENS ARE JUST JERKS SOMETIMES.
YEAH, I GUESS.
IT MAKES SENSE THAT YOU'D FEEL OUT OF PLACE.
YOU'RE PRETTY MATURE FOR YOUR AGE.
DIDN'T YOUR JOB APPLICATION SAY YOU'RE ALREADY IN COLLEGE?

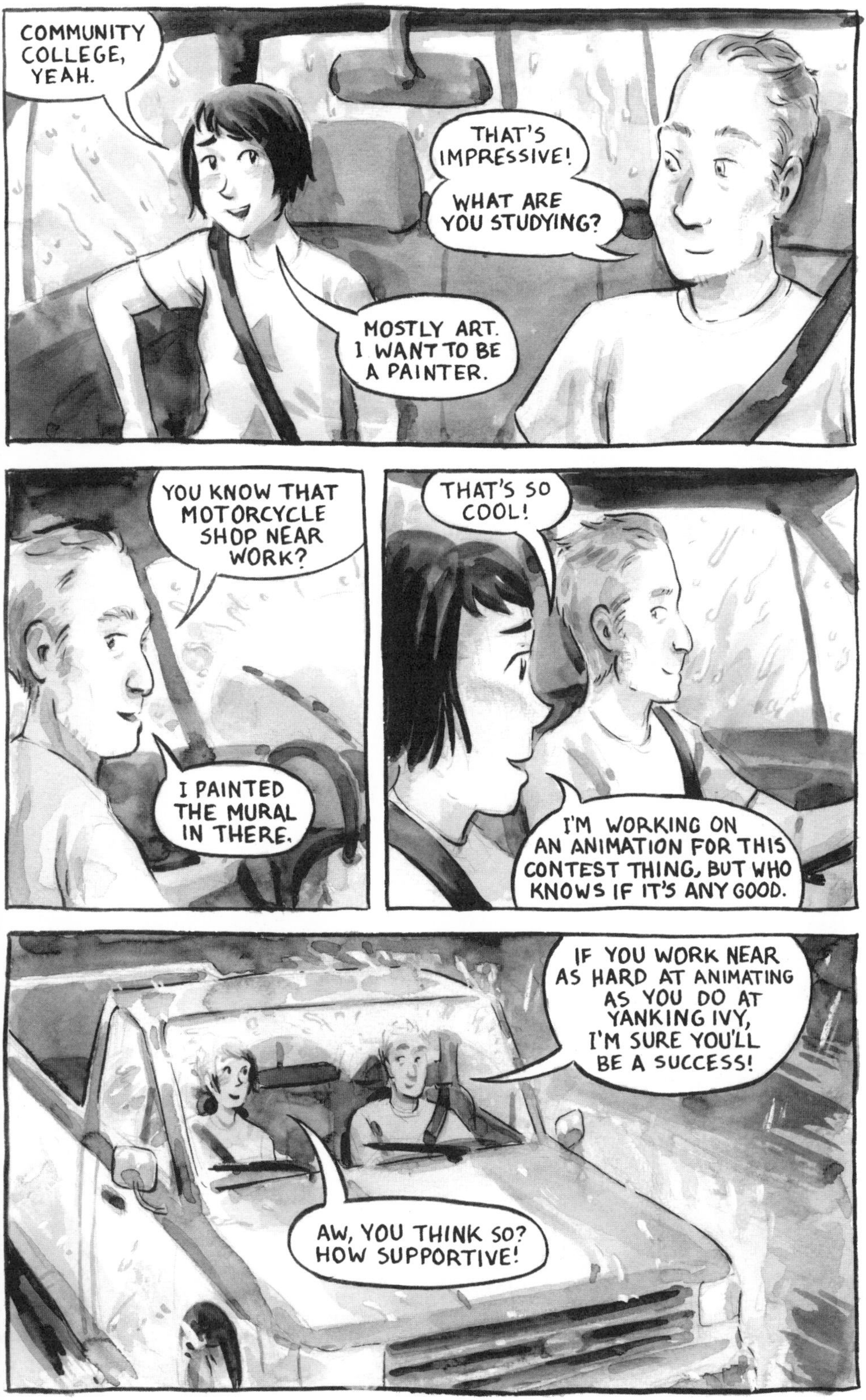
COMMUNITY COLLEGE, YEAH.
THAT'S IMPRESSIVE!
WHAT ARE YOU STUDYING?
MOSTLY ART. I WANT TO BE A PAINTER.
YOU KNOW THAT MOTORCYCLE SHOP NEAR WORK?
I PAINTED THE MURAL IN THERE.
THAT'S SO COOL!
I'M WORKING ON AN ANIMATION FOR THIS CONTEST THING, BUT WHO KNOWS IF IT'S ANY GOOD.
IF YOU WORK NEAR AS HARD AT ANIMATING AS YOU DO AT YANKING IVY, I'M SURE YOU'LL BE A SUCCESS!
AW, YOU THINK SO? HOW SUPPORTIVE!

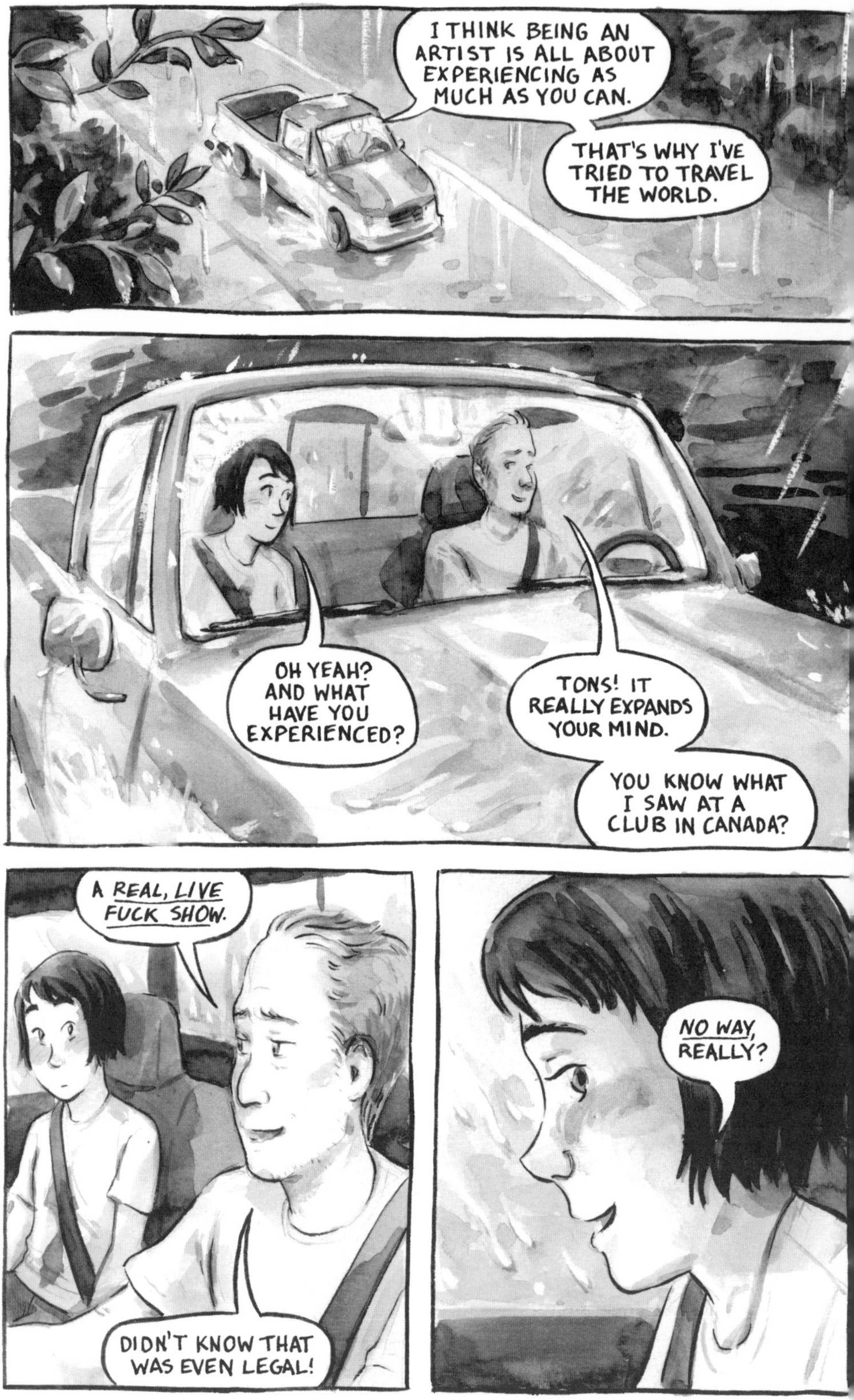
I THINK BEING AN ARTIST IS ALL ABOUT EXPERIENCING AS MUCH AS YOU CAN.
THAT'S WHY I'VE TRIED TO TRAVEL THE WORLD.
OH YEAH? AND WHAT HAVE YOU EXPERIENCED?
TONS! IT REALLY EXPANDS YOUR MIND.
YOU KNOW WHAT I SAW AT A CLUB IN CANADA?
A REAL, LIVE FUCK SHOW.
DIDN'T KNOW THAT WAS EVEN LEGAL!
NO WAY, REALLY?

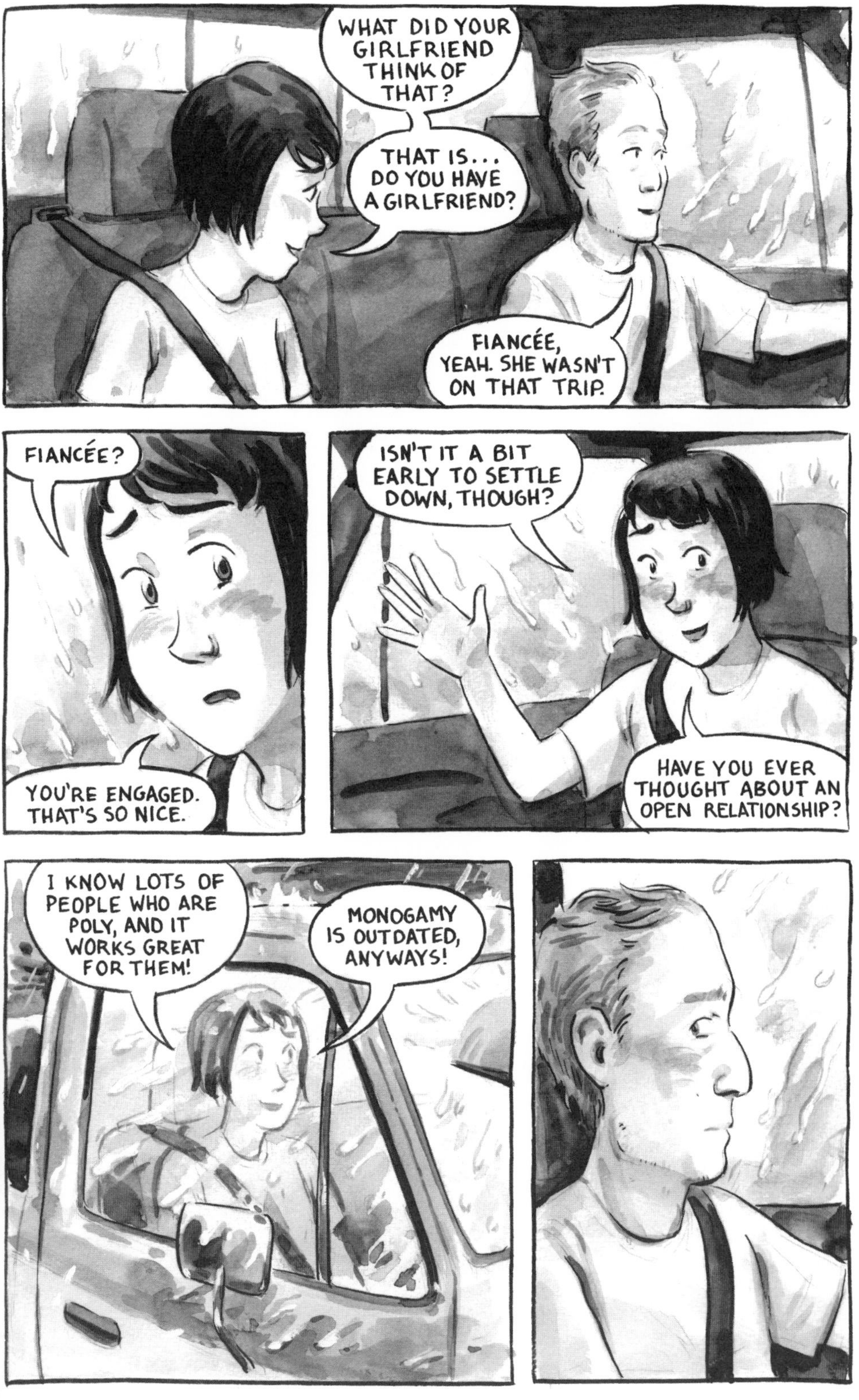
WHAT DID YOUR GIRLFRIEND THINK OF THAT?
THAT IS... DO YOU HAVE A GIRLFRIEND?
FIANCÉE, YEAH. SHE WASN'T ON THAT TRIP.
FIANCÉE?
YOU'RE ENGAGED. THAT'S SO NICE.
ISN'T IT A BIT EARLY TO SETTLE DOWN, THOUGH?
HAVE YOU EVER THOUGHT ABOUT AN OPEN RELATIONSHIP?
I KNOW LOTS OF PEOPLE WHO ARE POLY, AND IT WORKS GREAT FOR THEM!
MONOGAMY IS OUTDATED, ANYWAYS!

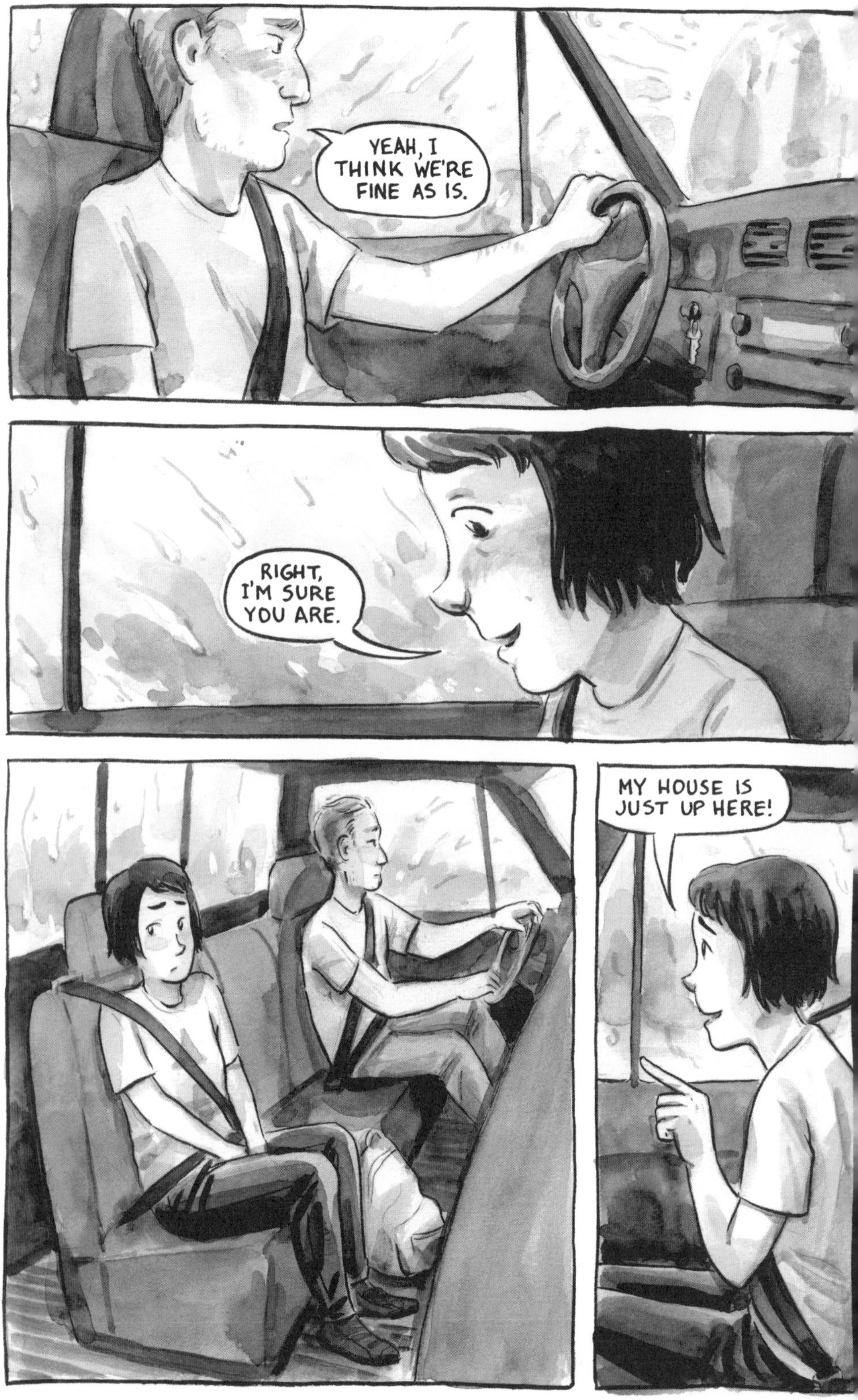
YEAH, I THINK WE'RE FINE AS IS.
RIGHT, I'M SURE YOU ARE.
MY HOUSE IS JUST UP HERE!

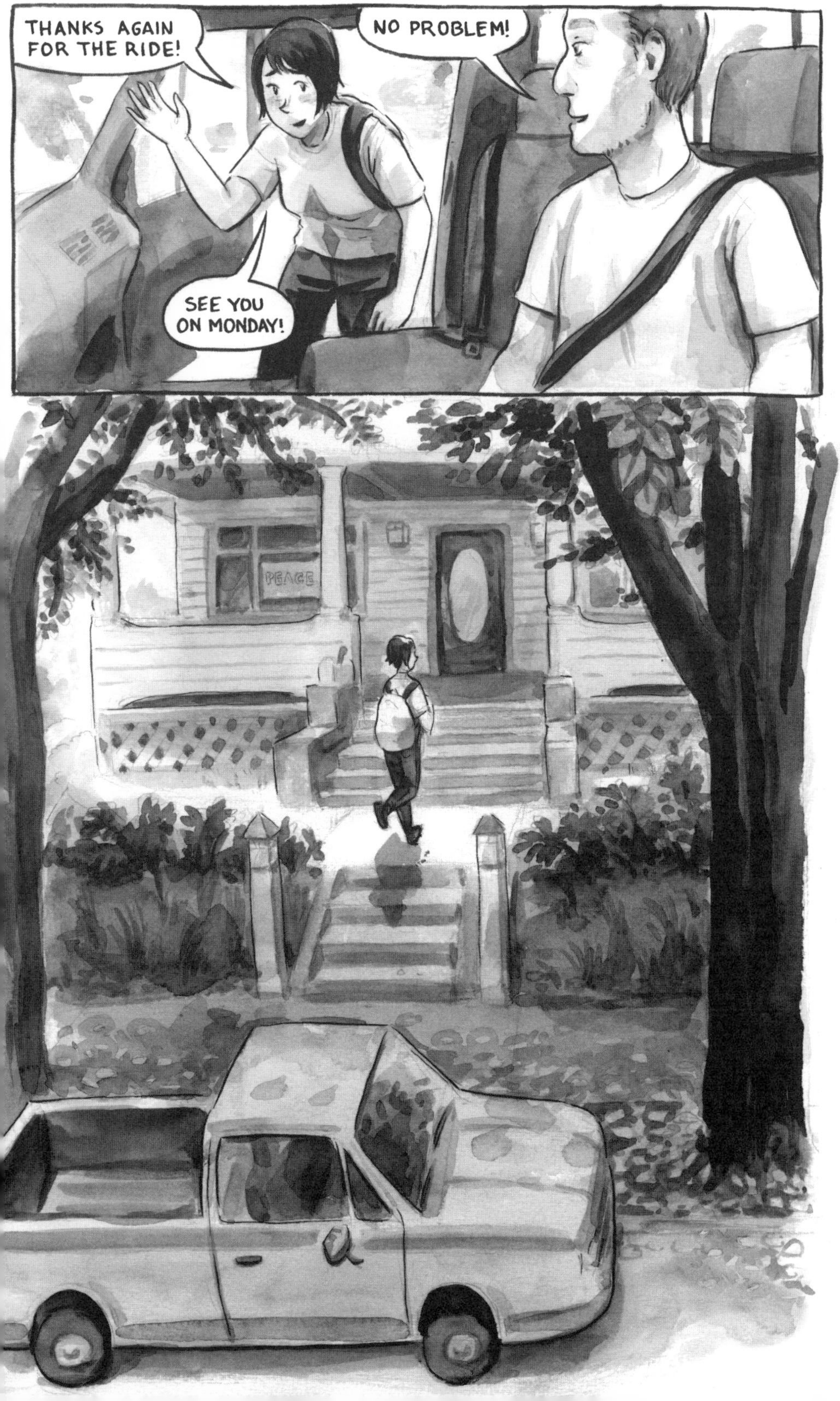
THANKS AGAIN FOR THE RIDE!
NO PROBLEM!
SEE YOU ON MONDAY!
PEACE

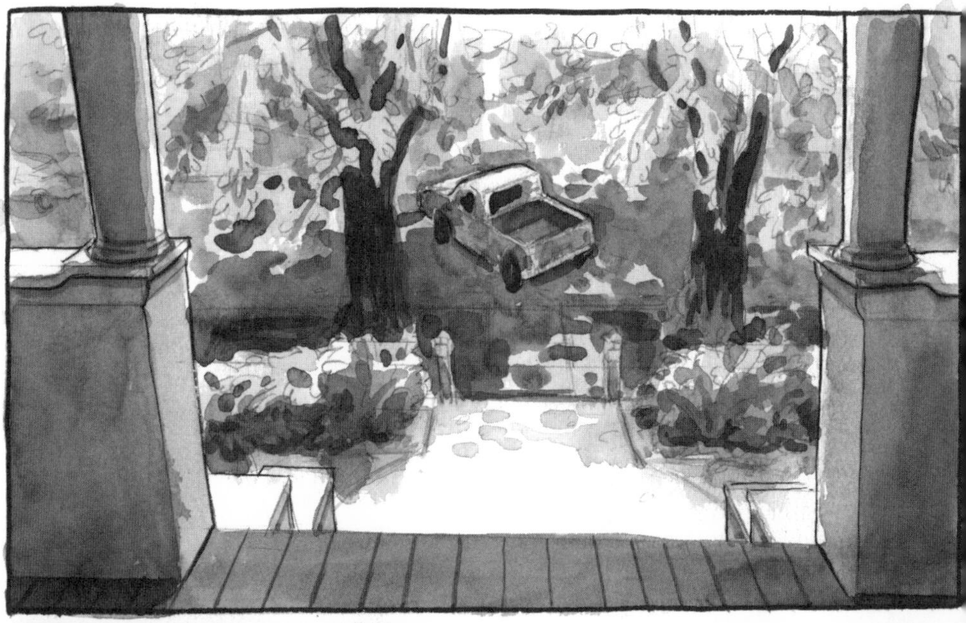

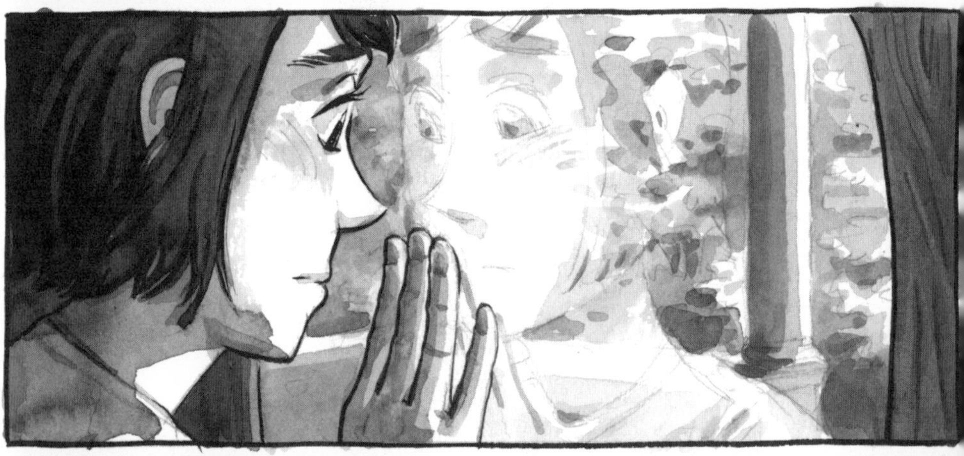

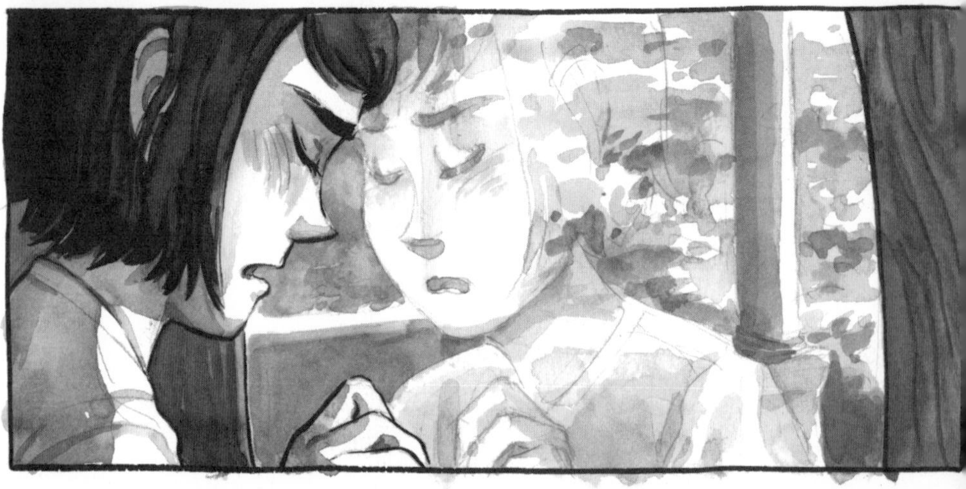

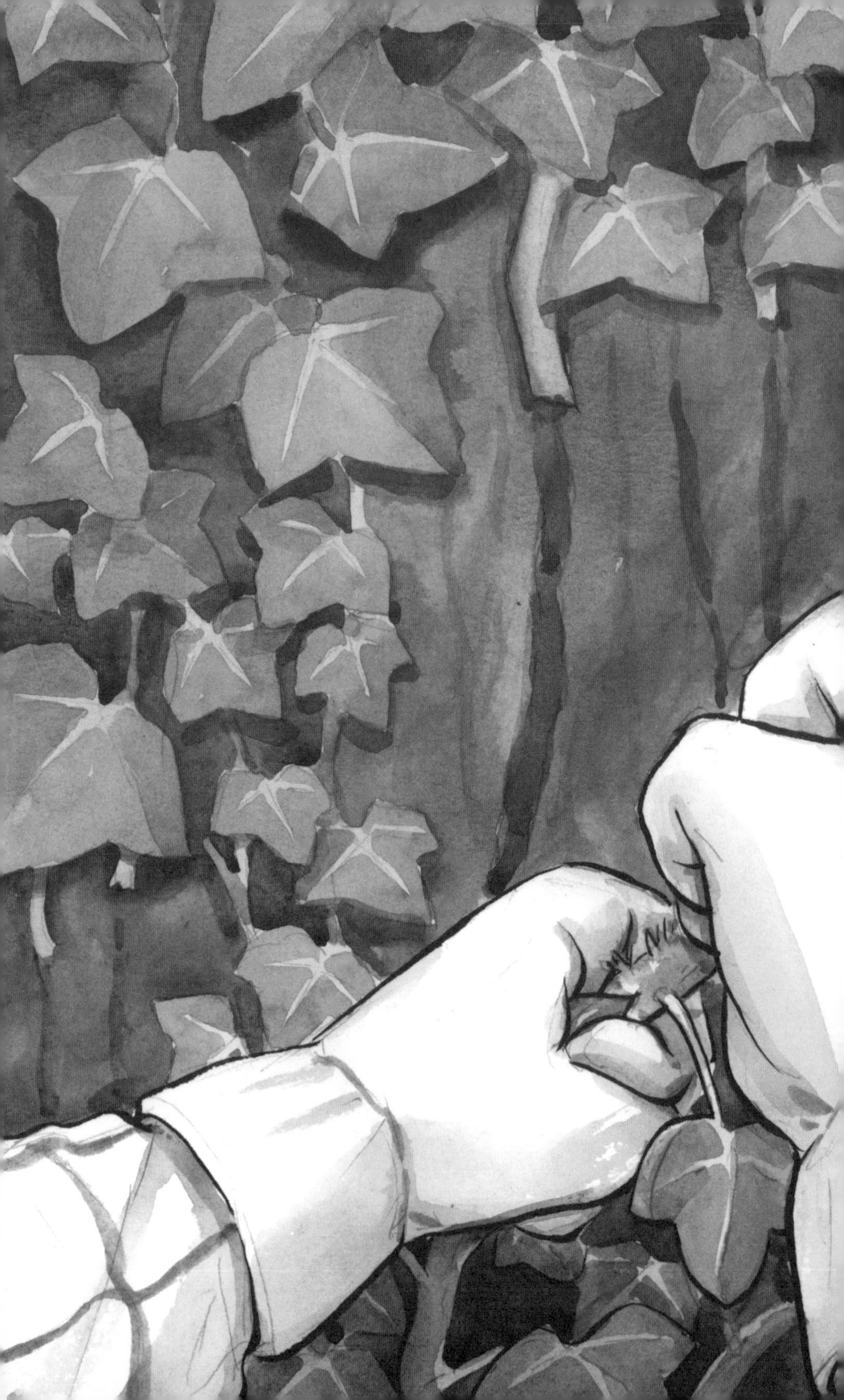

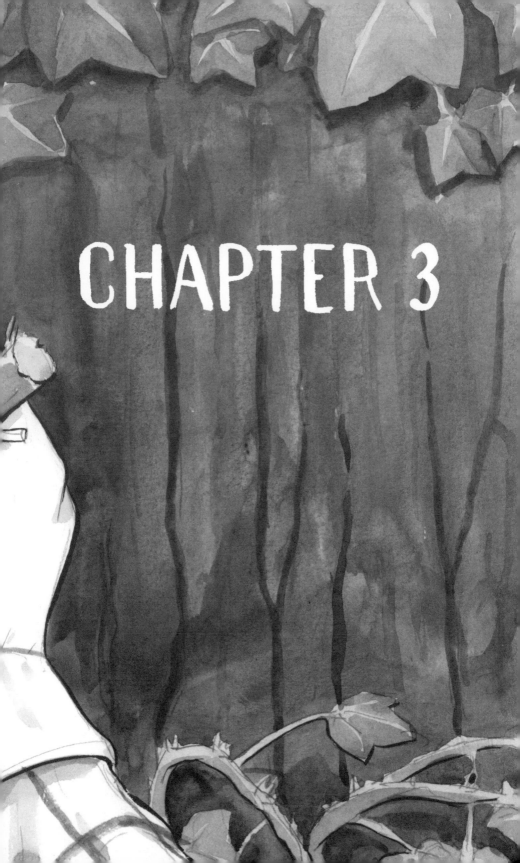

CHAPTER 3

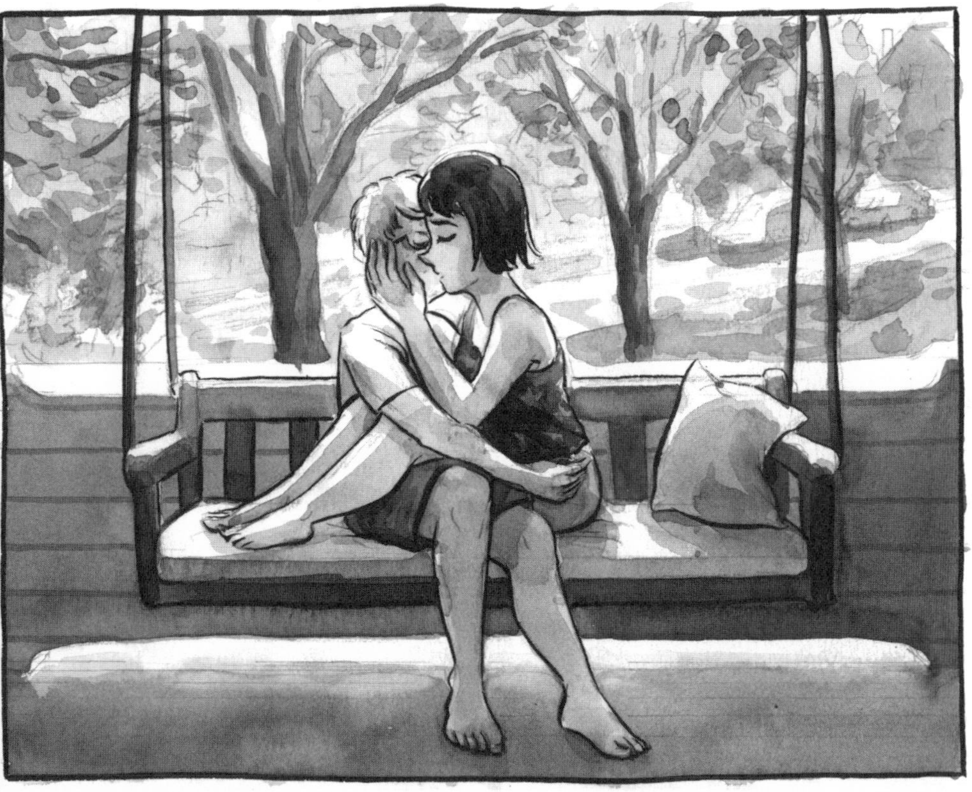

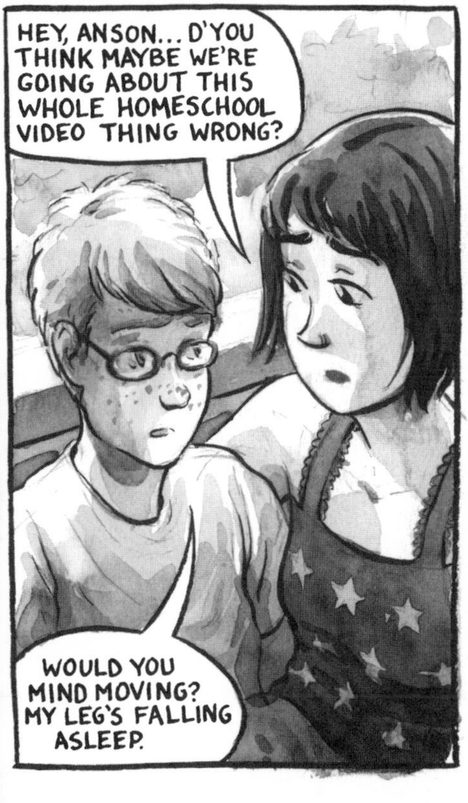
HEY, ANSON... D'YOU THINK MAYBE WE'RE GOING ABOUT THIS WHOLE HOMESCHOOL VIDEO THING WRONG?
WOULD YOU MIND MOVING? MY LEG'S FALLING ASLEEP.

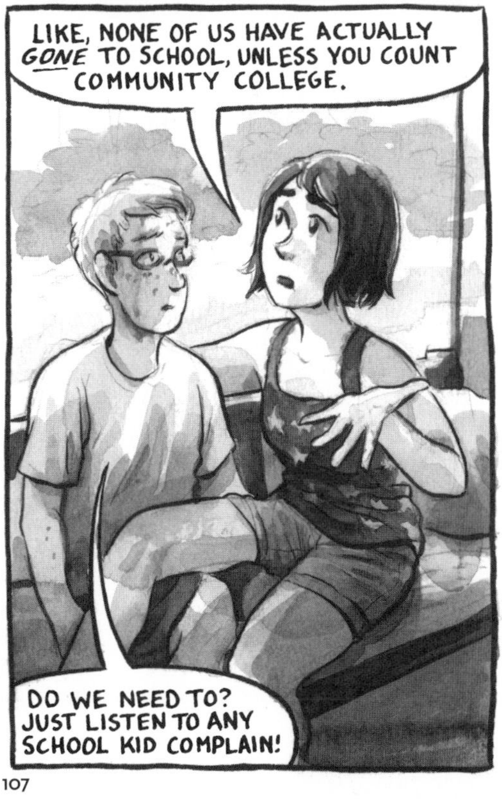
LIKE, NONE OF US HAVE ACTUALLY GONE TO SCHOOL, UNLESS YOU COUNT COMMUNITY COLLEGE.
DO WE NEED TO? JUST LISTEN TO ANY SCHOOL KID COMPLAIN!

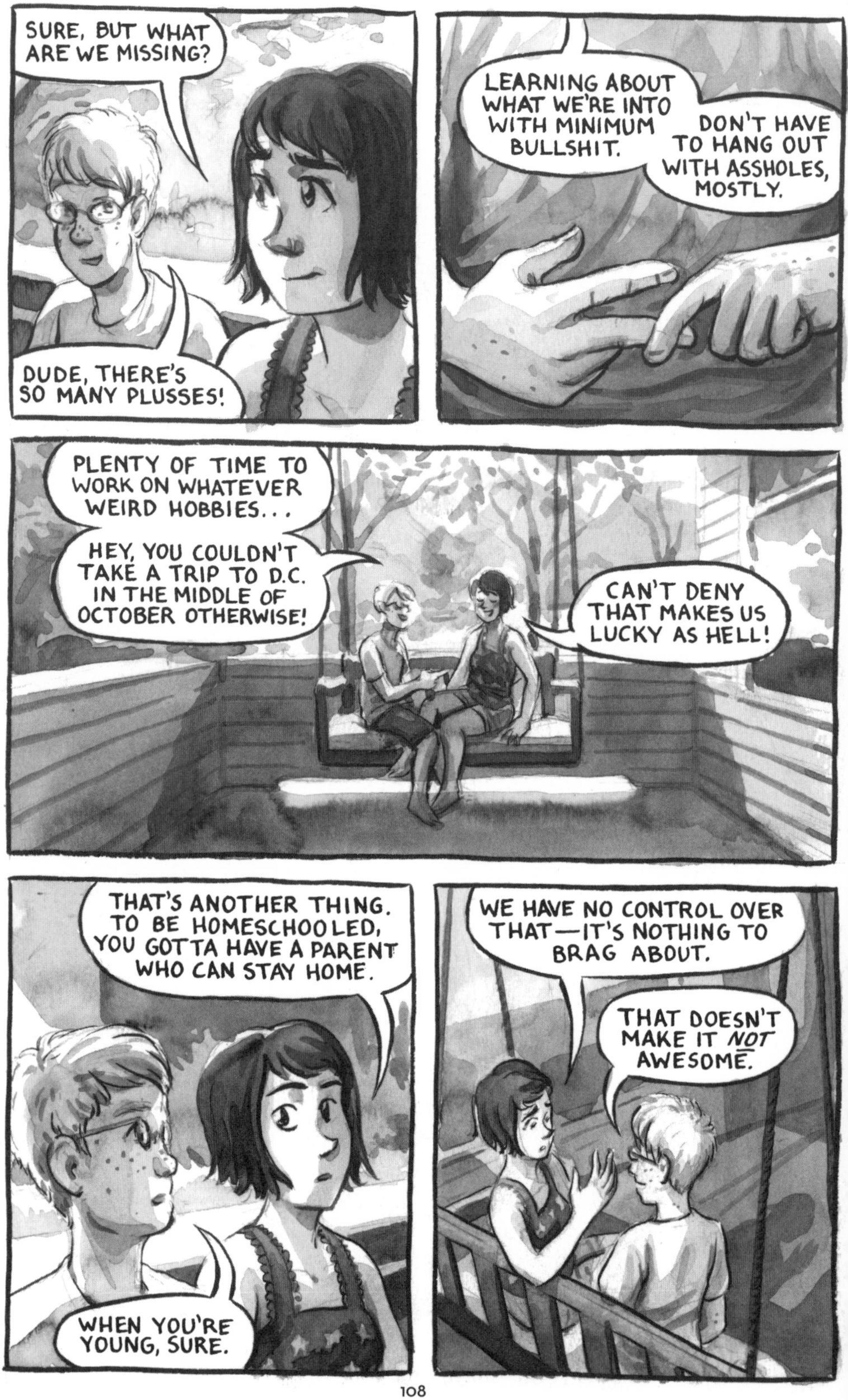
SURE, BUT WHAT ARE WE MISSING?
DUDE, THERE'S SO MANY PLUSSES!
LEARNING ABOUT WHAT WE'RE INTO WITH MINIMUM BULLSHIT.
DON'T HAVE TO HANG OUT WITH ASSHOLES, MOSTLY.
PLENTY OF TIME TO WORK ON WHATEVER WEIRD HOBBIES...
HEY, YOU COULDN'T TAKE A TRIP TO D.C. IN THE MIDDLE OF OCTOBER OTHERWISE!
CAN'T DENY THAT MAKES US LUCKY AS HELL!
THAT'S ANOTHER THING. TO BE HOMESCHOOLED, YOU GOTTA HAVE A PARENT WHO CAN STAY HOME.
WHEN YOU'RE YOUNG, SURE.
WE HAVE NO CONTROL OVER THAT—IT'S NOTHING TO BRAG ABOUT.
THAT DOESN'T MAKE IT *NOT* AWESOME.

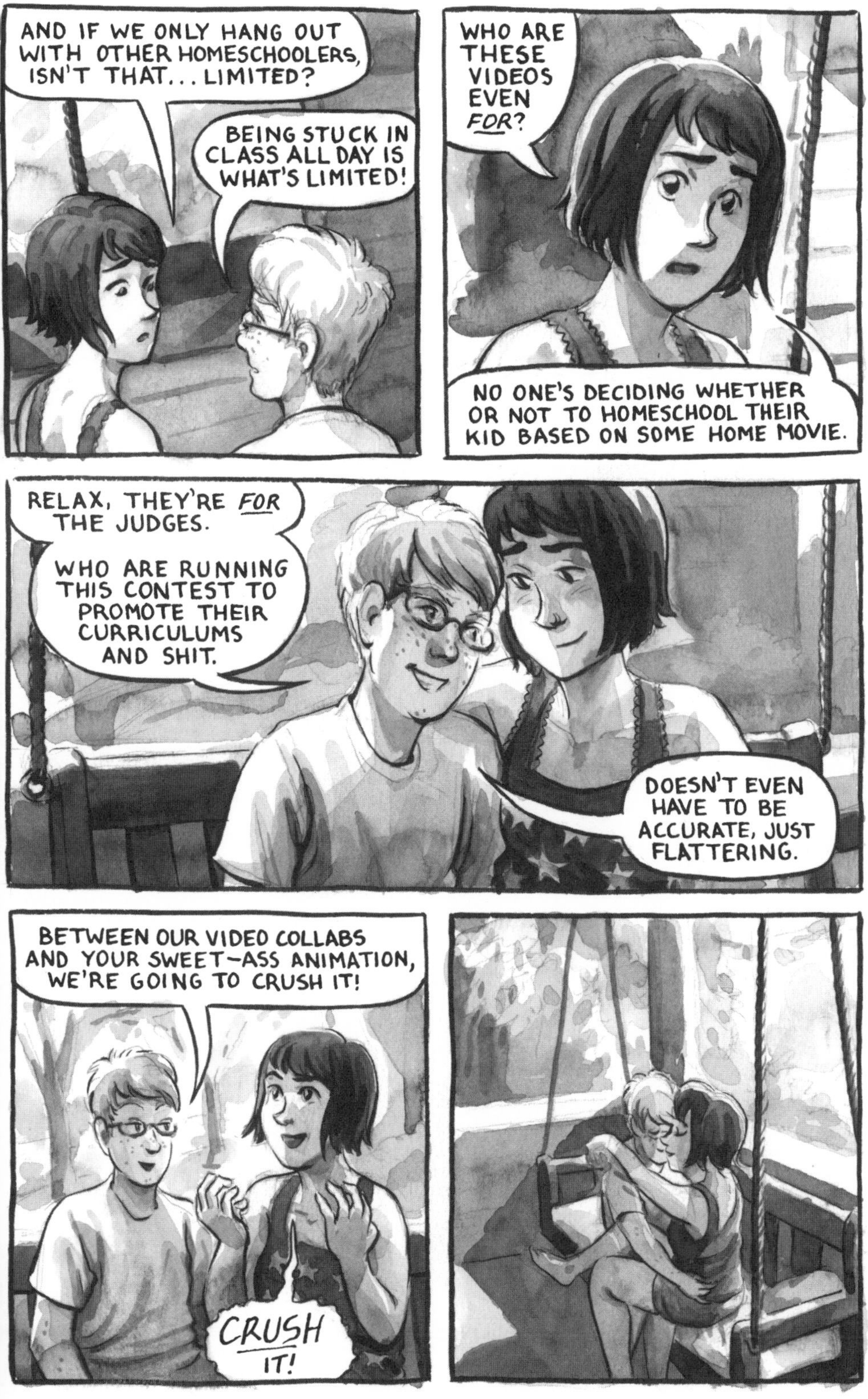
AND IF WE ONLY HANG OUT WITH OTHER HOMESCHOOLERS, ISN'T THAT... LIMITED?
BEING STUCK IN CLASS ALL DAY IS WHAT'S LIMITED!
WHO ARE THESE VIDEOS EVEN FOR?
NO ONE'S DECIDING WHETHER OR NOT TO HOMESCHOOL THEIR KID BASED ON SOME HOME MOVIE.
RELAX, THEY'RE FOR THE JUDGES.
WHO ARE RUNNING THIS CONTEST TO PROMOTE THEIR CURRICULUMS AND SHIT.
DOESN'T EVEN HAVE TO BE ACCURATE, JUST FLATTERING.
BETWEEN OUR VIDEO COLLABS AND YOUR SWEET-ASS ANIMATION, WE'RE GOING TO CRUSH IT!
CRUSH IT!

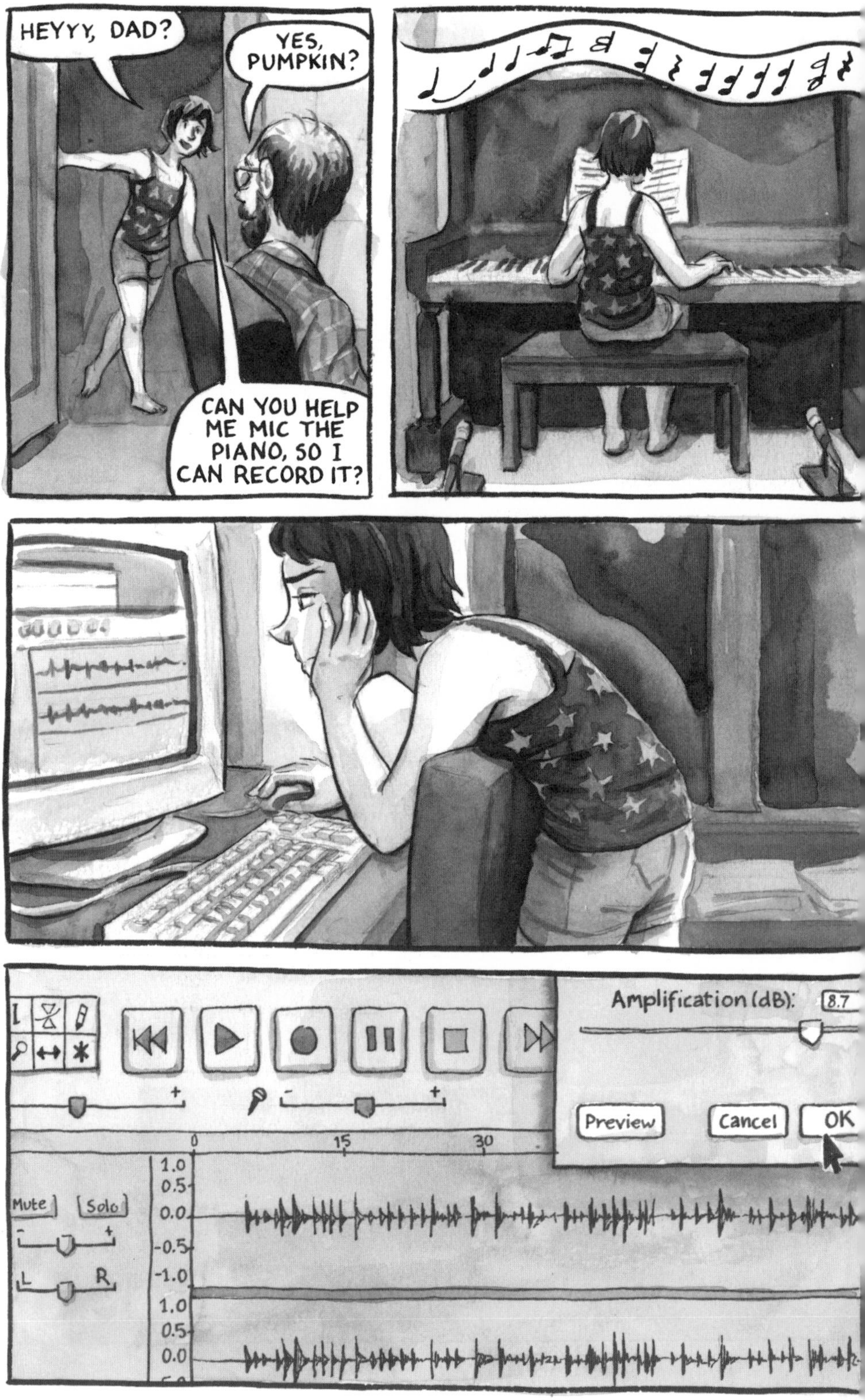
HEYYY, DAD?
YES, PUMPKIN?
CAN YOU HELP ME MIC THE PIANO, SO I CAN RECORD IT?
Amplification (dB):
8.7
Preview
Cancel
OK
Mute
Solo
L
R
0
15
30
1.0
0.5
0.0
-0.5
-1.0
1.0
0.5
0.0

TIMELINE
MOTION EDITOR
1 5 10 15 20 25 30 35 40 45 50 55
music
school
body
body med
Teacher
face close
clock
head turn
montage
item 1
Local Disc (C:)
Flash Video
Music
psd's
vid
movie.avi
movie edit.avi
movie FINAL.a
movie FINALFI
movie 2.avi
movie 2 edit.a
WHAT I LIKE
ABOUT HOMESCO
OOPS!
WHAT I LIKE
ABOUT HOMESCHO

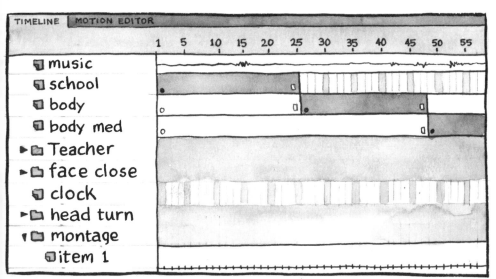

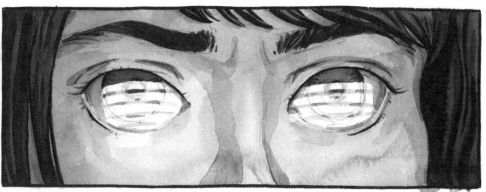

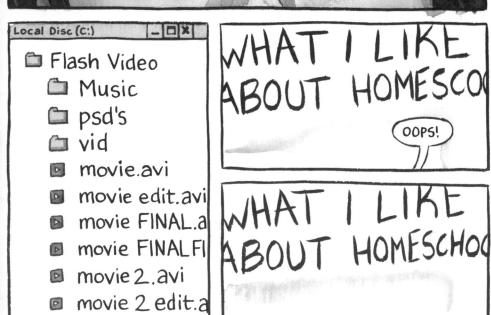

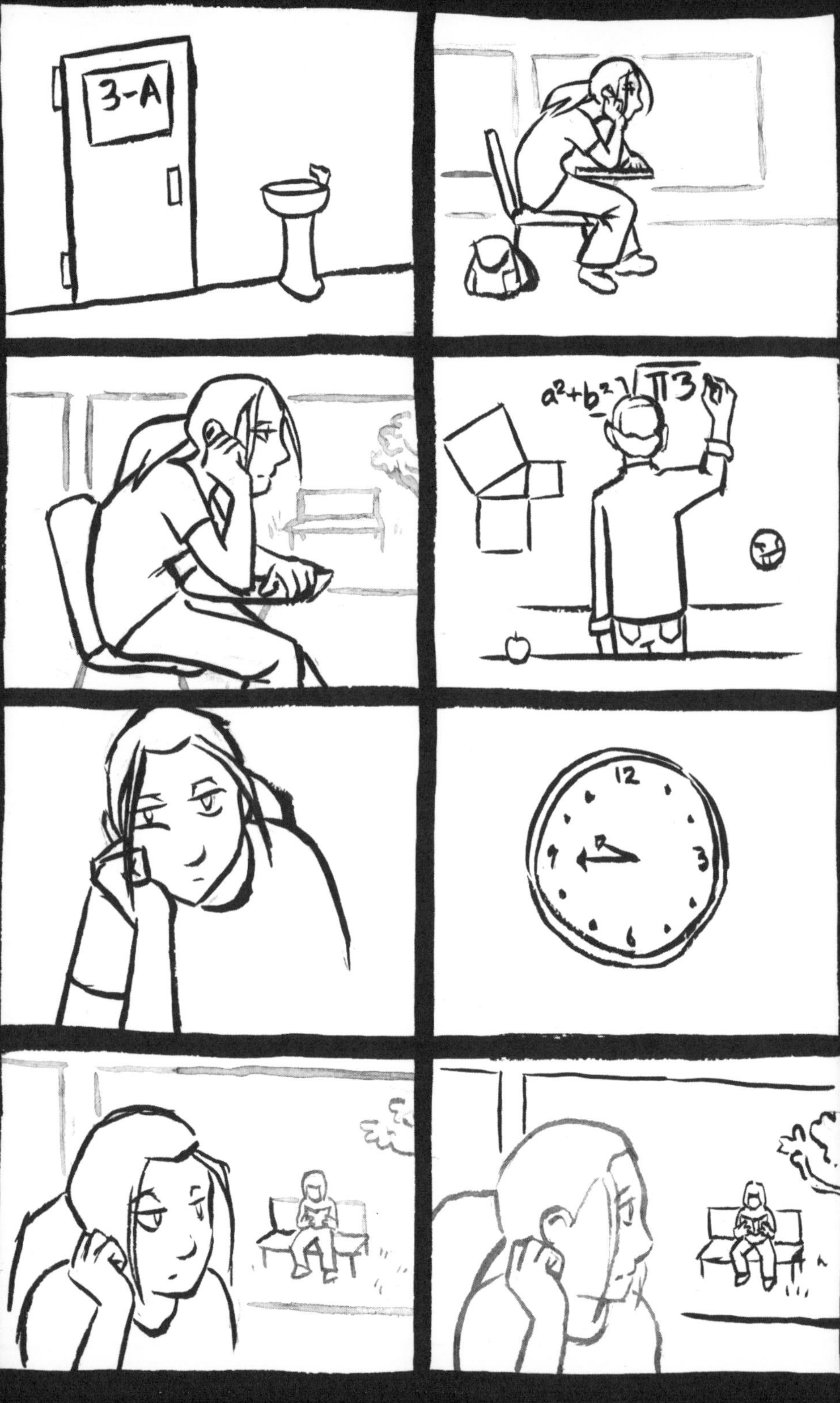
3-A

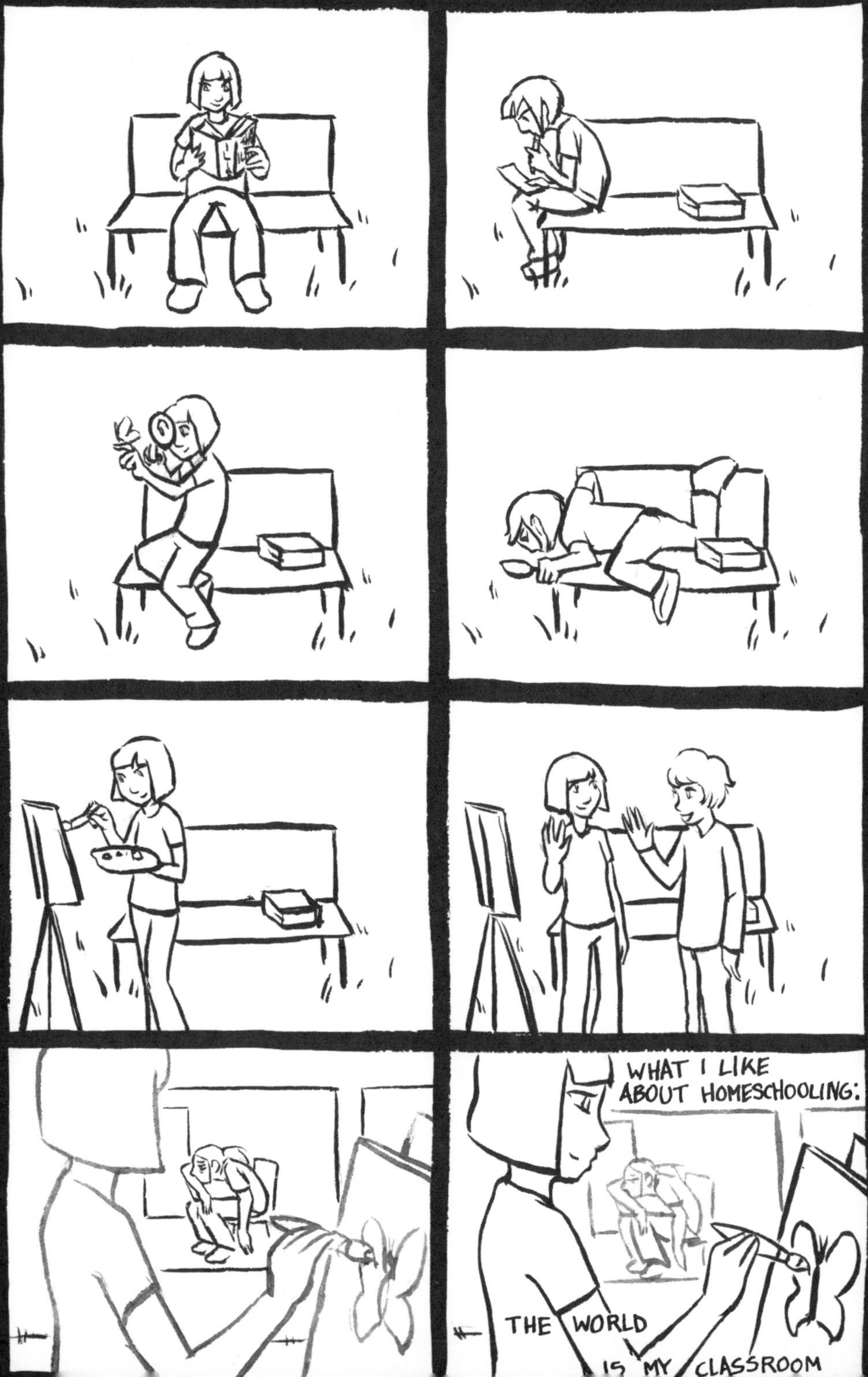
WHAT I LIKE ABOUT HOMESCHOOLING:
THE WORLD
IS MY CLASSROOM

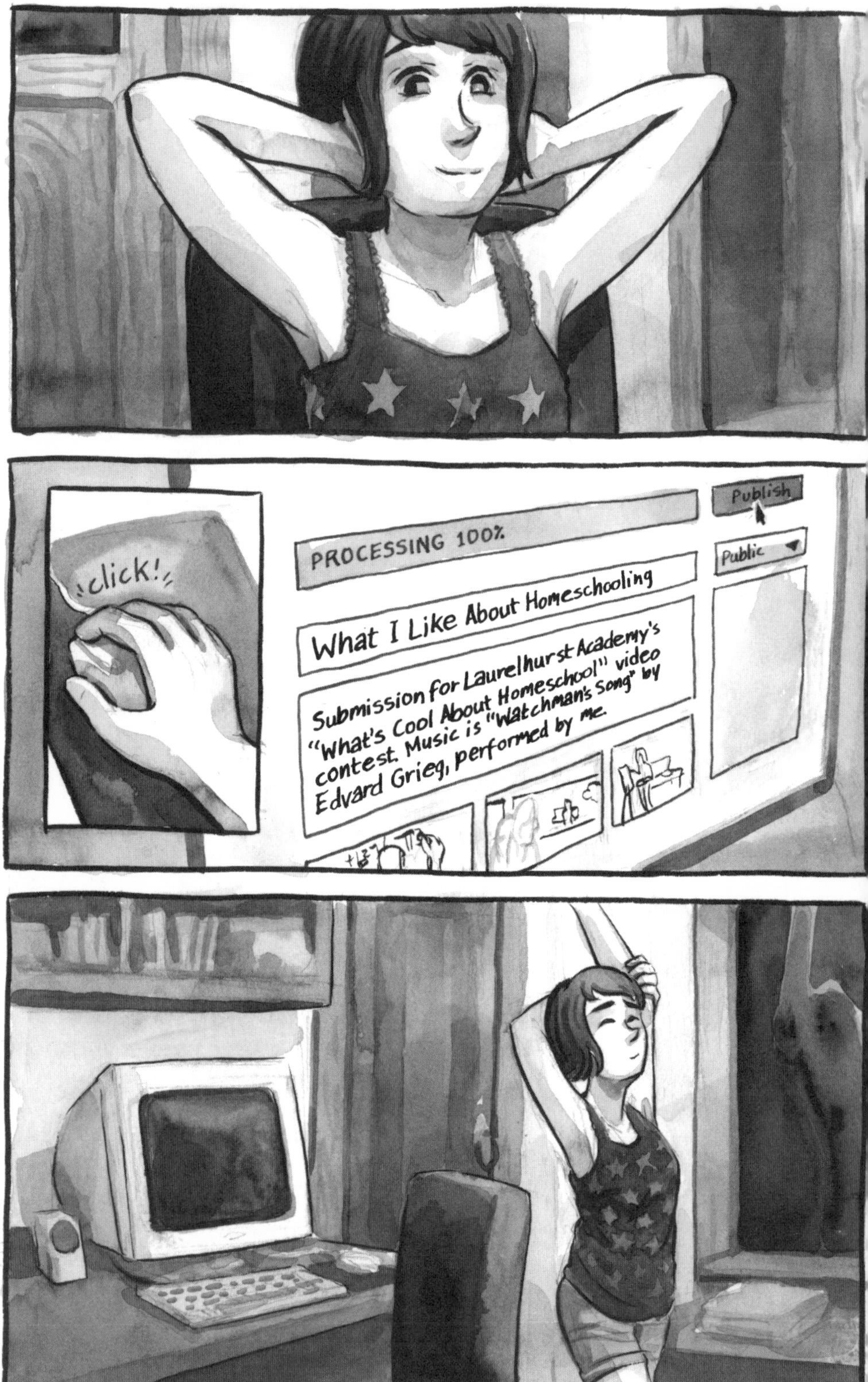
click!
Publish
PROCESSING 100%
Public
What I Like About Homeschooling
Submission for Laurelhurst Academy's "What's Cool About Homeschool" video contest. Music is "Watchman's Song" by Edvard Grieg, performed by me.

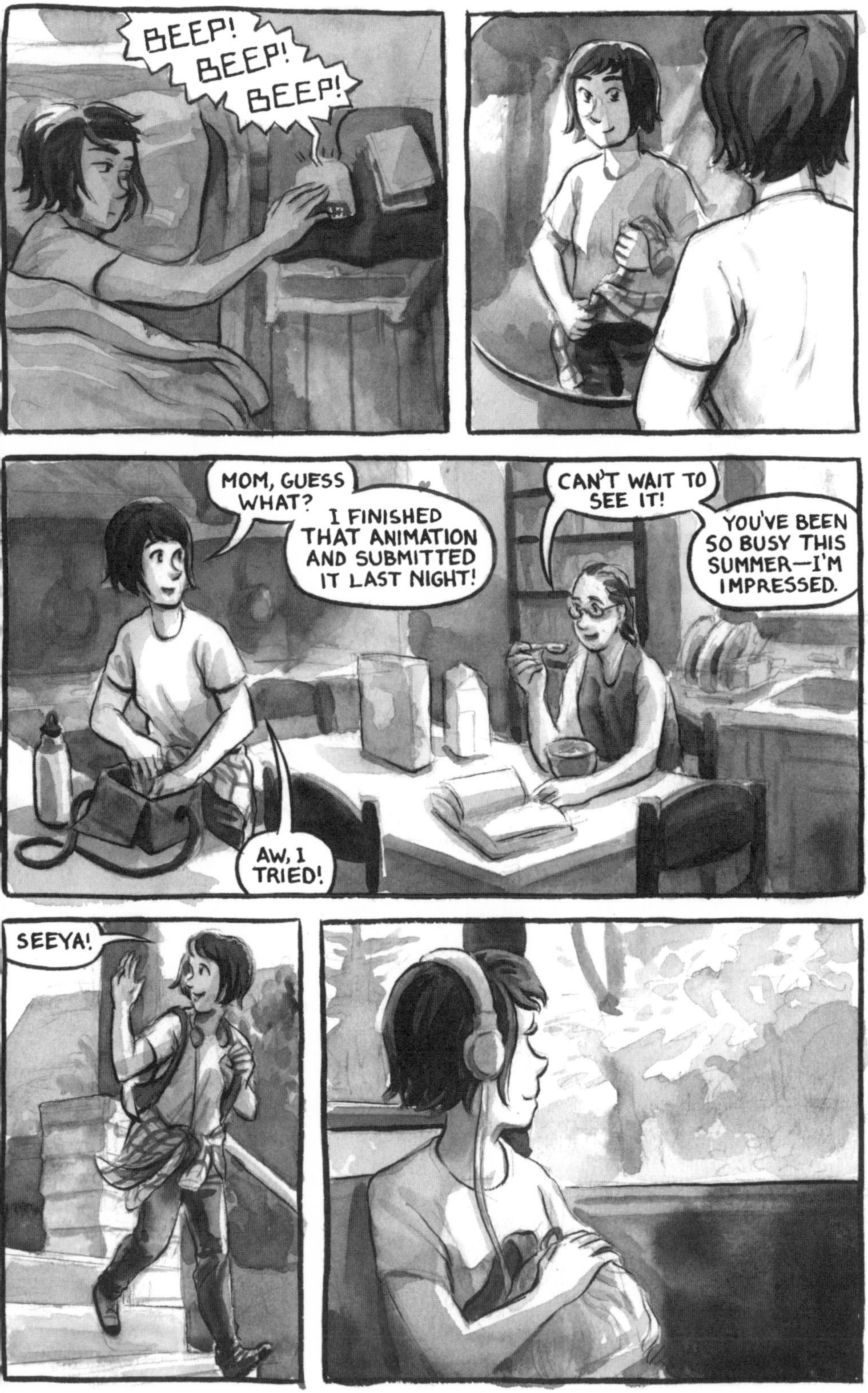
BEEP! BEEP! BEEP!
MOM, GUESS WHAT?
I FINISHED THAT ANIMATION AND SUBMITTED IT LAST NIGHT!
CAN'T WAIT TO SEE IT!
YOU'VE BEEN SO BUSY THIS SUMMER—I'M IMPRESSED.
AW, I TRIED!
SEEYA!

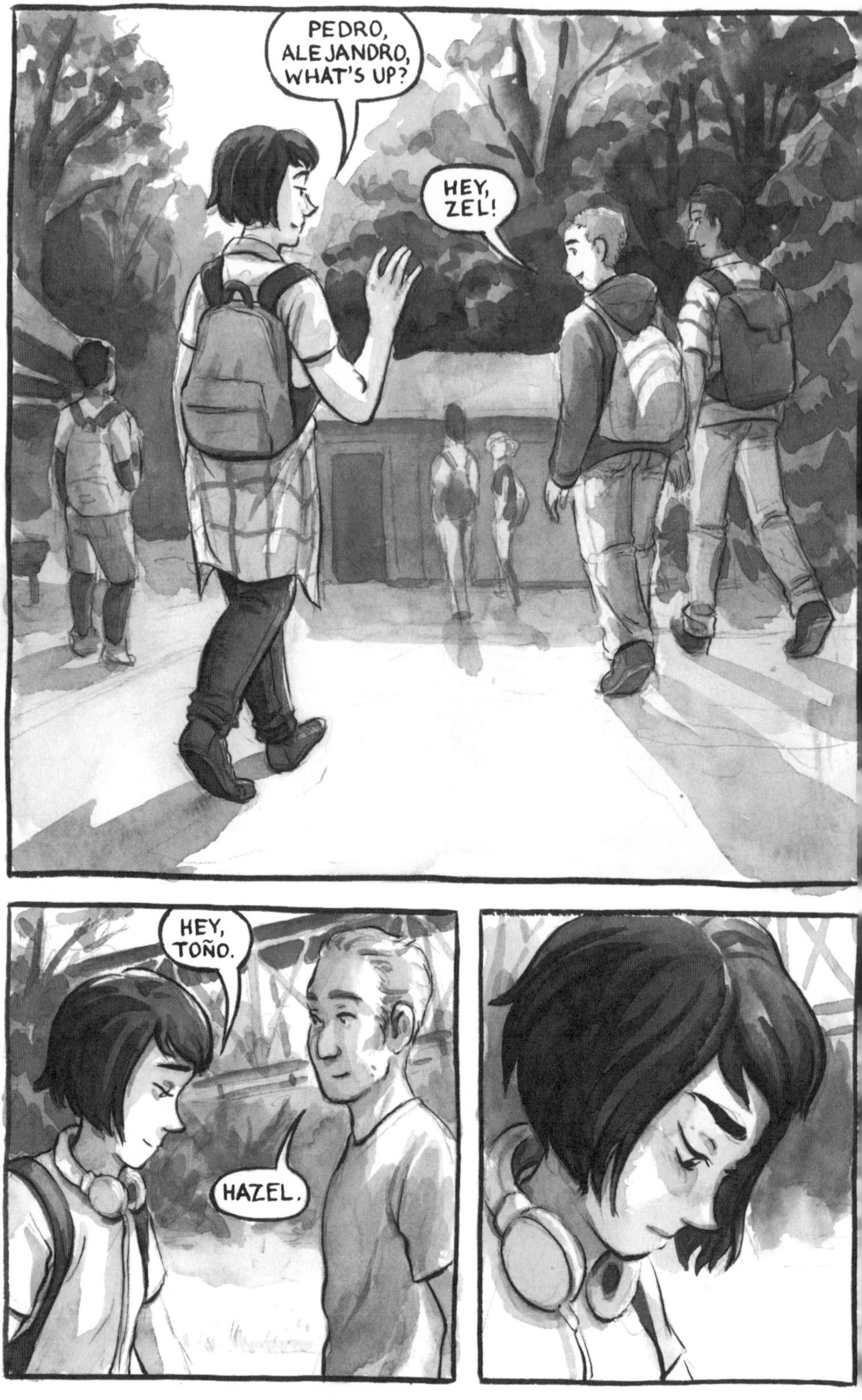
PEDRO, ALEJANDRO, WHAT'S UP?
HEY, ZEL!
HEY, TOÑO.
HAZEL.

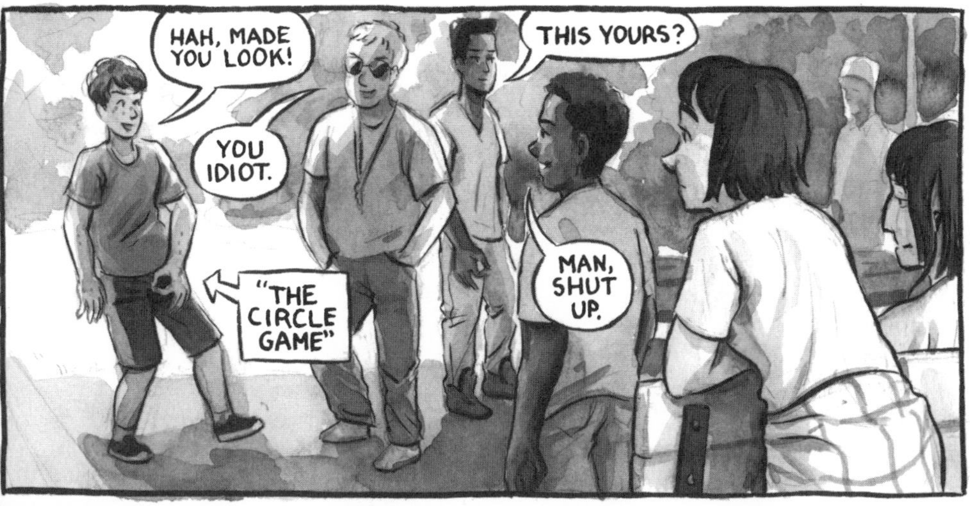
HAH, MADE YOU LOOK!
YOU IDIOT.
THIS YOURS?
MAN, SHUT UP.
"THE CIRCLE GAME"

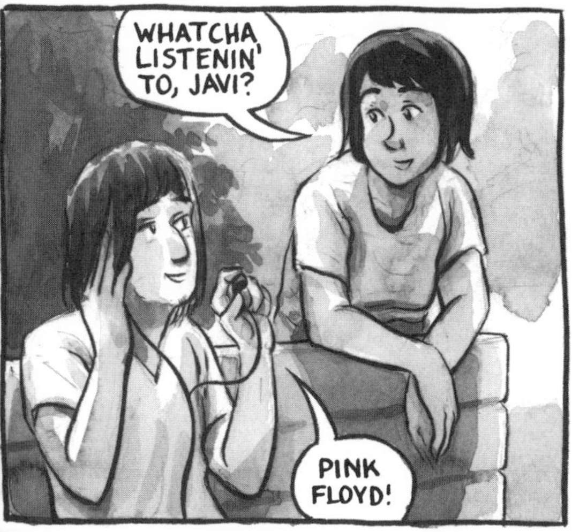
WHATCHA LISTENIN' TO, JAVI?
PINK FLOYD!

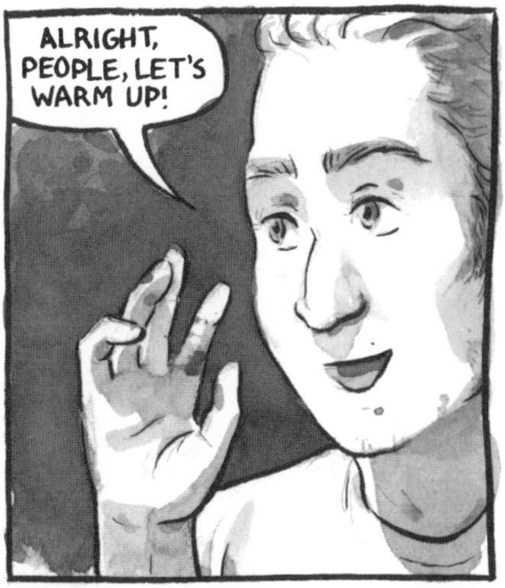
ALRIGHT, PEOPLE, LET'S WARM UP!

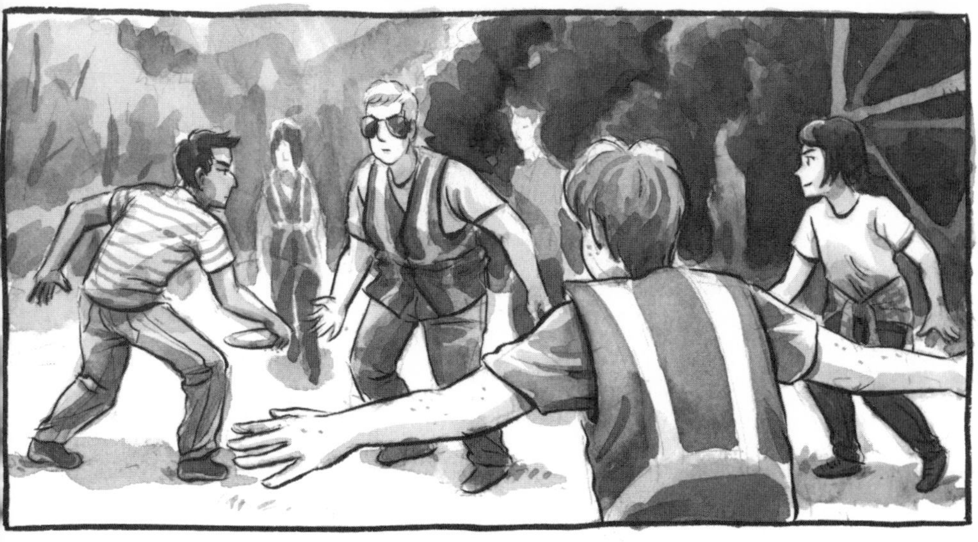

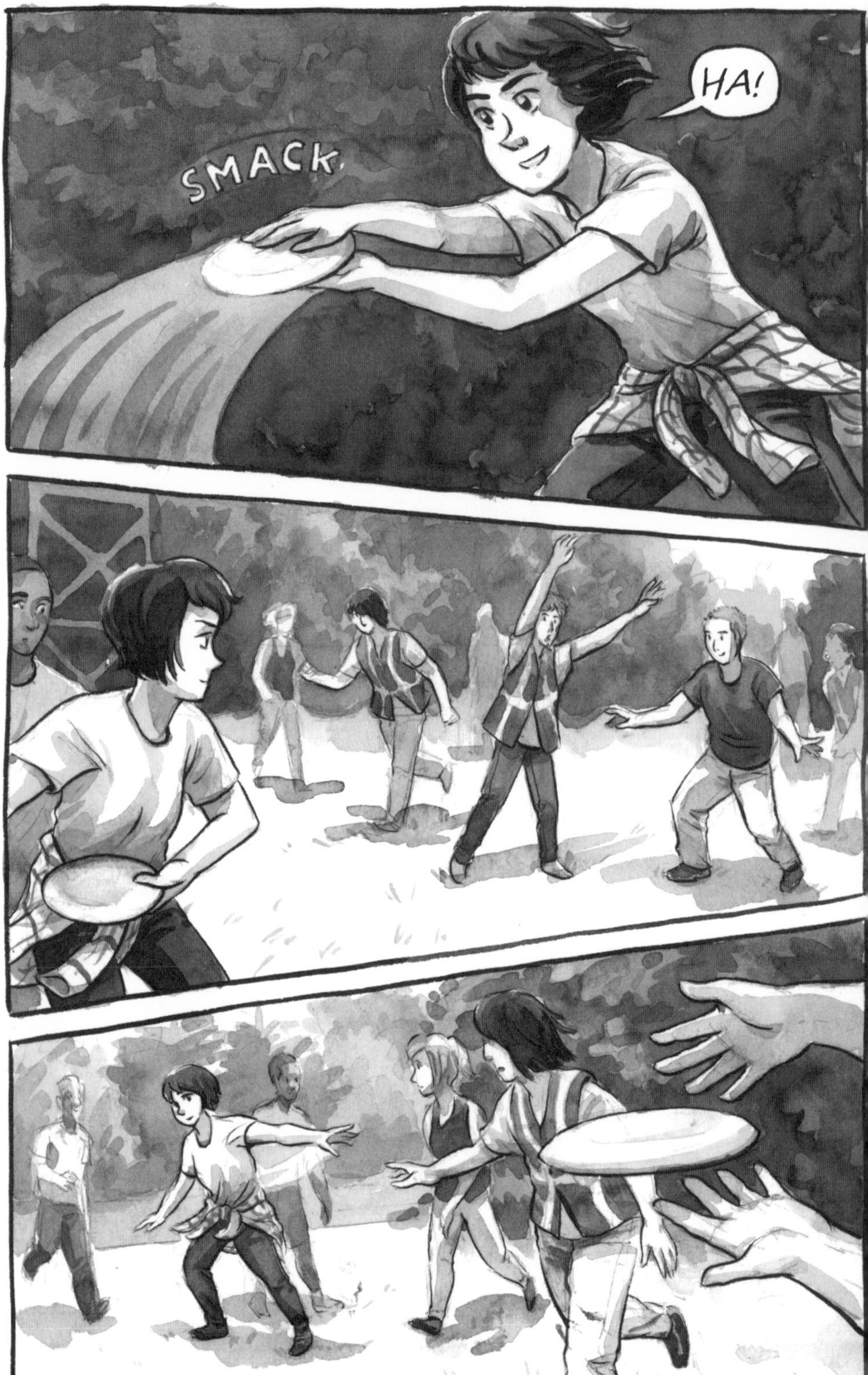
SMACK
HA!

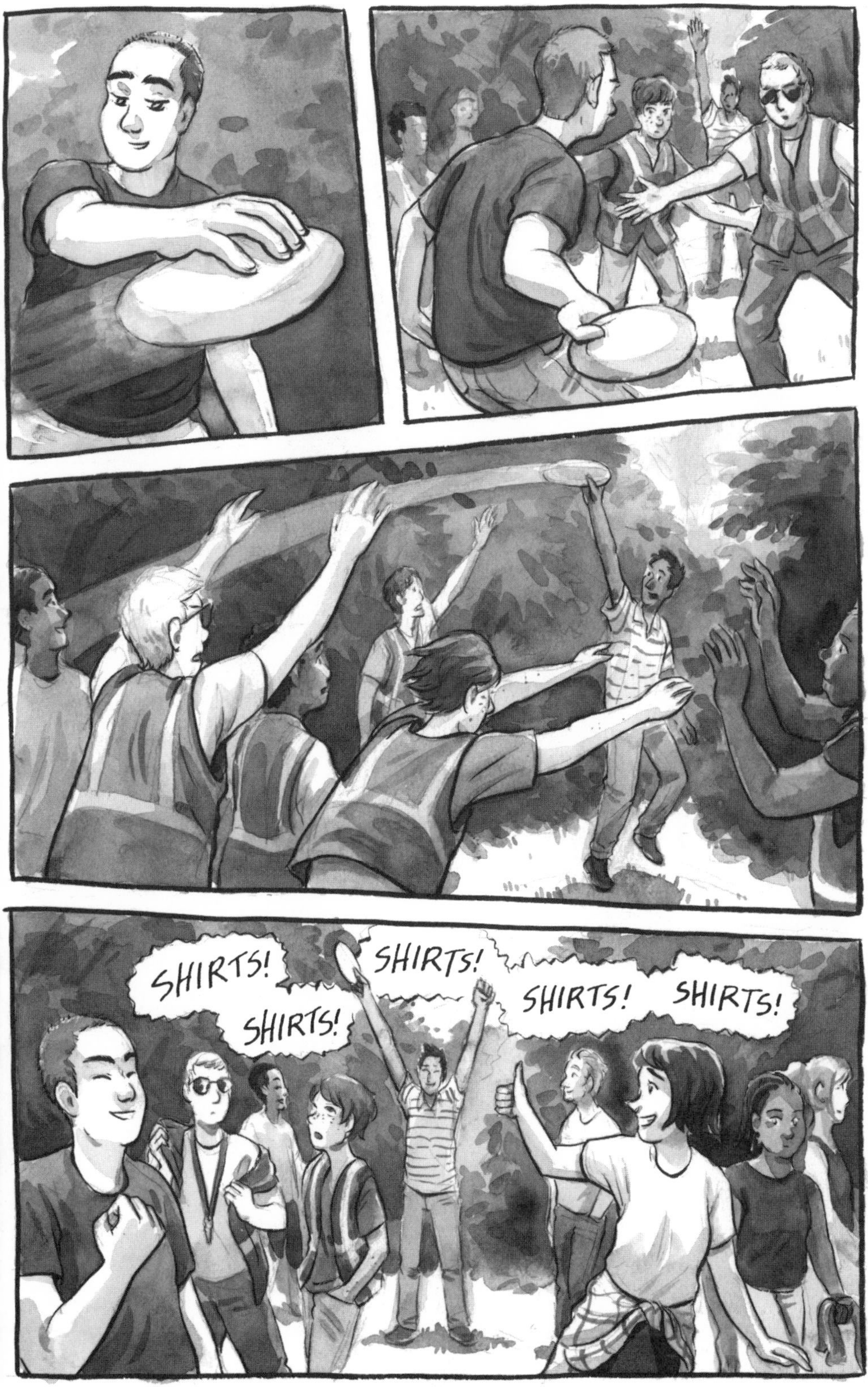
SHIRTS!
SHIRTS!
SHIRTS!
SHIRTS!
SHIRTS!

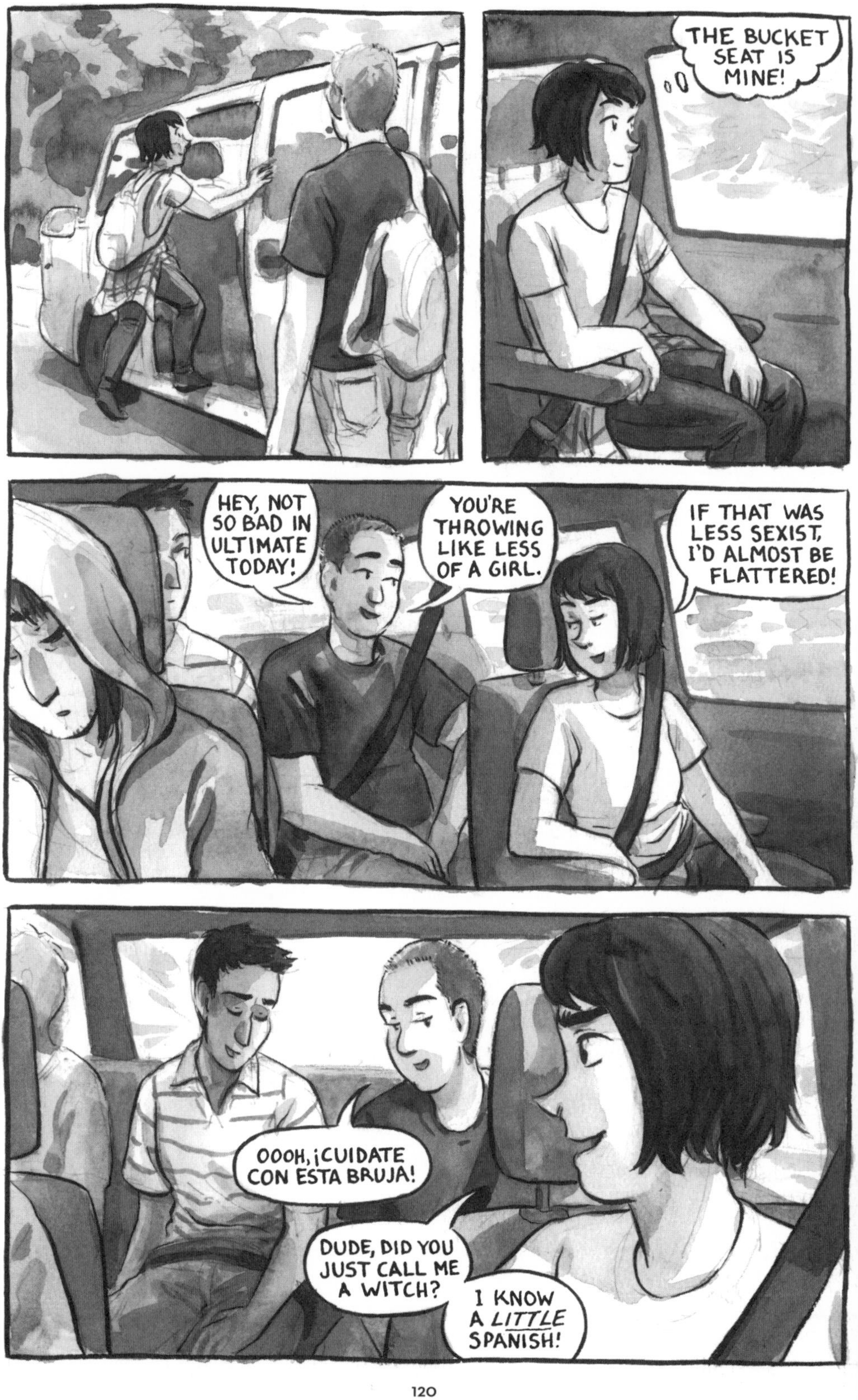
THE BUCKET SEAT IS MINE!
HEY, NOT SO BAD IN ULTIMATE TODAY!
YOU'RE THROWING LIKE LESS OF A GIRL.
IF THAT WAS LESS SEXIST, I'D ALMOST BE FLATTERED!
OOOH, ¡CUIDATE CON ESTA BRUJA!
DUDE, DID YOU JUST CALL ME A WITCH?
I KNOW A *LITTLE* SPANISH!

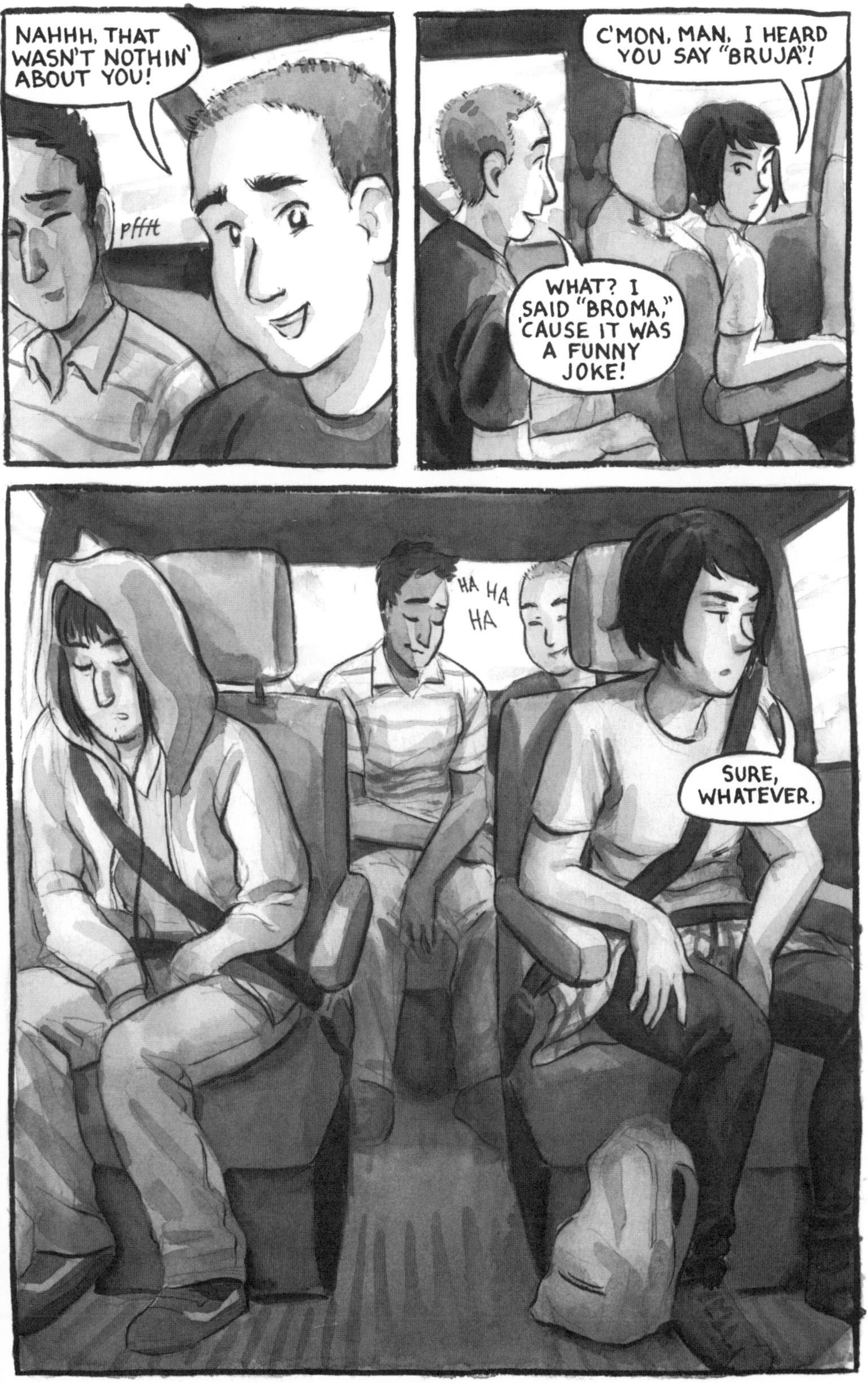
NAHHH, THAT WASN'T NOTHIN' ABOUT YOU!
pffft
C'MON, MAN, I HEARD YOU SAY "BRUJA"!
WHAT? I SAID "BROMA," 'CAUSE IT WAS A FUNNY JOKE!
HA HA HA
SURE, WHATEVER.

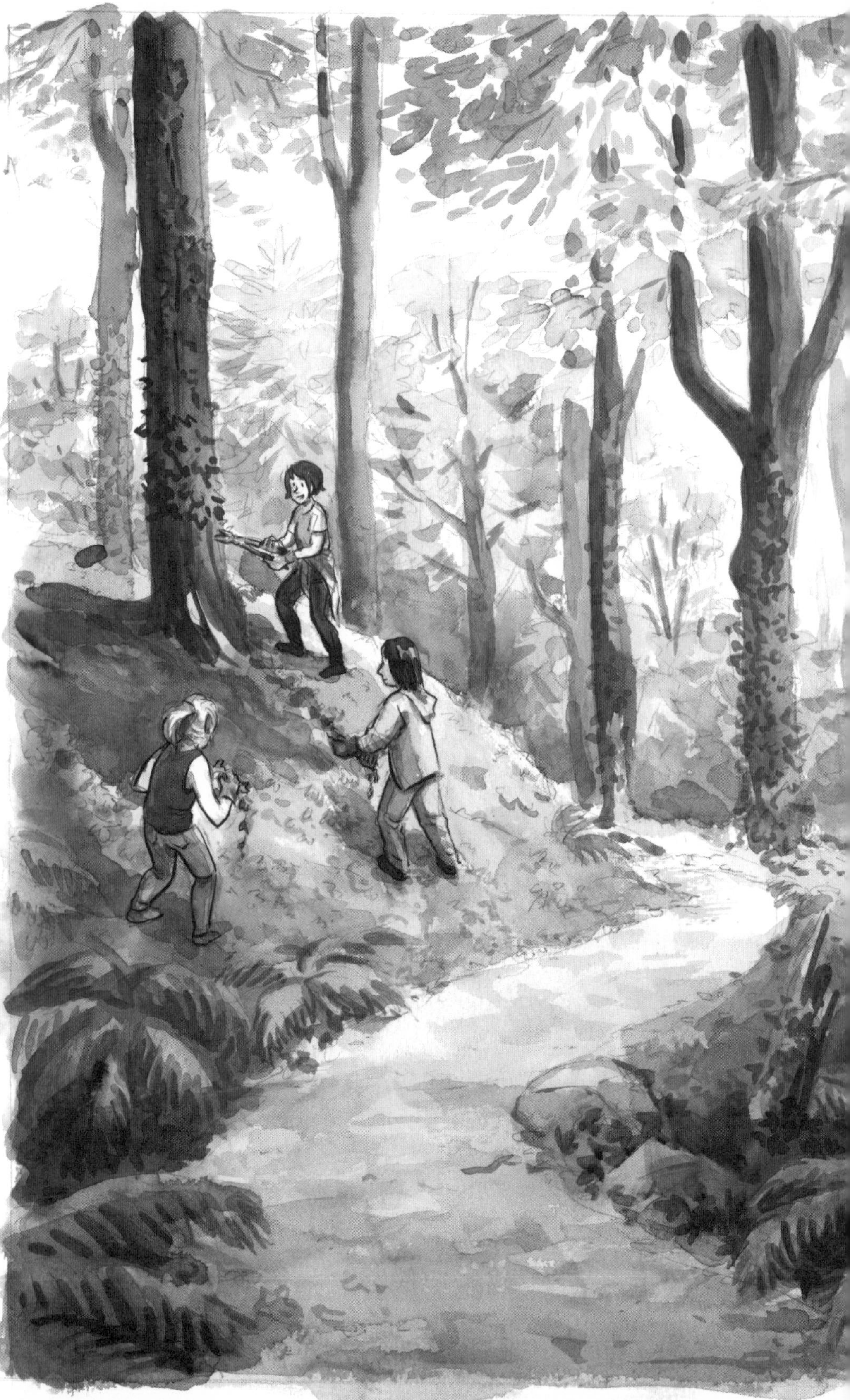

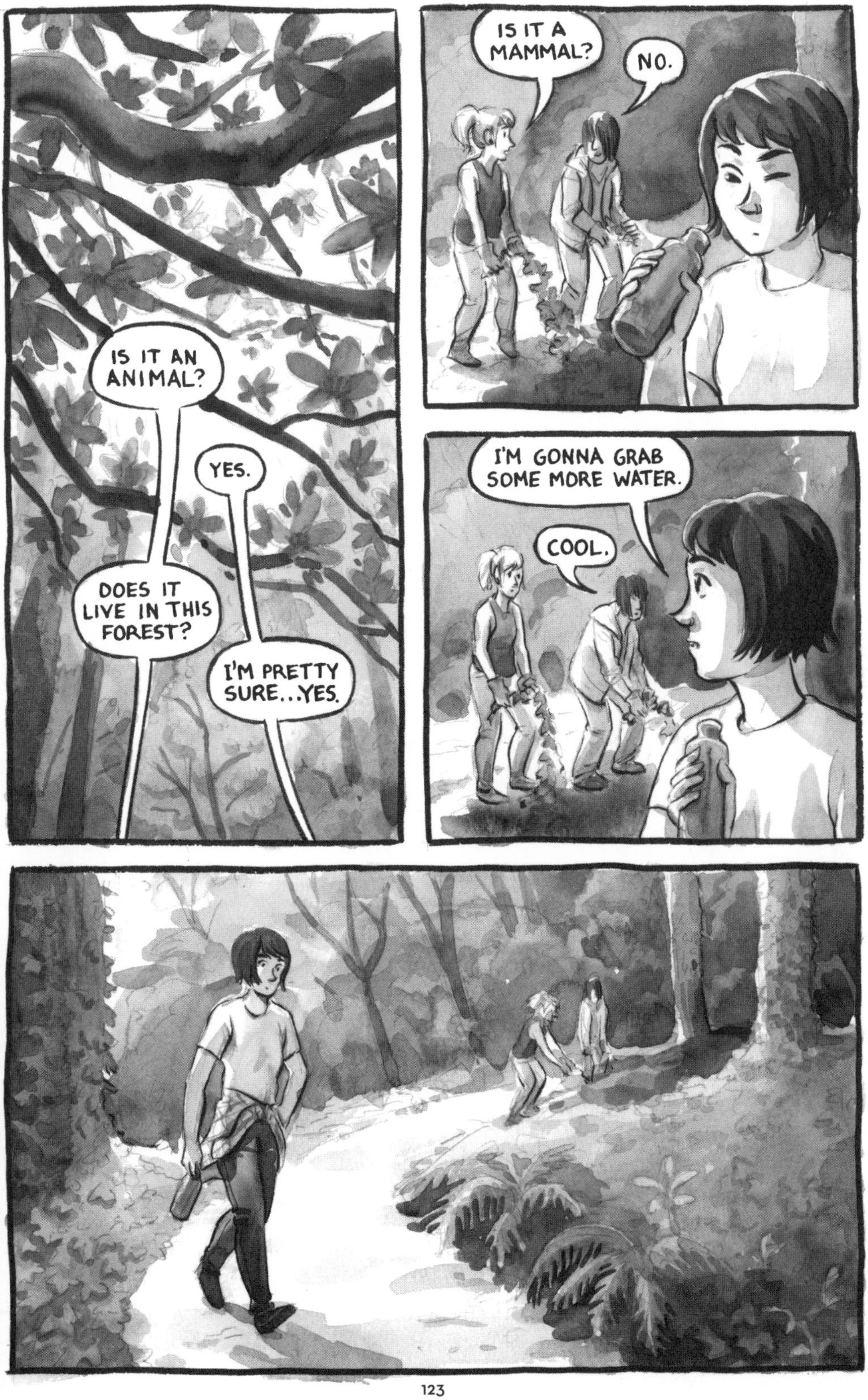
IS IT AN ANIMAL?
YES.
DOES IT LIVE IN THIS FOREST?
I'M PRETTY SURE...YES.
IS IT A MAMMAL?
NO.
I'M GONNA GRAB SOME MORE WATER.
COOL.

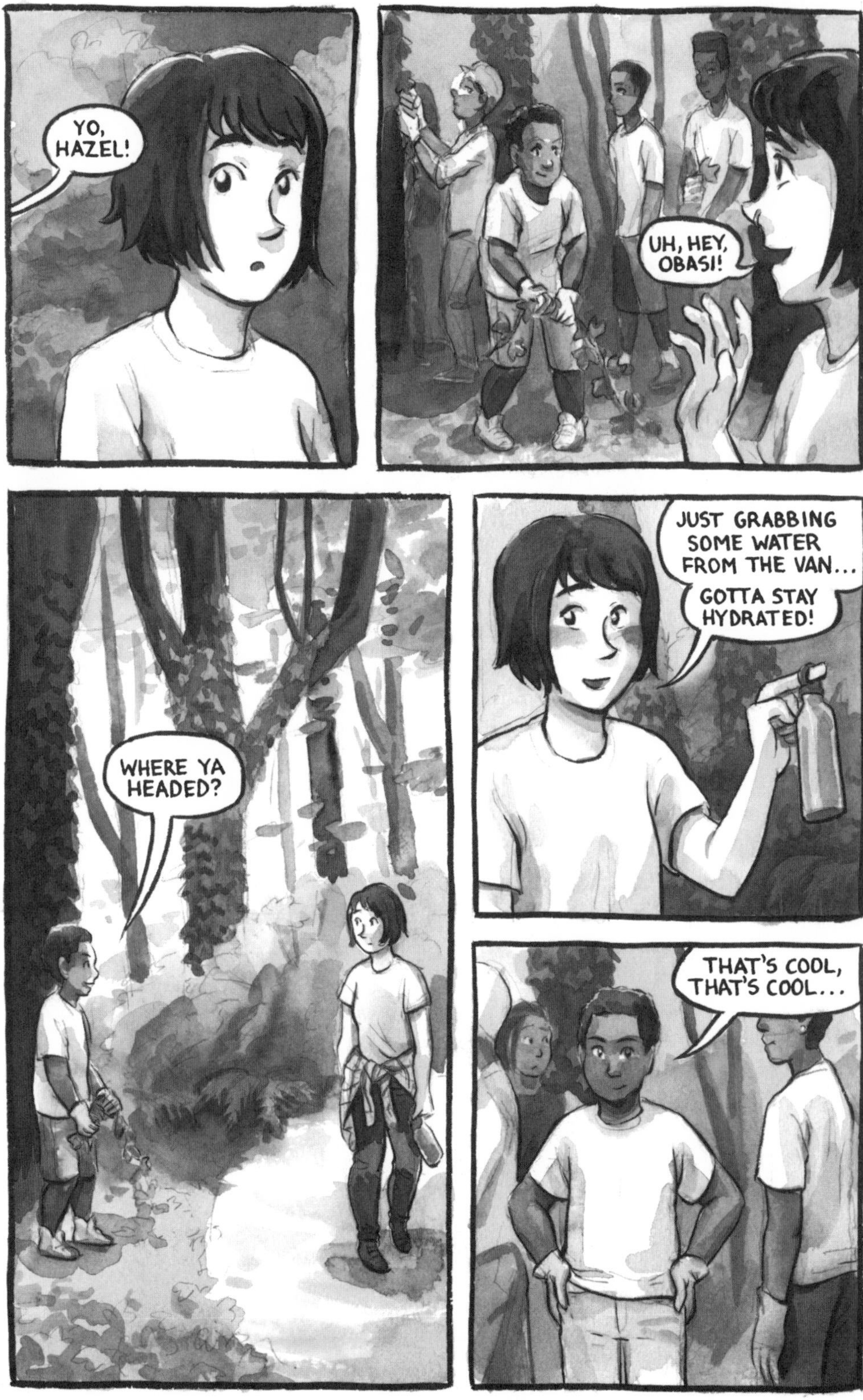
YO, HAZEL!
UH, HEY, OBASI!
WHERE YA HEADED?
JUST GRABBING SOME WATER FROM THE VAN...
GOTTA STAY HYDRATED!
THAT'S COOL, THAT'S COOL...

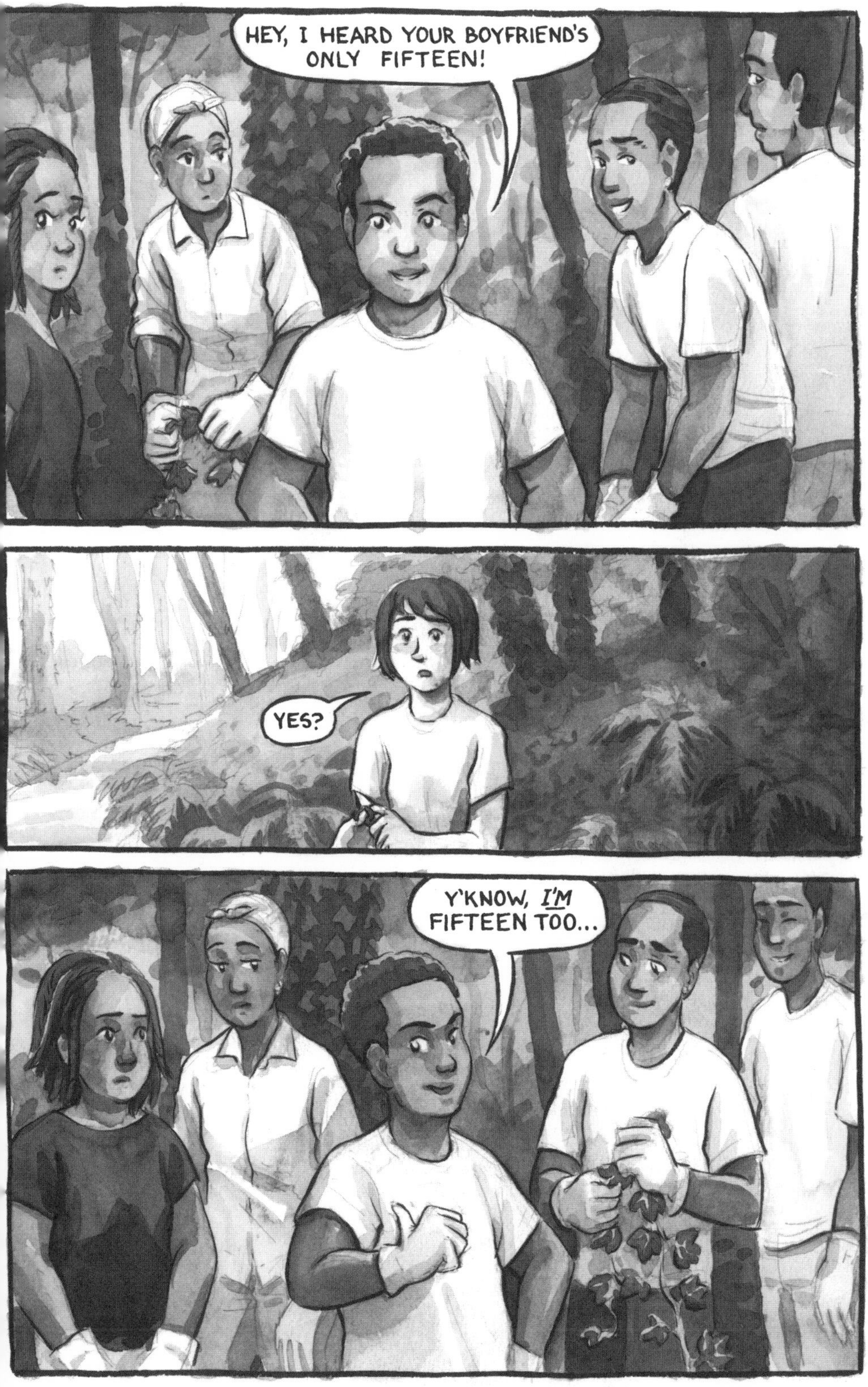
HEY, I HEARD YOUR BOYFRIEND'S ONLY FIFTEEN!
YES?
Y'KNOW, I'M FIFTEEN TOO...

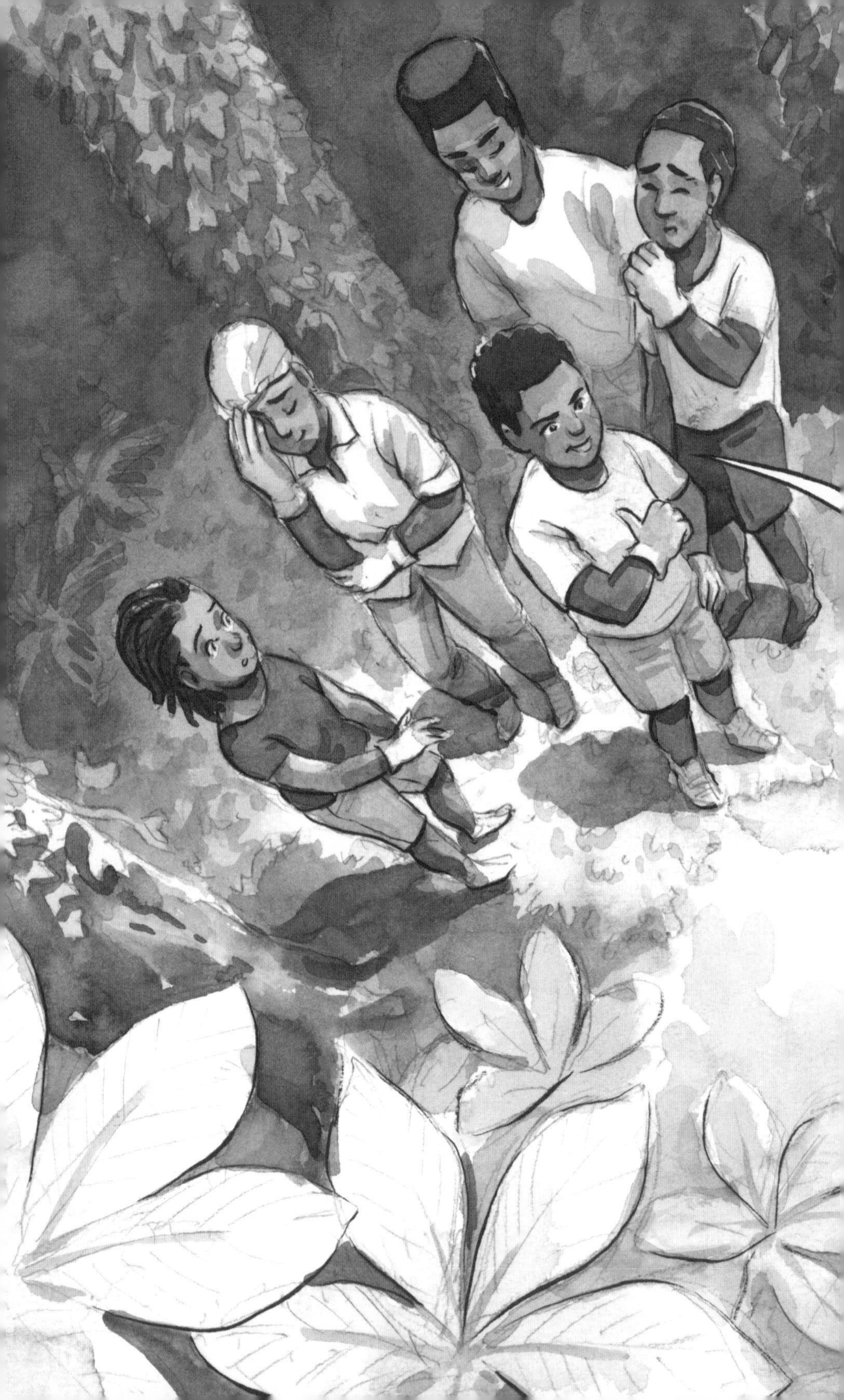

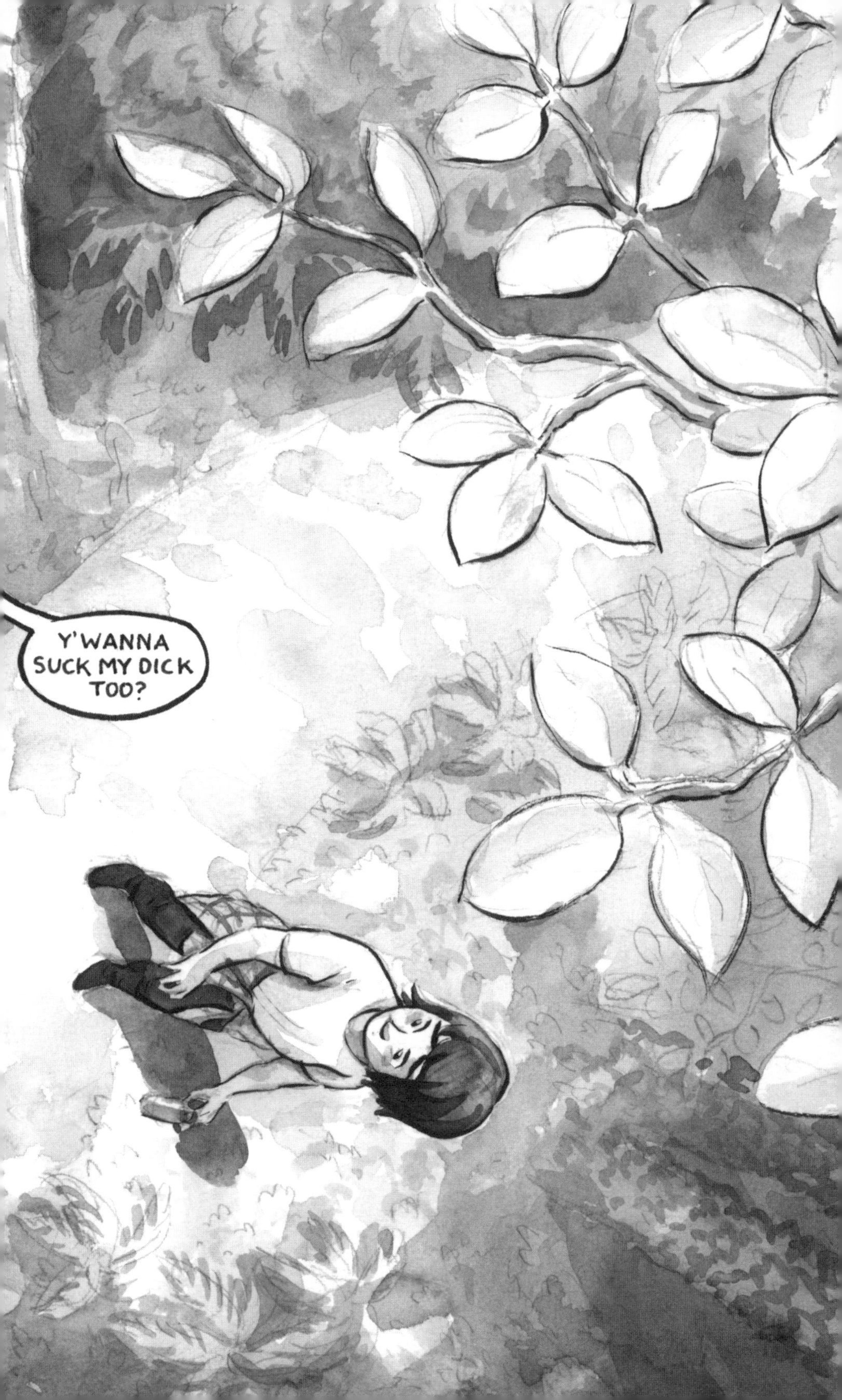
Y'WANNA SUCK MY DICK TOO?

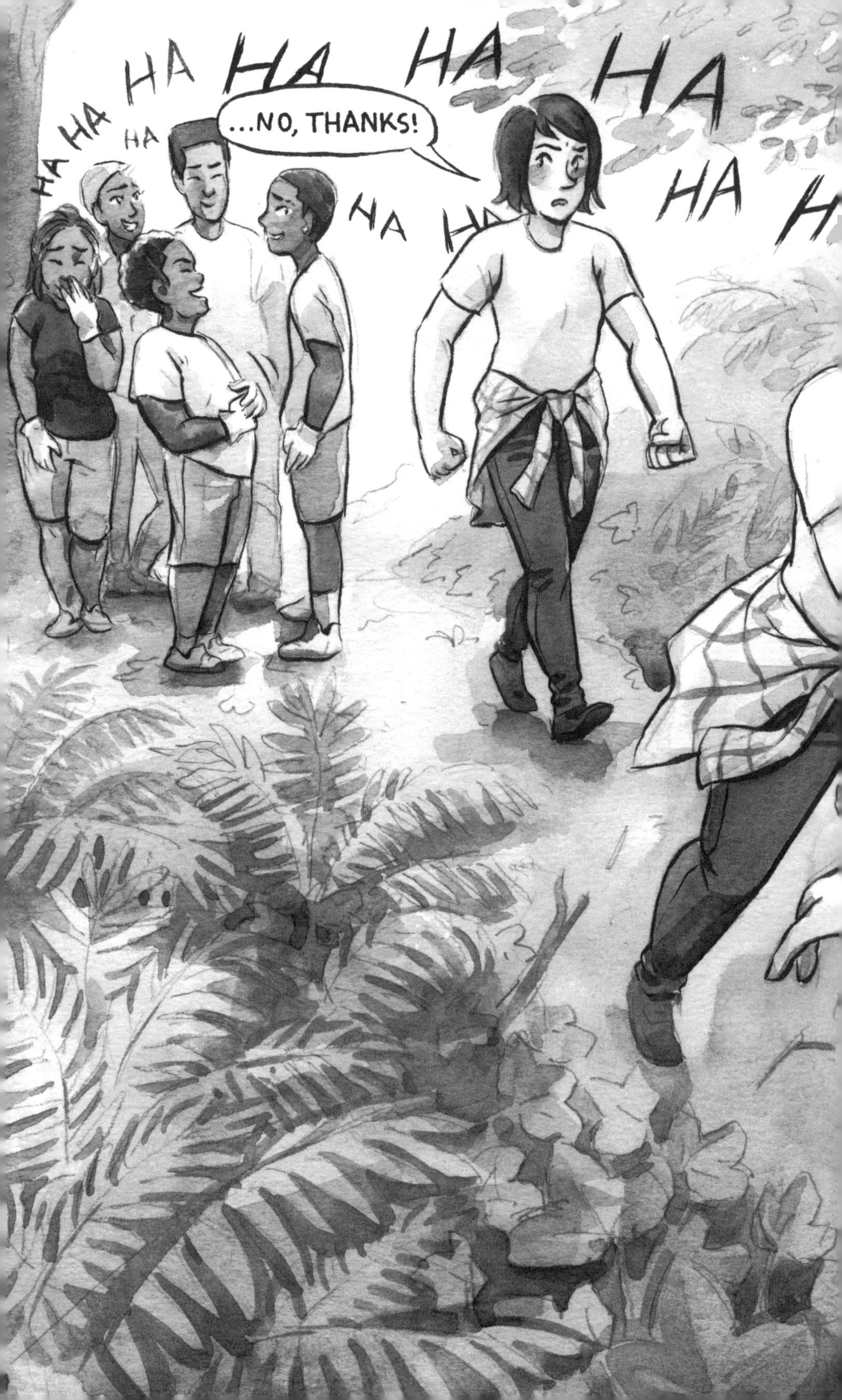
HA HA HA HA HA HA HA HA
...NO, THANKS!
HA HA HA HA HA

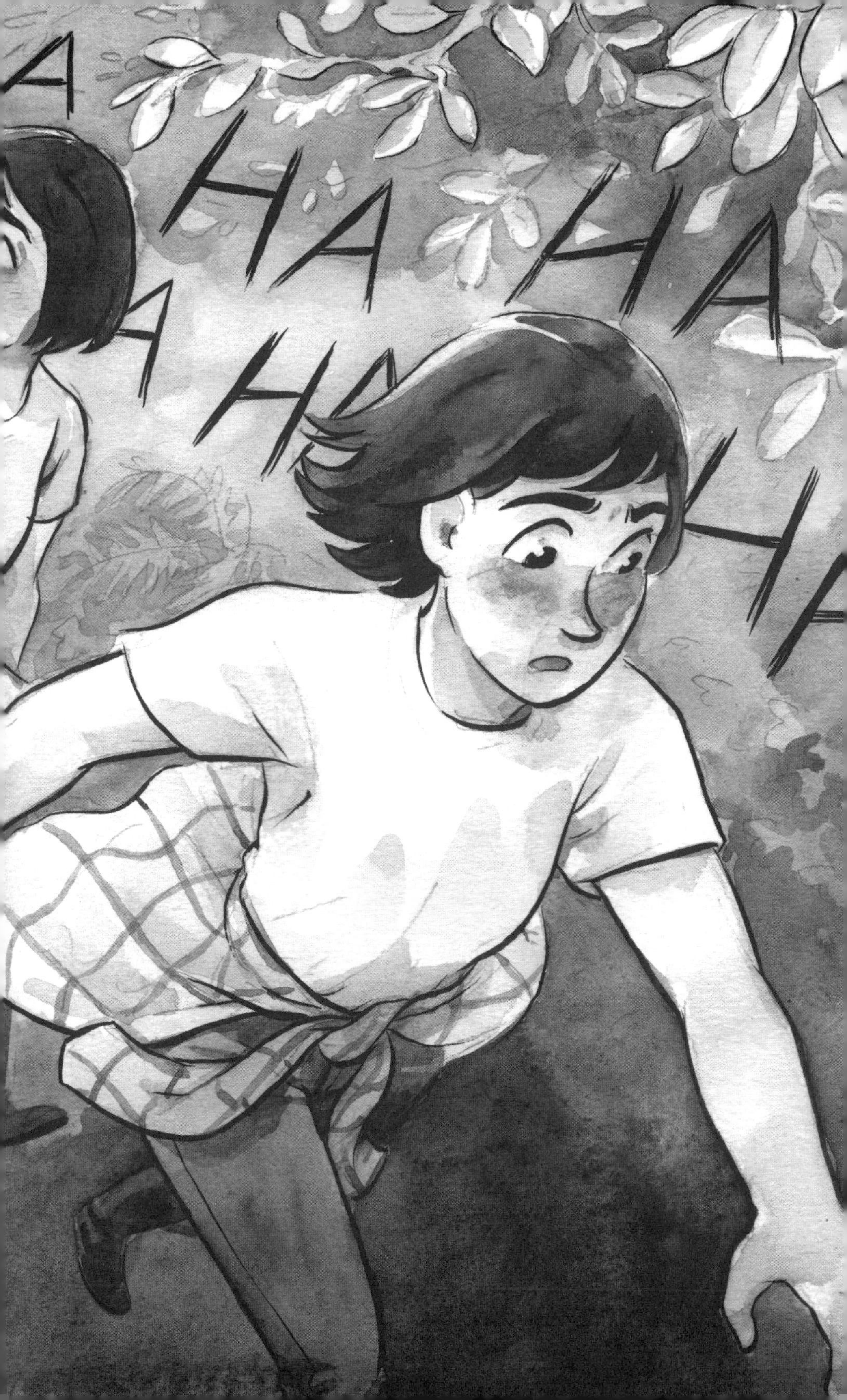
A
HA HA
A HA
HA

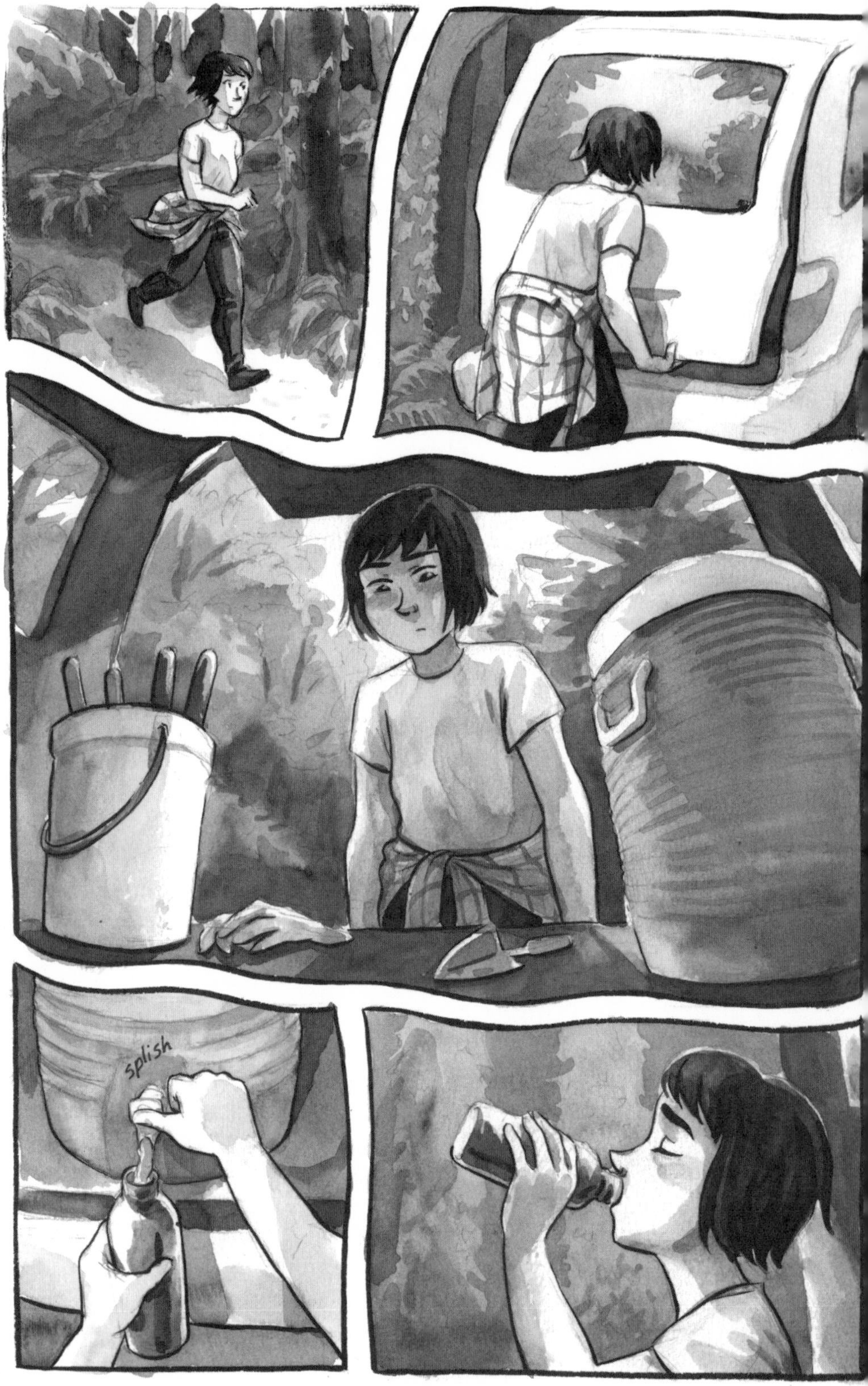
splish

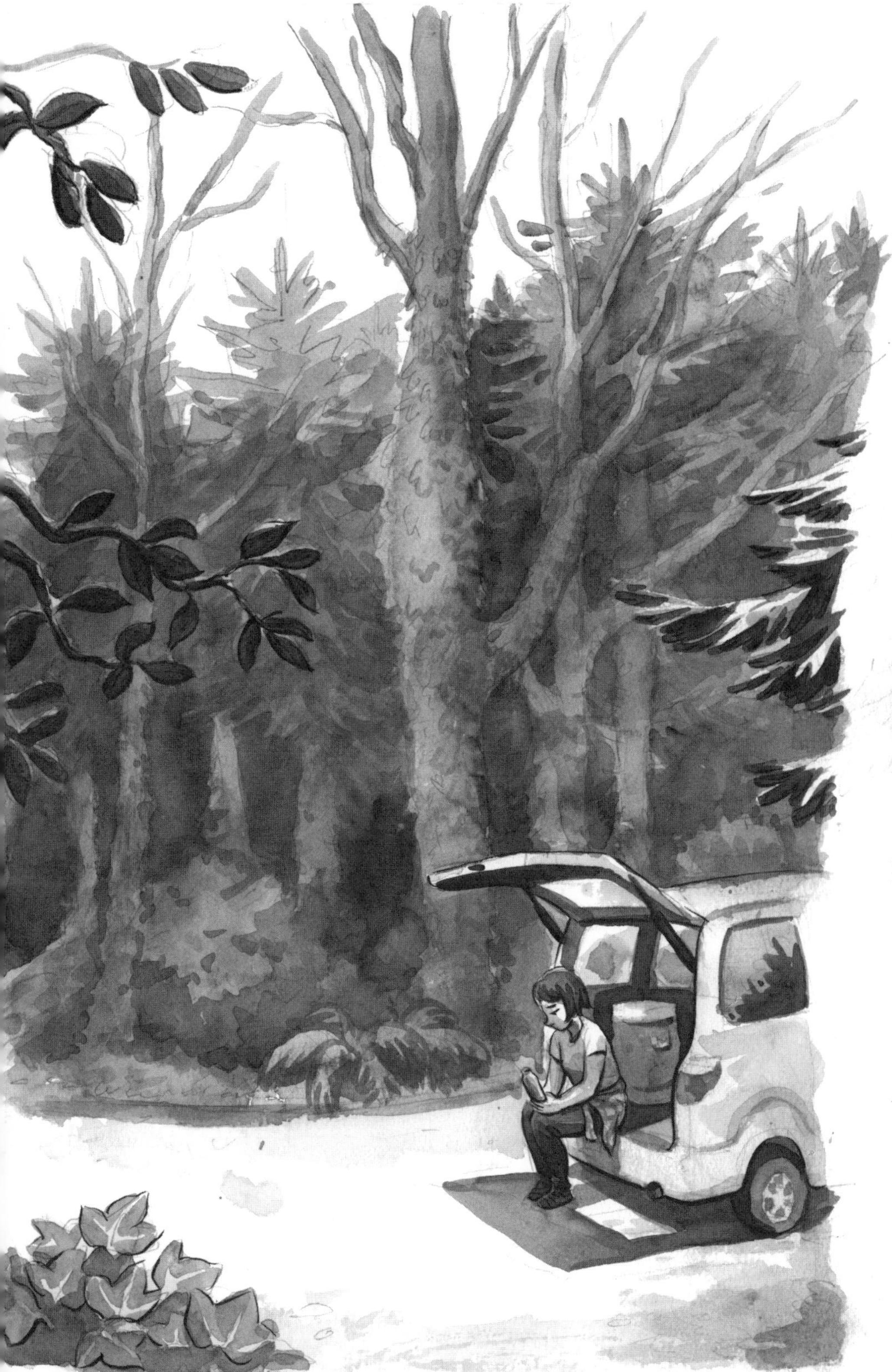

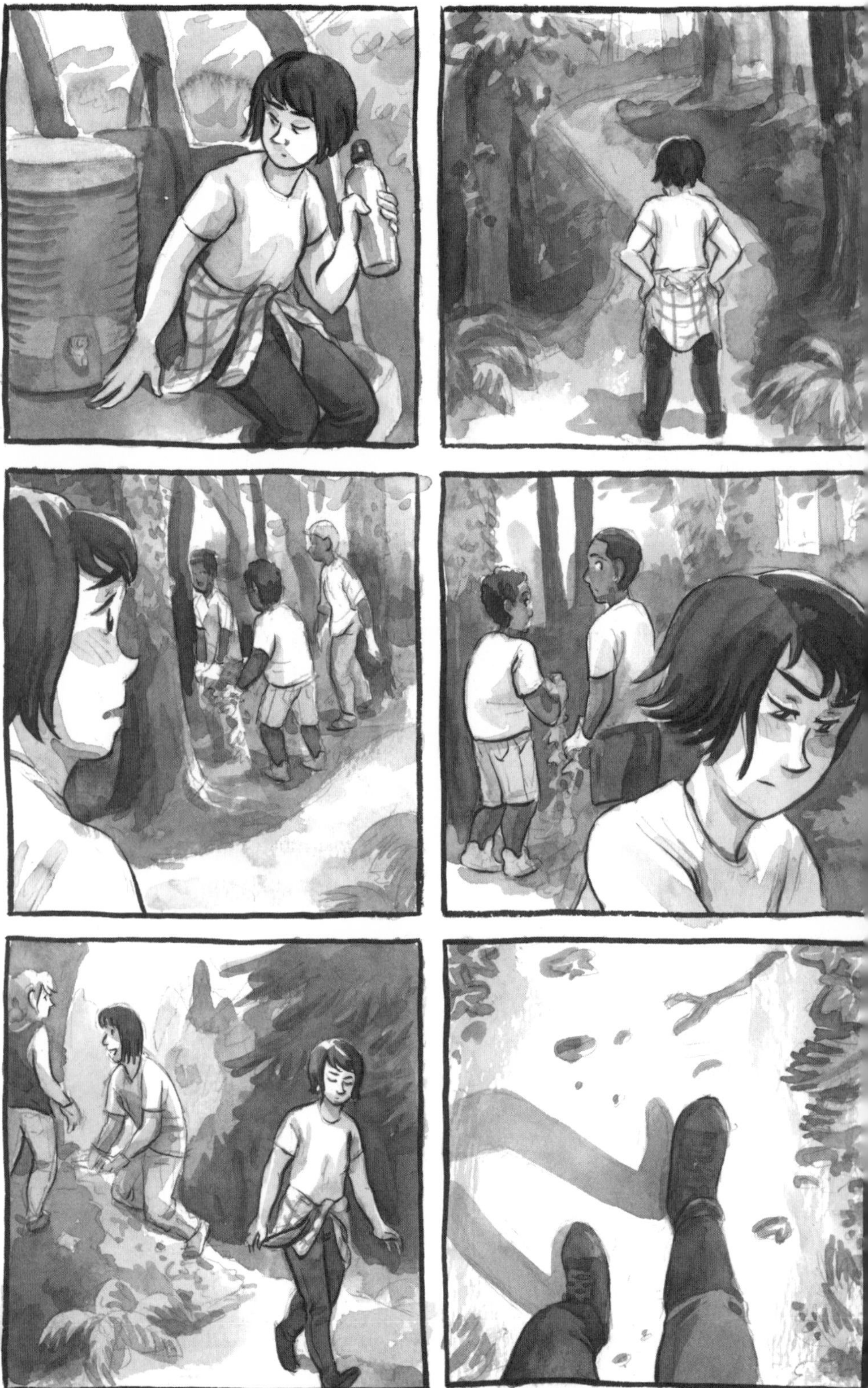

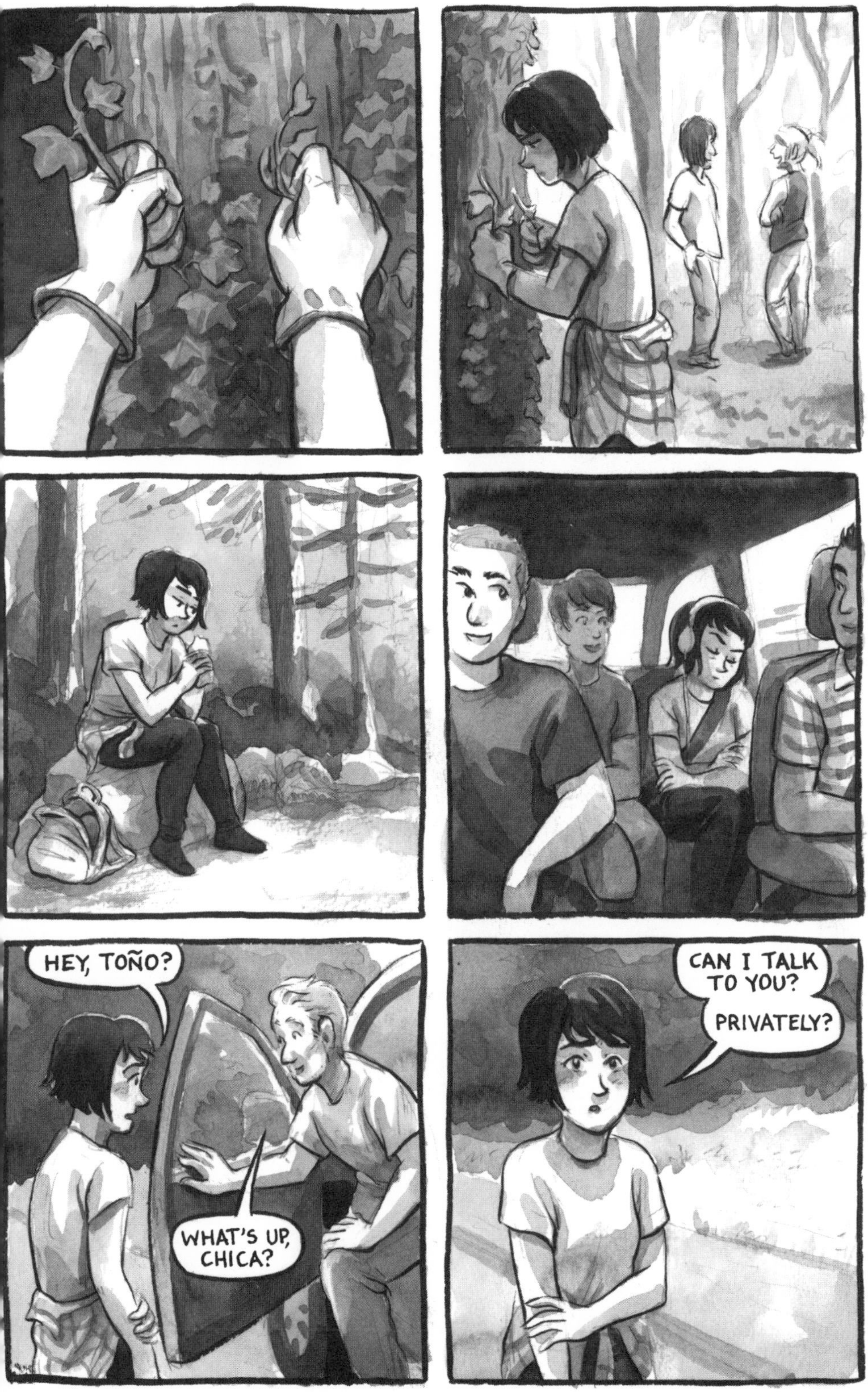
HEY, TOÑO?
WHAT'S UP, CHICA?
CAN I TALK TO YOU?
PRIVATELY?

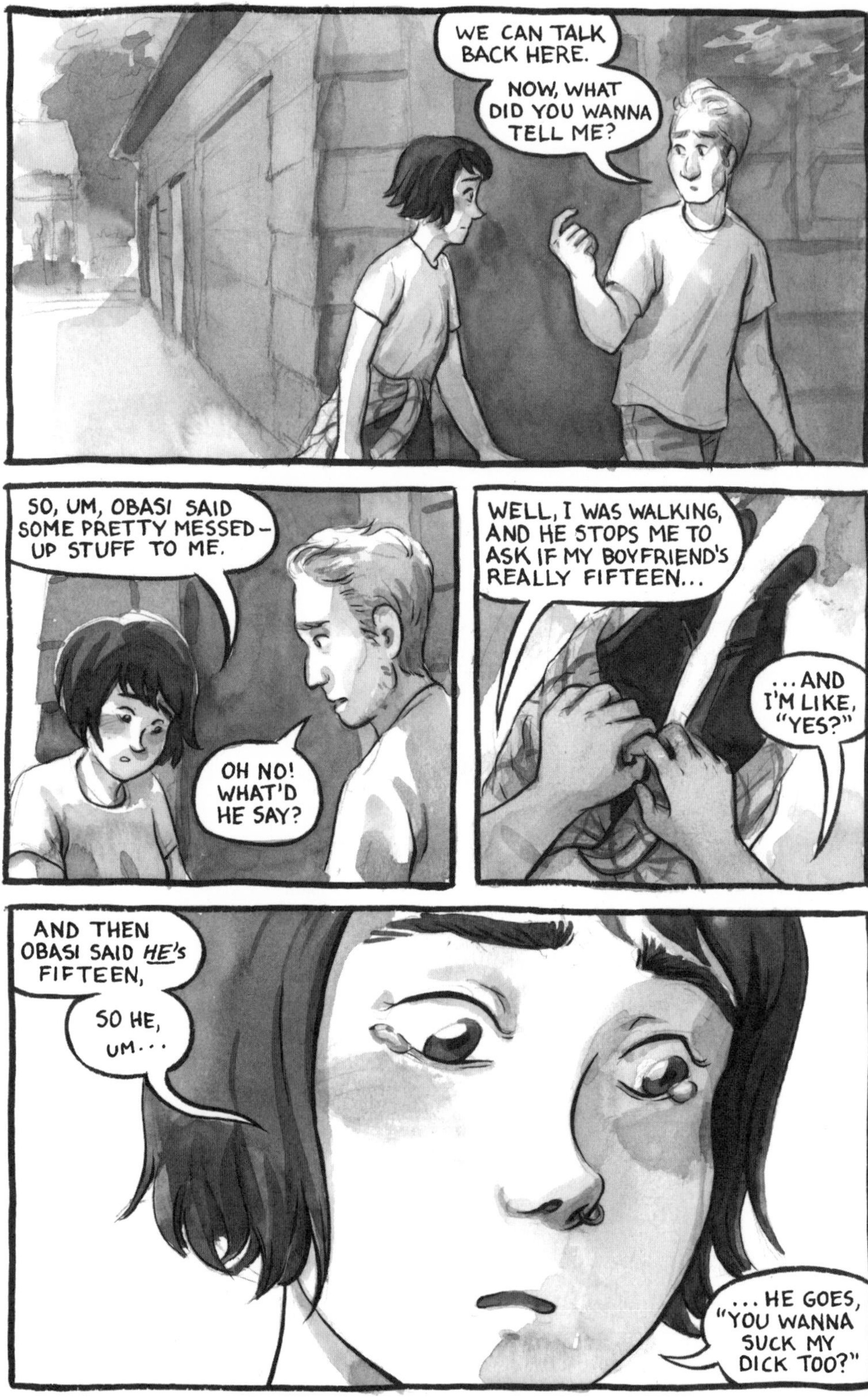

WE CAN TALK BACK HERE.
NOW, WHAT DID YOU WANNA TELL ME?
SO, UM, OBASI SAID SOME PRETTY MESSED-UP STUFF TO ME.
OH NO! WHAT'D HE SAY?
WELL, I WAS WALKING, AND HE STOPS ME TO ASK IF MY BOYFRIEND'S REALLY FIFTEEN...
...AND I'M LIKE, "YES?"
AND THEN OBASI SAID *HE*'s FIFTEEN,
SO HE, UM...
...HE GOES, "YOU WANNA SUCK MY DICK TOO?"

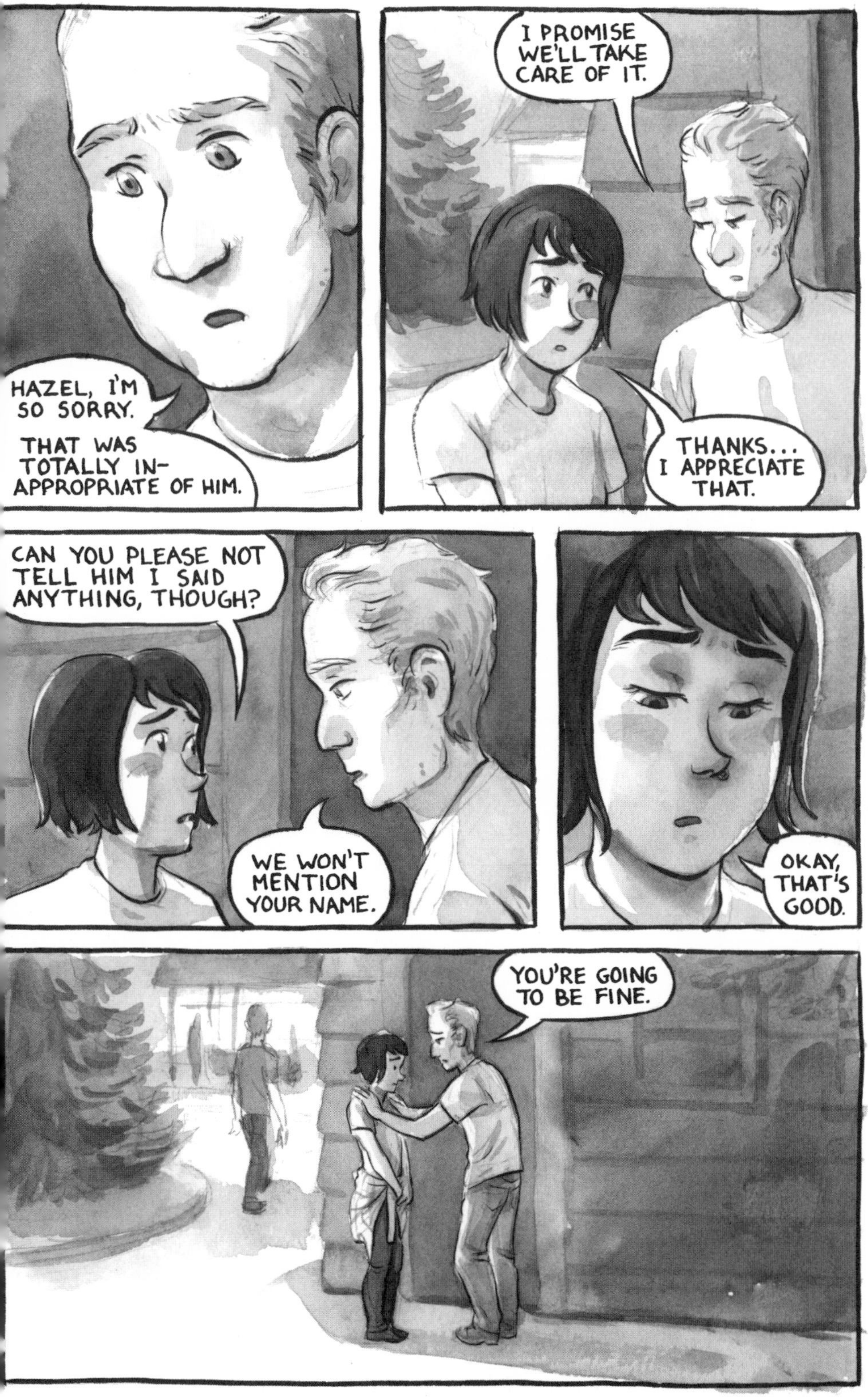
HAZEL, I'M SO SORRY.
THAT WAS TOTALLY IN-APPROPRIATE OF HIM.
I PROMISE WE'LL TAKE CARE OF IT.
THANKS... I APPRECIATE THAT.
CAN YOU PLEASE NOT TELL HIM I SAID ANYTHING, THOUGH?
WE WON'T MENTION YOUR NAME.
OKAY, THAT'S GOOD.
YOU'RE GOING TO BE FINE.

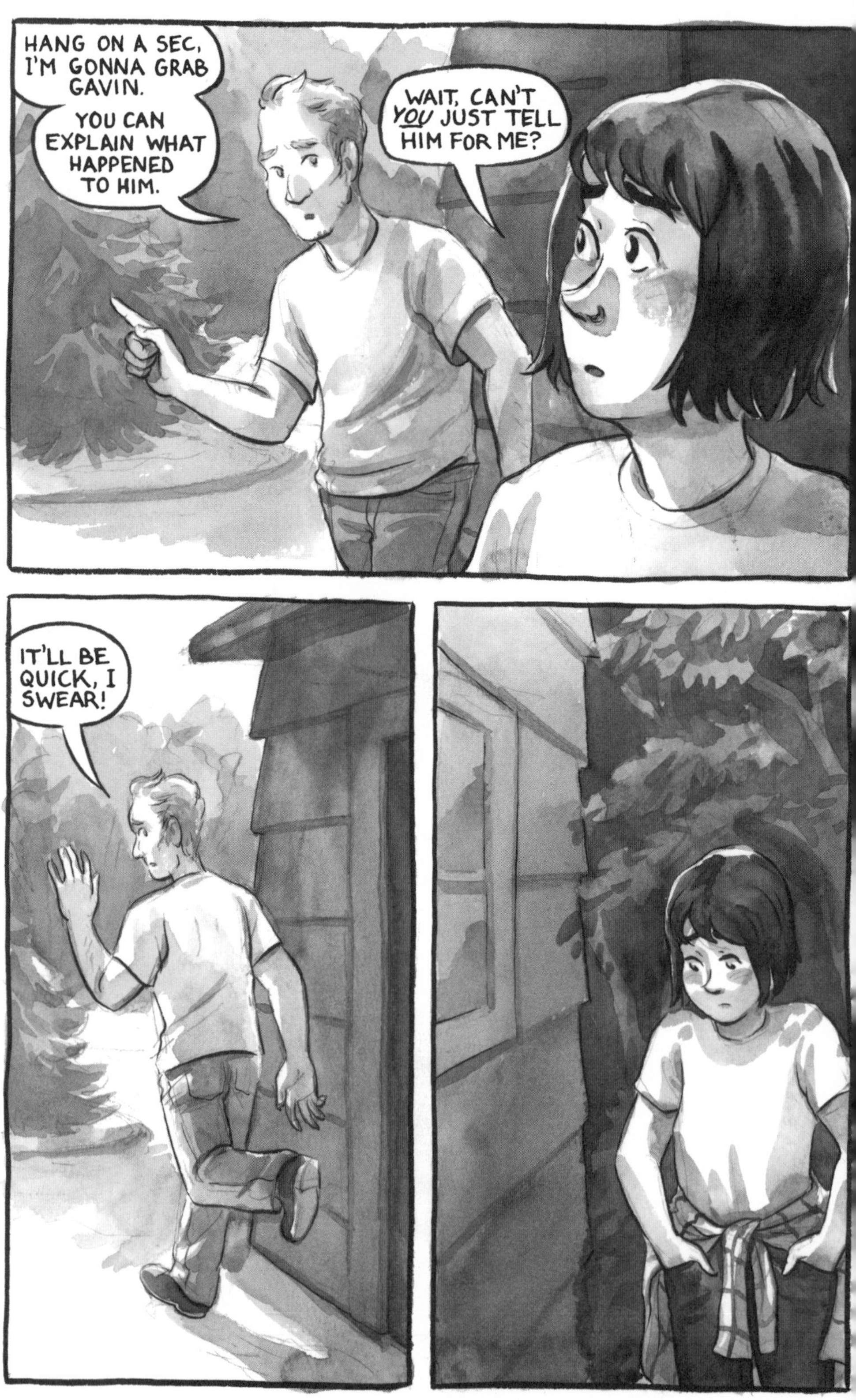
HANG ON A SEC, I'M GONNA GRAB GAVIN.
YOU CAN EXPLAIN WHAT HAPPENED TO HIM.
WAIT, CAN'T YOU JUST TELL HIM FOR ME?
IT'LL BE QUICK, I SWEAR!

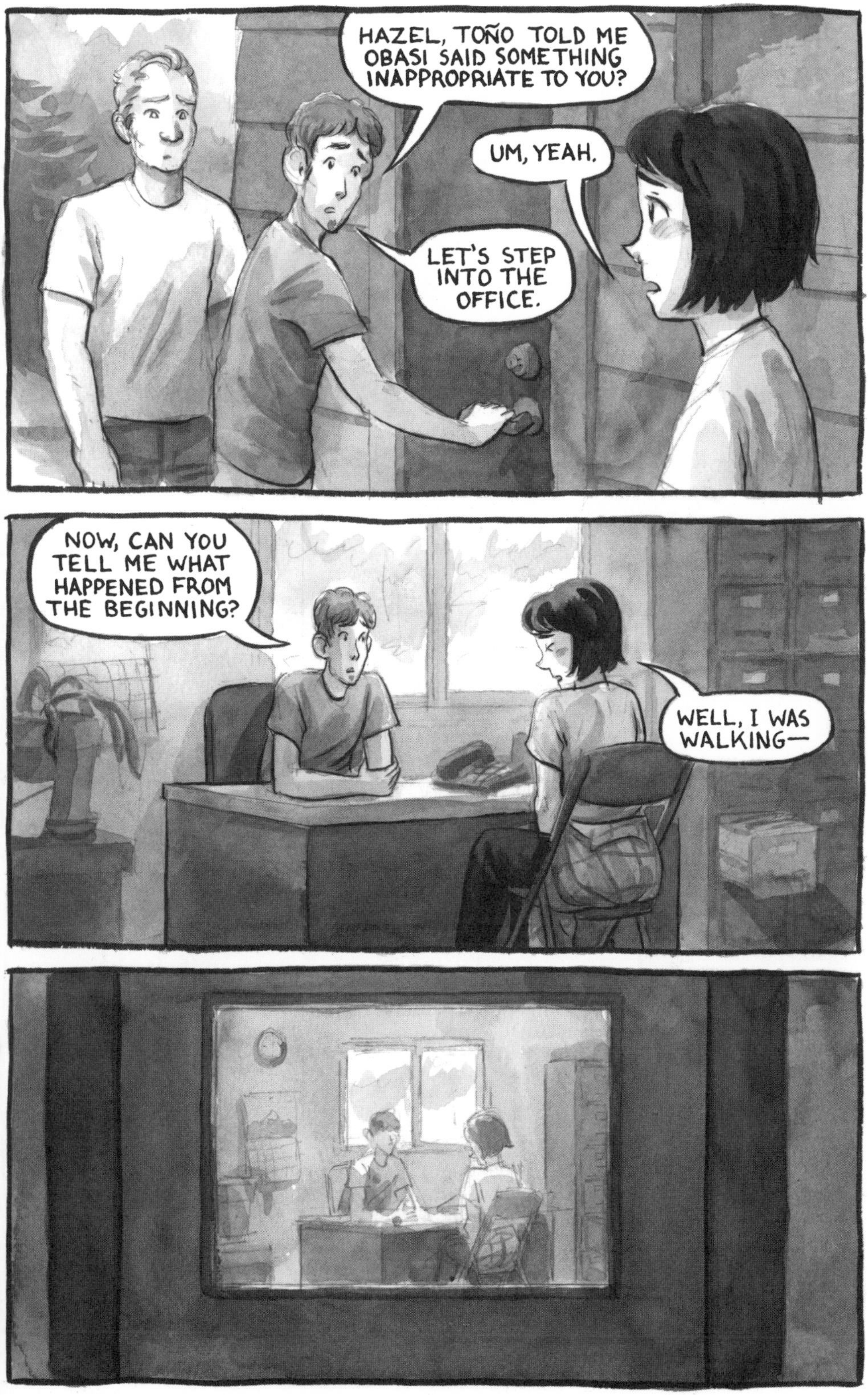
HAZEL, TOÑO TOLD ME OBASI SAID SOMETHING INAPPROPRIATE TO YOU?
UM, YEAH.
LET'S STEP INTO THE OFFICE.
NOW, CAN YOU TELL ME WHAT HAPPENED FROM THE BEGINNING?
WELL, I WAS WALKING—

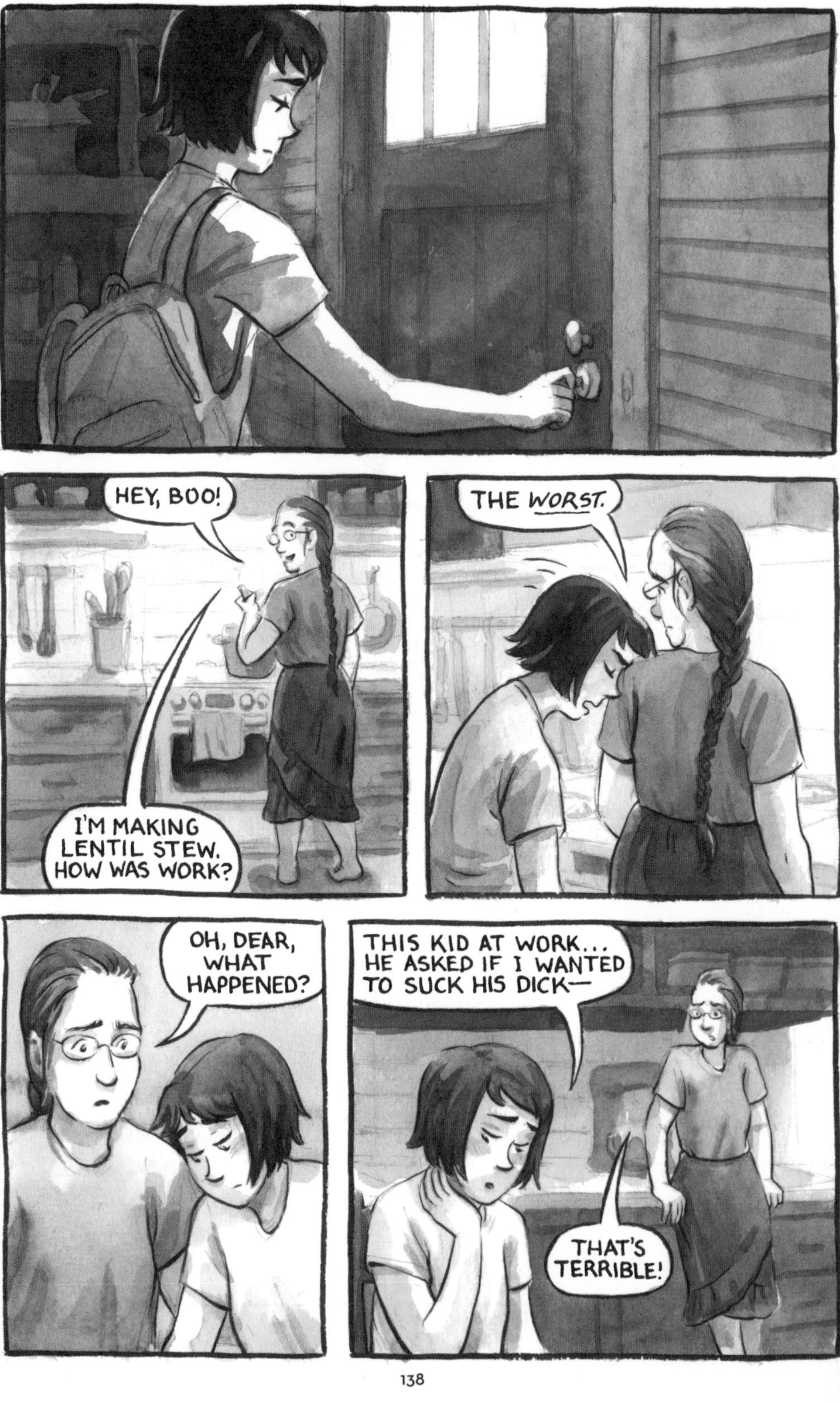

HEY, BOO!
I'M MAKING LENTIL STEW. HOW WAS WORK?
THE WORST.
OH, DEAR, WHAT HAPPENED?
THIS KID AT WORK... HE ASKED IF I WANTED TO SUCK HIS DICK—
THAT'S TERRIBLE!

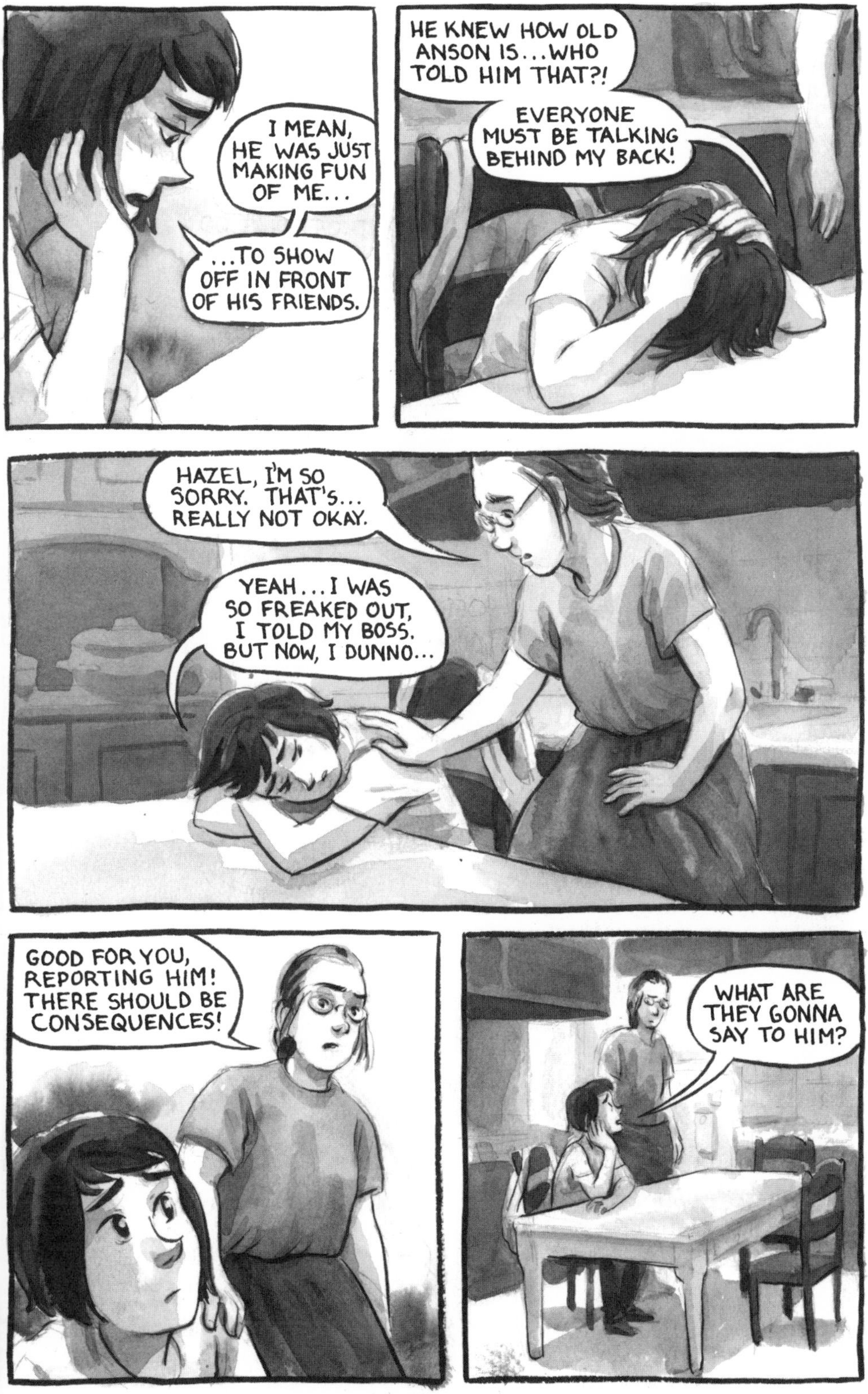
I MEAN, HE WAS JUST MAKING FUN OF ME...
...TO SHOW OFF IN FRONT OF HIS FRIENDS.
HE KNEW HOW OLD ANSON IS...WHO TOLD HIM THAT?!
EVERYONE MUST BE TALKING BEHIND MY BACK!
HAZEL, I'M SO SORRY. THAT'S... REALLY NOT OKAY.
YEAH...I WAS SO FREAKED OUT, I TOLD MY BOSS. BUT NOW, I DUNNO...
GOOD FOR YOU, REPORTING HIM! THERE SHOULD BE CONSEQUENCES!
WHAT ARE THEY GONNA SAY TO HIM?

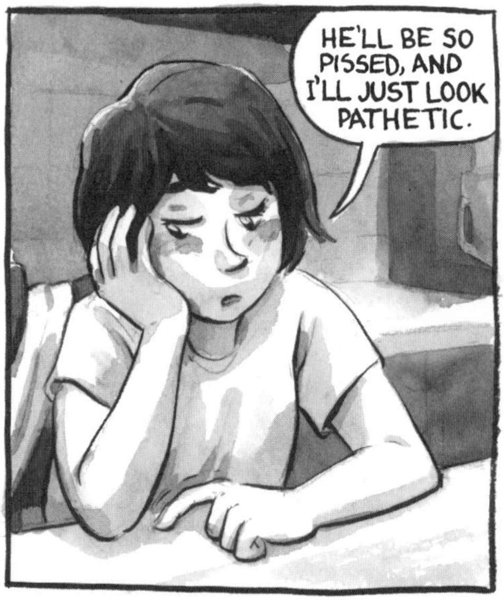
HE'LL BE SO PISSED, AND I'LL JUST LOOK PATHETIC.

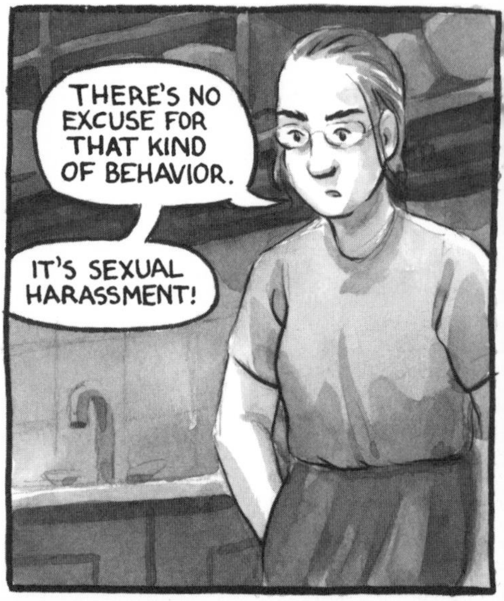
THERE'S NO EXCUSE FOR THAT KIND OF BEHAVIOR.
IT'S SEXUAL HARASSMENT!

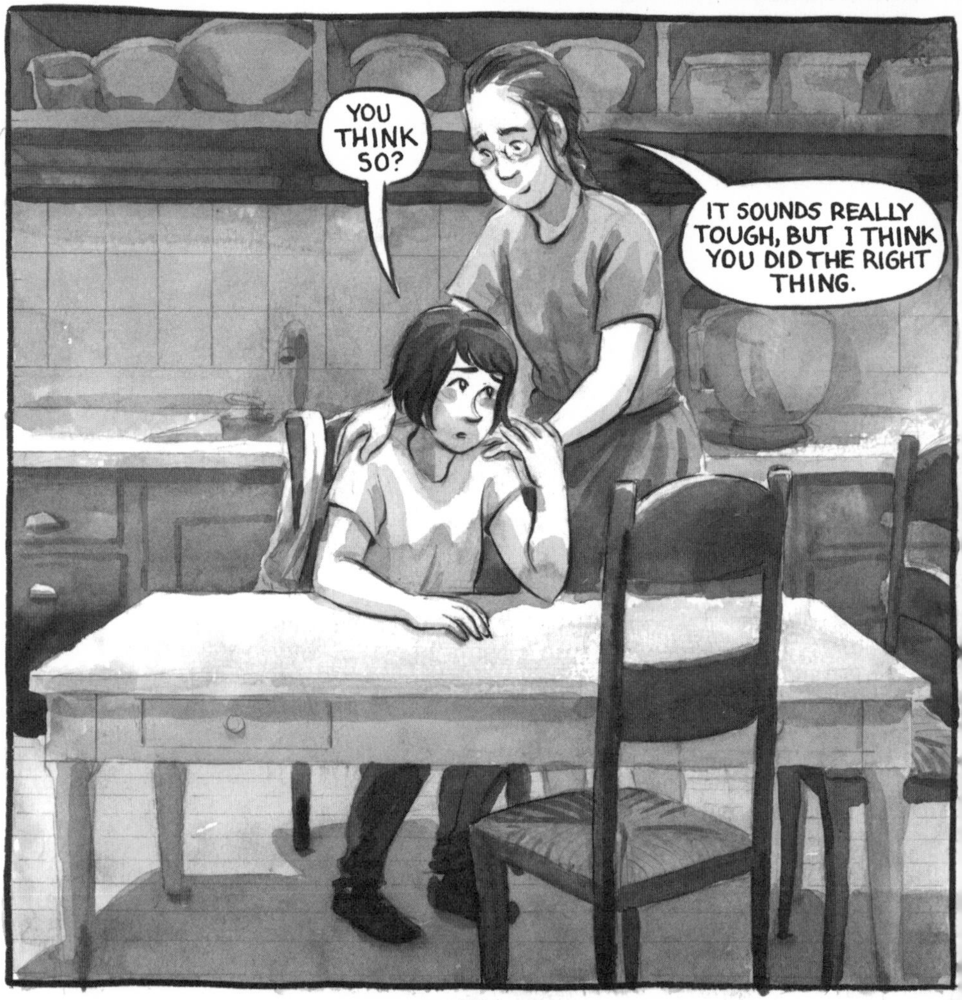
YOU THINK SO?
IT SOUNDS REALLY TOUGH, BUT I THINK YOU DID THE RIGHT THING.

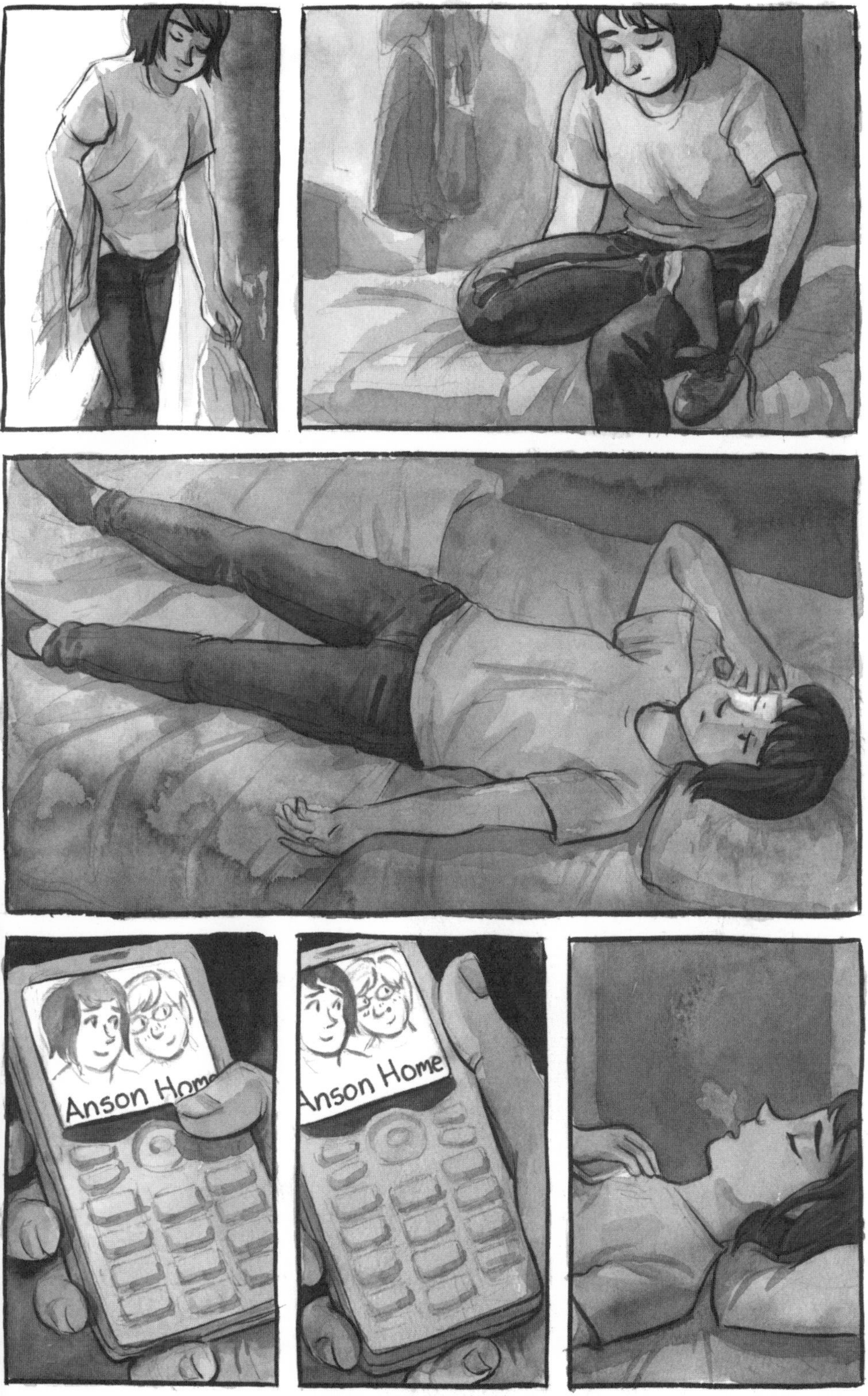
Anson Home
Anson Home

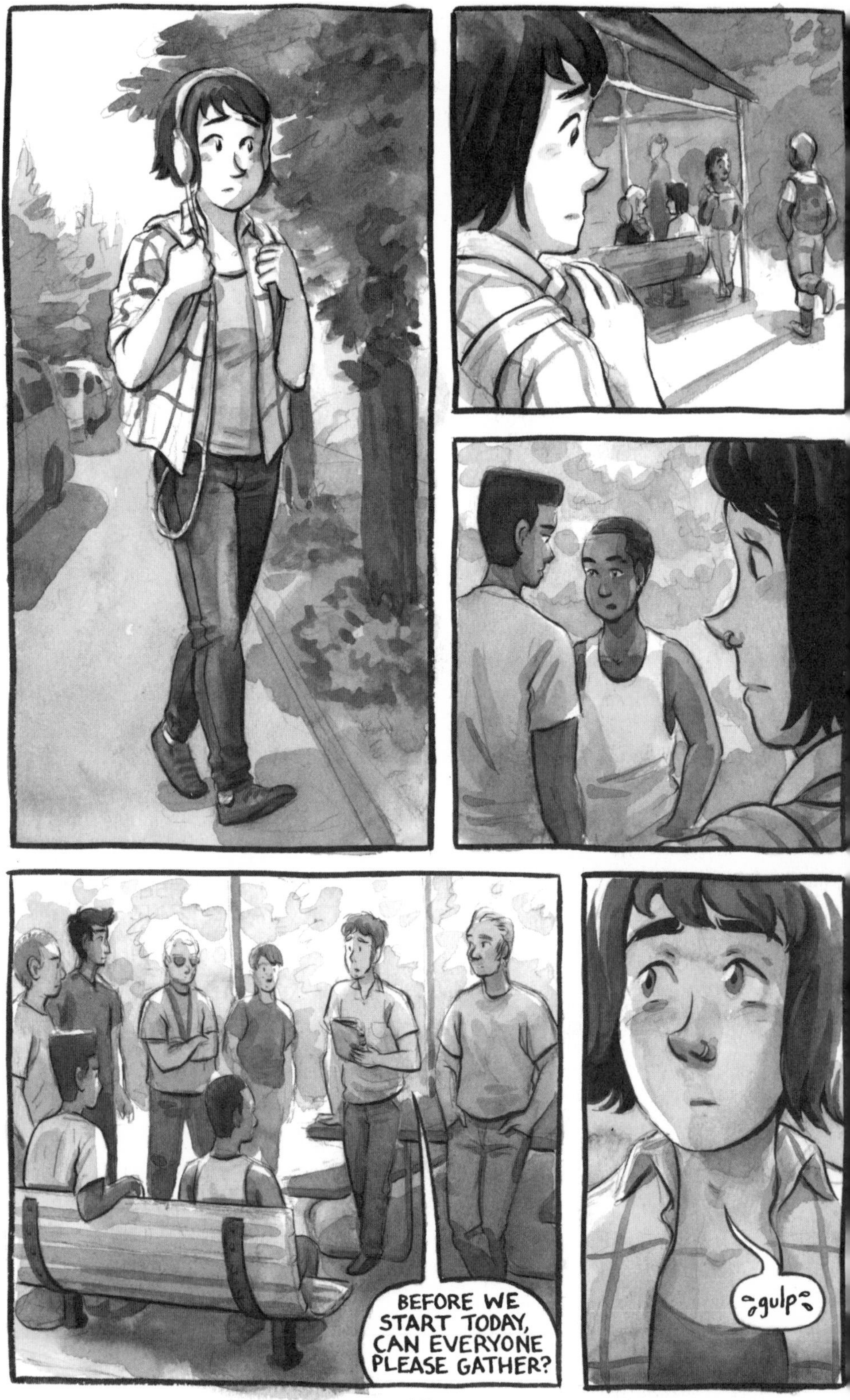
BEFORE WE START TODAY, CAN EVERYONE PLEASE GATHER?
gulp

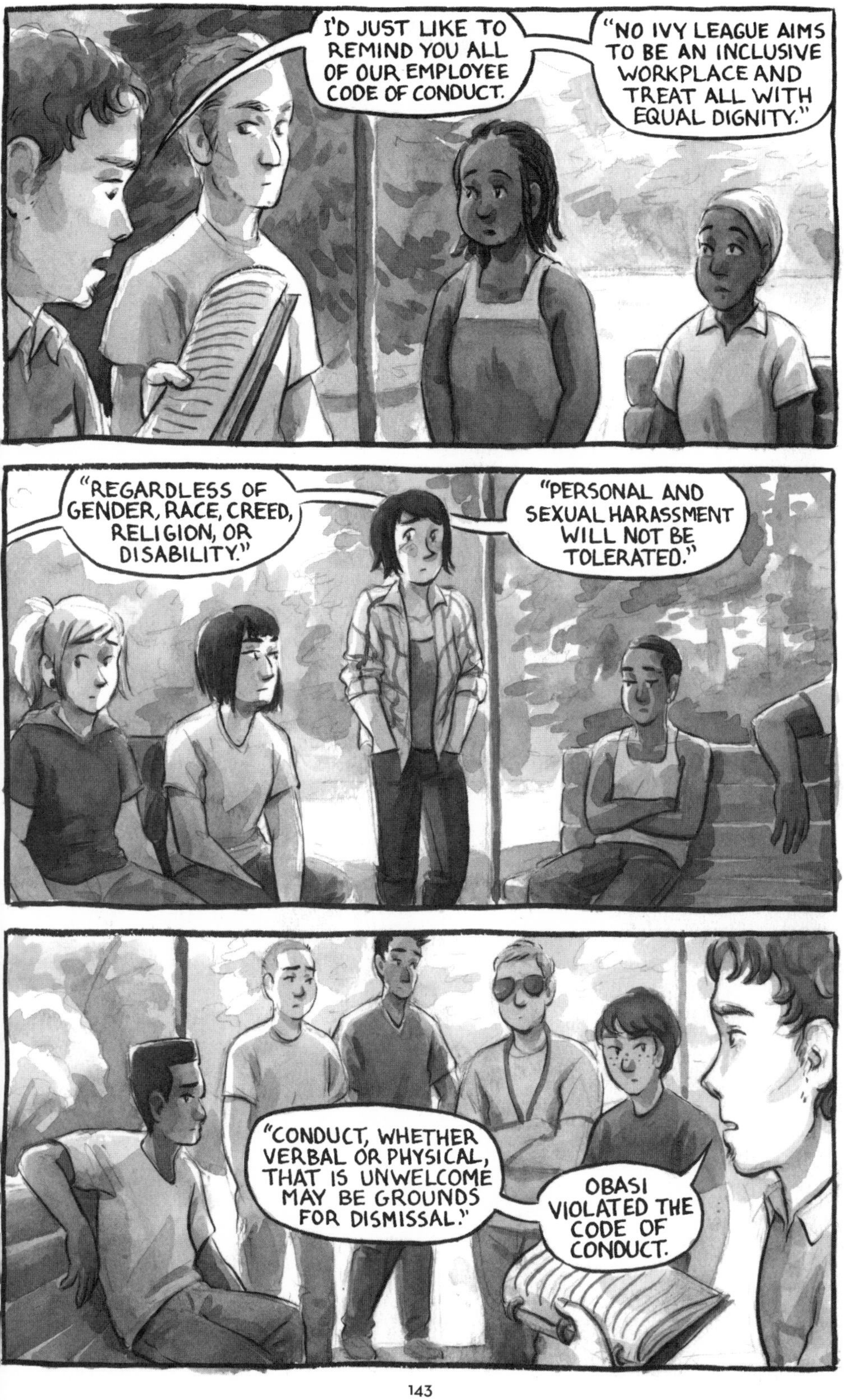
I'D JUST LIKE TO REMIND YOU ALL OF OUR EMPLOYEE CODE OF CONDUCT.
"NO IVY LEAGUE AIMS TO BE AN INCLUSIVE WORKPLACE AND TREAT ALL WITH EQUAL DIGNITY."
"REGARDLESS OF GENDER, RACE, CREED, RELIGION, OR DISABILITY."
"PERSONAL AND SEXUAL HARASSMENT WILL NOT BE TOLERATED."
"CONDUCT, WHETHER VERBAL OR PHYSICAL, THAT IS UNWELCOME MAY BE GROUNDS FOR DISMISSAL."
OBASI VIOLATED THE CODE OF CONDUCT.

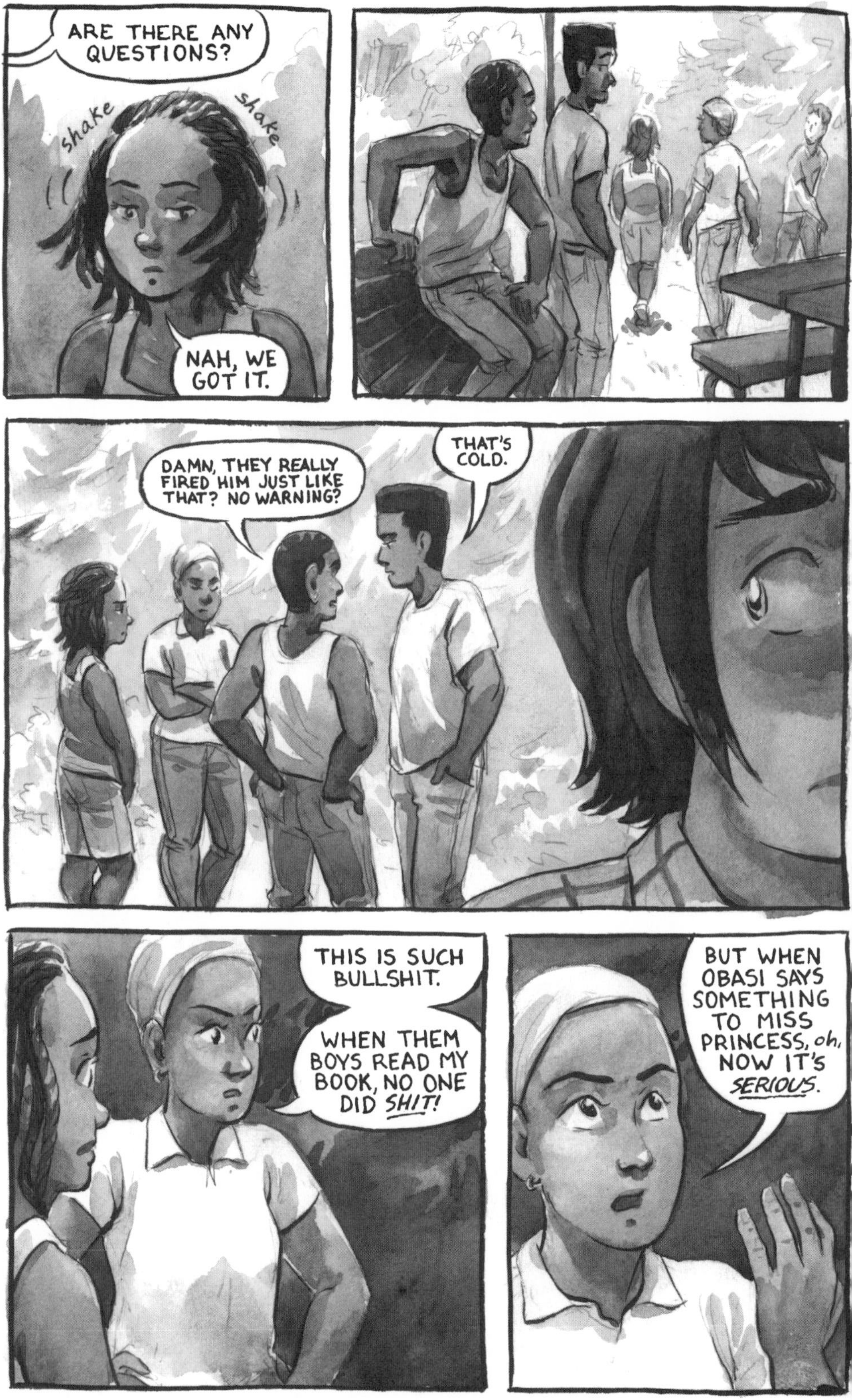
ARE THERE ANY QUESTIONS?
shake
shake
NAH, WE GOT IT.
DAMN, THEY REALLY FIRED HIM JUST LIKE THAT? NO WARNING?
THAT'S COLD.
THIS IS SUCH BULLSHIT.
WHEN THEM BOYS READ MY BOOK, NO ONE DID SHIT!
BUT WHEN OBASI SAYS SOMETHING TO MISS PRINCESS, oh, NOW IT'S SERIOUS.

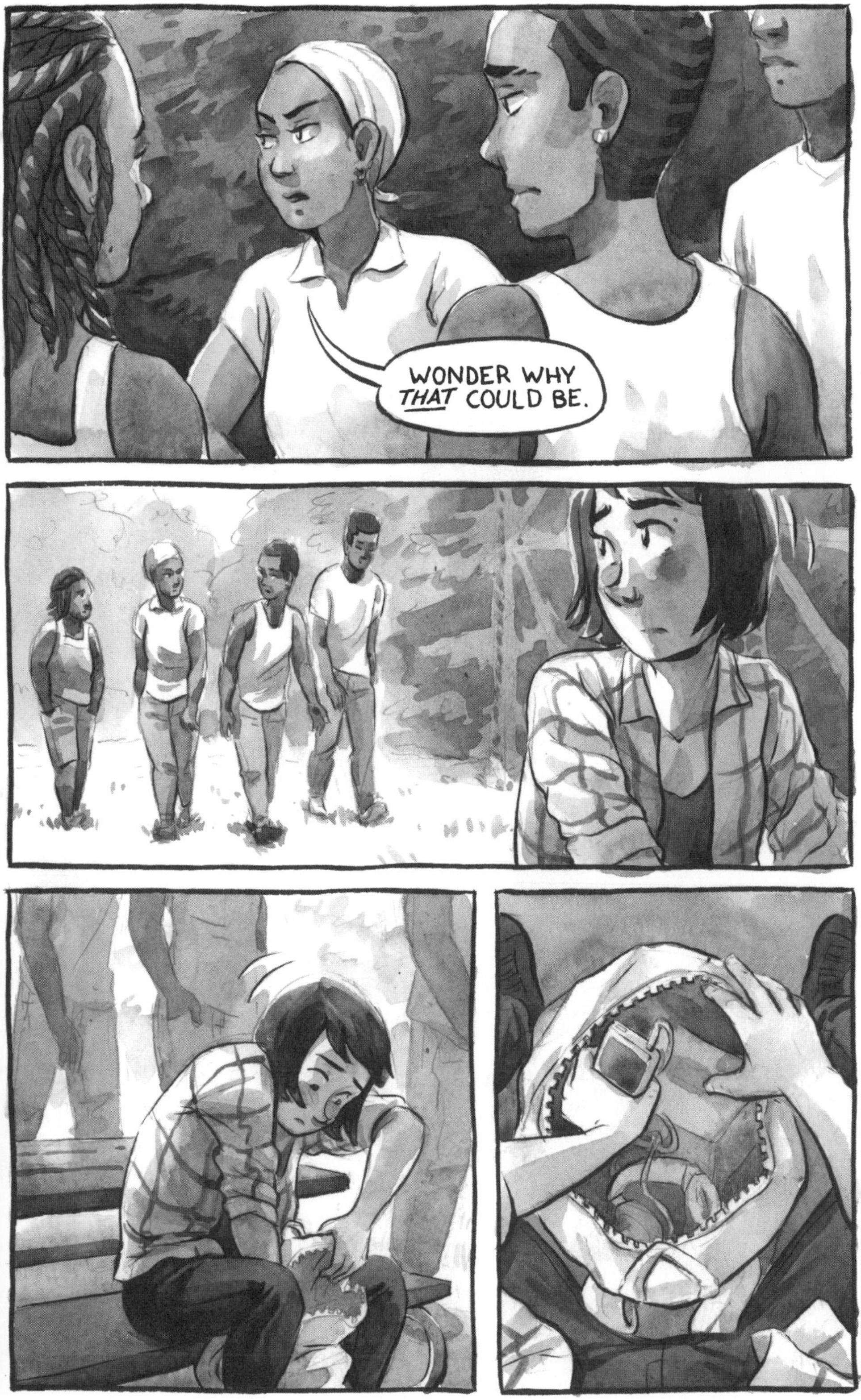
WONDER WHY THAT COULD BE.

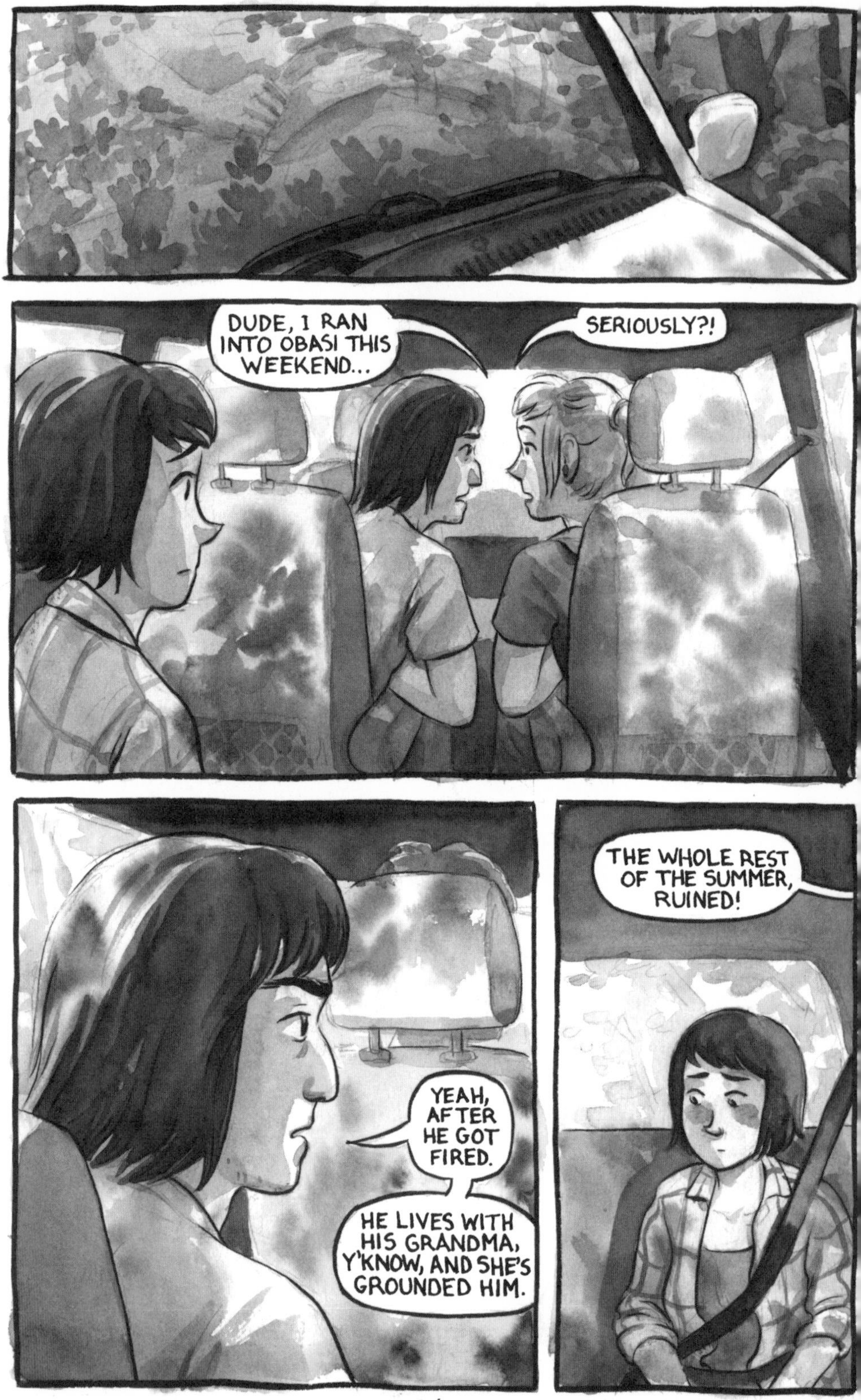
DUDE, I RAN INTO OBASI THIS WEEKEND...
SERIOUSLY?!
YEAH, AFTER HE GOT FIRED.
HE LIVES WITH HIS GRANDMA, Y'KNOW, AND SHE'S GROUNDED HIM.
THE WHOLE REST OF THE SUMMER, RUINED!

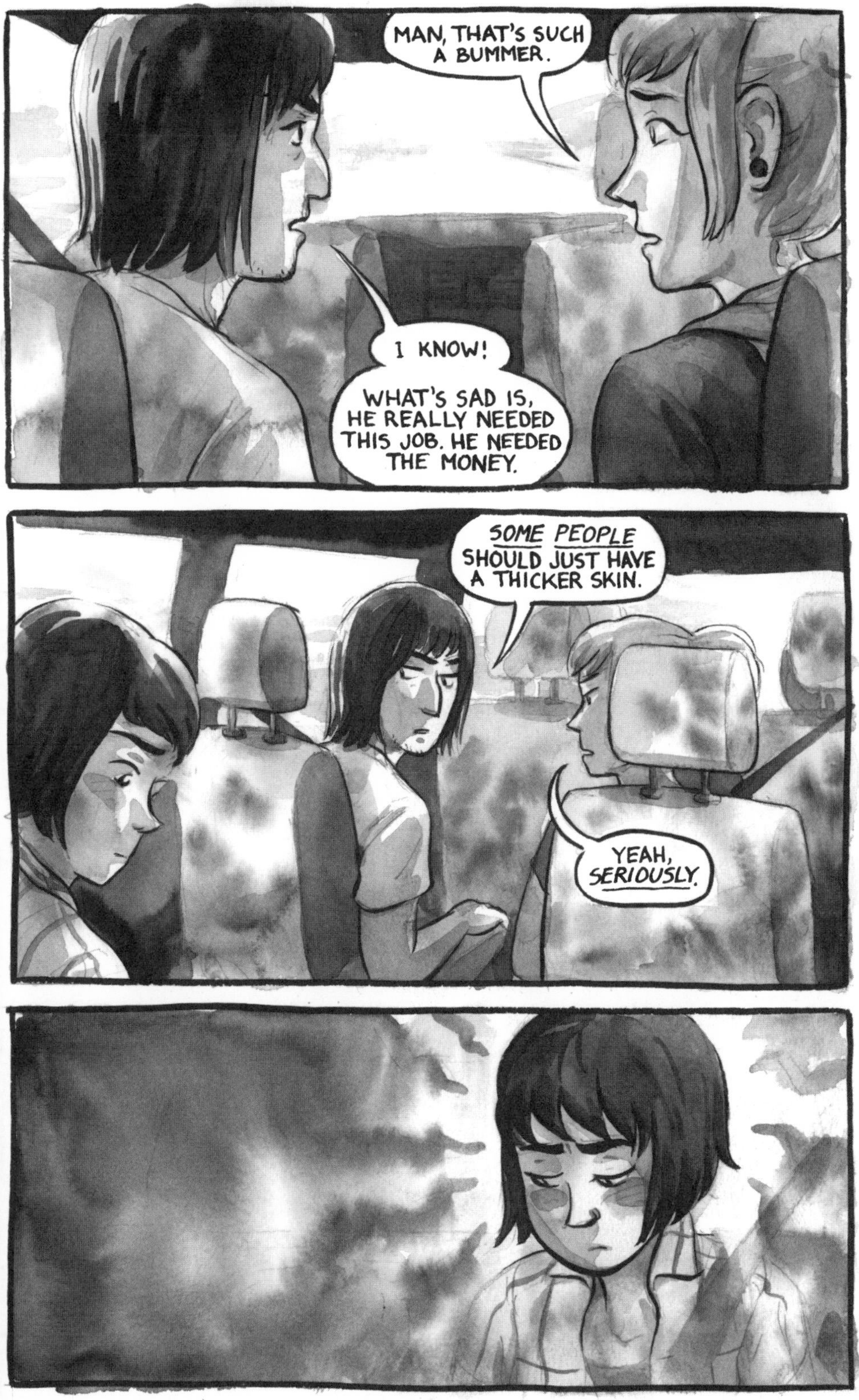
MAN, THAT'S SUCH A BUMMER.
I KNOW!
WHAT'S SAD IS, HE REALLY NEEDED THIS JOB. HE NEEDED THE MONEY.
SOME PEOPLE SHOULD JUST HAVE A THICKER SKIN.
YEAH, SERIOUSLY.

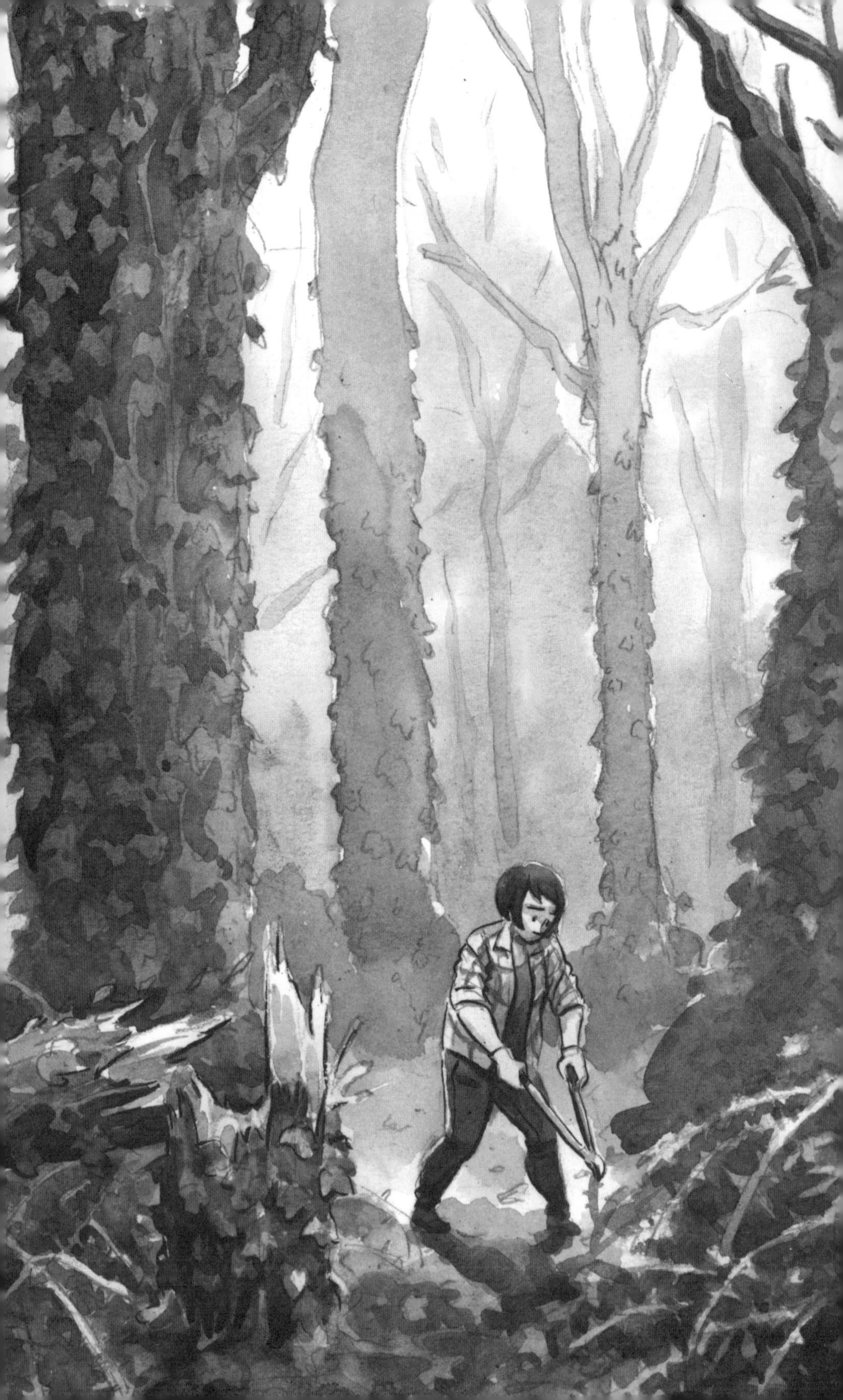

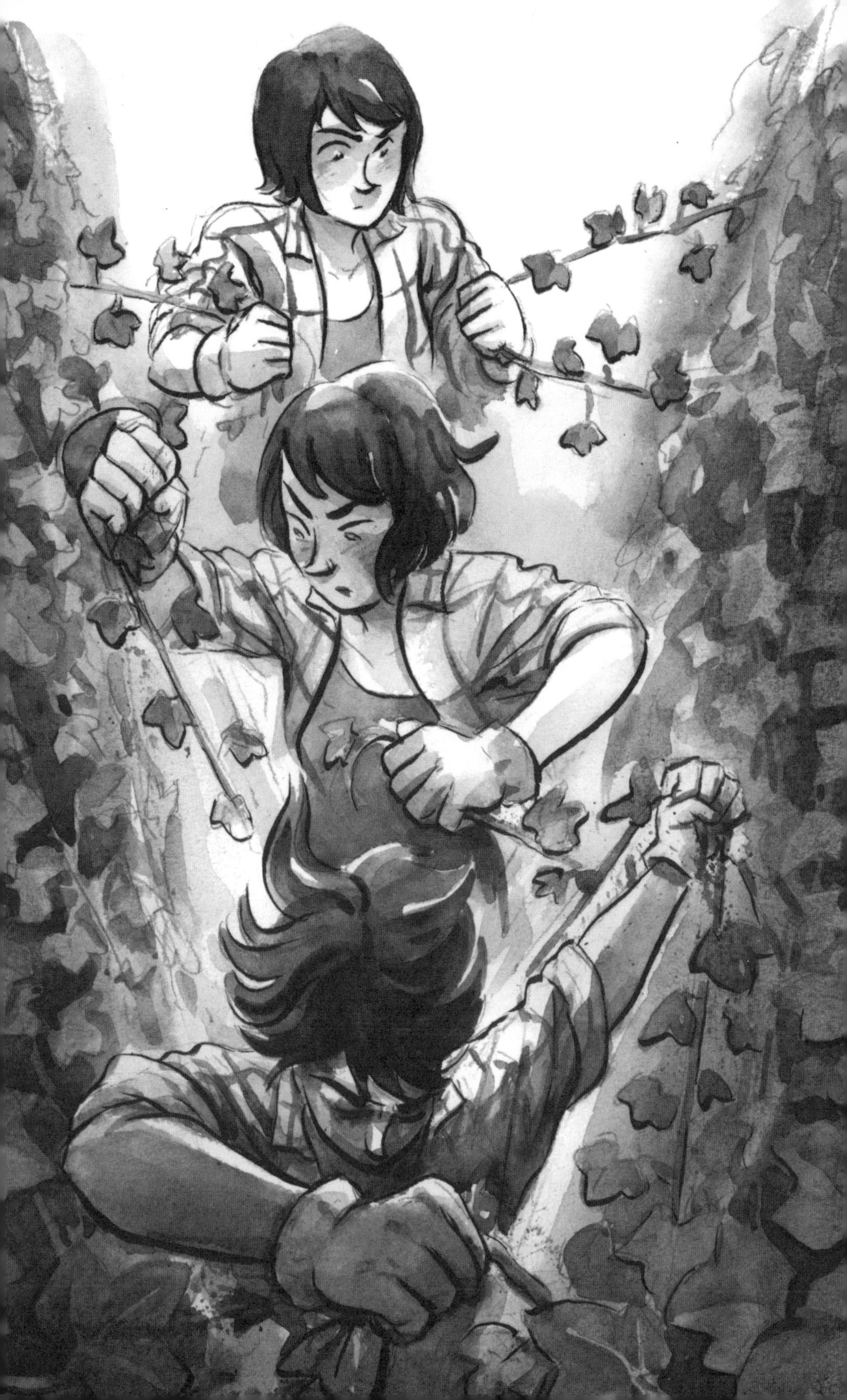

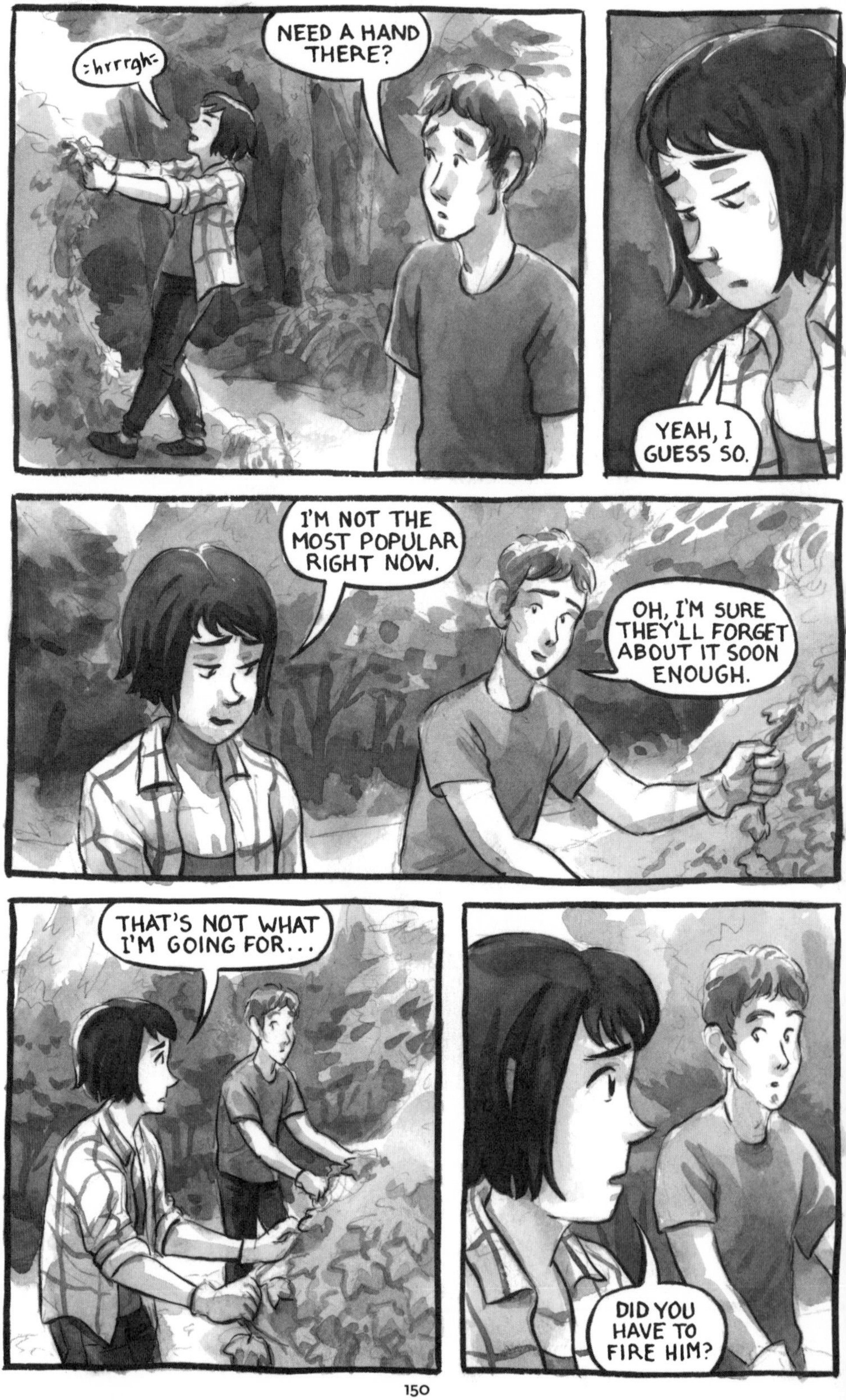
:hrrrgh:
NEED A HAND THERE?
YEAH, I GUESS SO.
I'M NOT THE MOST POPULAR RIGHT NOW.
OH, I'M SURE THEY'LL FORGET ABOUT IT SOON ENOUGH.
THAT'S NOT WHAT I'M GOING FOR...
DID YOU HAVE TO FIRE HIM?

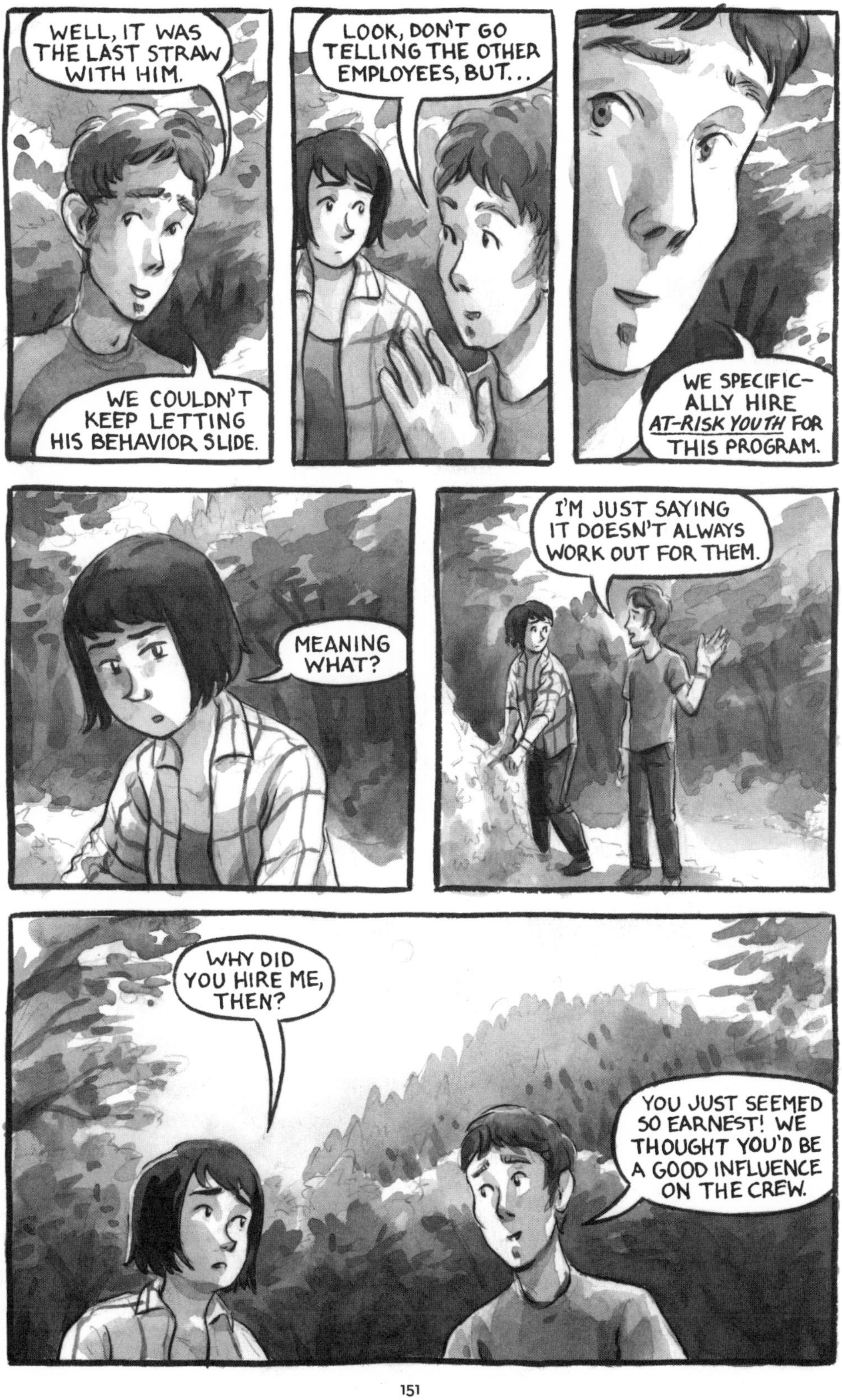
WELL, IT WAS THE LAST STRAW WITH HIM.
WE COULDN'T KEEP LETTING HIS BEHAVIOR SLIDE.
LOOK, DON'T GO TELLING THE OTHER EMPLOYEES, BUT...
WE SPECIFICALLY HIRE AT-RISK YOUTH FOR THIS PROGRAM.
MEANING WHAT?
I'M JUST SAYING IT DOESN'T ALWAYS WORK OUT FOR THEM.
WHY DID YOU HIRE ME, THEN?
YOU JUST SEEMED SO EARNEST! WE THOUGHT YOU'D BE A GOOD INFLUENCE ON THE CREW.

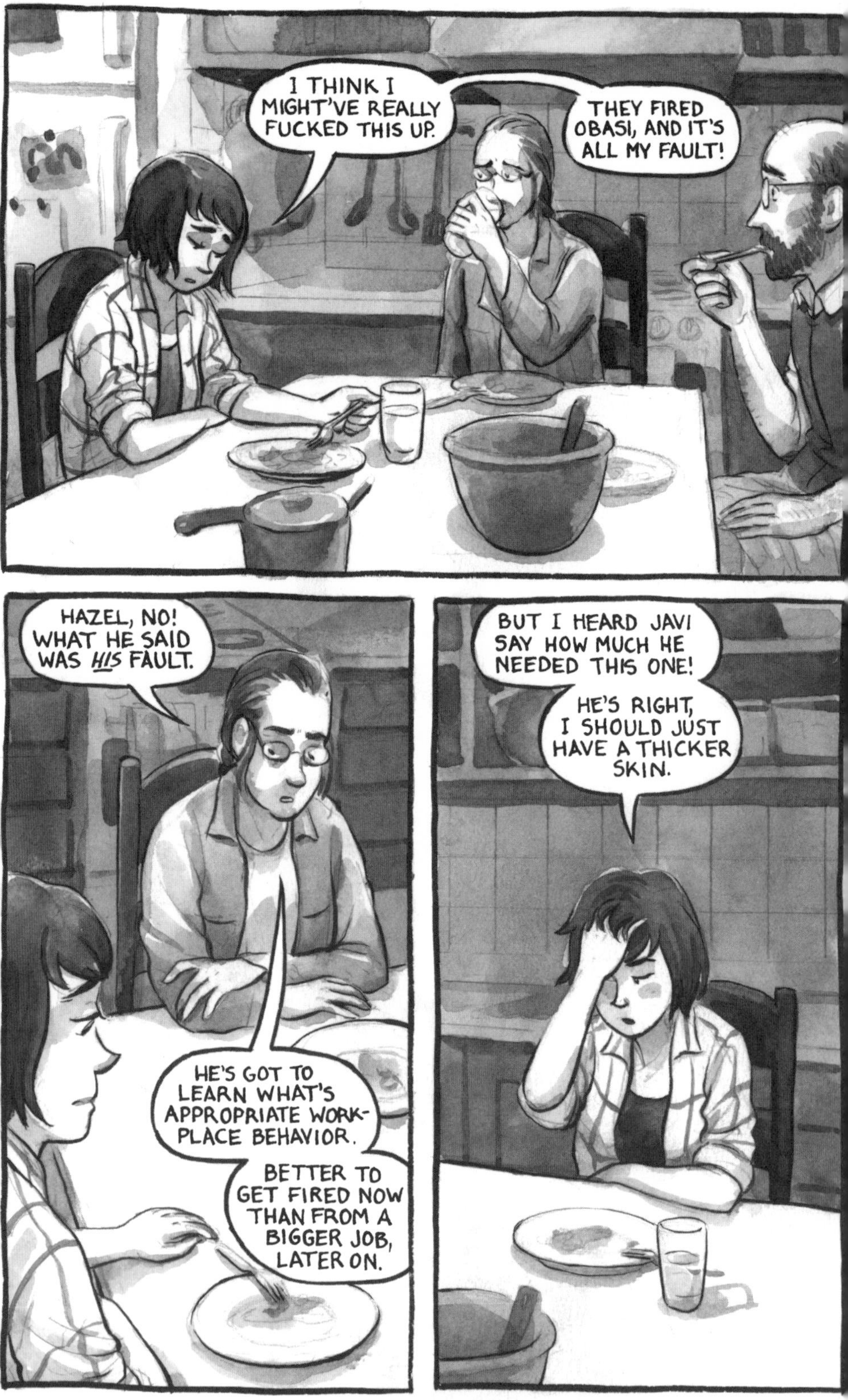
I THINK I MIGHT'VE REALLY FUCKED THIS UP.
THEY FIRED OBASI, AND IT'S ALL MY FAULT!
HAZEL, NO! WHAT HE SAID WAS HIS FAULT.
HE'S GOT TO LEARN WHAT'S APPROPRIATE WORK-PLACE BEHAVIOR.
BETTER TO GET FIRED NOW THAN FROM A BIGGER JOB, LATER ON.
BUT I HEARD JAVI SAY HOW MUCH HE NEEDED THIS ONE!
HE'S RIGHT, I SHOULD JUST HAVE A THICKER SKIN.

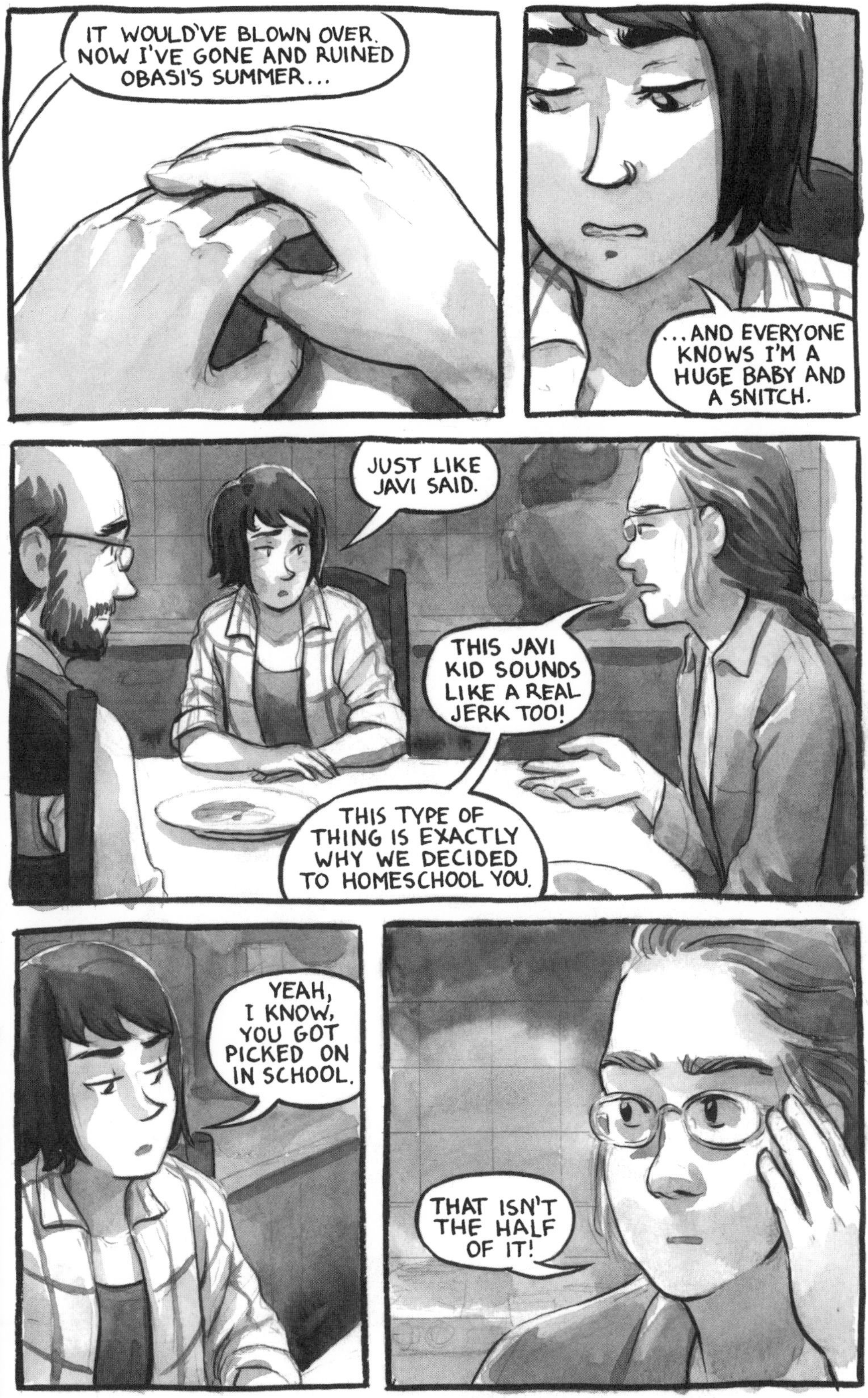
IT WOULD'VE BLOWN OVER. NOW I'VE GONE AND RUINED OBASI'S SUMMER...
...AND EVERYONE KNOWS I'M A HUGE BABY AND A SNITCH.
JUST LIKE JAVI SAID.
THIS JAVI KID SOUNDS LIKE A REAL JERK TOO!
THIS TYPE OF THING IS EXACTLY WHY WE DECIDED TO HOMESCHOOL YOU.
YEAH, I KNOW, YOU GOT PICKED ON IN SCHOOL.
THAT ISN'T THE HALF OF IT!

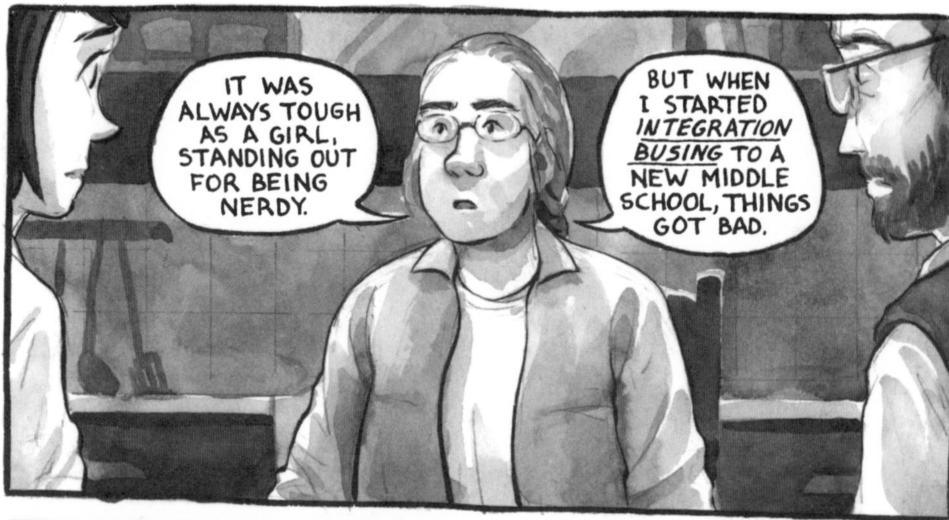
IT WAS ALWAYS TOUGH AS A GIRL, STANDING OUT FOR BEING NERDY.
BUT WHEN I STARTED INTEGRATION BUSING TO A NEW MIDDLE SCHOOL, THINGS GOT BAD.

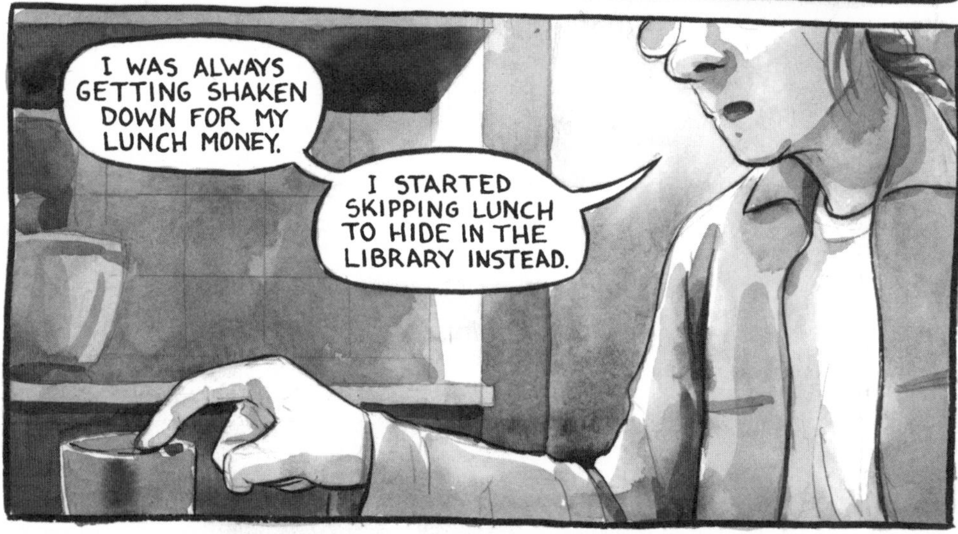
I WAS ALWAYS GETTING SHAKEN DOWN FOR MY LUNCH MONEY.
I STARTED SKIPPING LUNCH TO HIDE IN THE LIBRARY INSTEAD.

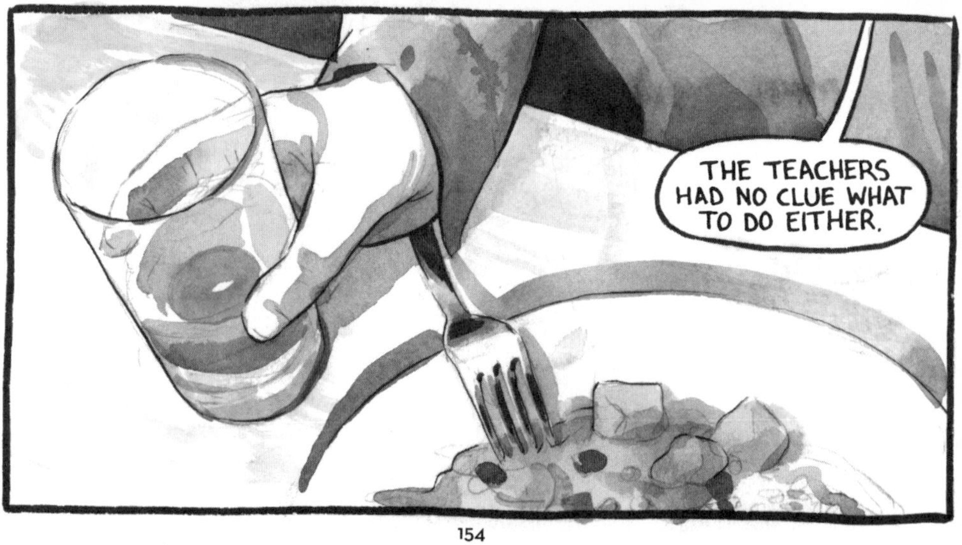
THE TEACHERS HAD NO CLUE WHAT TO DO EITHER.

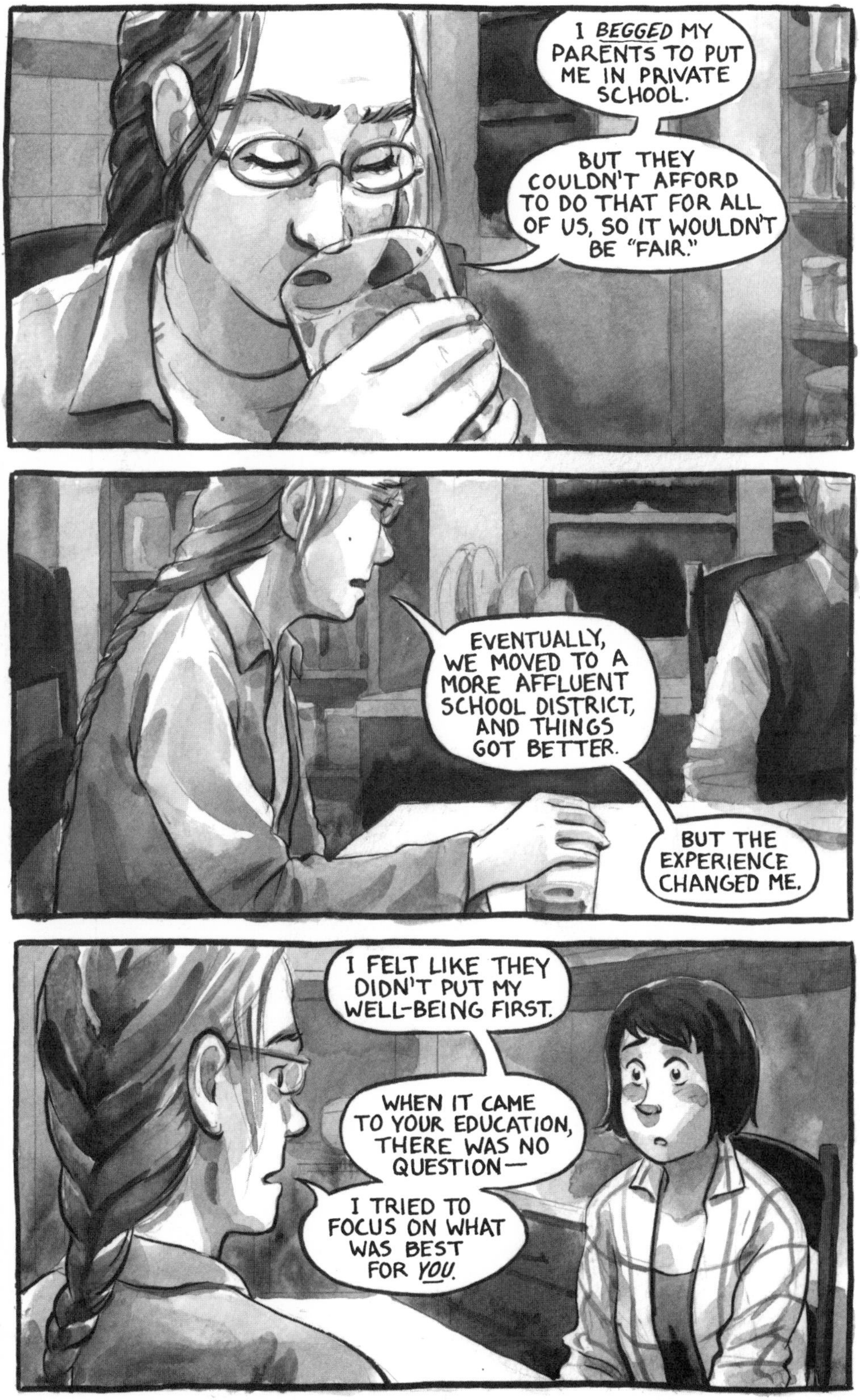
I BEGGED MY PARENTS TO PUT ME IN PRIVATE SCHOOL.
BUT THEY COULDN'T AFFORD TO DO THAT FOR ALL OF US, SO IT WOULDN'T BE "FAIR."
EVENTUALLY, WE MOVED TO A MORE AFFLUENT SCHOOL DISTRICT, AND THINGS GOT BETTER.
BUT THE EXPERIENCE CHANGED ME.
I FELT LIKE THEY DIDN'T PUT MY WELL-BEING FIRST.
WHEN IT CAME TO YOUR EDUCATION, THERE WAS NO QUESTION—
I TRIED TO FOCUS ON WHAT WAS BEST FOR YOU.

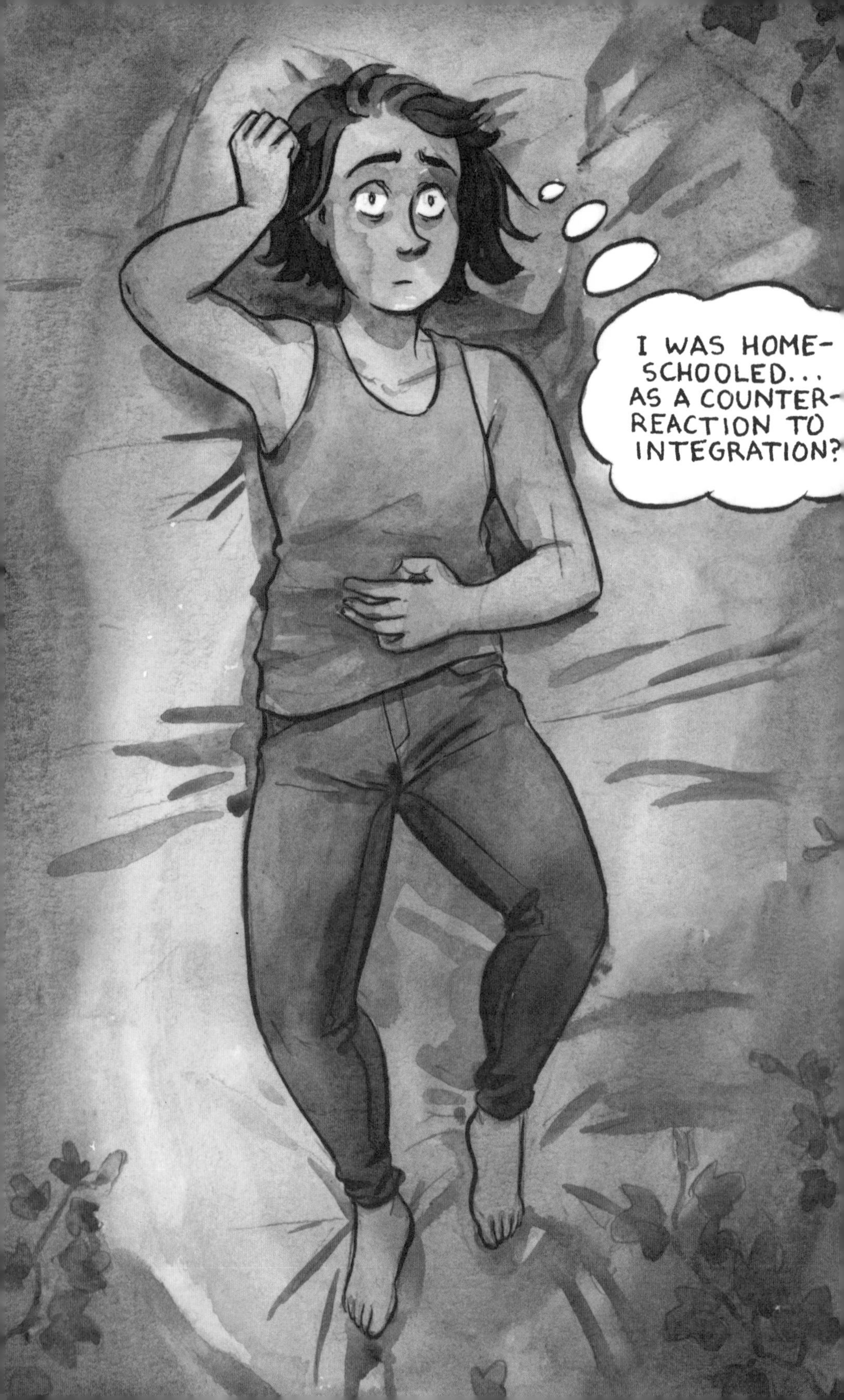
I WAS HOME-SCHOOLED... AS A COUNTER-REACTION TO INTEGRATION?

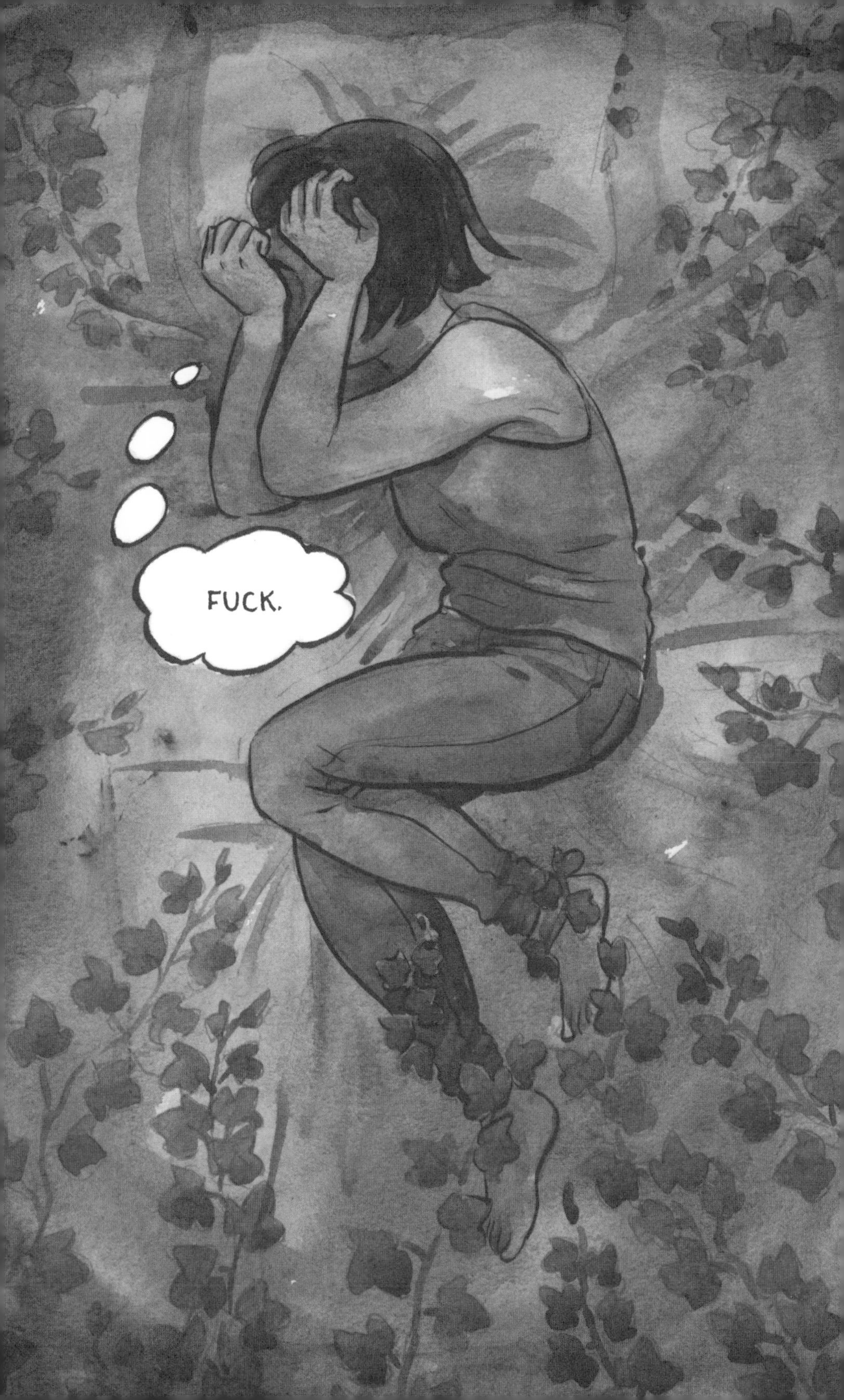
FUCK.

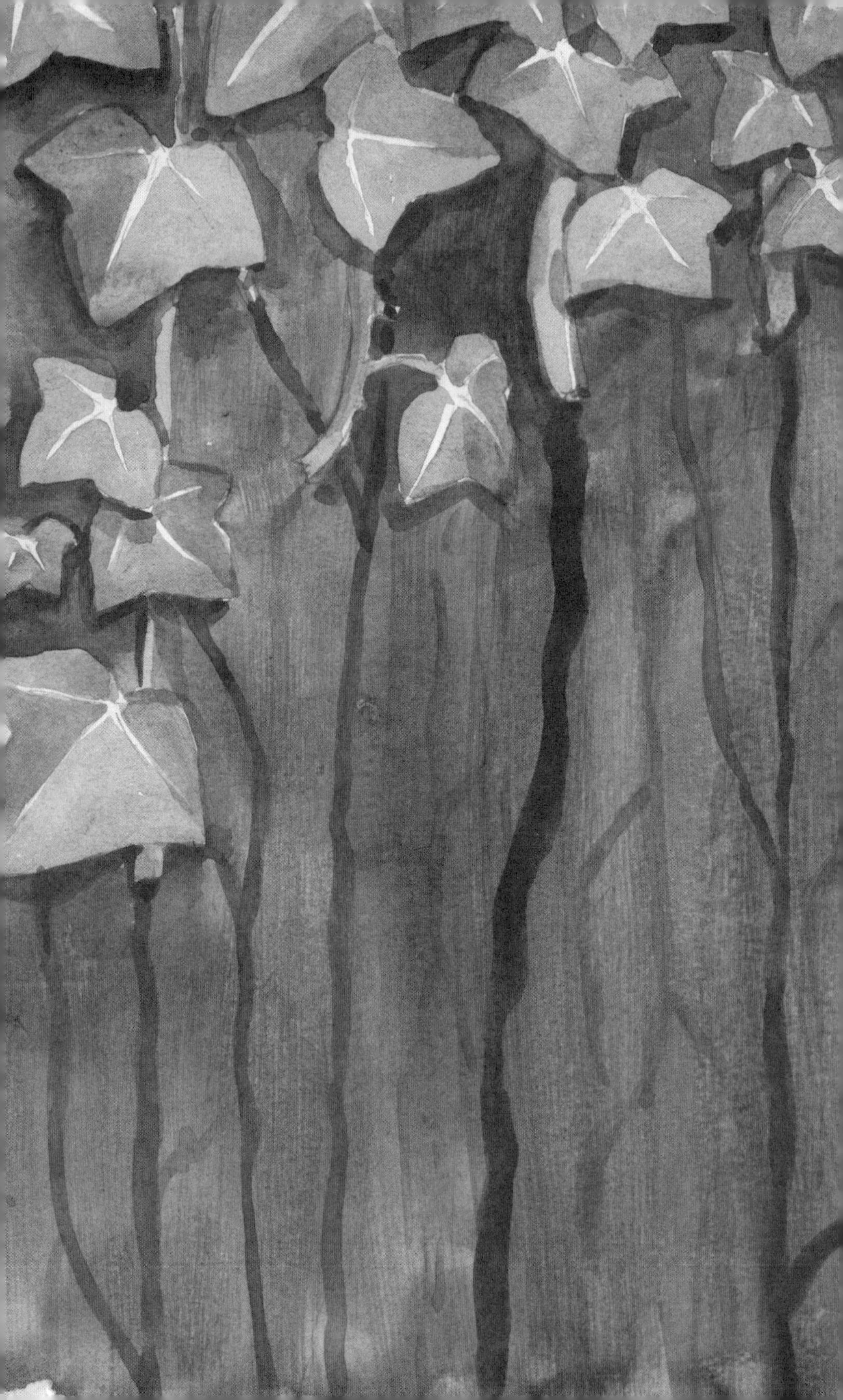

CHAPTER 4

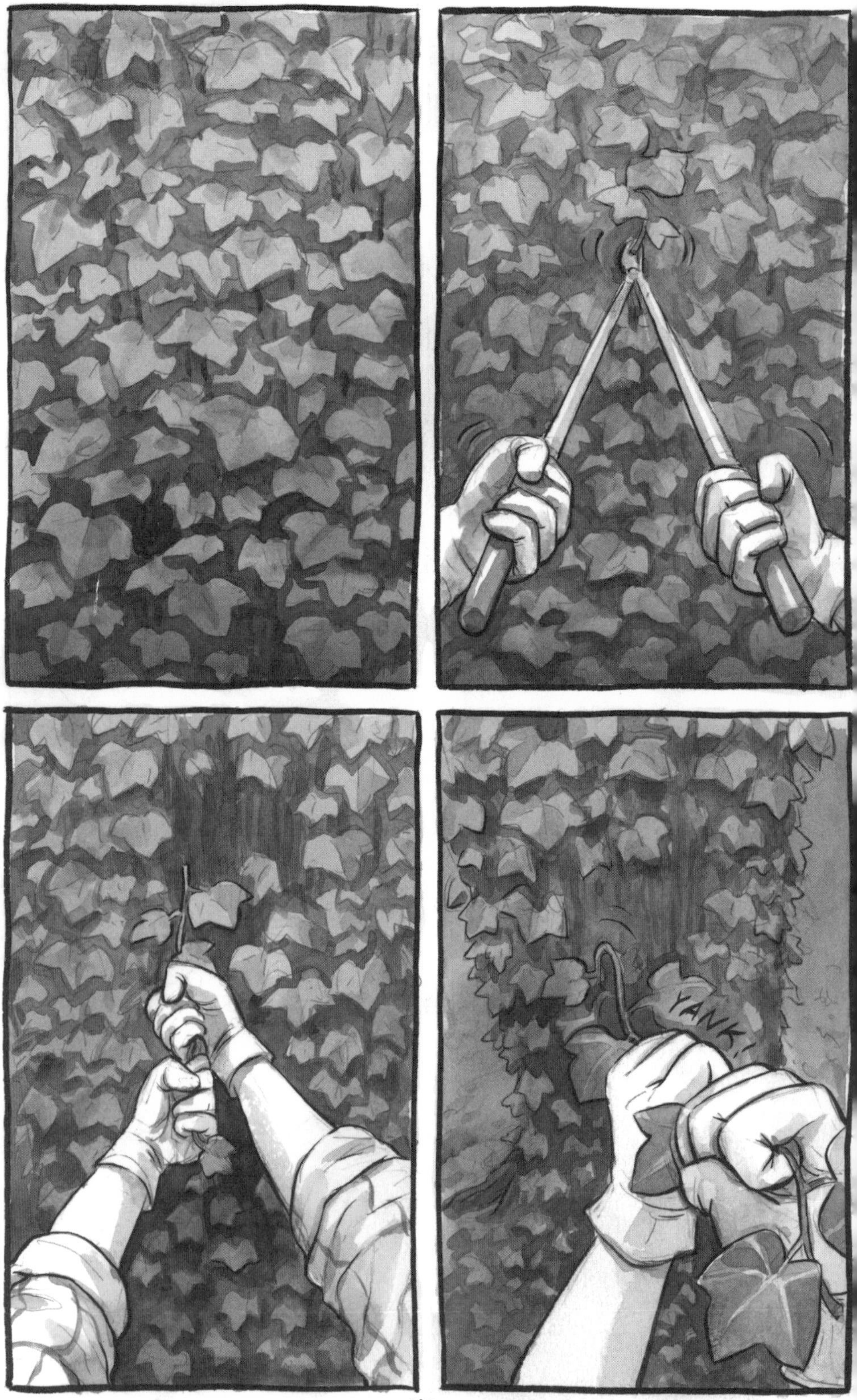
YANK!

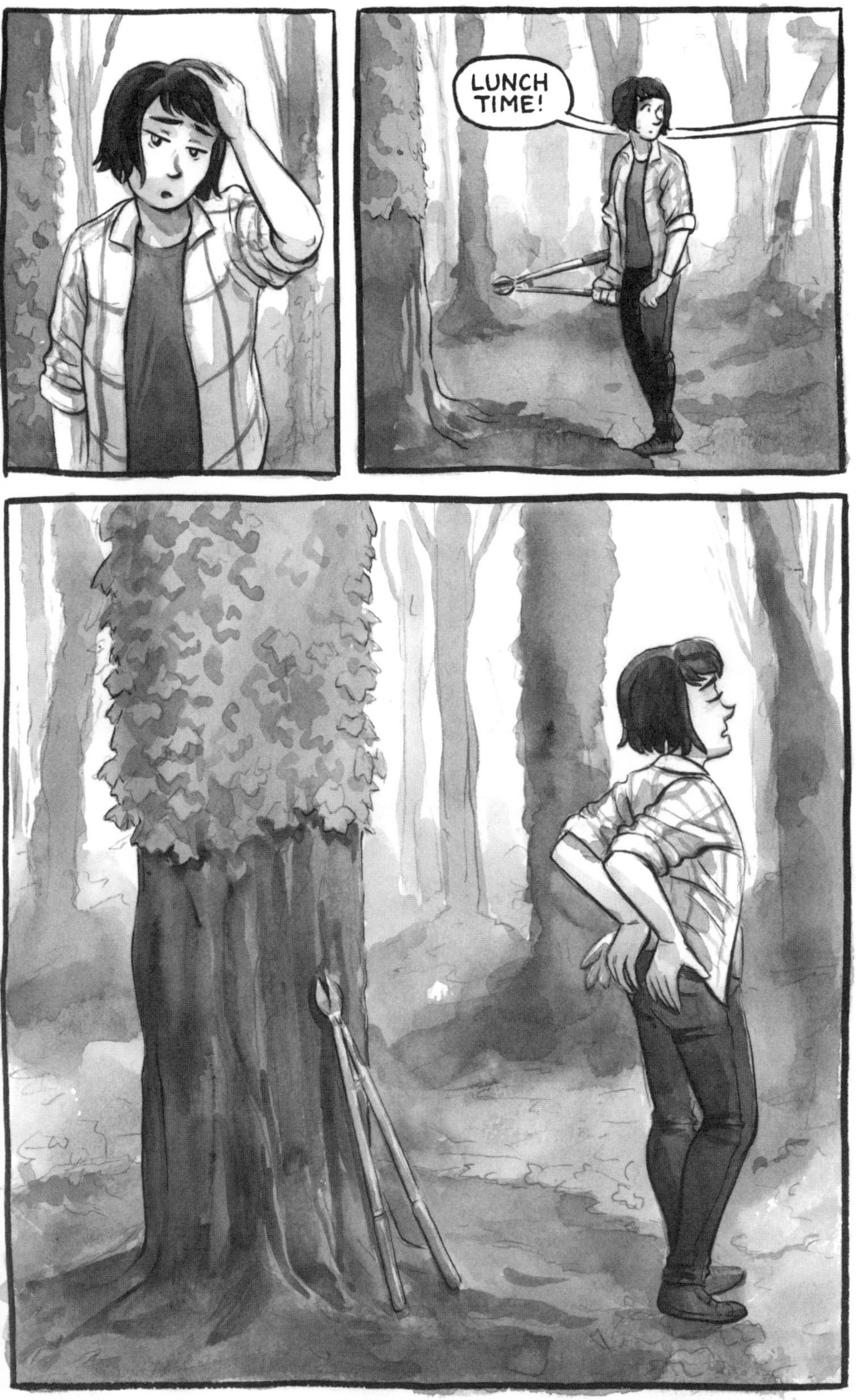
LUNCH TIME!

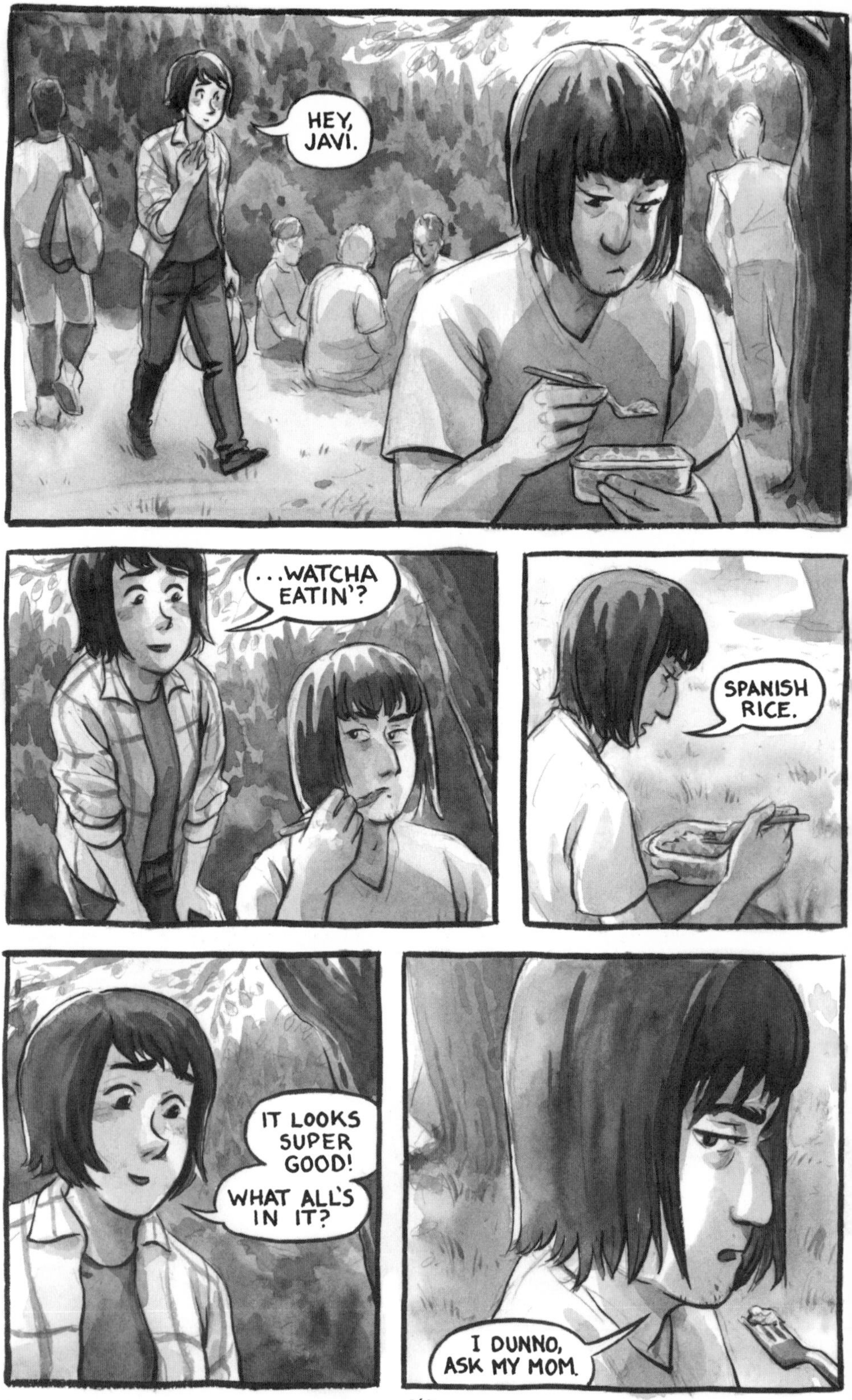
HEY, JAVI.
...WATCHA EATIN'?
SPANISH RICE.
IT LOOKS SUPER GOOD!
WHAT ALL'S IN IT?
I DUNNO, ASK MY MOM.

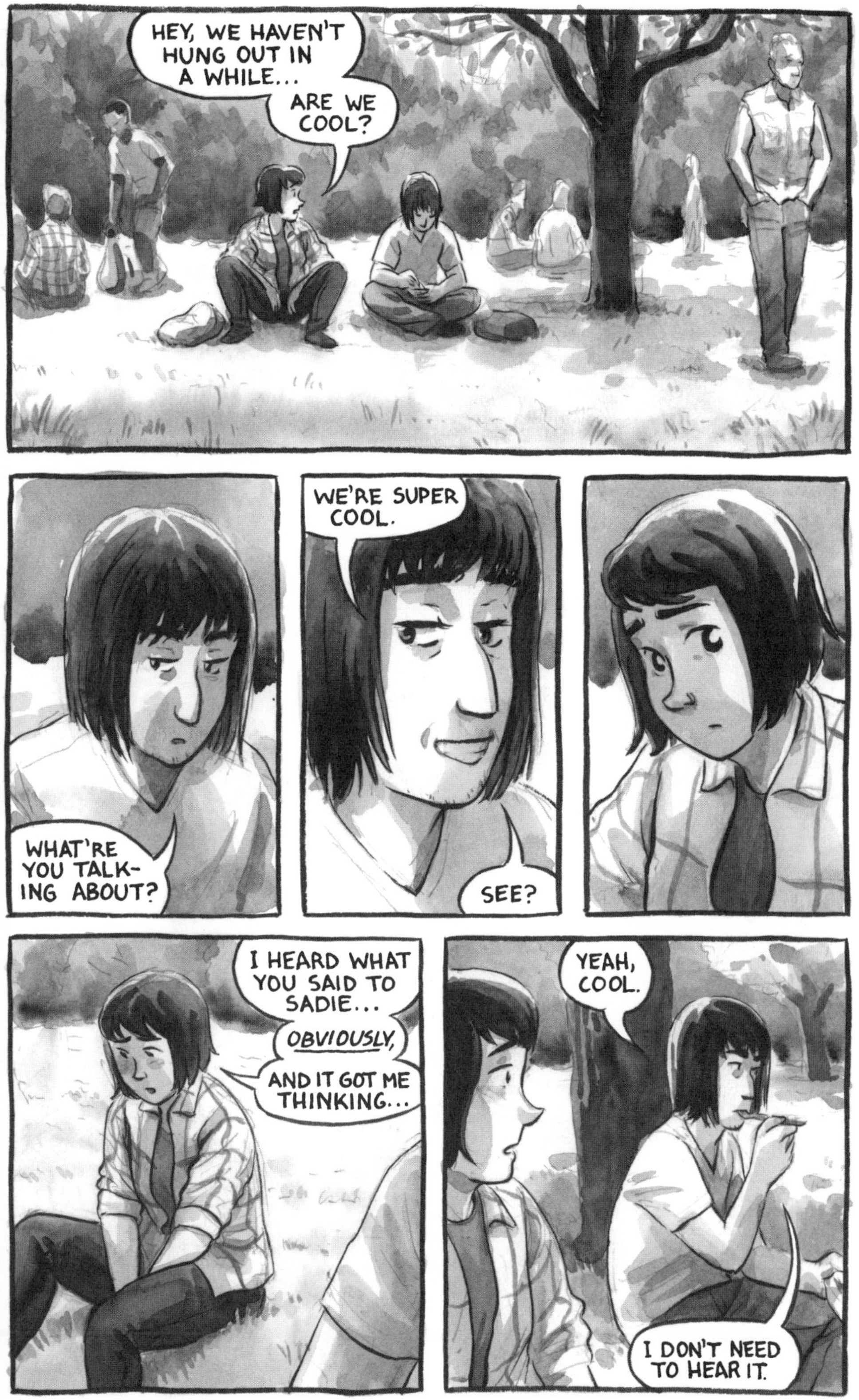
HEY, WE HAVEN'T HUNG OUT IN A WHILE...
ARE WE COOL?
WHAT'RE YOU TALK-ING ABOUT?
WE'RE SUPER COOL.
SEE?
I HEARD WHAT YOU SAID TO SADIE...
OBVIOUSLY,
AND IT GOT ME THINKING...
YEAH, COOL.
I DON'T NEED TO HEAR IT.

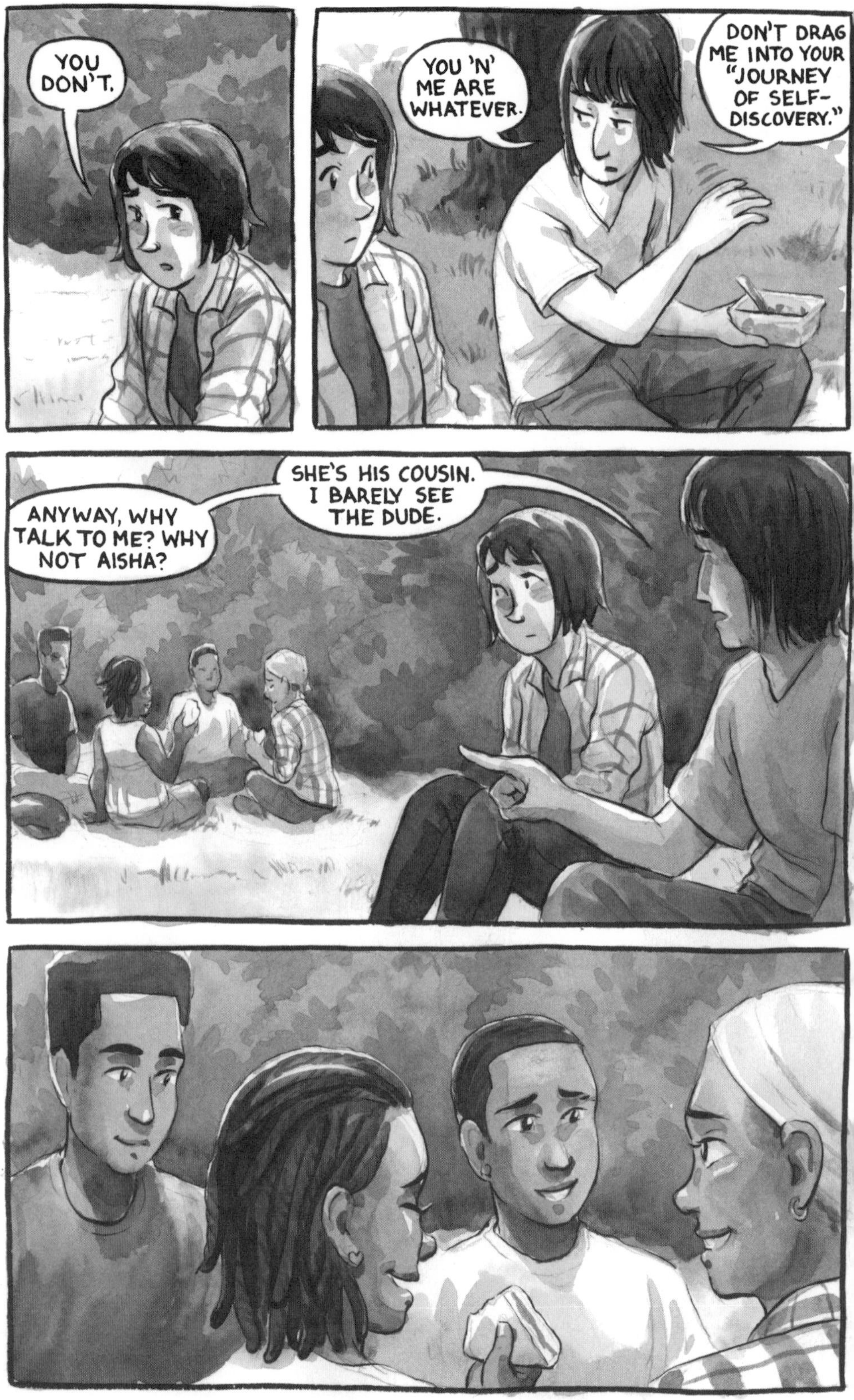
YOU DON'T.
YOU 'N' ME ARE WHATEVER.
DON'T DRAG ME INTO YOUR "JOURNEY OF SELF-DISCOVERY."
ANYWAY, WHY TALK TO ME? WHY NOT AISHA?
SHE'S HIS COUSIN. I BARELY SEE THE DUDE.

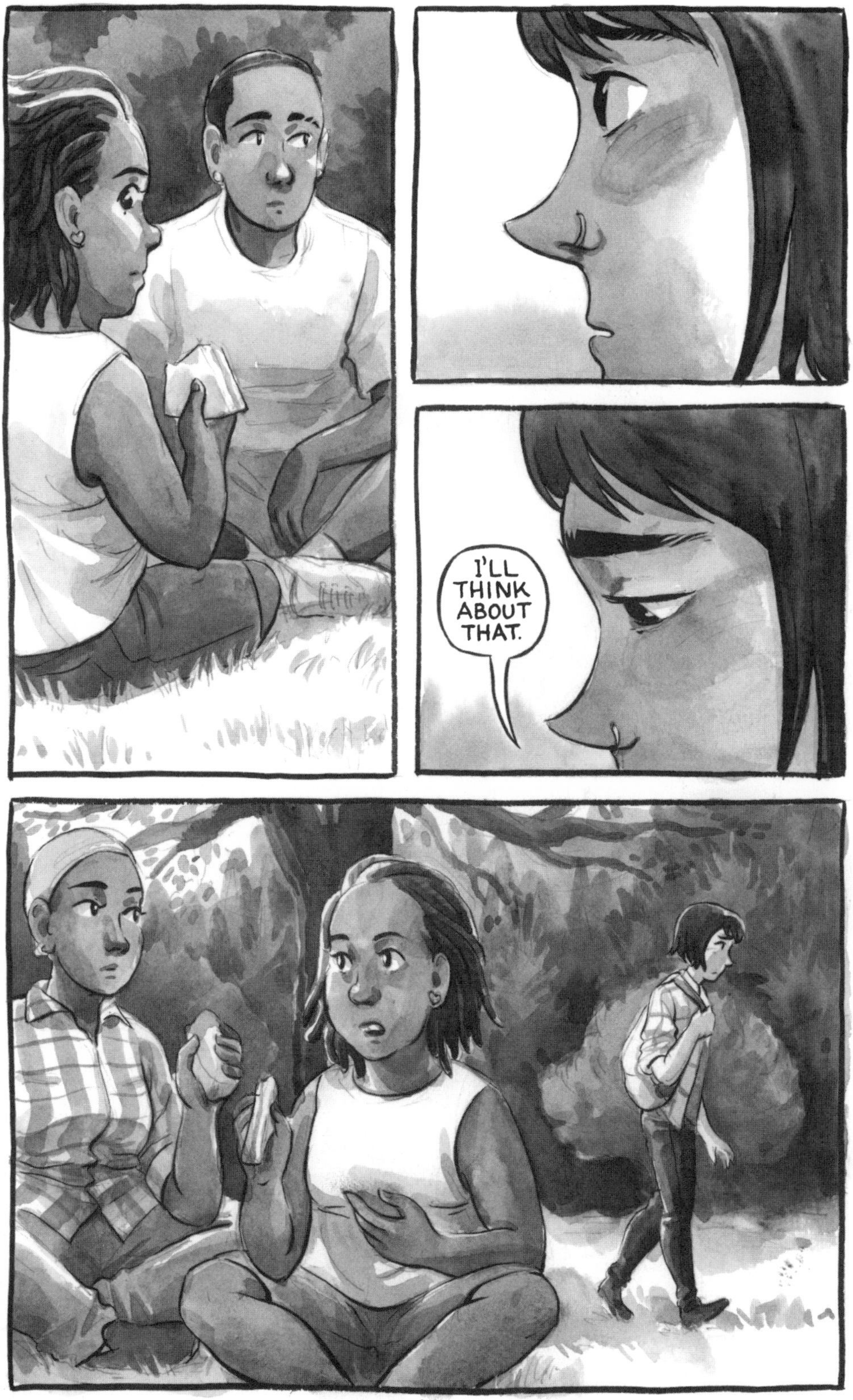
I'LL THINK ABOUT THAT.

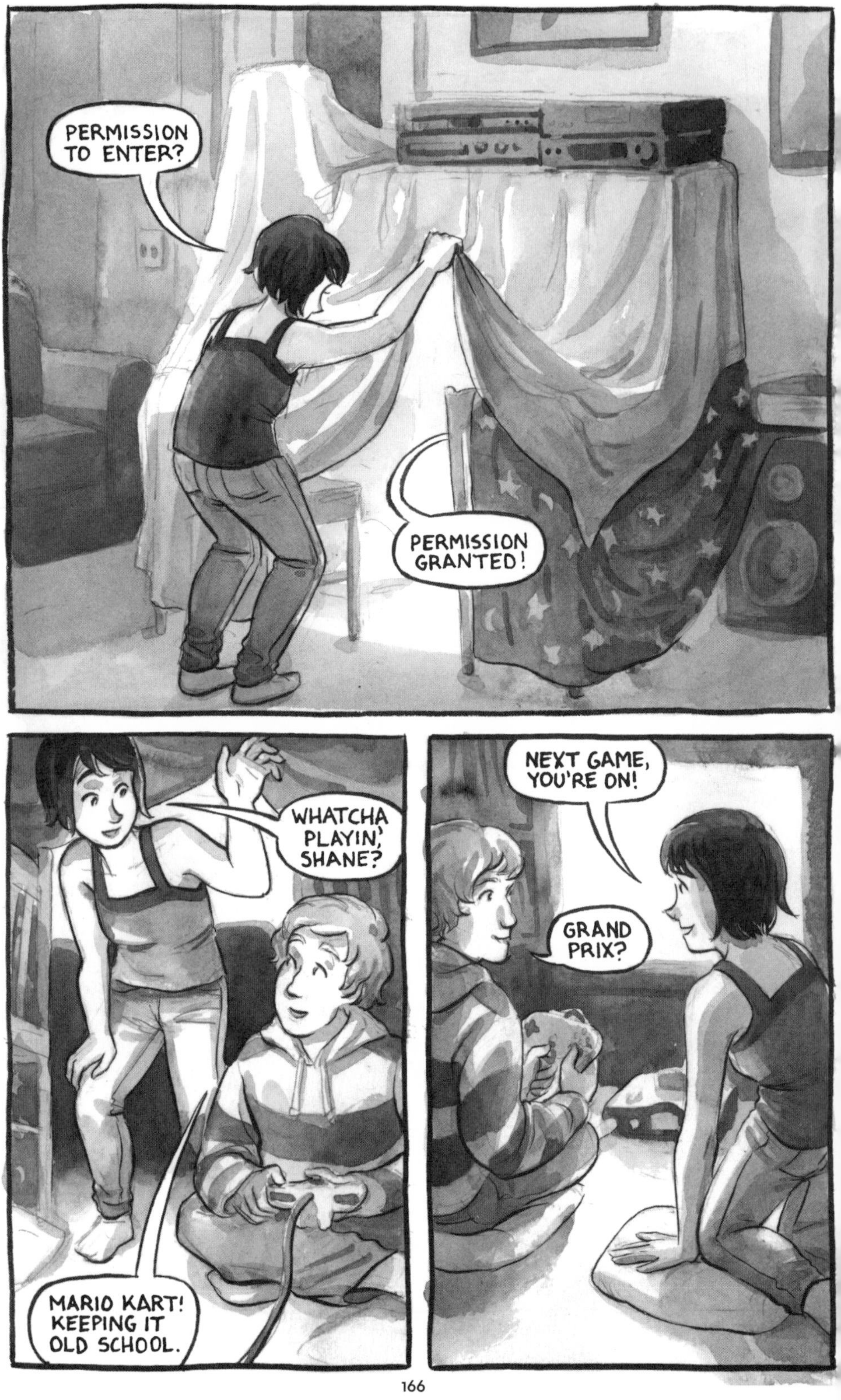
PERMISSION TO ENTER?
PERMISSION GRANTED!
WHATCHA PLAYIN', SHANE?
MARIO KART! KEEPING IT OLD SCHOOL.
NEXT GAME, YOU'RE ON!
GRAND PRIX?

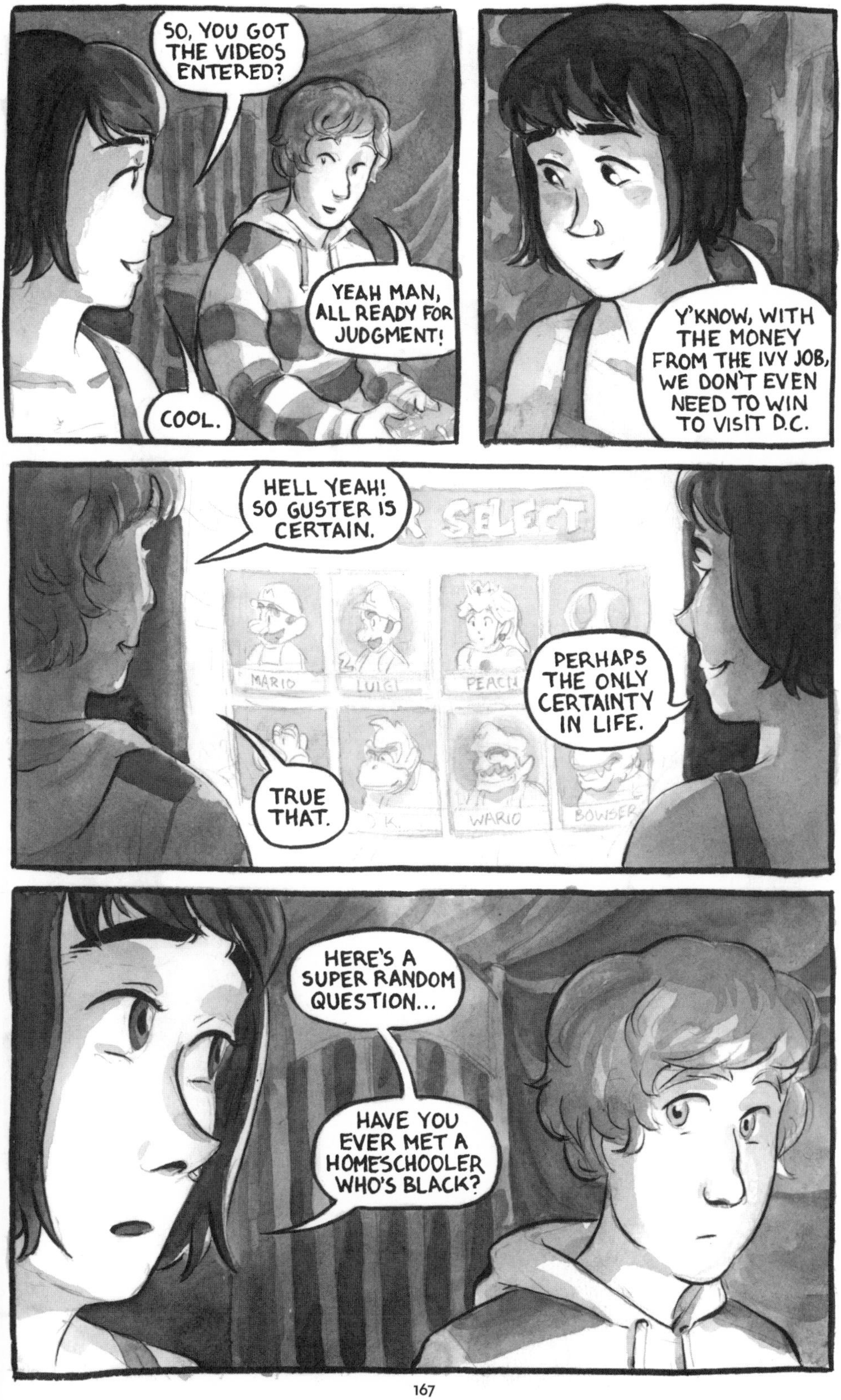
SO, YOU GOT THE VIDEOS ENTERED?
YEAH MAN, ALL READY FOR JUDGMENT!
COOL.
Y'KNOW, WITH THE MONEY FROM THE IVY JOB, WE DON'T EVEN NEED TO WIN TO VISIT D.C.
HELL YEAH! SO GUSTER IS CERTAIN.
R SELECT
MARIO
LUIGI
PEACH
WARIO
BOWSER
PERHAPS THE ONLY CERTAINTY IN LIFE.
TRUE THAT.
HERE'S A SUPER RANDOM QUESTION...
HAVE YOU EVER MET A HOMESCHOOLER WHO'S BLACK?

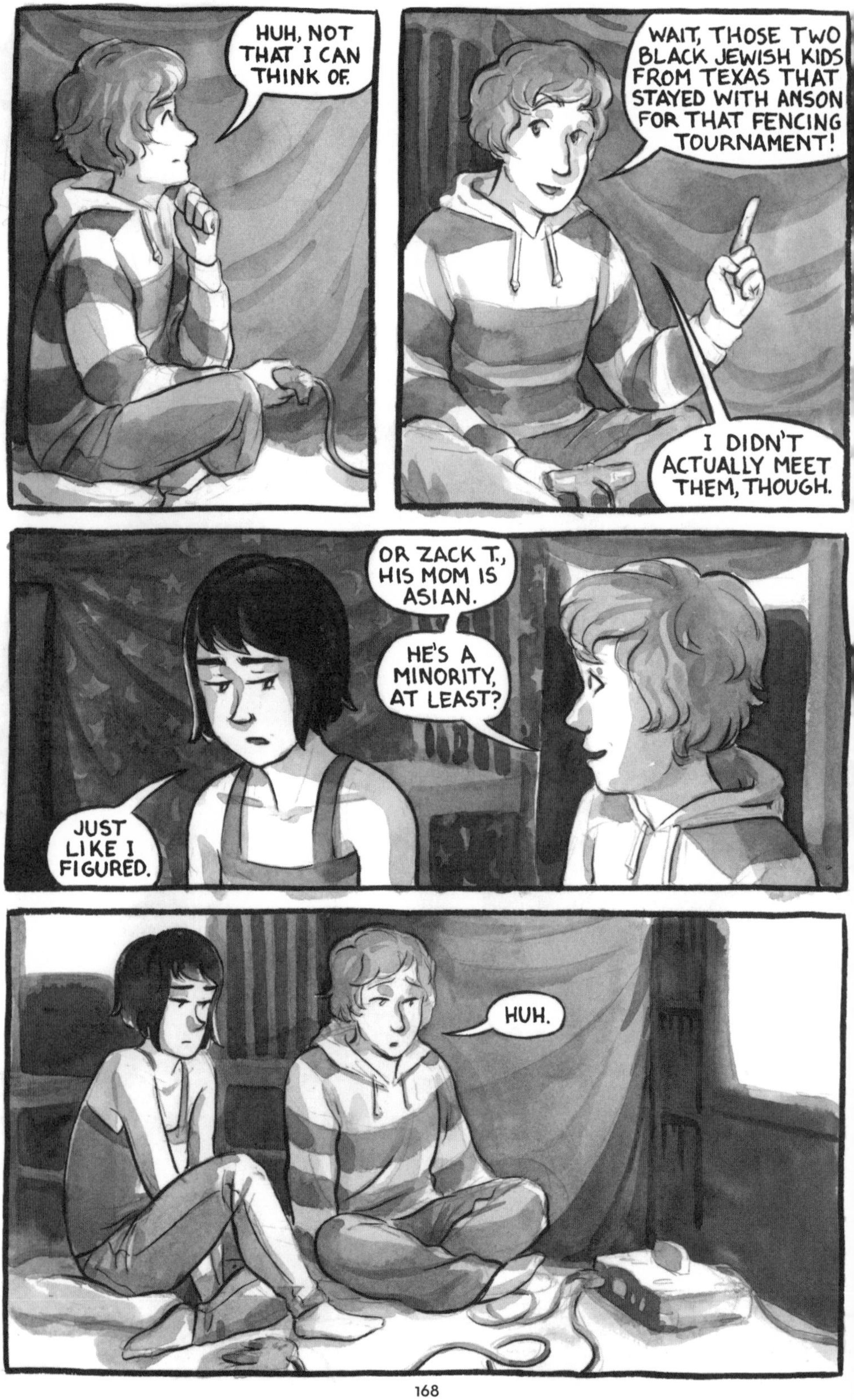
HUH, NOT THAT I CAN THINK OF.
WAIT, THOSE TWO BLACK JEWISH KIDS FROM TEXAS THAT STAYED WITH ANSON FOR THAT FENCING TOURNAMENT!
I DIDN'T ACTUALLY MEET THEM, THOUGH.
OR ZACK T., HIS MOM IS ASIAN.
HE'S A MINORITY, AT LEAST?
JUST LIKE I FIGURED.
HUH.

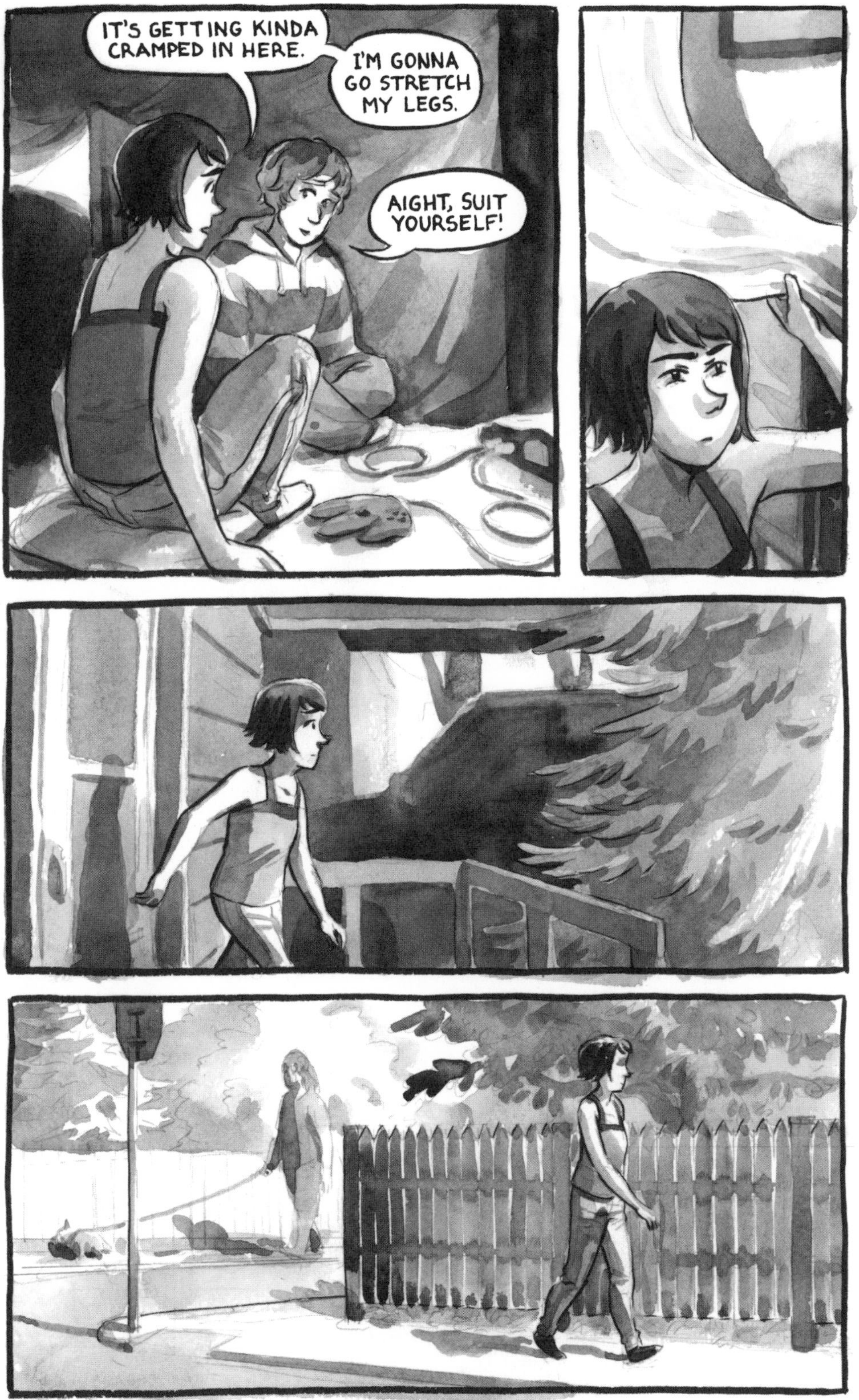
IT'S GETTING KINDA CRAMPED IN HERE.
I'M GONNA GO STRETCH MY LEGS.
AIGHT, SUIT YOURSELF!

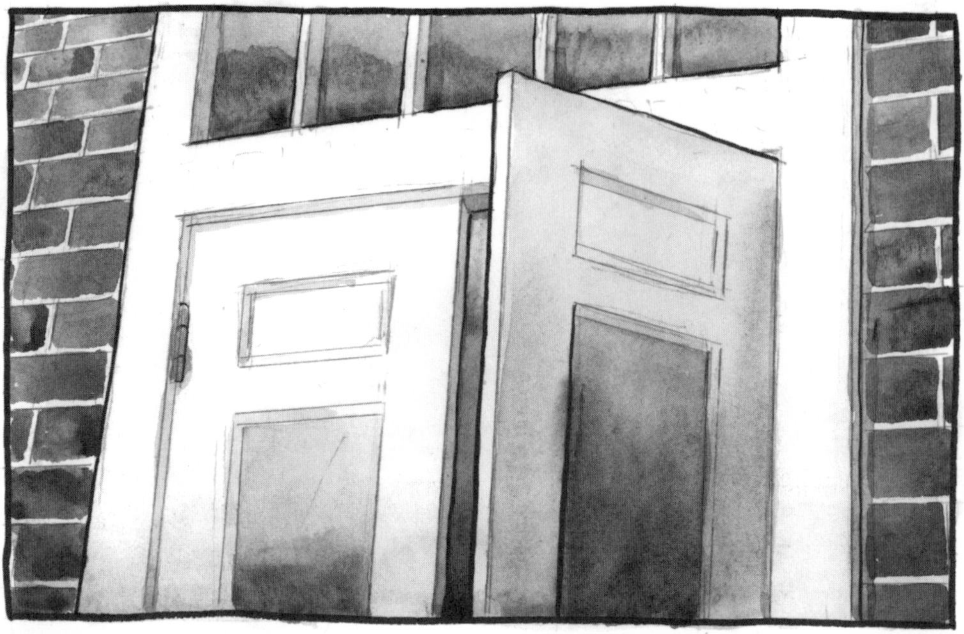

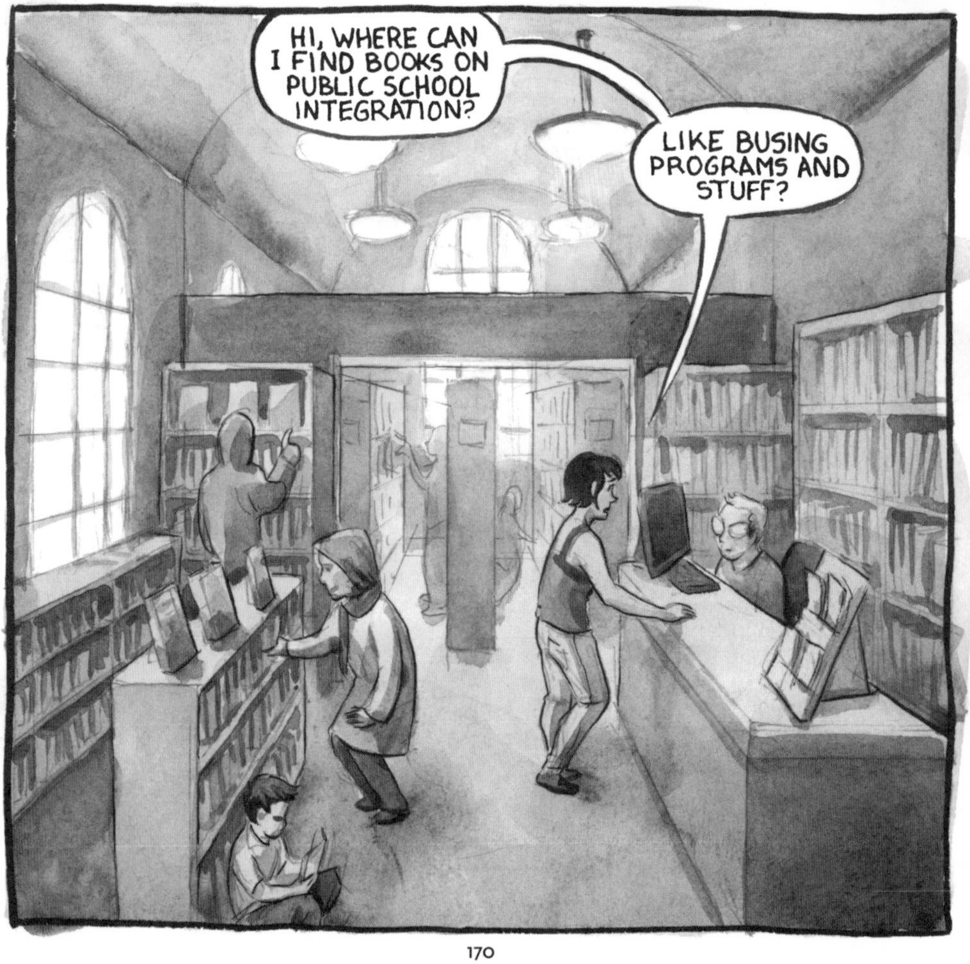
HI, WHERE CAN I FIND BOOKS ON PUBLIC SCHOOL INTEGRATION?
LIKE BUSING PROGRAMS AND STUFF?

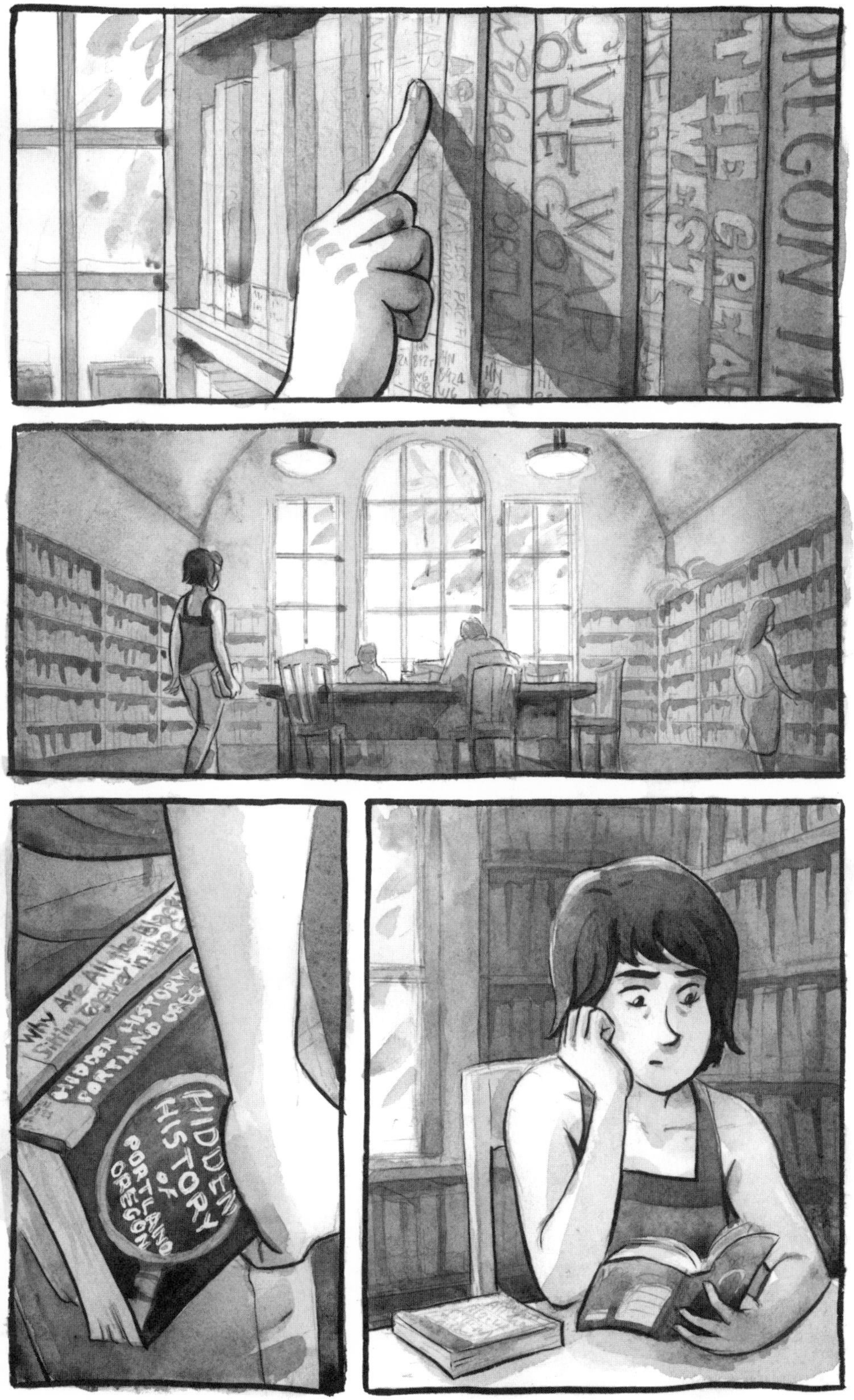
HIDDEN HISTORY OF PORTLAND OREGON

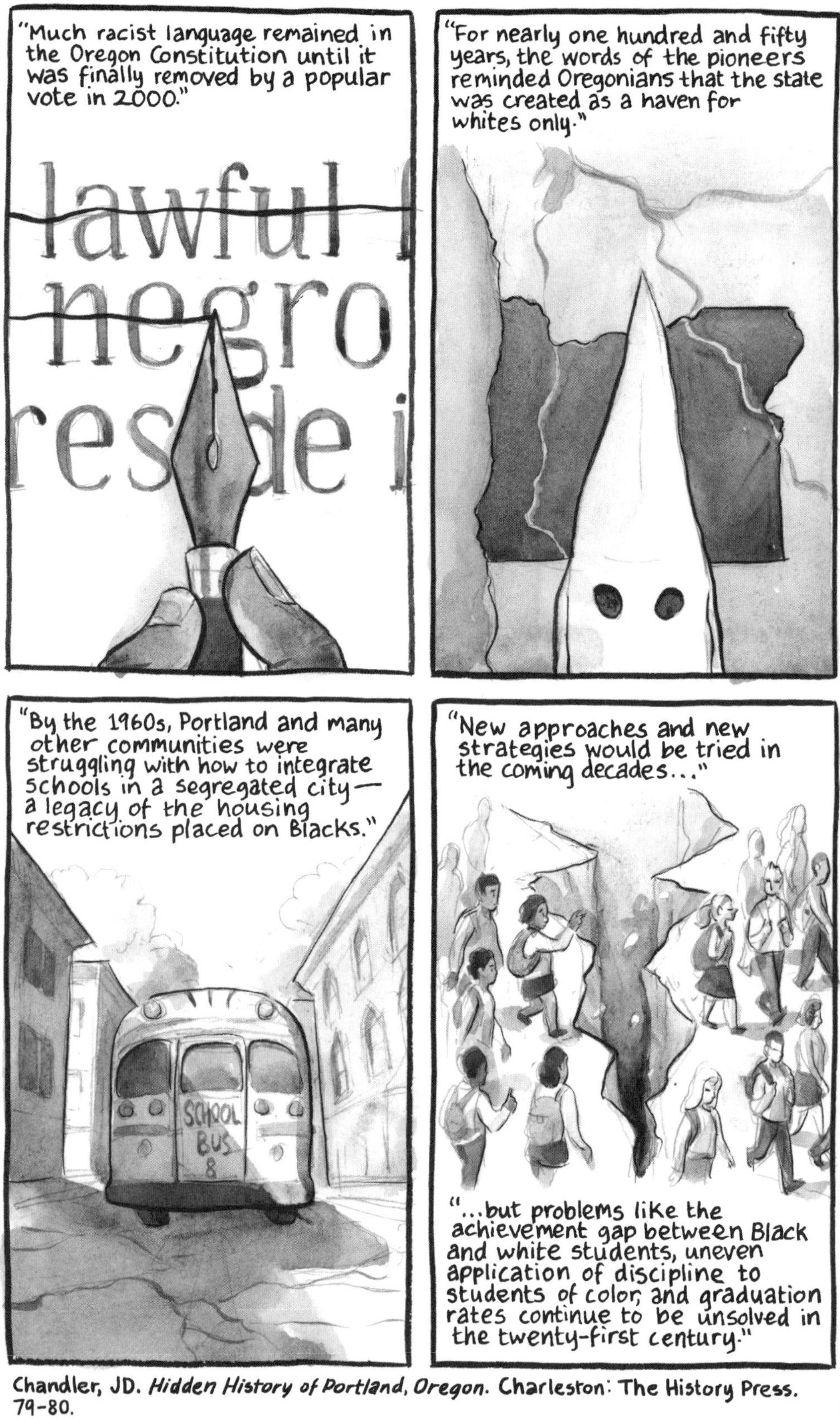
"Much racist language remained in the Oregon Constitution until it was finally removed by a popular vote in 2000."
lawful
negro
reside
"For nearly one hundred and fifty years, the words of the pioneers reminded Oregonians that the state was created as a haven for whites only."
"By the 1960s, Portland and many other communities were struggling with how to integrate schools in a segregated city—a legacy of the housing restrictions placed on Blacks."
SCHOOL BUS 8
"New approaches and new strategies would be tried in the coming decades..."
"...but problems like the achievement gap between Black and white students, uneven application of discipline to students of color, and graduation rates continue to be unsolved in the twenty-first century."

Chandler, JD. *Hidden History of Portland, Oregon*. Charleston: The History Press. 79–80.

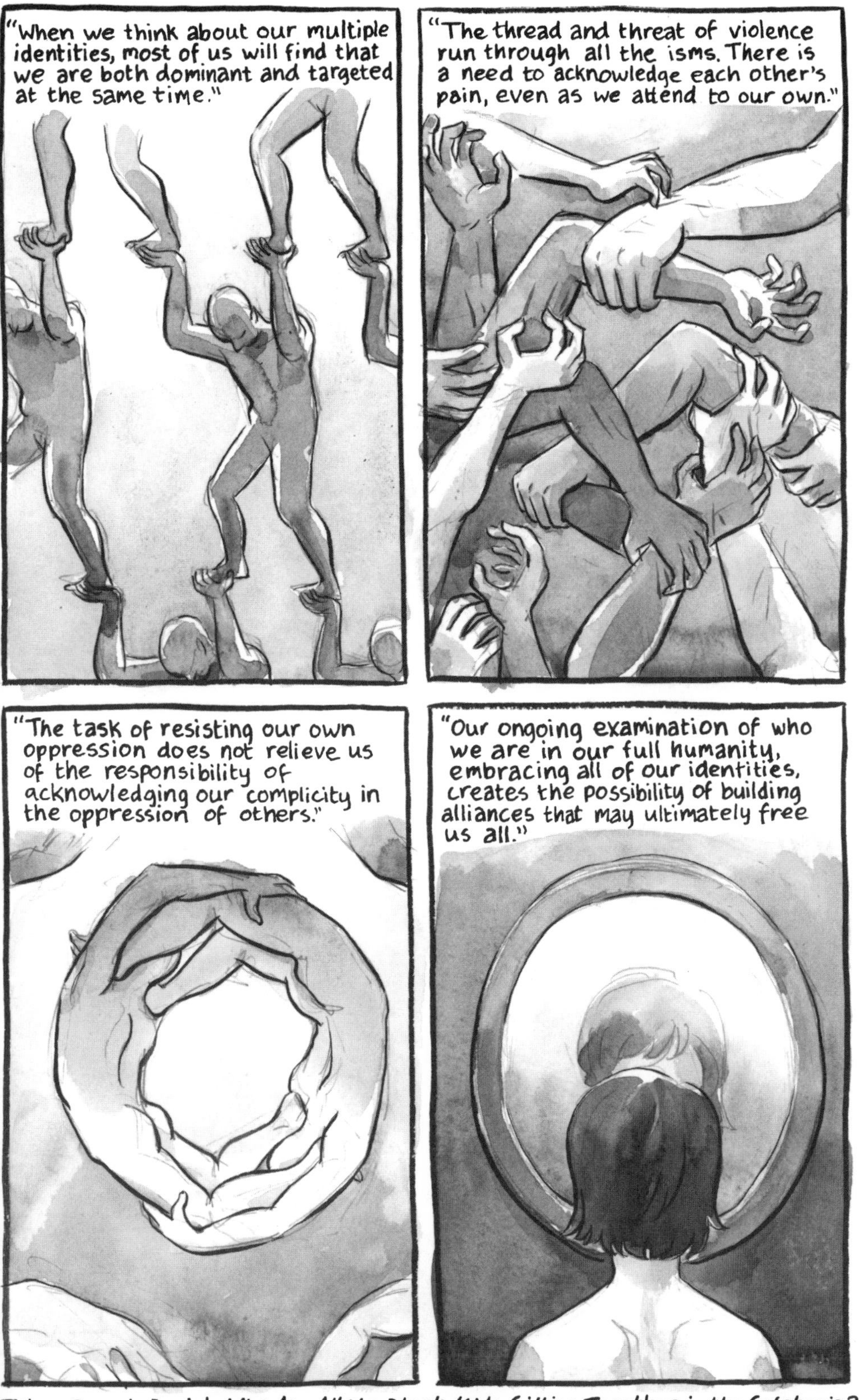

"When we think about our multiple identities, most of us will find that we are both dominant and targeted at the same time."

"The thread and threat of violence run through all the isms. There is a need to acknowledge each other's pain, even as we attend to our own."

"The task of resisting our own oppression does not relieve us of the responsibility of acknowledging our complicity in the oppression of others."

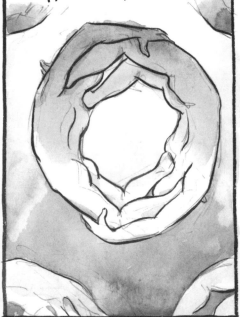

"Our ongoing examination of who we are in our full humanity, embracing all of our identities, creates the possibility of building alliances that may ultimately free us all."

Tatum, Beverly Daniel. *Why Are All the Black Kids Sitting Together in the Cafeteria?: And Other Conversations About Race.* New York: Basic Books. 22-28.

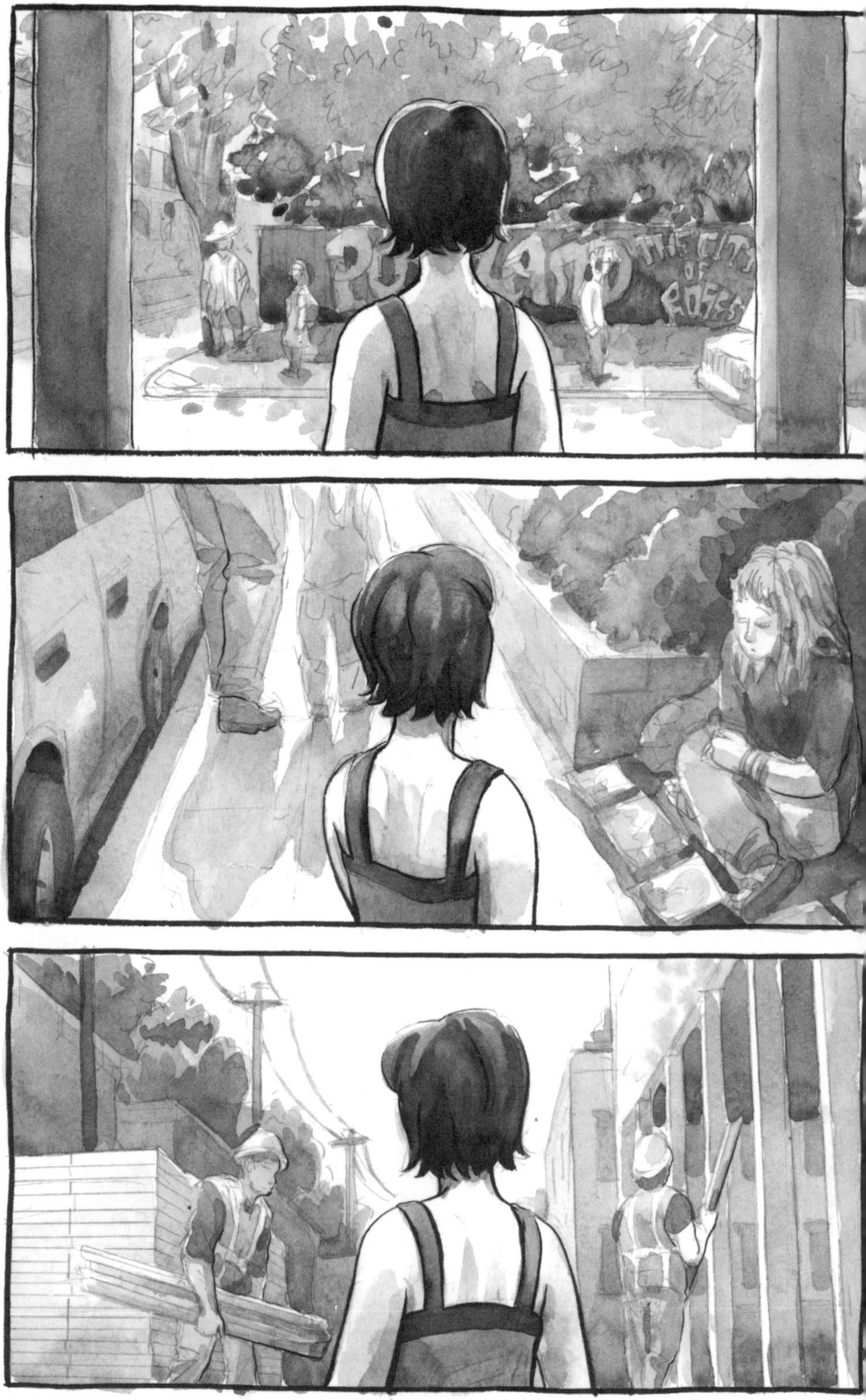
THE CITY OF ROSES

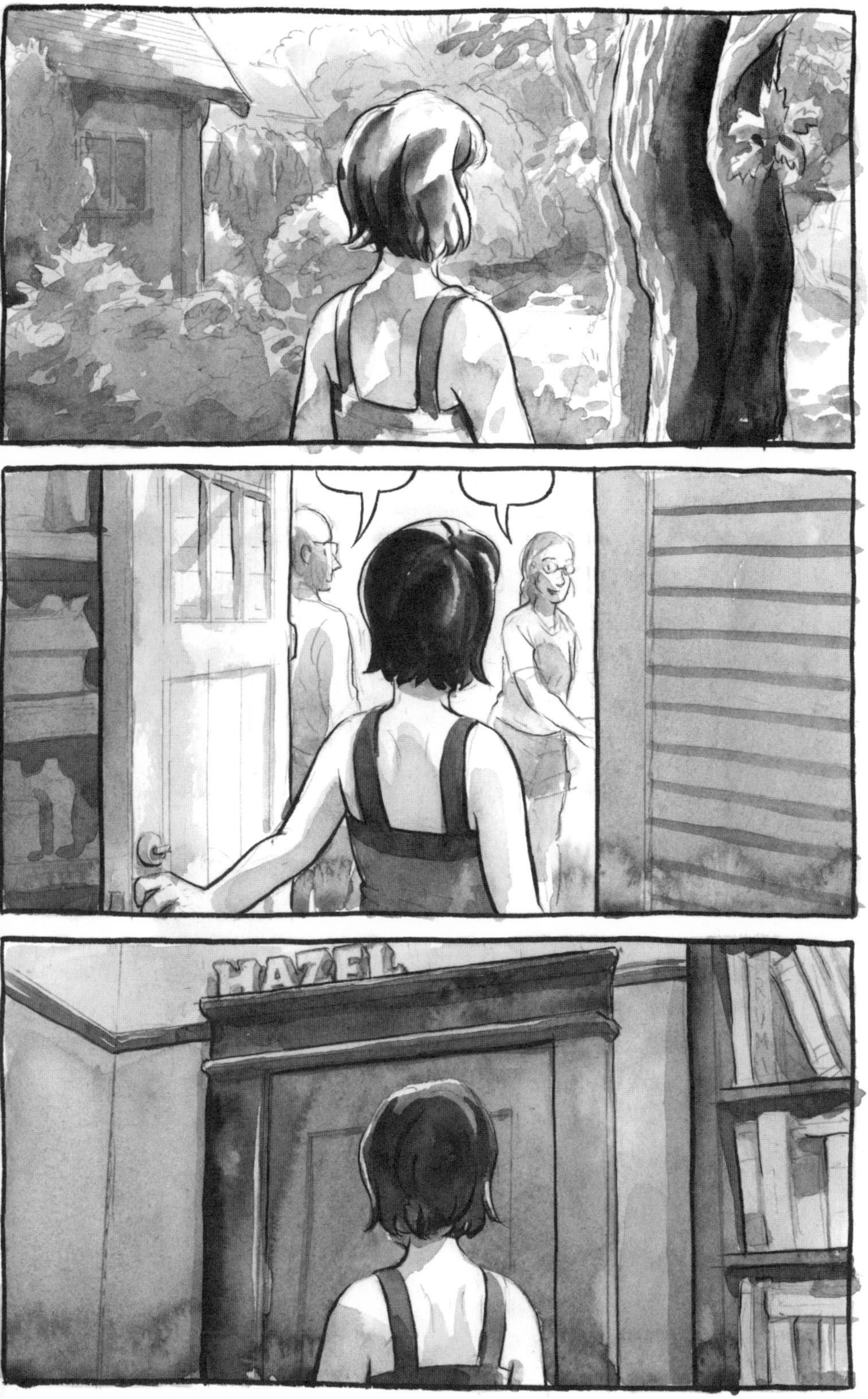
HAZEL
RUMI

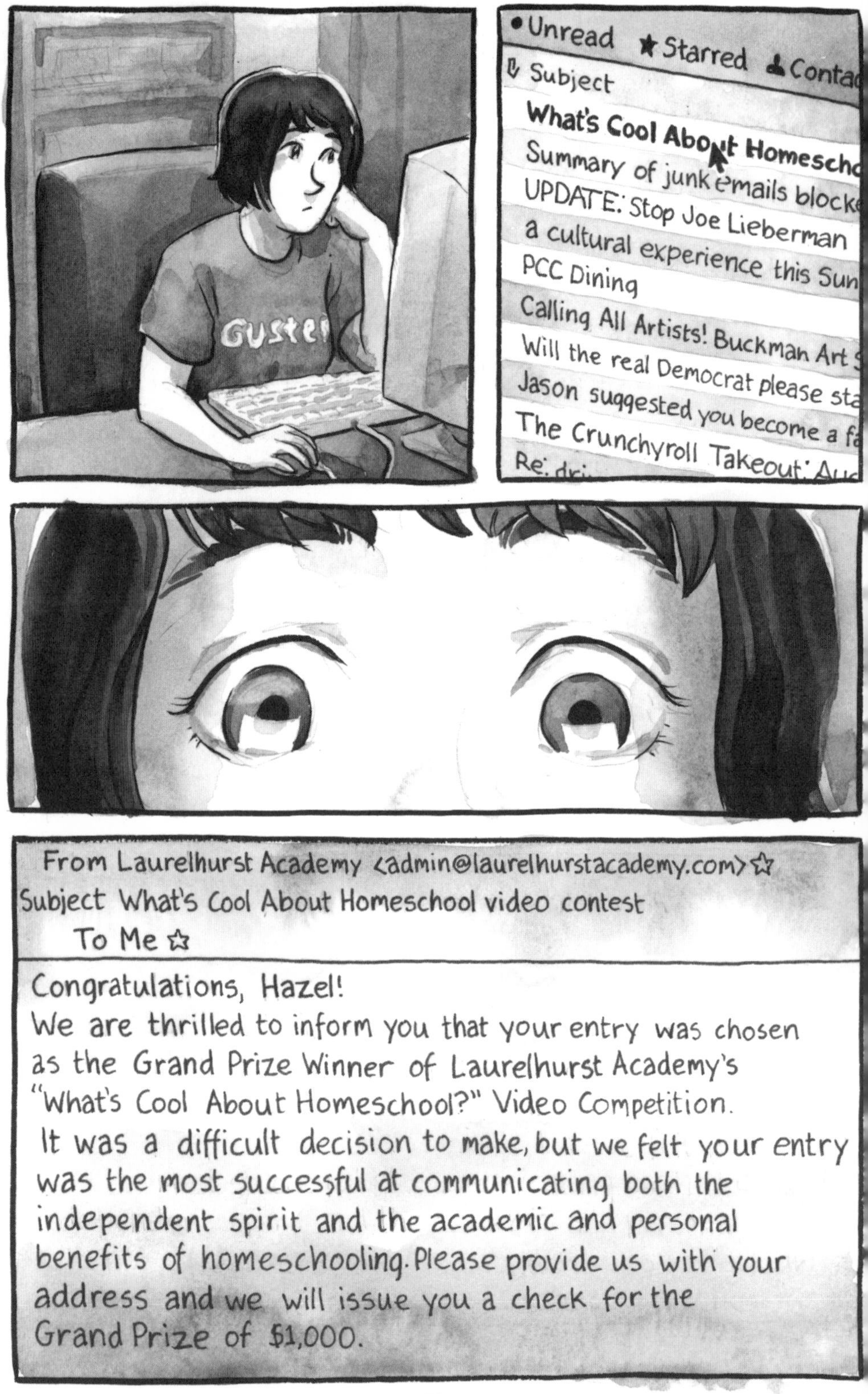
GUSTER
• Unread ★ Starred Contac
Subject
What's Cool About Homeschc
Summary of junk emails block
UPDATE: Stop Joe Lieberman
a cultural experience this Sun
PCC Dining
Calling All Artists! Buckman Art
Will the real Democrat please sta
Jason suggested you become a f
The Crunchyroll Takeout: Au
From Laurelhurst Academy <admin@laurelhurstacademy.com> ☆
Subject What's Cool About Homeschool video contest
To Me ☆
Congratulations, Hazel!
We are thrilled to inform you that your entry was chosen as the Grand Prize Winner of Laurelhurst Academy's "What's Cool About Homeschool?" Video Competition.
It was a difficult decision to make, but we felt your entry was the most successful at communicating both the independent spirit and the academic and personal benefits of homeschooling. Please provide us with your address and we will issue you a check for the Grand Prize of $1,000.

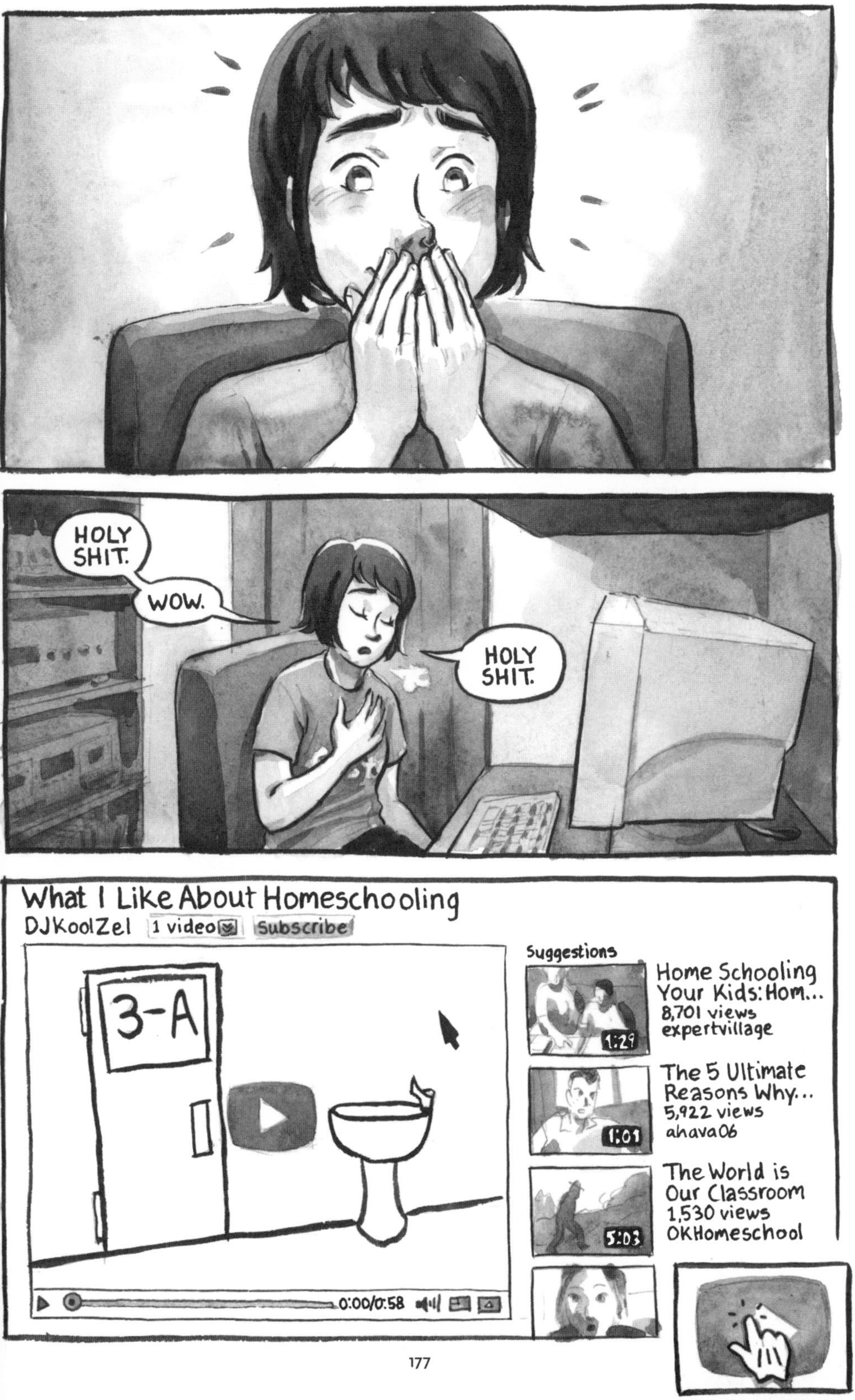
HOLY SHIT.
WOW.
HOLY SHIT.
What I Like About Homeschooling
DJKoolZel
1 video
Subscribe
3-A
0:00/0:58
Suggestions
Home Schooling Your Kids: Hom...
8,701 views
expertvillage
1:29
The 5 Ultimate Reasons Why...
5,922 views
ahava06
1:01
The World is Our Classroom
1,530 views
OKHomeschool
5:03

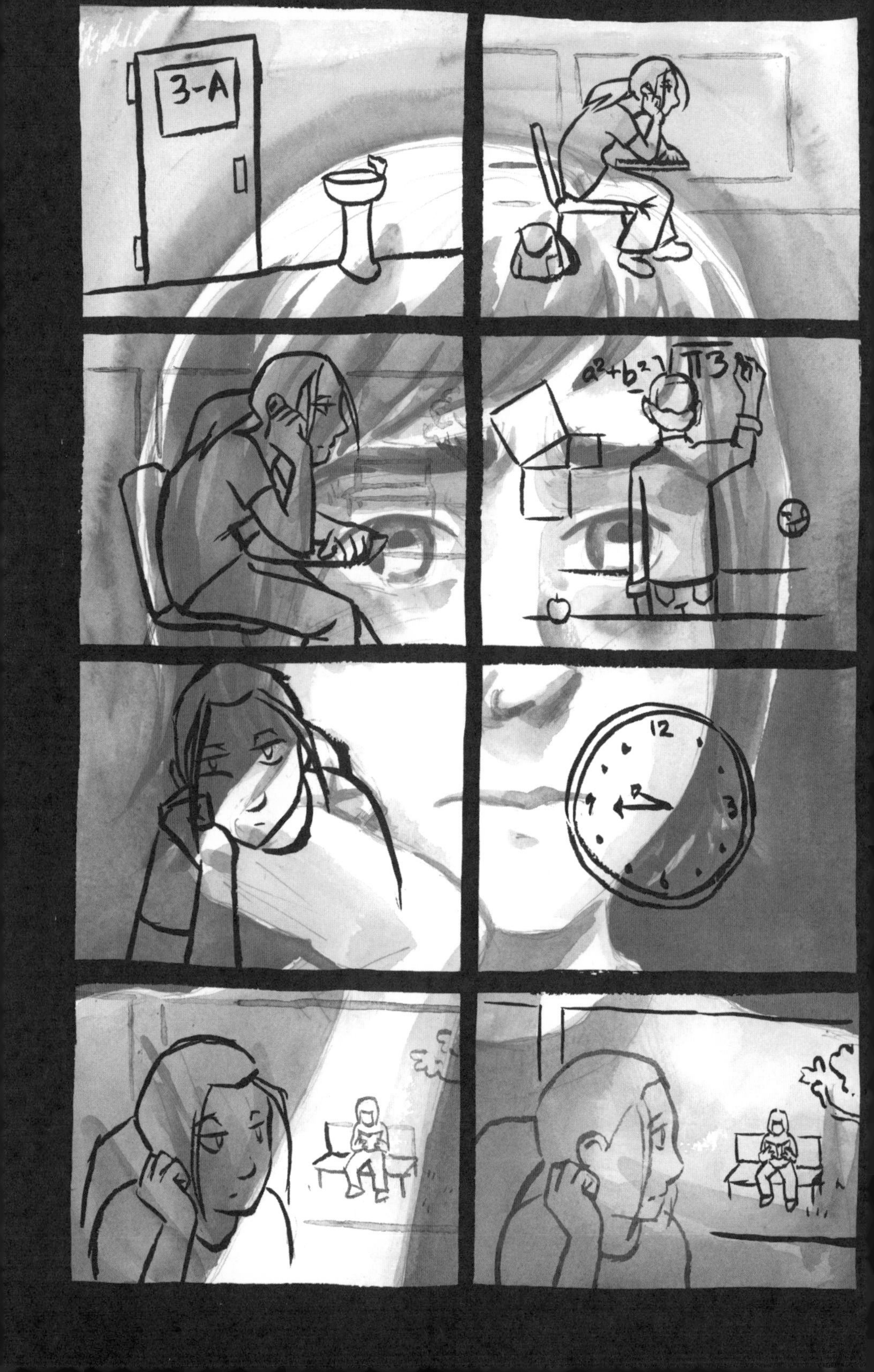
3-A

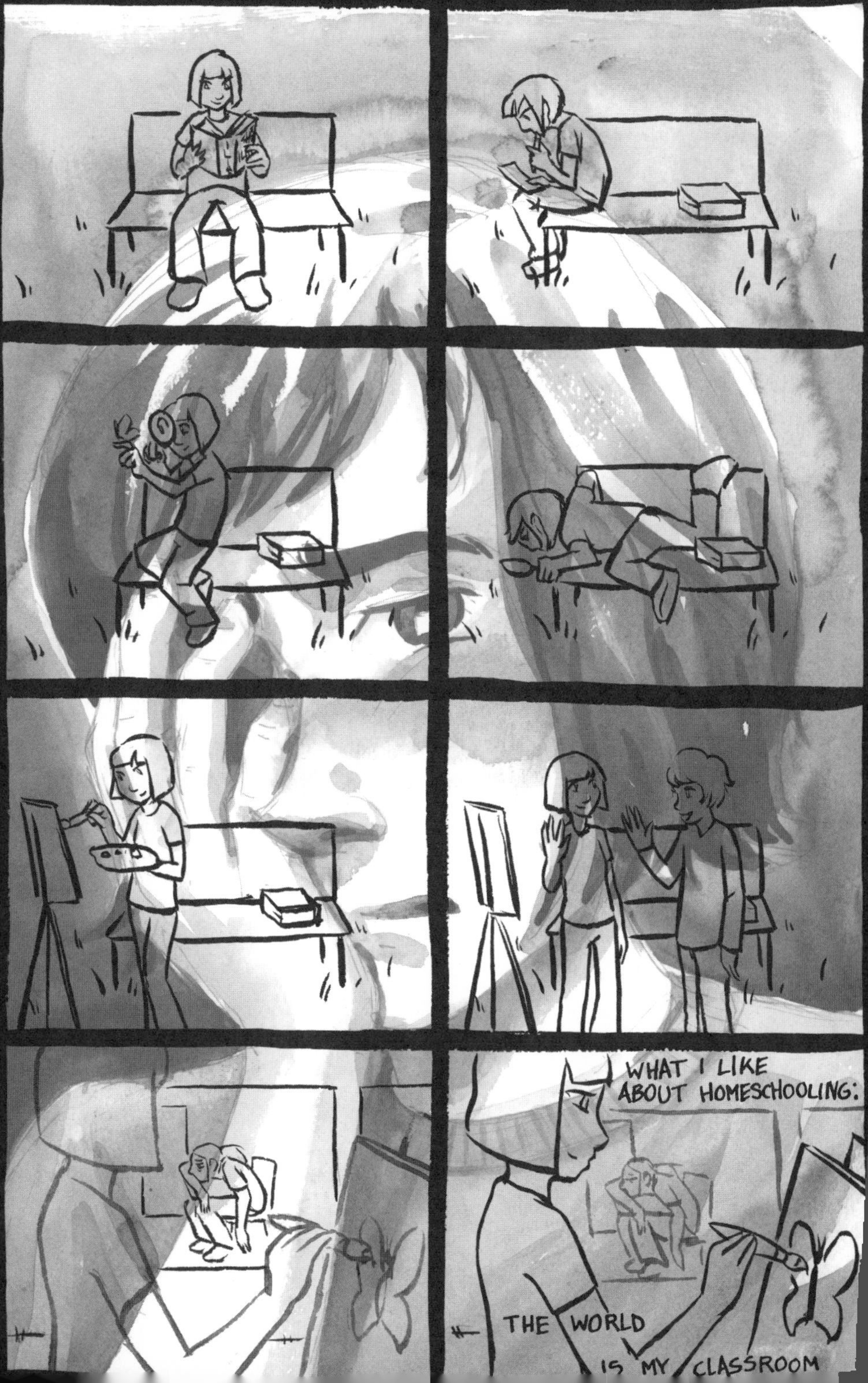
WHAT I LIKE
ABOUT HOMESCHOOLING:
THE WORLD
IS MY CLASSROOM

YIKES. WHAT A BUNCH OF NAÏVE CRAP.

BUT THEY ATE IT UP.

AT LEAST IT LOOKS NICE.

Contest Winners

GRAND PRIZE	HAZEL NEWLEVA
0-8	MADISON PARKE ETHAN COLEMAN SAMANTHA BAIL
9-12	JACOB SCHUES ALEXIS GREENL LAUREN LONG
13-15	JESSICA ANDE ZACHARY MILL BRANDON POW
16-18	AMBER GARCIA RACHEL PHILN

HEY, SHANE?

DUDE, I JUST GOT THE EMAIL!

MY ANIMATION WON THE GRAND PRIZE!

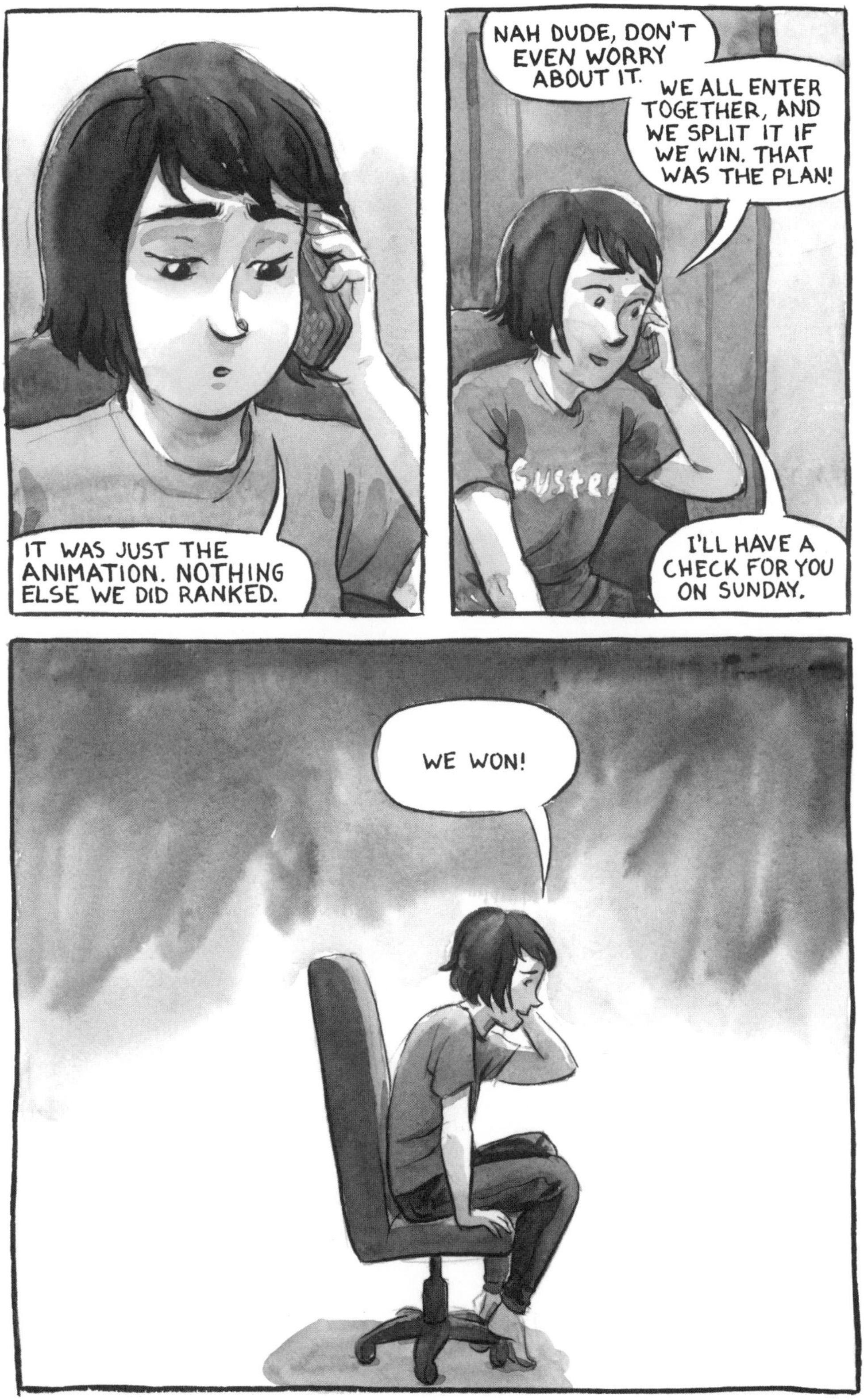
IT WAS JUST THE ANIMATION. NOTHING ELSE WE DID RANKED.
NAH DUDE, DON'T EVEN WORRY ABOUT IT.
WE ALL ENTER TOGETHER, AND WE SPLIT IT IF WE WIN. THAT WAS THE PLAN!
I'LL HAVE A CHECK FOR YOU ON SUNDAY.
WE WON!

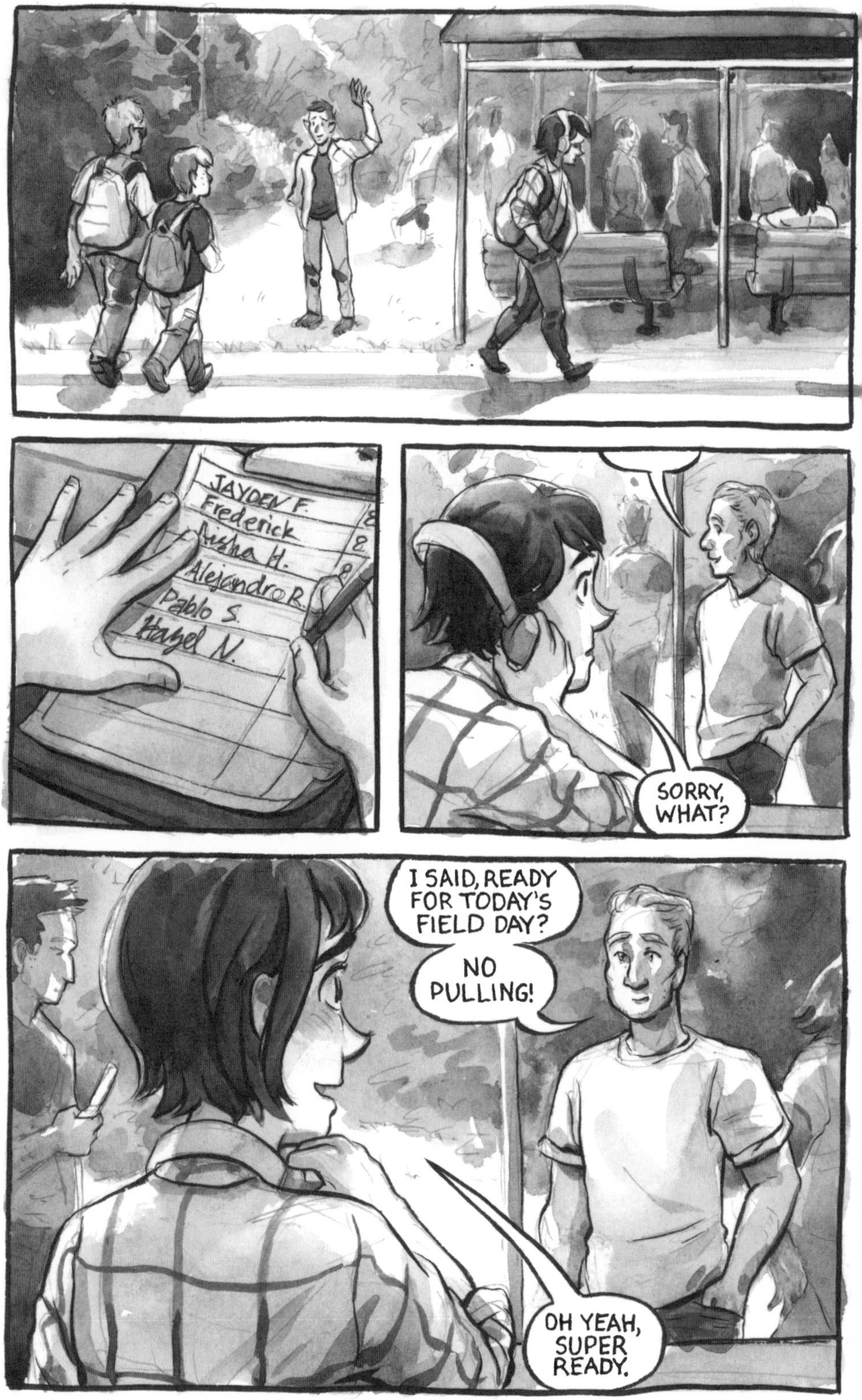
JAYDEN F.
Frederick
Aisha H.
Alejandro R.
Pablo S.
Hazel N.
SORRY, WHAT?
I SAID, READY FOR TODAY'S FIELD DAY?
NO PULLING!
OH YEAH, SUPER READY.

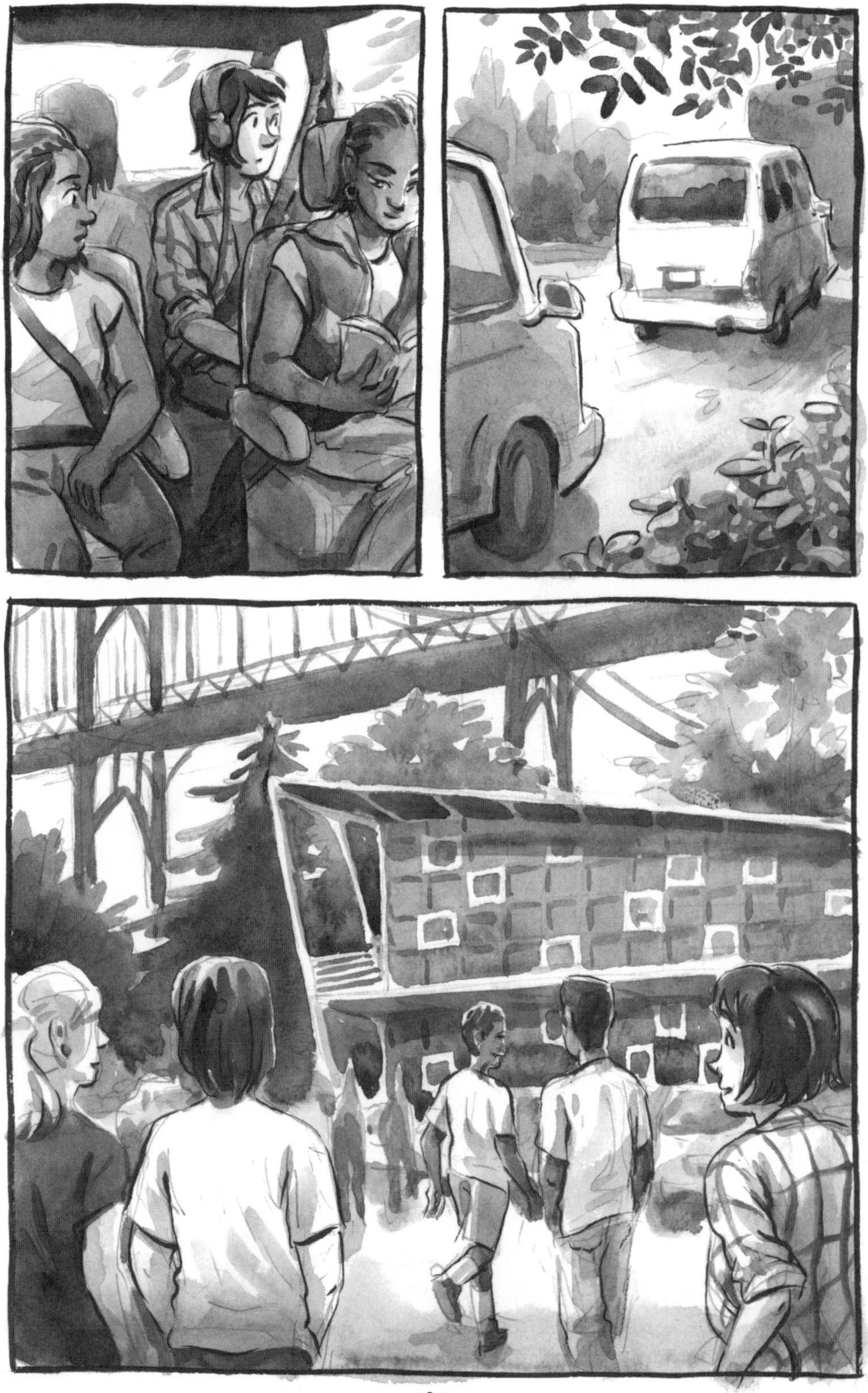

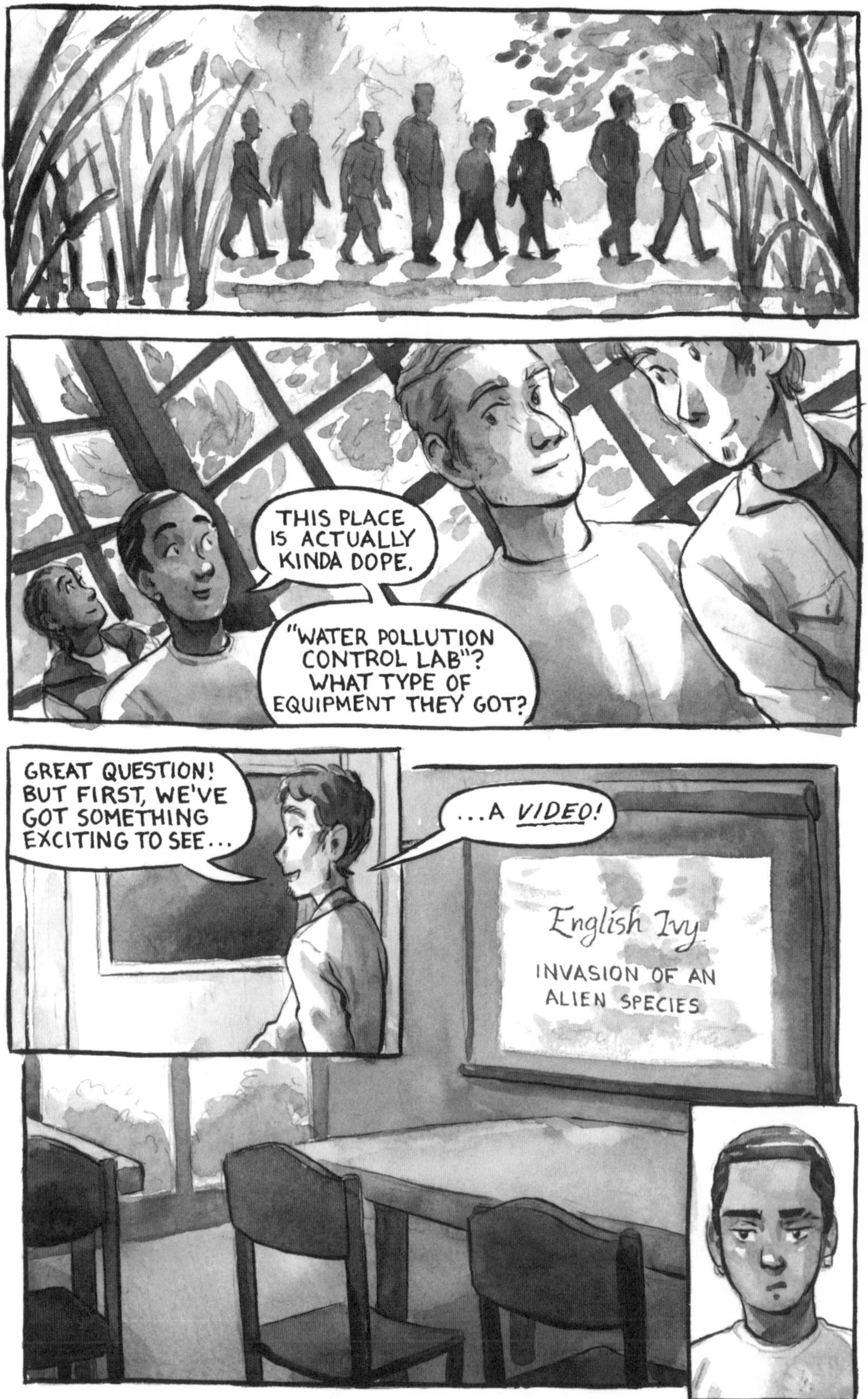
THIS PLACE IS ACTUALLY KINDA DOPE.
"WATER POLLUTION CONTROL LAB"? WHAT TYPE OF EQUIPMENT THEY GOT?
GREAT QUESTION! BUT FIRST, WE'VE GOT SOMETHING EXCITING TO SEE...
...A *VIDEO!*
English Ivy
INVASION OF AN ALIEN SPECIES

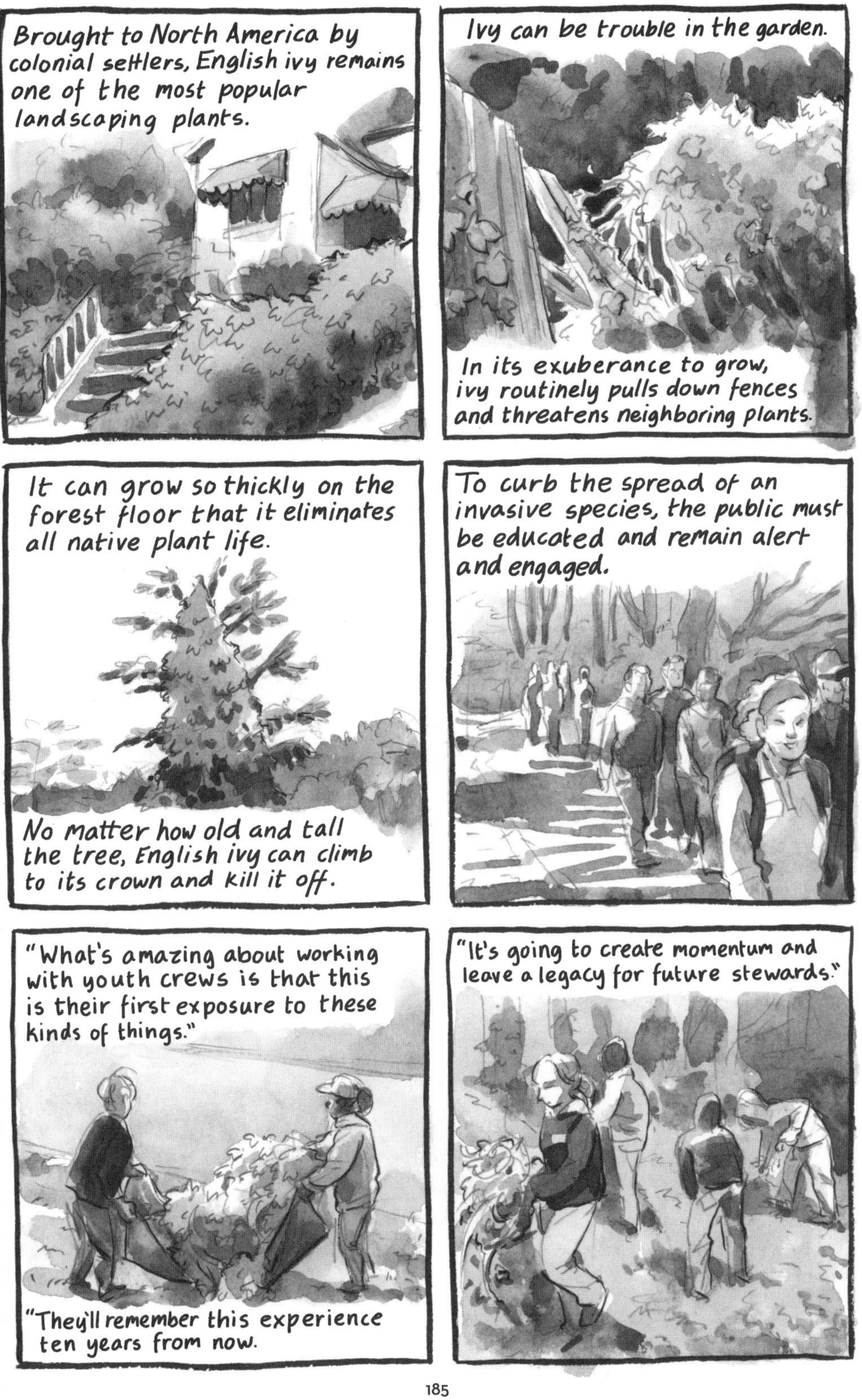
Brought to North America by colonial settlers, English ivy remains one of the most popular landscaping plants.
Ivy can be trouble in the garden.
In its exuberance to grow, ivy routinely pulls down fences and threatens neighboring plants.
It can grow so thickly on the forest floor that it eliminates all native plant life.
No matter how old and tall the tree, English ivy can climb to its crown and kill it off.
To curb the spread of an invasive species, the public must be educated and remain alert and engaged.
"What's amazing about working with youth crews is that this is their first exposure to these kinds of things."
"They'll remember this experience ten years from now.
"It's going to create momentum and leave a legacy for future stewards."

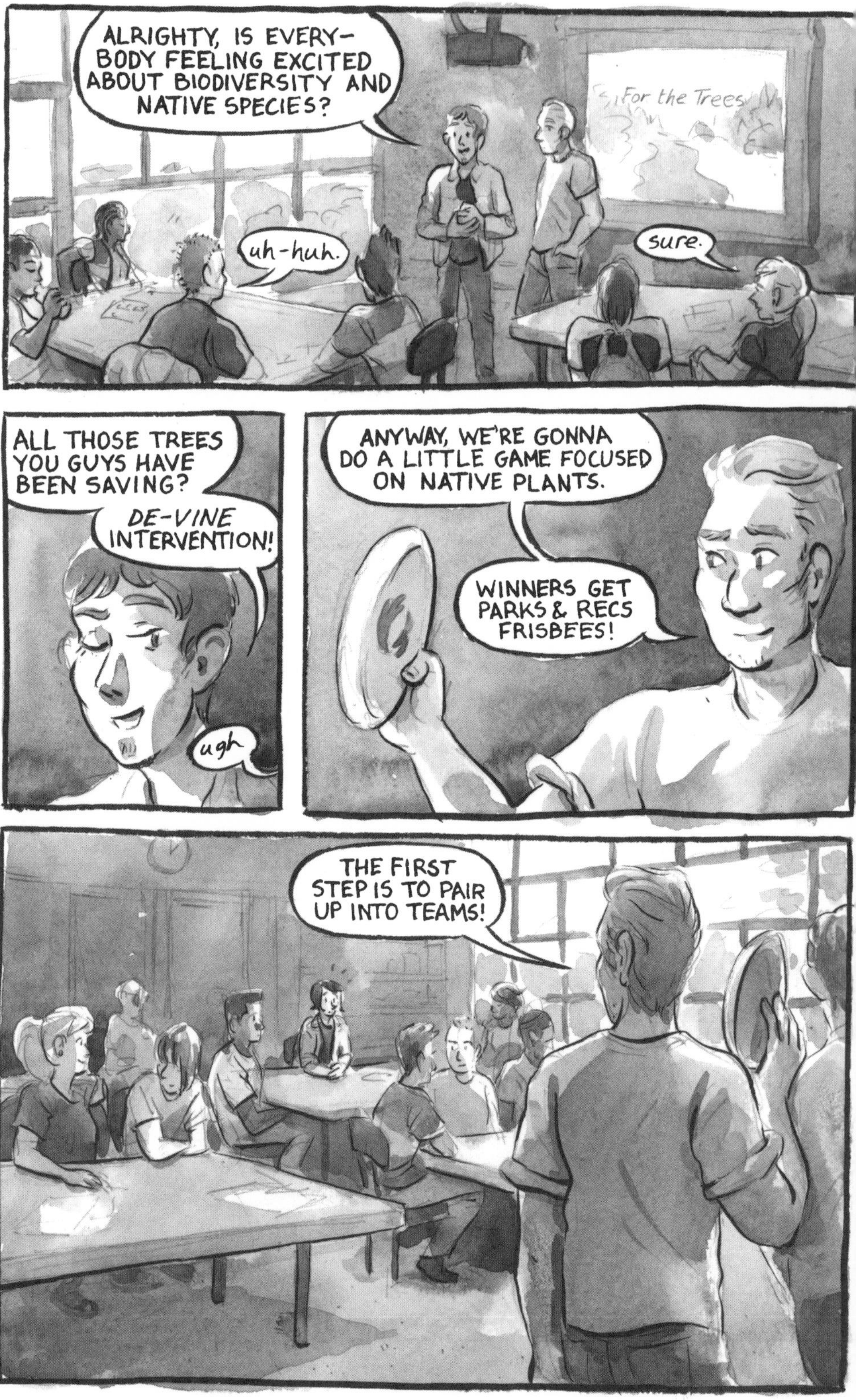
ALRIGHTY, IS EVERY-BODY FEELING EXCITED ABOUT BIODIVERSITY AND NATIVE SPECIES?
For the Trees
uh-huh.
sure.
ALL THOSE TREES YOU GUYS HAVE BEEN SAVING?
DE-VINE INTERVENTION!
ugh
ANYWAY, WE'RE GONNA DO A LITTLE GAME FOCUSED ON NATIVE PLANTS.
WINNERS GET PARKS & RECS FRISBEES!
THE FIRST STEP IS TO PAIR UP INTO TEAMS!

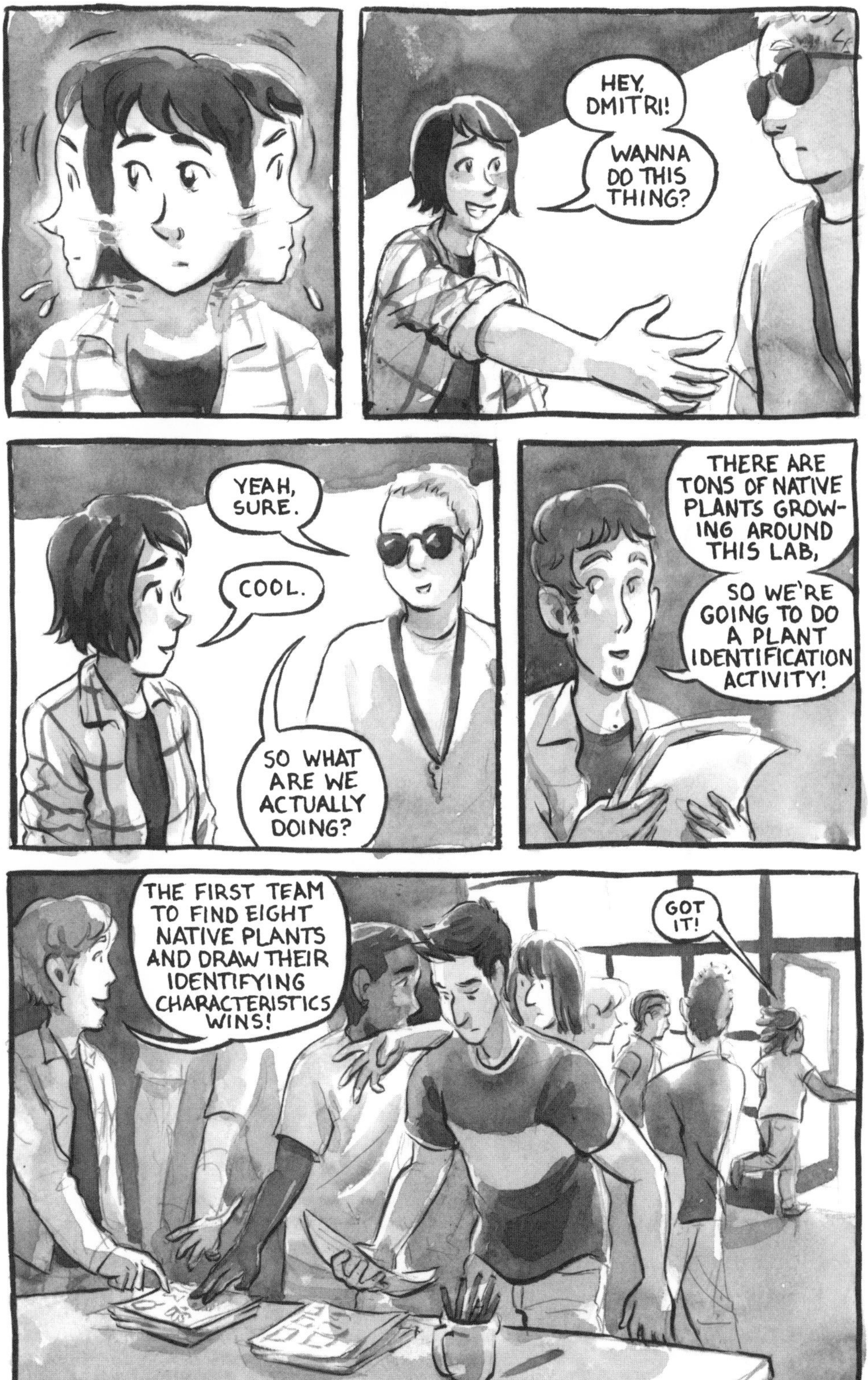
HEY, DMITRI!
WANNA DO THIS THING?
YEAH, SURE.
COOL.
SO WHAT ARE WE ACTUALLY DOING?
THERE ARE TONS OF NATIVE PLANTS GROWING AROUND THIS LAB,
SO WE'RE GOING TO DO A PLANT IDENTIFICATION ACTIVITY!
THE FIRST TEAM TO FIND EIGHT NATIVE PLANTS AND DRAW THEIR IDENTIFYING CHARACTERISTICS WINS!
GOT IT!

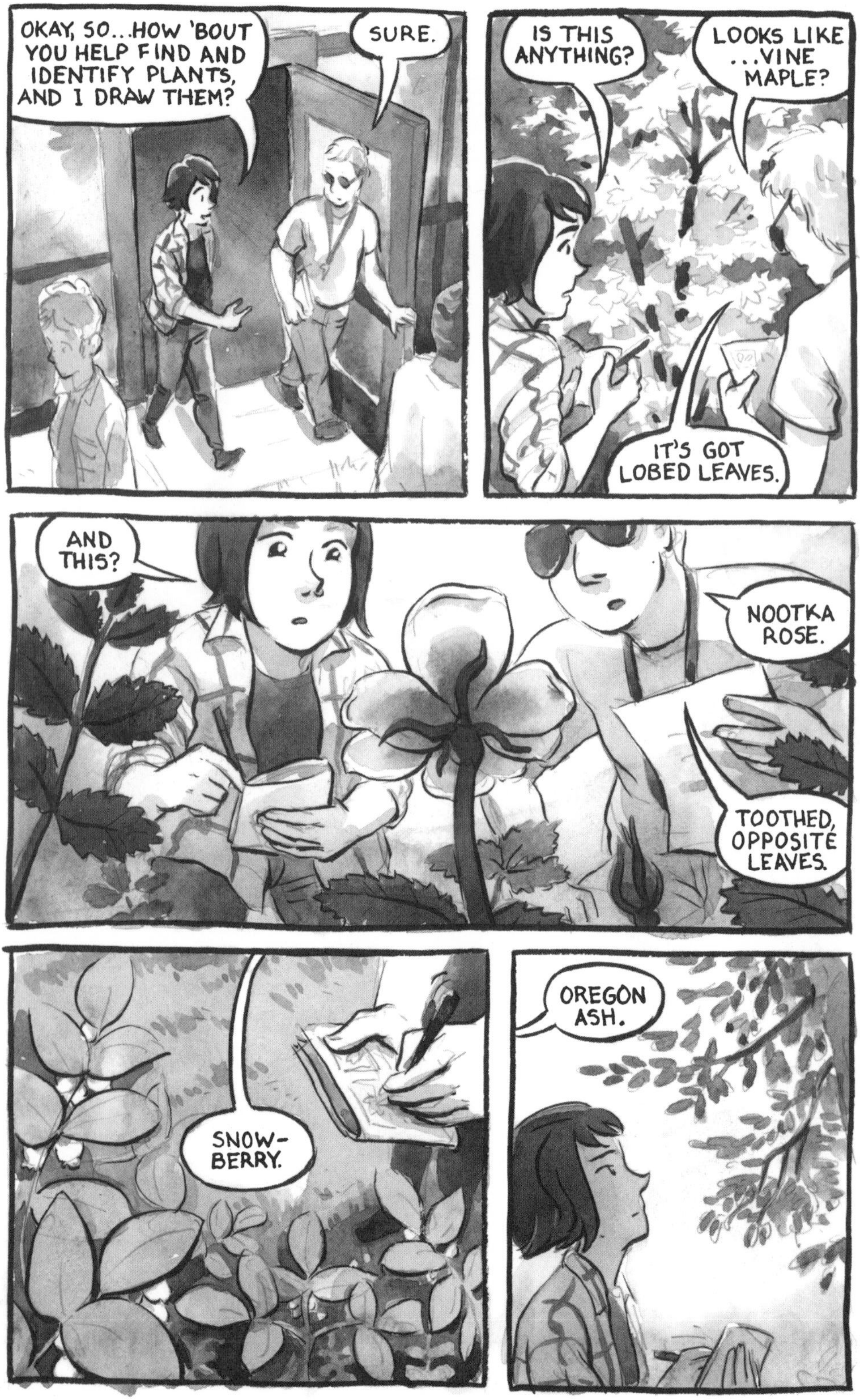
OKAY, SO...HOW 'BOUT YOU HELP FIND AND IDENTIFY PLANTS, AND I DRAW THEM?
SURE.
IS THIS ANYTHING?
LOOKS LIKE ...VINE MAPLE?
IT'S GOT LOBED LEAVES.
AND THIS?
NOOTKA ROSE.
TOOTHED, OPPOSITE LEAVES.
SNOW-BERRY.
OREGON ASH.

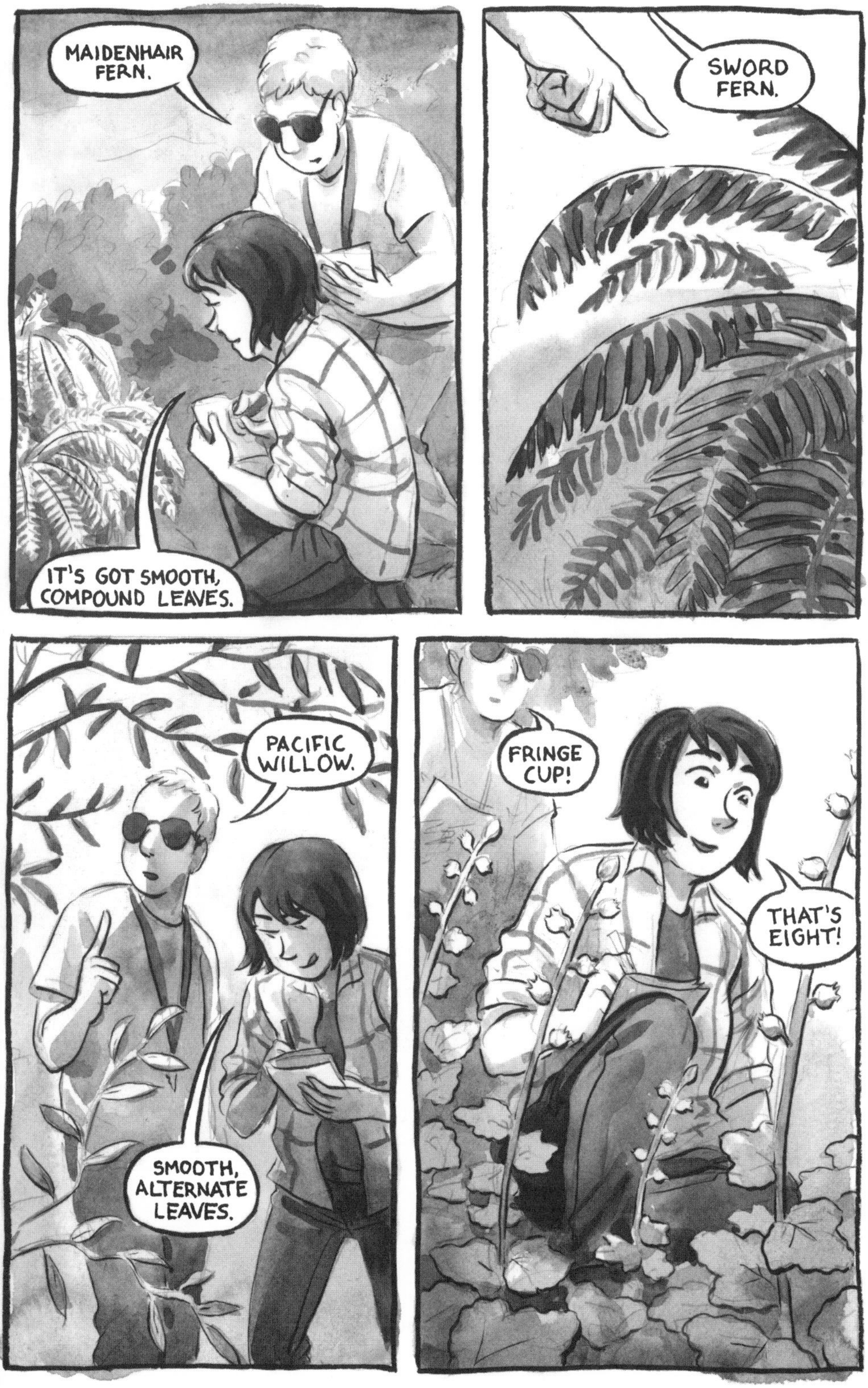
MAIDENHAIR FERN.
IT'S GOT SMOOTH, COMPOUND LEAVES.
SWORD FERN.
PACIFIC WILLOW.
SMOOTH, ALTERNATE LEAVES.
FRINGE CUP!
THAT'S EIGHT!

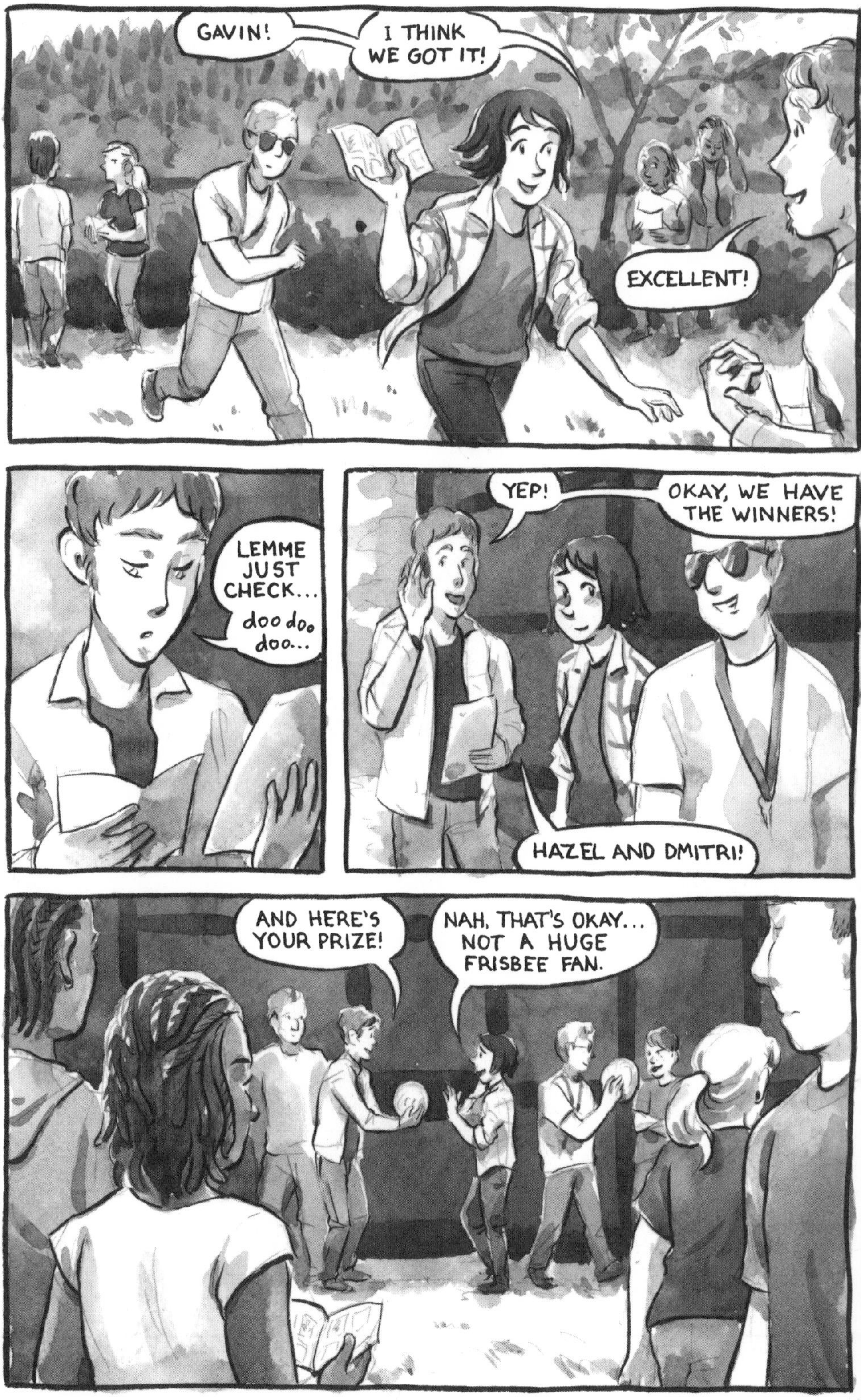
GAVIN!
I THINK WE GOT IT!
EXCELLENT!
LEMME JUST CHECK... doo doo doo...
YEP!
OKAY, WE HAVE THE WINNERS!
HAZEL AND DMITRI!
AND HERE'S YOUR PRIZE!
NAH, THAT'S OKAY... NOT A HUGE FRISBEE FAN.

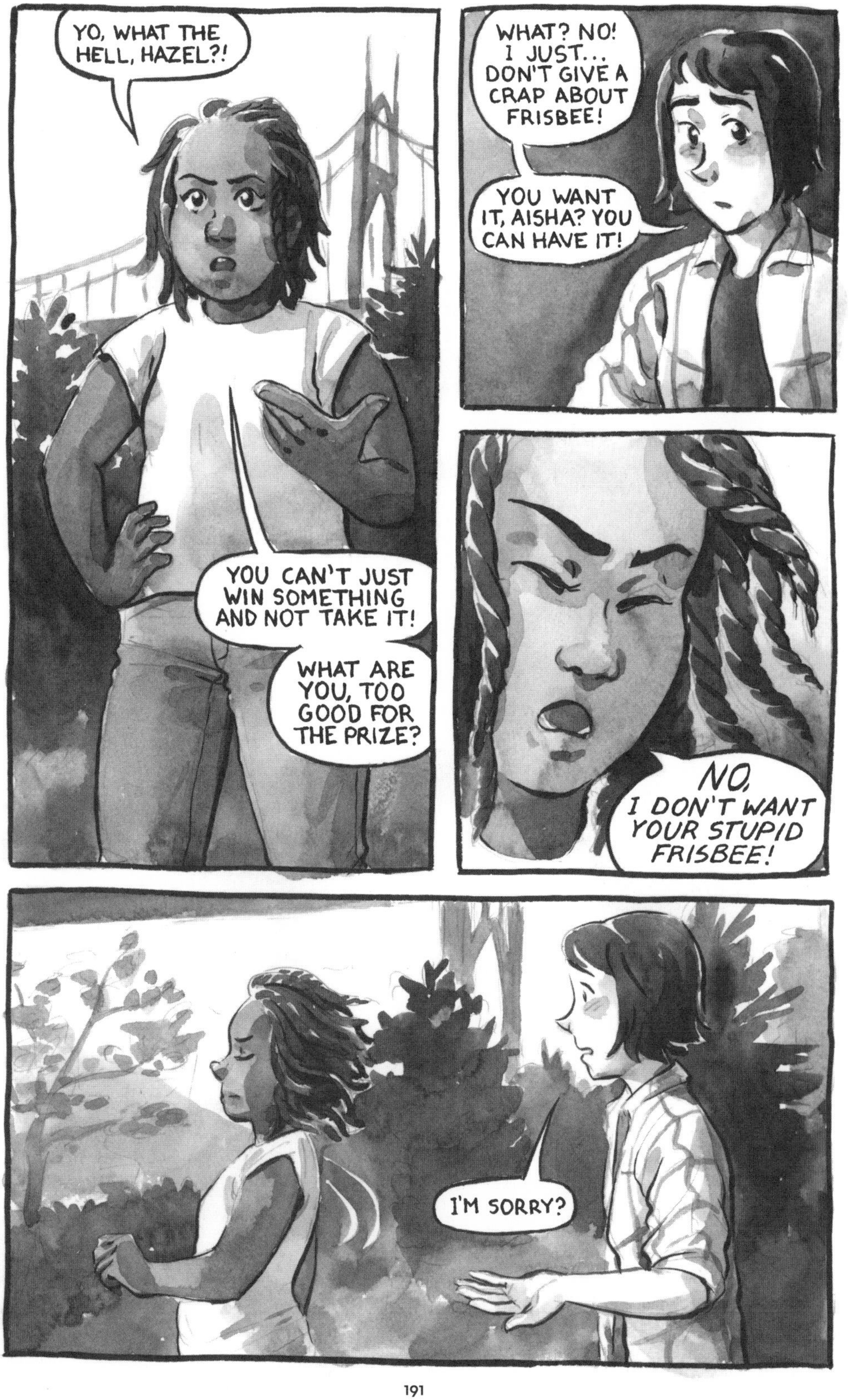
YO, WHAT THE HELL, HAZEL?!
YOU CAN'T JUST WIN SOMETHING AND NOT TAKE IT!
WHAT ARE YOU, TOO GOOD FOR THE PRIZE?
WHAT? NO! I JUST... DON'T GIVE A CRAP ABOUT FRISBEE!
YOU WANT IT, AISHA? YOU CAN HAVE IT!
NO, I DON'T WANT YOUR STUPID FRISBEE!
I'M SORRY?

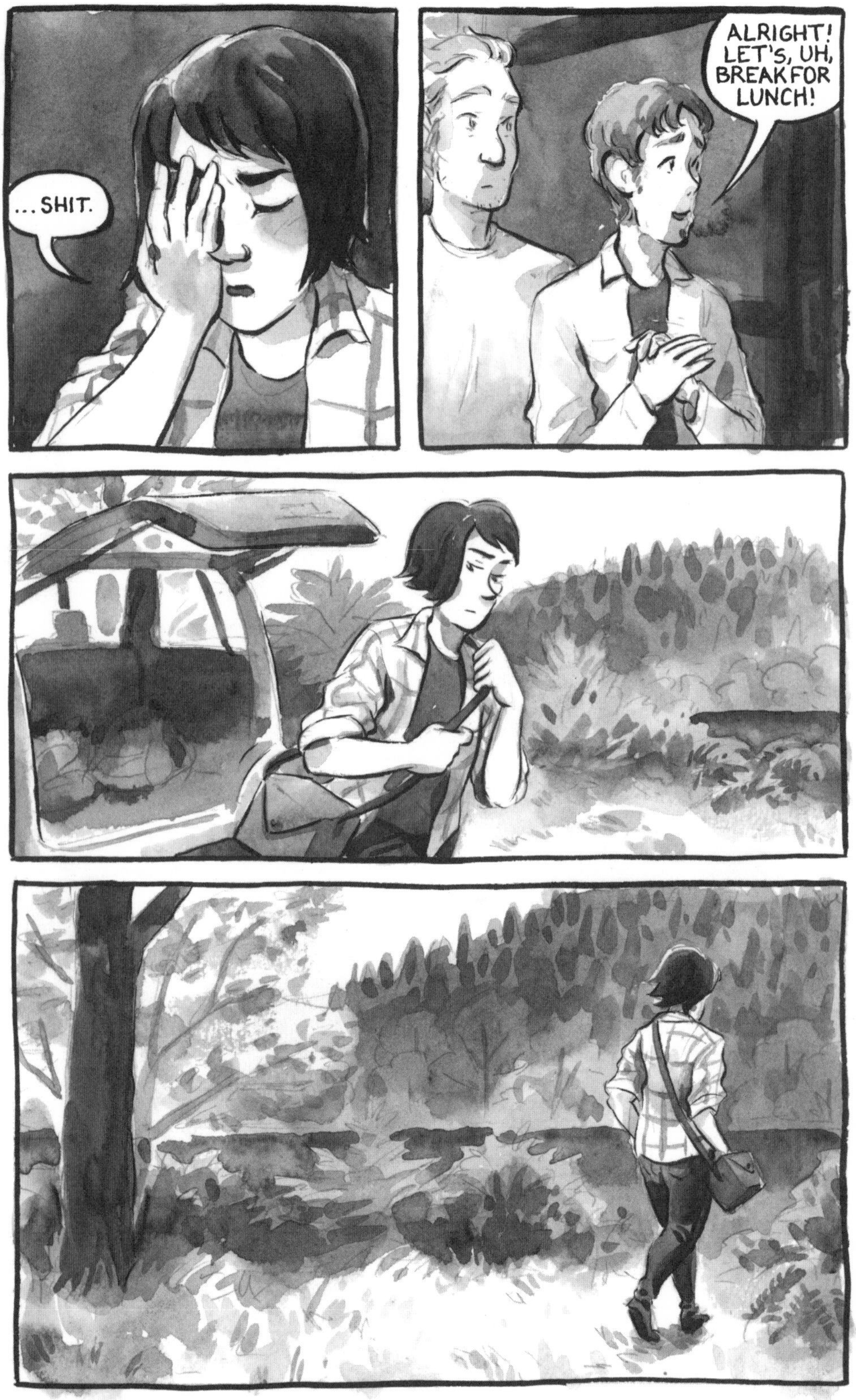
...SHIT.
ALRIGHT! LET'S, UH, BREAK FOR LUNCH!

HEY.

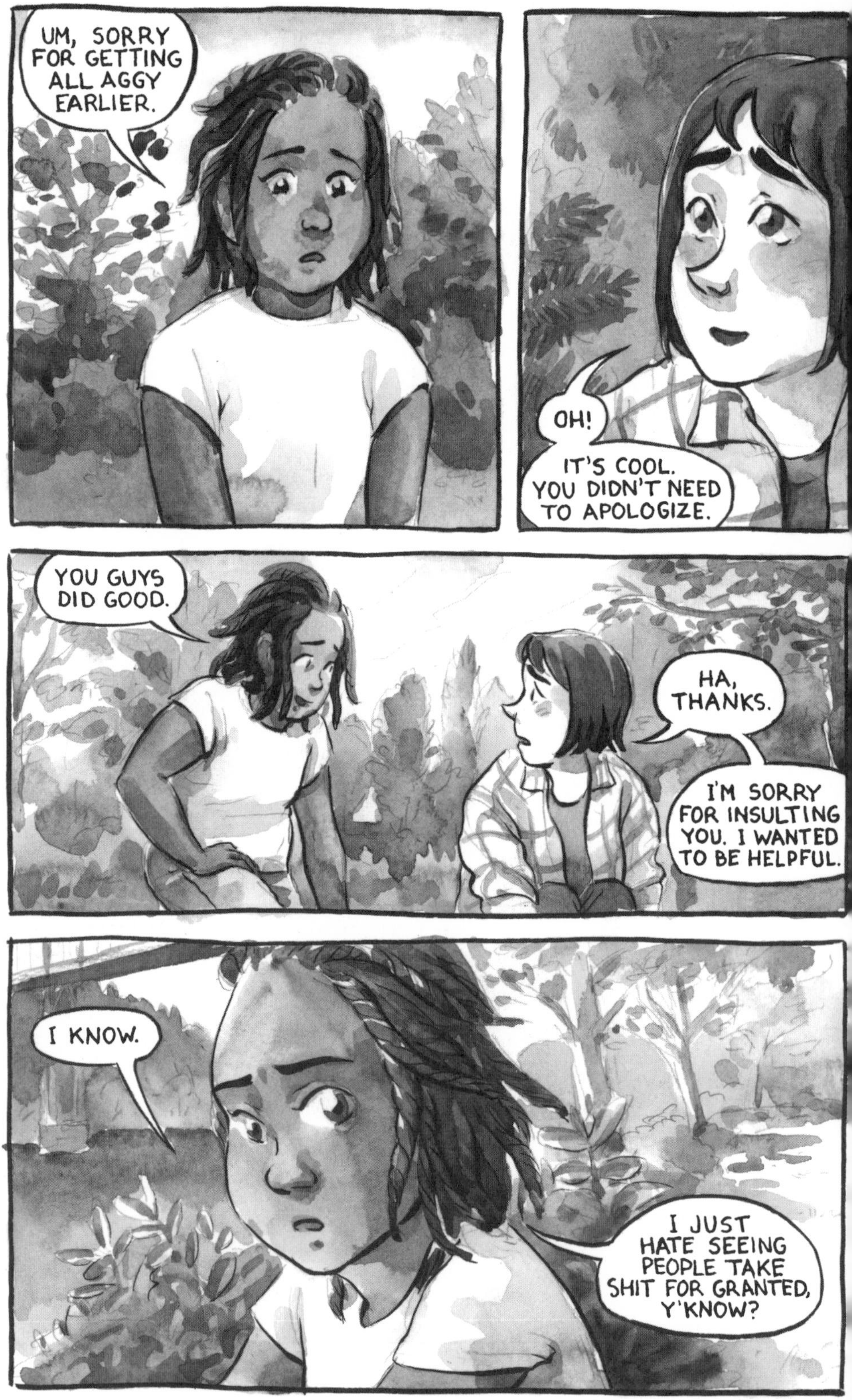
UM, SORRY FOR GETTING ALL AGGY EARLIER.
OH!
IT'S COOL. YOU DIDN'T NEED TO APOLOGIZE.
YOU GUYS DID GOOD.
HA, THANKS.
I'M SORRY FOR INSULTING YOU. I WANTED TO BE HELPFUL.
I KNOW.
I JUST HATE SEEING PEOPLE TAKE SHIT FOR GRANTED, Y'KNOW?

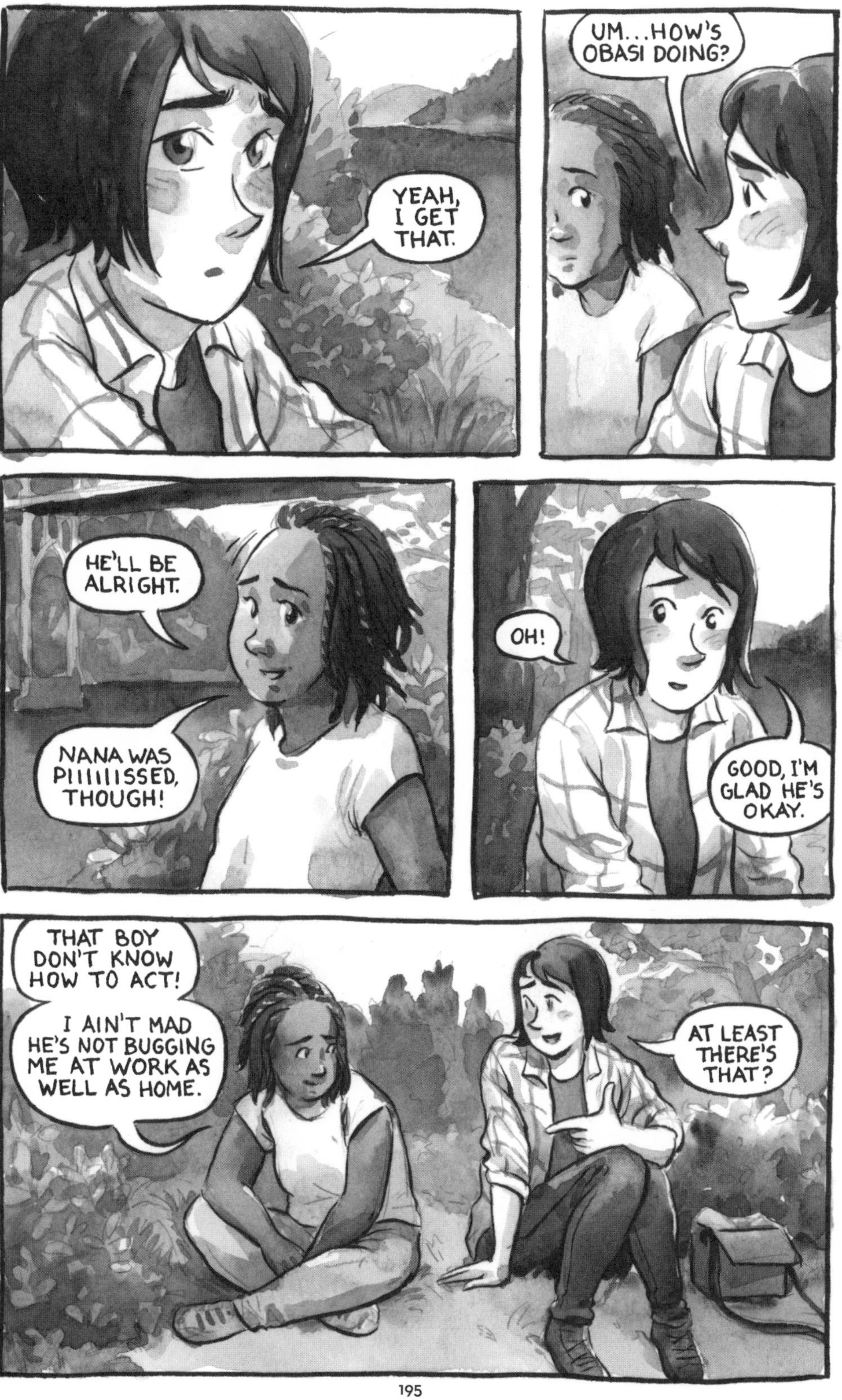
YEAH, I GET THAT.
UM...HOW'S OBASI DOING?
HE'LL BE ALRIGHT.
NANA WAS PIIIIIISSED, THOUGH!
OH!
GOOD, I'M GLAD HE'S OKAY.
THAT BOY DON'T KNOW HOW TO ACT!
I AIN'T MAD HE'S NOT BUGGING ME AT WORK AS WELL AS HOME.
AT LEAST THERE'S THAT?

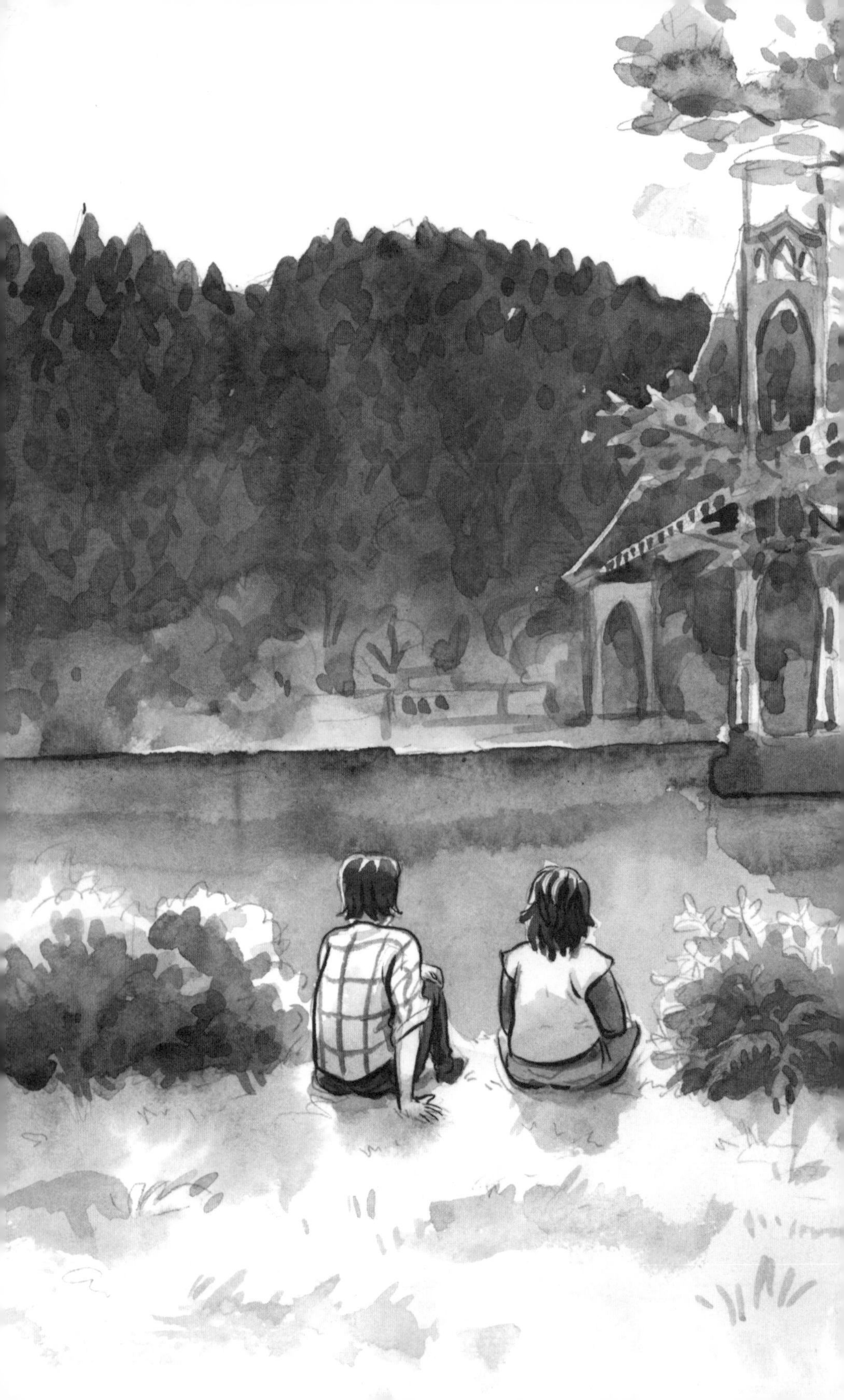

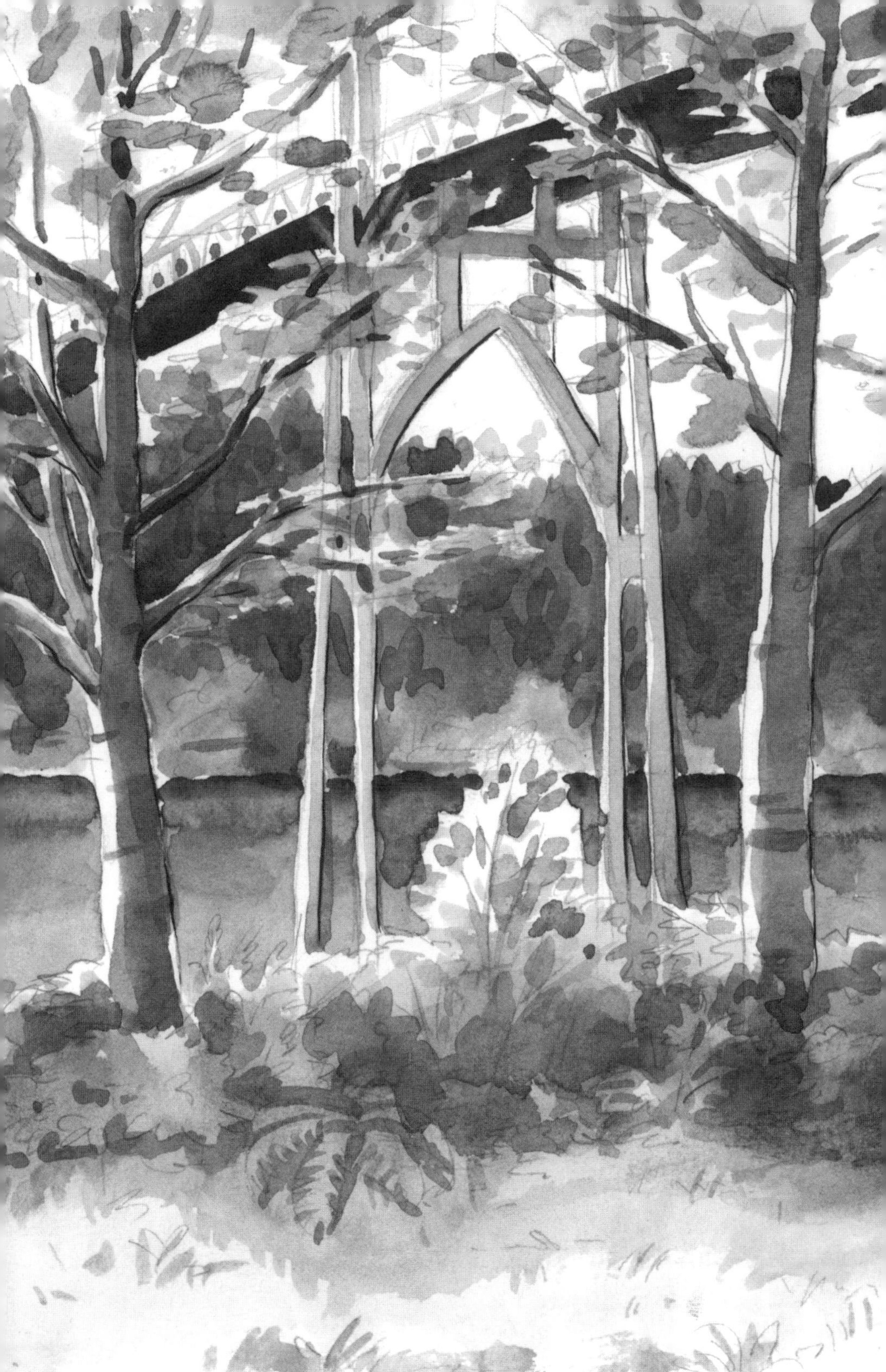

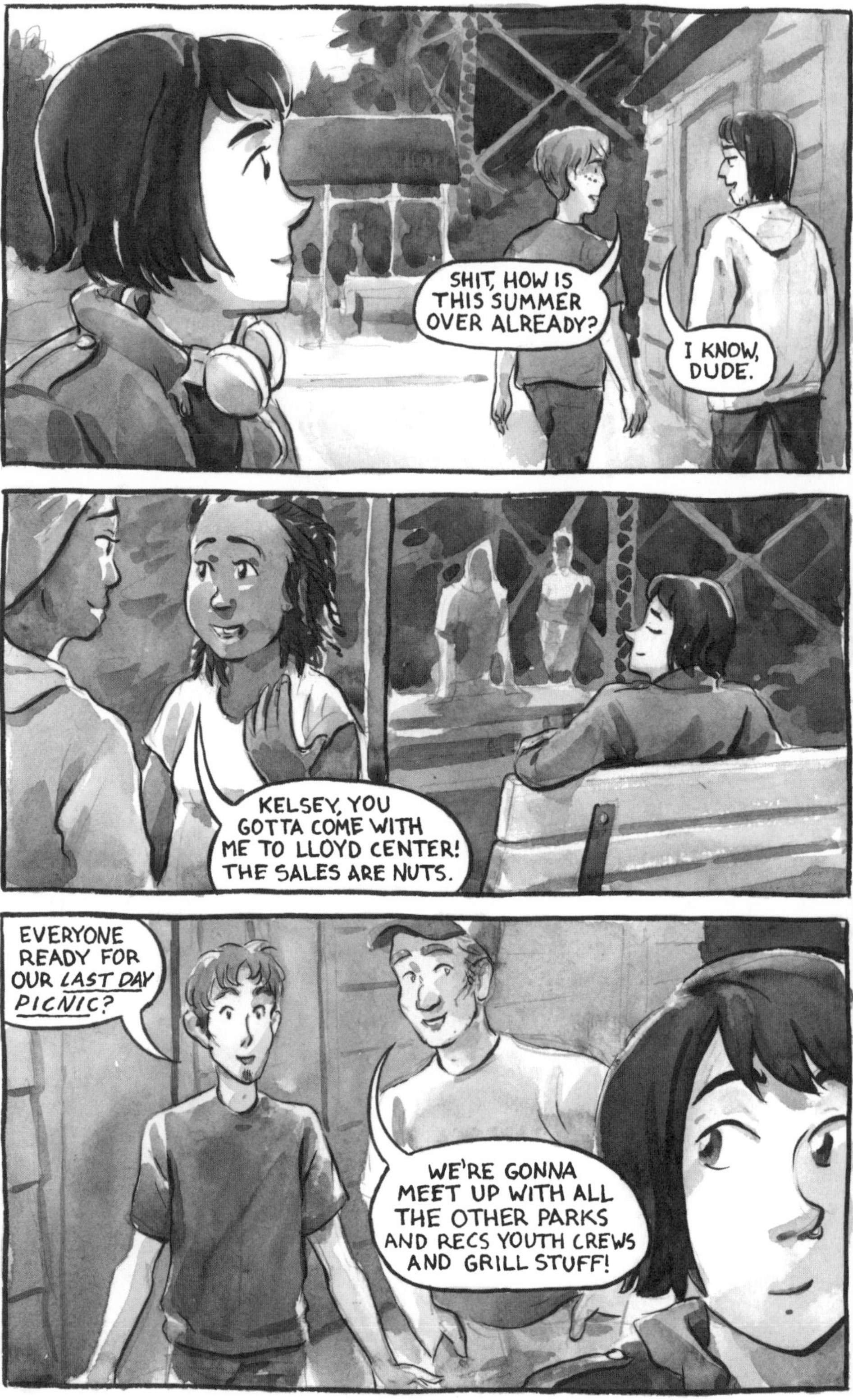
SHIT, HOW IS THIS SUMMER OVER ALREADY?
I KNOW, DUDE.
KELSEY, YOU GOTTA COME WITH ME TO LLOYD CENTER! THE SALES ARE NUTS.
EVERYONE READY FOR OUR *LAST DAY PICNIC*?
WE'RE GONNA MEET UP WITH ALL THE OTHER PARKS AND RECS YOUTH CREWS AND GRILL STUFF!

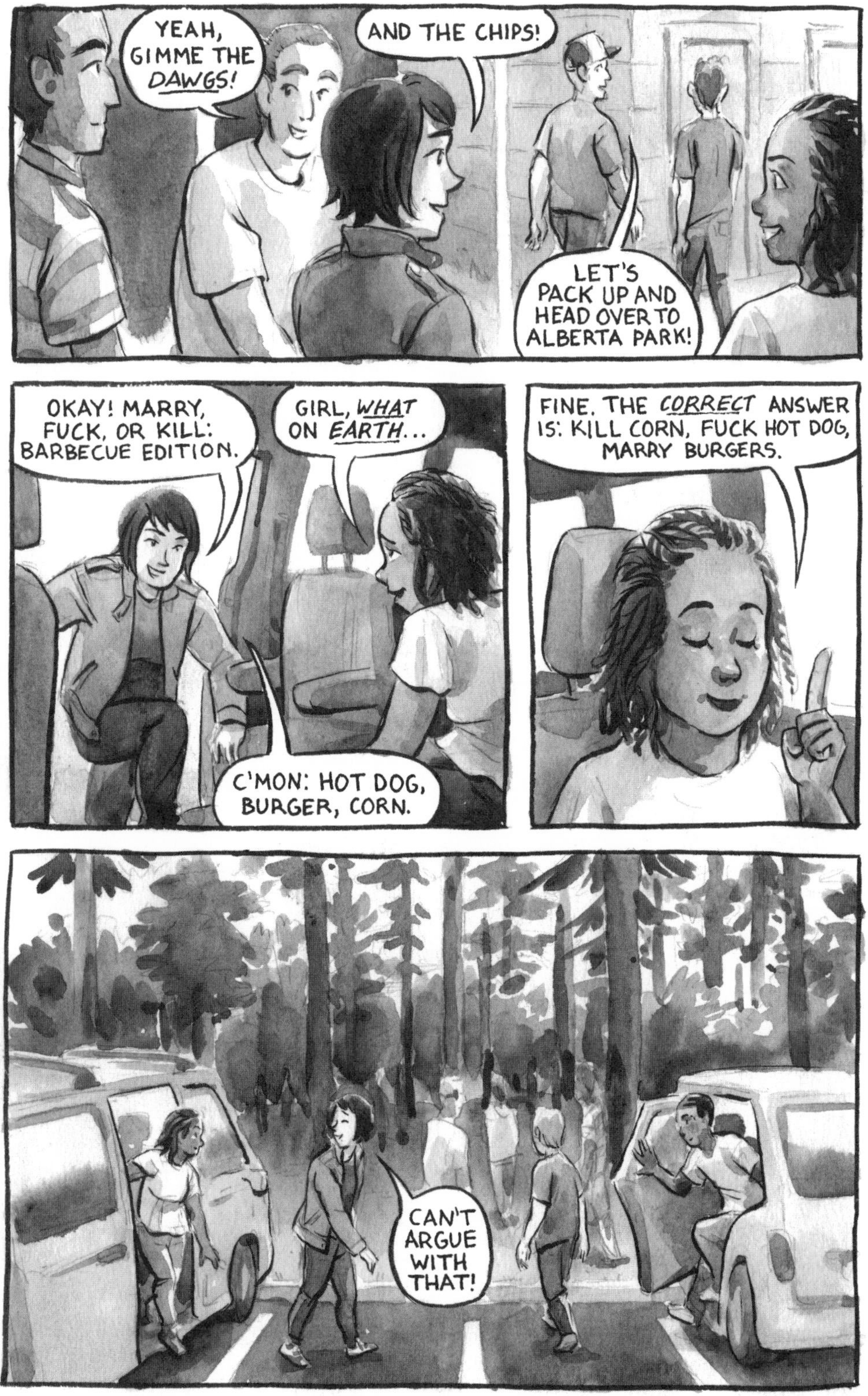
YEAH, GIMME THE DAWGS!
AND THE CHIPS!
LET'S PACK UP AND HEAD OVER TO ALBERTA PARK!
OKAY! MARRY, FUCK, OR KILL: BARBECUE EDITION.
GIRL, WHAT ON EARTH...
C'MON: HOT DOG, BURGER, CORN.
FINE. THE CORRECT ANSWER IS: KILL CORN, FUCK HOT DOG, MARRY BURGERS.
CAN'T ARGUE WITH THAT!

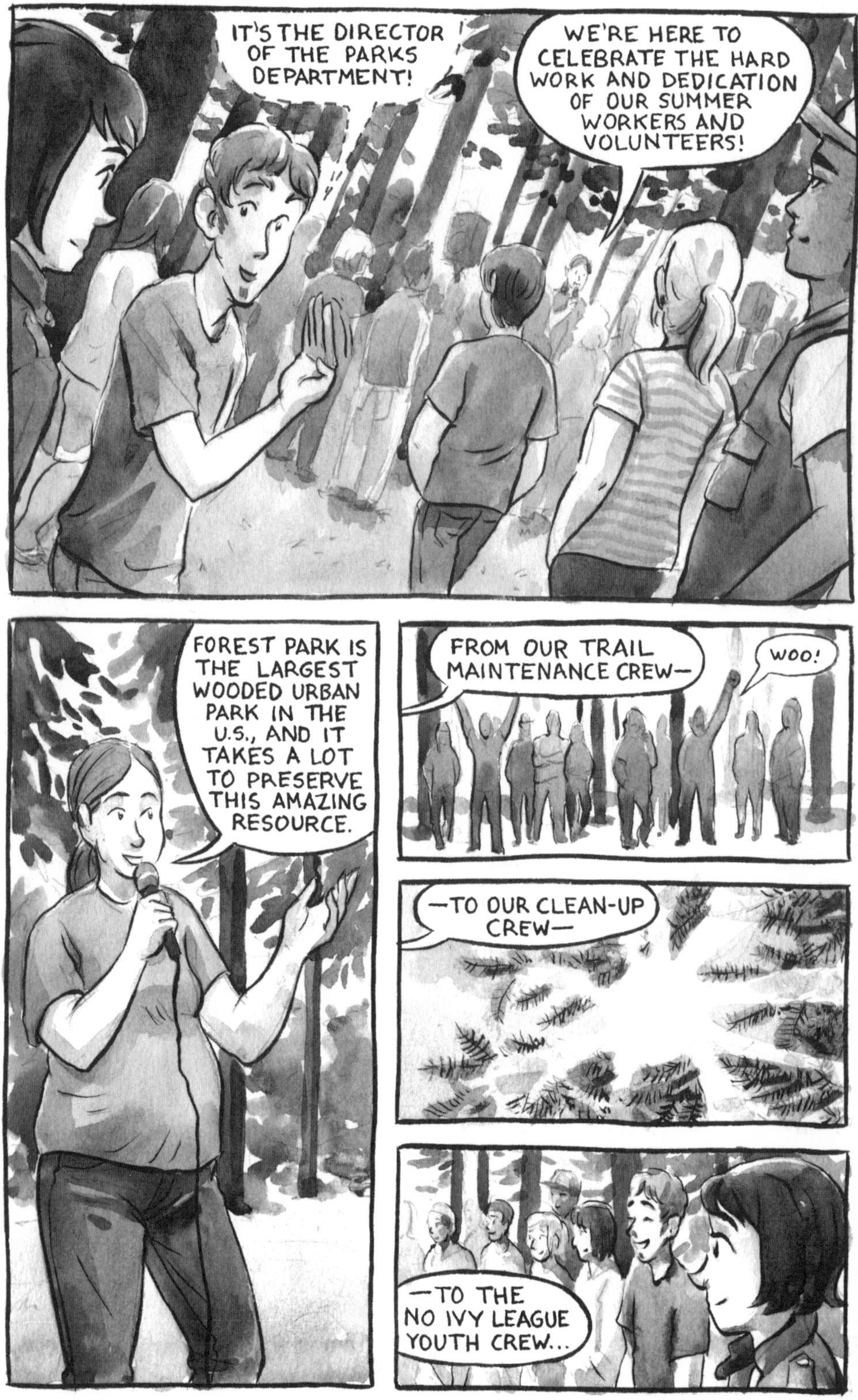
IT'S THE DIRECTOR OF THE PARKS DEPARTMENT!
WE'RE HERE TO CELEBRATE THE HARD WORK AND DEDICATION OF OUR SUMMER WORKERS AND VOLUNTEERS!
FOREST PARK IS THE LARGEST WOODED URBAN PARK IN THE U.S., AND IT TAKES A LOT TO PRESERVE THIS AMAZING RESOURCE.
FROM OUR TRAIL MAINTENANCE CREW—
WOO!
—TO OUR CLEAN-UP CREW—
—TO THE NO IVY LEAGUE YOUTH CREW...

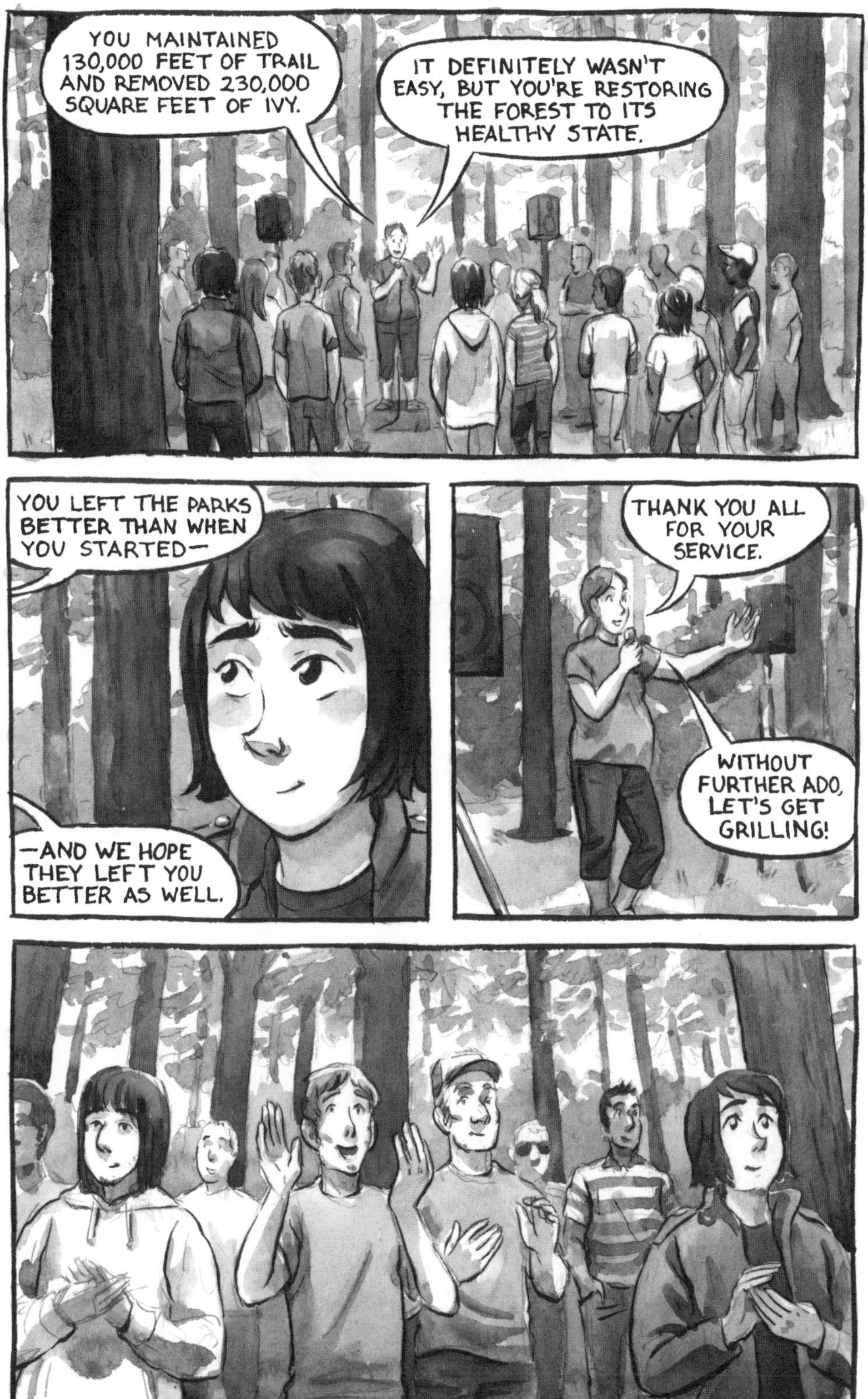
YOU MAINTAINED 130,000 FEET OF TRAIL AND REMOVED 230,000 SQUARE FEET OF IVY.
IT DEFINITELY WASN'T EASY, BUT YOU'RE RESTORING THE FOREST TO ITS HEALTHY STATE.
YOU LEFT THE PARKS BETTER THAN WHEN YOU STARTED—
—AND WE HOPE THEY LEFT YOU BETTER AS WELL.
THANK YOU ALL FOR YOUR SERVICE.
WITHOUT FURTHER ADO, LET'S GET GRILLING!

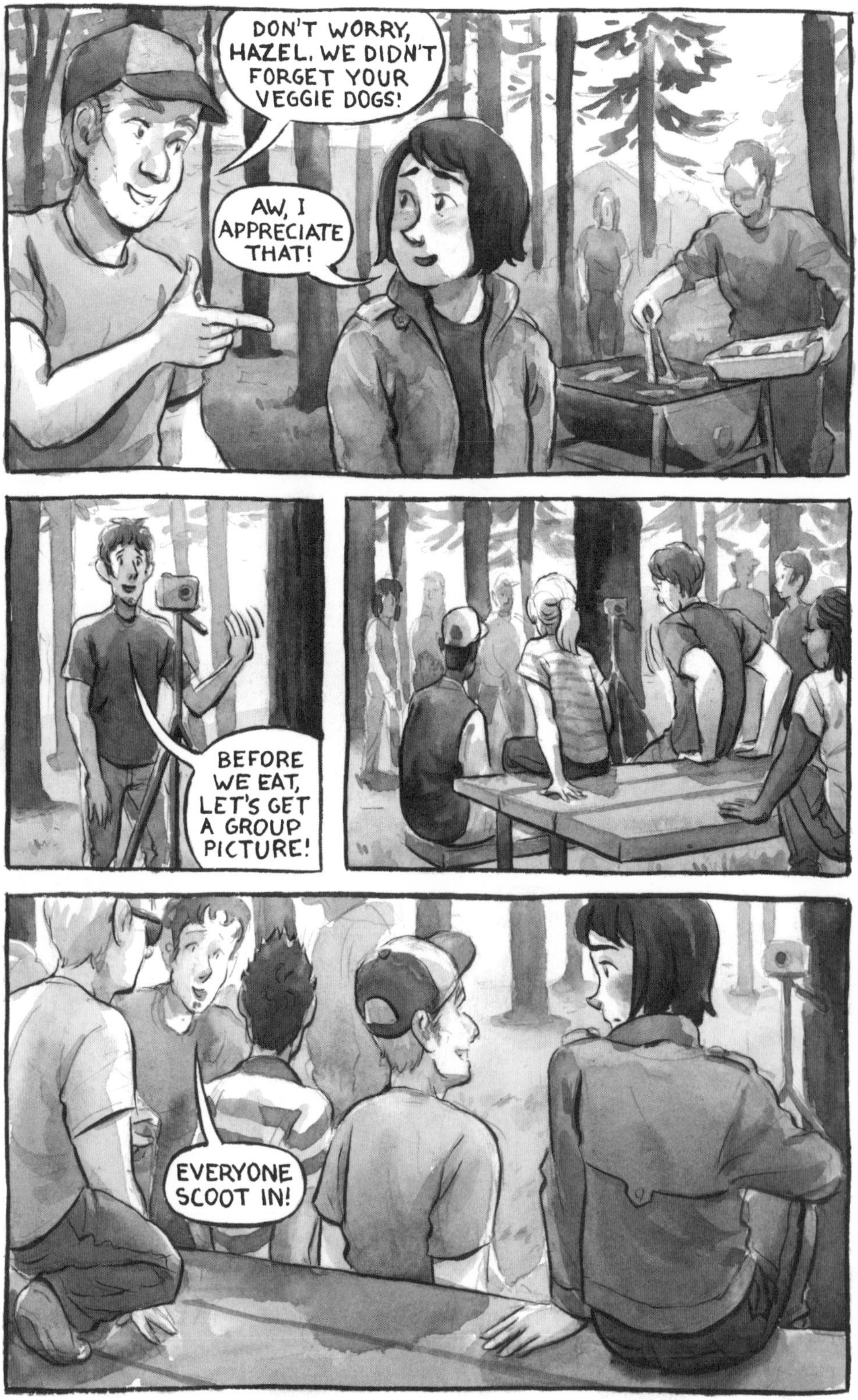
DON'T WORRY, HAZEL. WE DIDN'T FORGET YOUR VEGGIE DOGS!
AW, I APPRECIATE THAT!
BEFORE WE EAT, LET'S GET A GROUP PICTURE!
EVERYONE SCOOT IN!

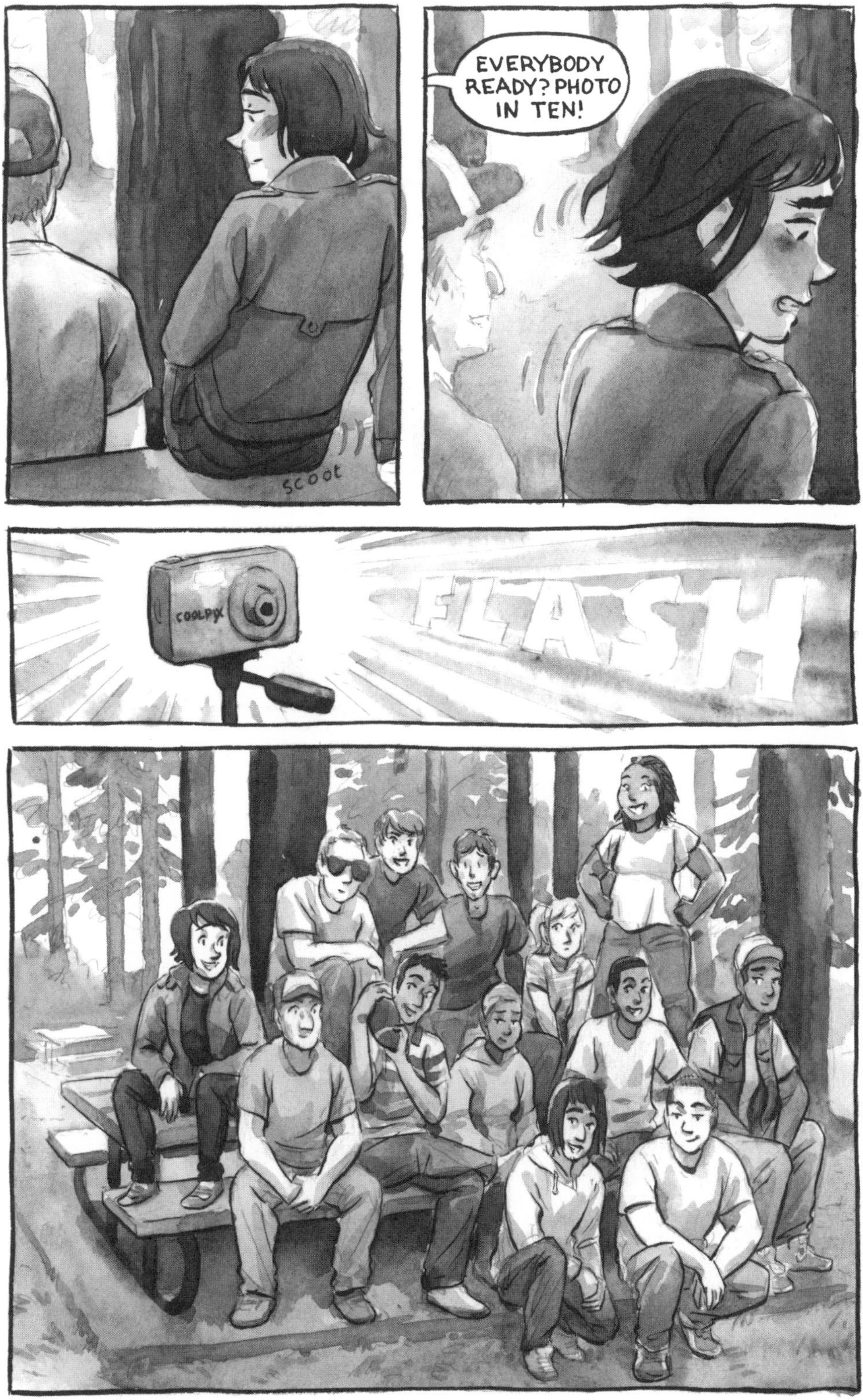
scoot
EVERYBODY READY? PHOTO IN TEN!
COOLPIX
FLASH

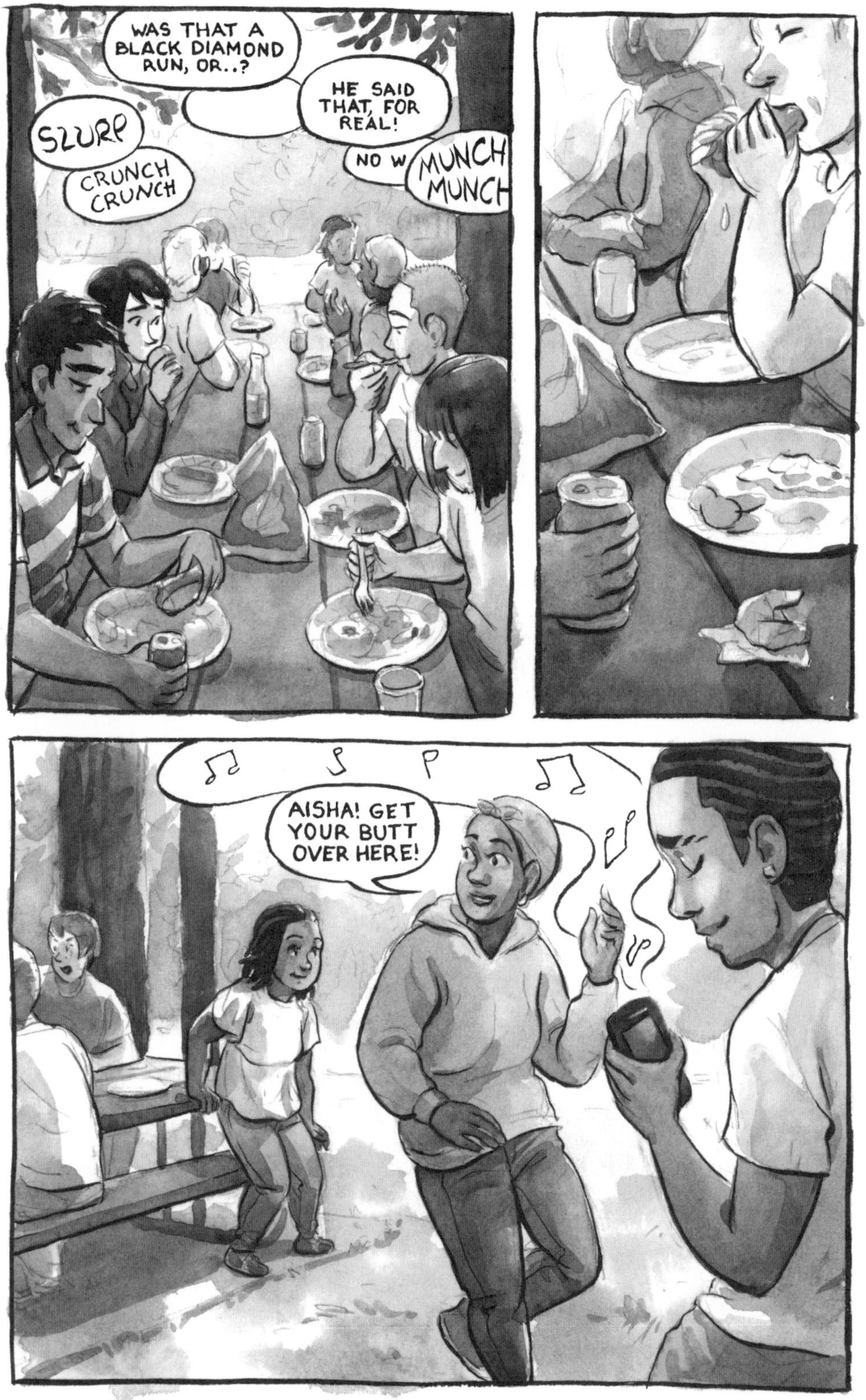
WAS THAT A BLACK DIAMOND RUN, OR..?
HE SAID THAT, FOR REAL!
SLURP
CRUNCH CRUNCH
NO W
MUNCH MUNCH
AISHA! GET YOUR BUTT OVER HERE!

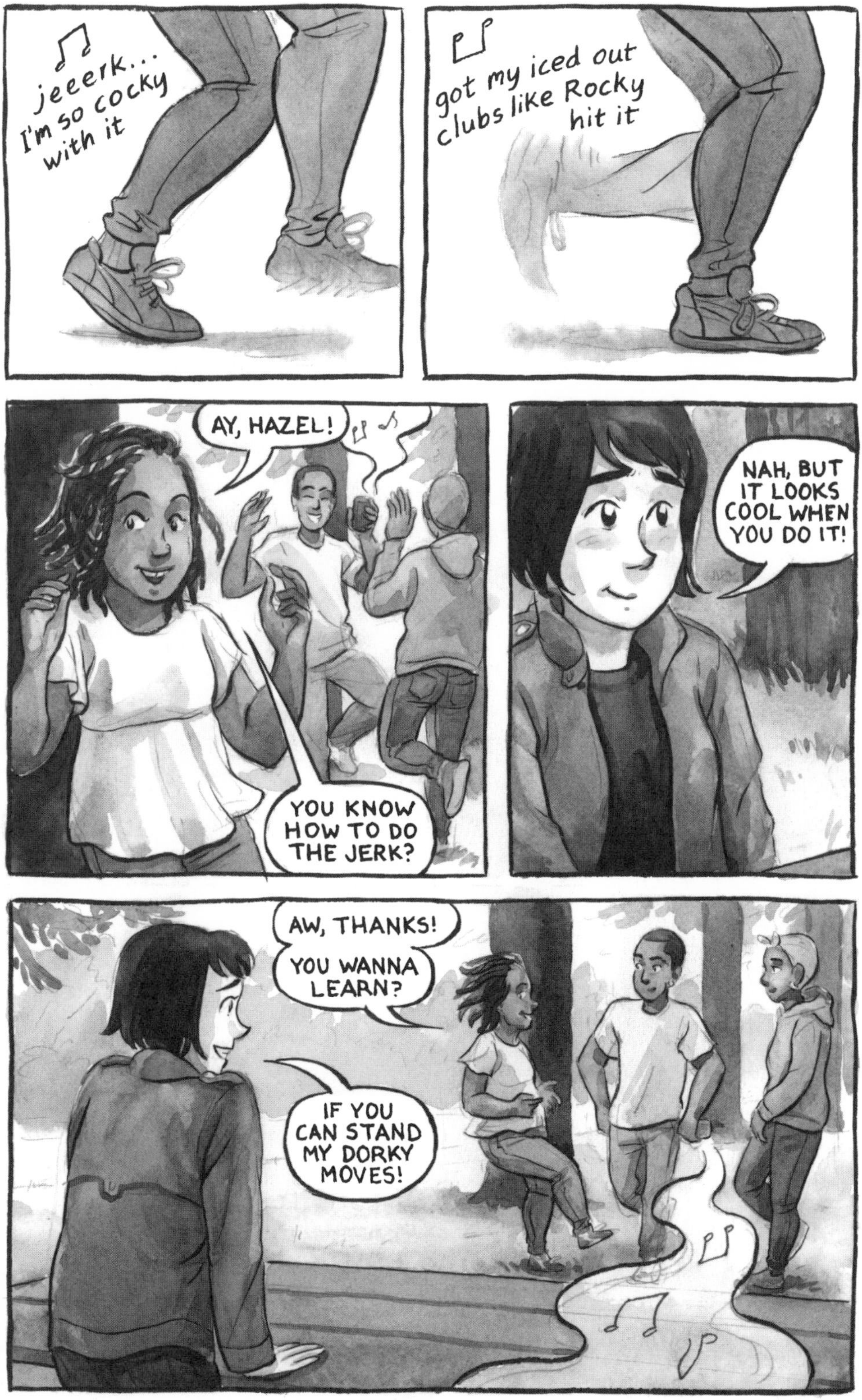
jeeerk... I'm so cocky with it
got my iced out clubs like Rocky hit it
AY, HAZEL!
YOU KNOW HOW TO DO THE JERK?
NAH, BUT IT LOOKS COOL WHEN YOU DO IT!
AW, THANKS!
YOU WANNA LEARN?
IF YOU CAN STAND MY DORKY MOVES!

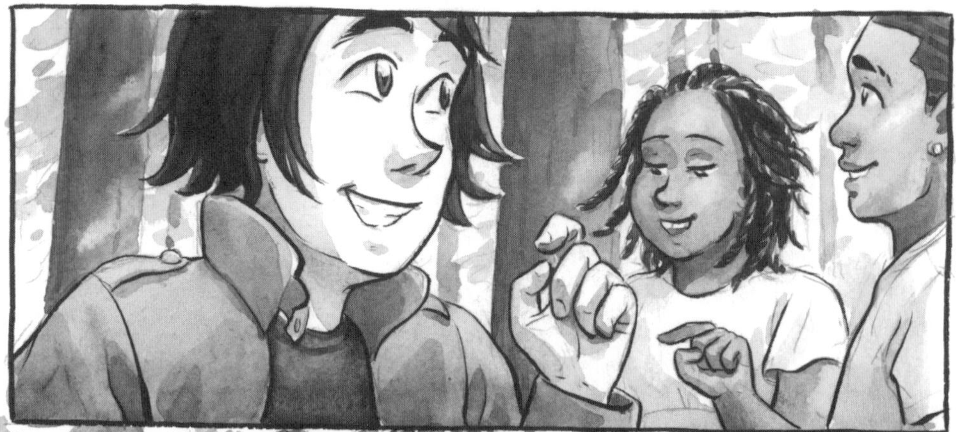

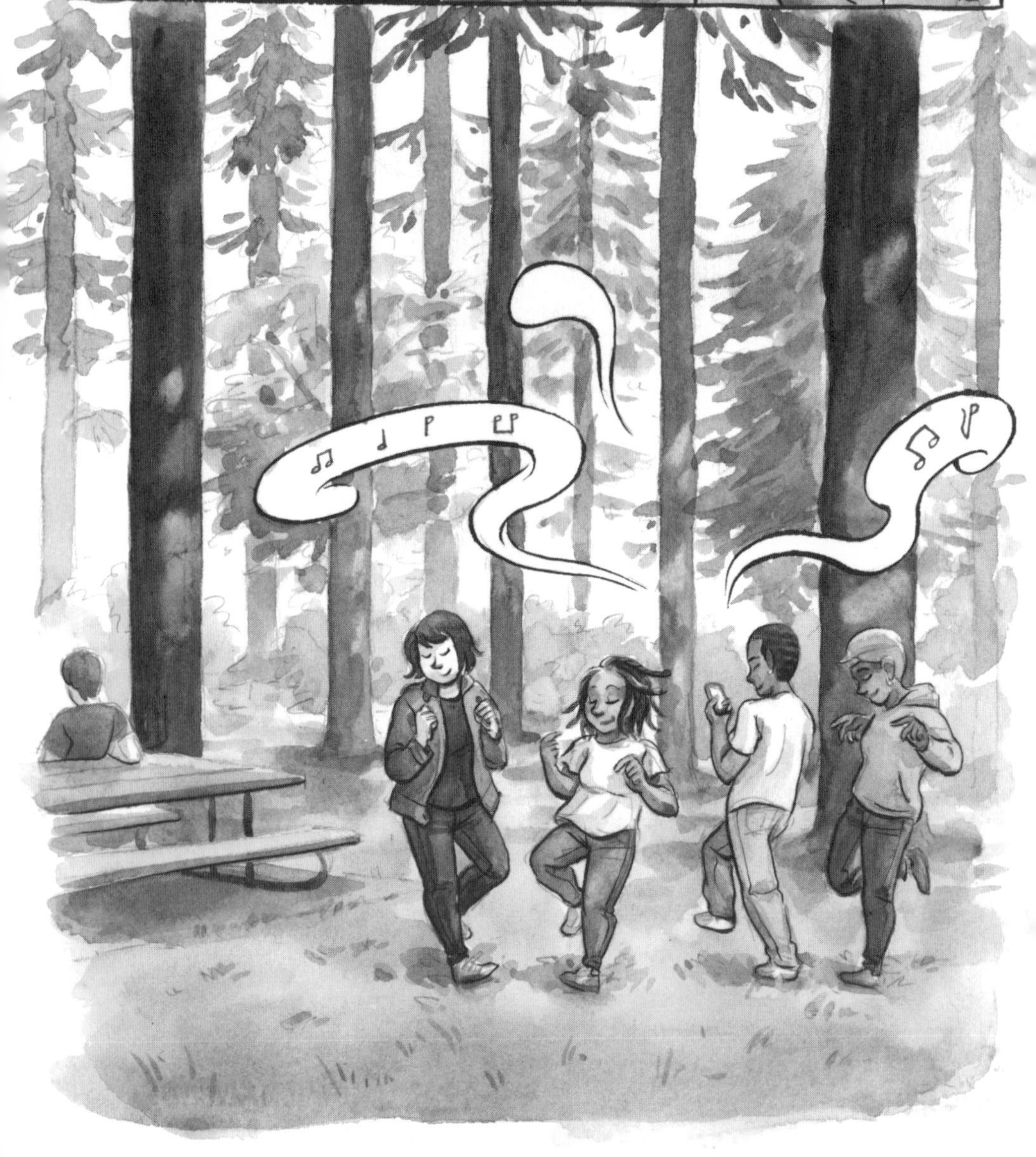

THE END

SPECIAL THANKS TO...

My parents, whose love buoys me up, and who have always encouraged and supported my art-making.

Jordan Michael Iannucci, who invited me to draw a series of minicomics for him to publish, and encouraged me to develop *No Ivy League*.

Ahren Swanson, who helped me take reference photos of Forest Park, and whose friendship is a cherished connection between my past and present.

George O'Connor, the original #1 fan of this comic, who I was always thrilled to share thumbnails with.

My agent, Tanya McKinnon, who believed in the importance of a coming-of-age story about reckoning with white privilege, and offered me a metric ton of story feedback.

Andrea Colvin, who brought the graphic novel to Lion Forge, and pushed me to include more about homeschooling, which added an essential layer to the story.

Christina "Steenz" Stewart, who gave me an excellent critical reading and helped me not fall flat on my face when inventing AAVE dialogue.

Robin Enrico and EMi Spicer, who gave me artistic feedback, emotional support, and were very patient with me doing less than my share of the chores while finishing this book.

Gretchen Felker-Martin, my constant companion, who has helped me in more ways than I can say.

Without everyone's advocacy, support, and critical feedback, *No Ivy League* wouldn't be the book it turned out to be, or wouldn't exist at all.

AUTHOR'S NOTE

This book is about a pivotal summer in my life. It poked a hole in my familiar bubbles and complicated my understanding of the world. It was a multi-car pileup of race, class, gender, and teen hormones. I started working on *No Ivy League* five years after the events that inspired it. Now, as I finish the book, it's been a decade. I thought I started out with a complete and mature understanding of my past. It's incredible, believing over and over again that you've figured things out—only to stumble on new ways your place in society shields you from the truth. I didn't really know anything. Maybe I still don't.

How true-to-life is this memoir? All the characters' names have been changed aside from my own. Most of the dialogue isn't remembered word-for-word, except in the most emotionally searing moments, which I remember clearly and I've tried to convey accurately. I wish that I could fully know and paint a picture of the experiences of my friends, my coworkers, and my parents—everyone who's been transmuted into a character in my own coming-of-age narrative. But I won't pretend that I can. Taking the reader into the feelings I was grappling with is the truest way I can tell the story.

It was a hard summer. In many ways it destroyed my image of myself as a fundamentally "good," "well-liked" person, but grappling with those experiences has helped me become the somewhat better person I am today.

It's intimidating to publish a story about my younger self doing and saying so many profoundly embarrassing and regrettable things, but I hope that it helps those who see their own shame reflected in mine resolve to move forward with compassion.

—Hazel

MY PROCESS

I started by drawing all my co-workers from memory and coming up with appropriate pseudonyms. (None of these are their real names.) When I looked at photos from that summer, I realized I'd forgotten quite a few people! But I continued to leave them out, because they didn't play a role in my story.

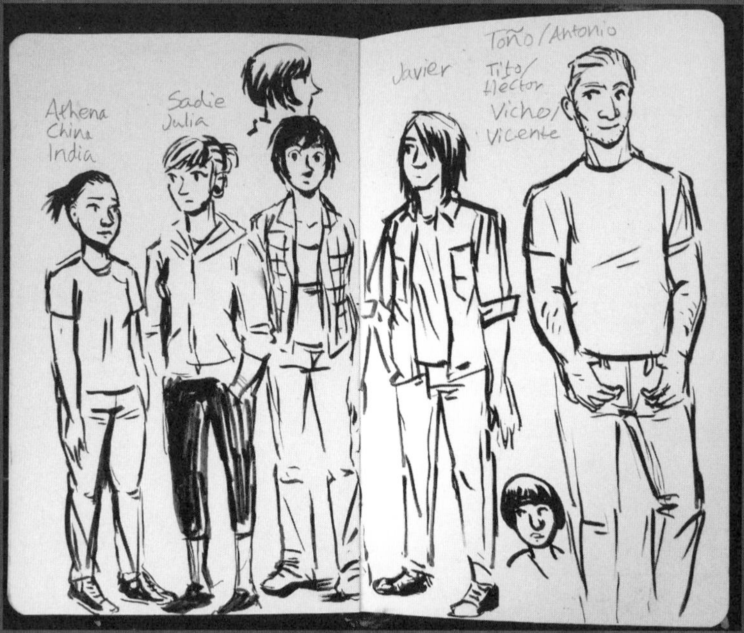

Athena
China
India
Sadie
Julia
Javier
Toño/Antonio
Tito/
Hector
Vicho/
Vicente

I brainstormed memories of the job and jotted them on index cards so I could reorder them. Sometimes I'd include an associated visual.

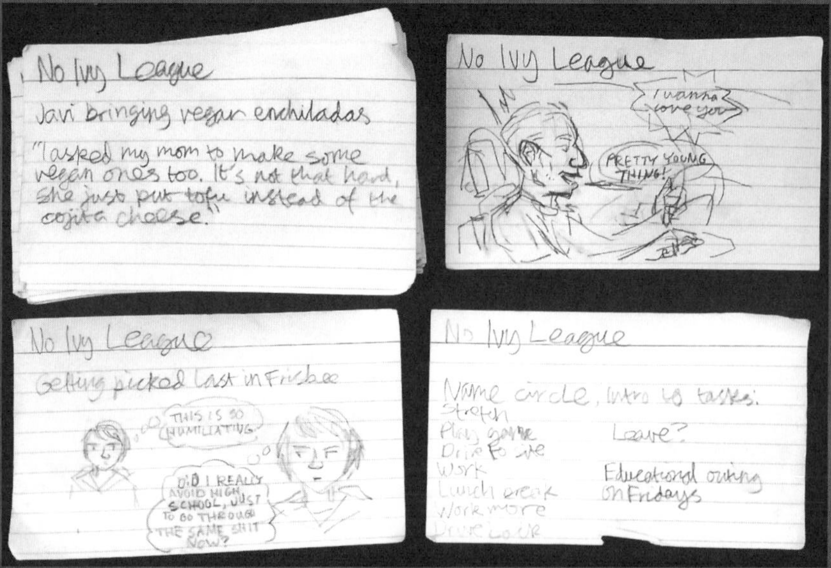

No Ivy League
Javi bringing vegan enchiladas
"I asked my mom to make some vegan ones too. It's not that hard, she just put tofu instead of the cojita cheese."
No Ivy League
I wanna love you
PRETTY YOUNG THING!
No Ivy League
Getting picked last in Frisbee
THIS IS SO HUMILIATING
DID I REALLY AVOID HIGH SCHOOL, JUST TO GO THROUGH THE SAME SHIT NOW?
No Ivy League
Name circle, intro to tasks:
Stretch
Play game
Drive to site
Work
Lunch break
Work more
Drive back
Leave?
Educational outing on Fridays

Next, I started "thumbnailing" pages (doing smaller, rough sketches) in Moleskine notebooks and on printer paper folded in half. I don't write scripts first, because I enjoy drawing much more than writing dialogue, and prefer to come up with page layouts, writing, and expressions as one.

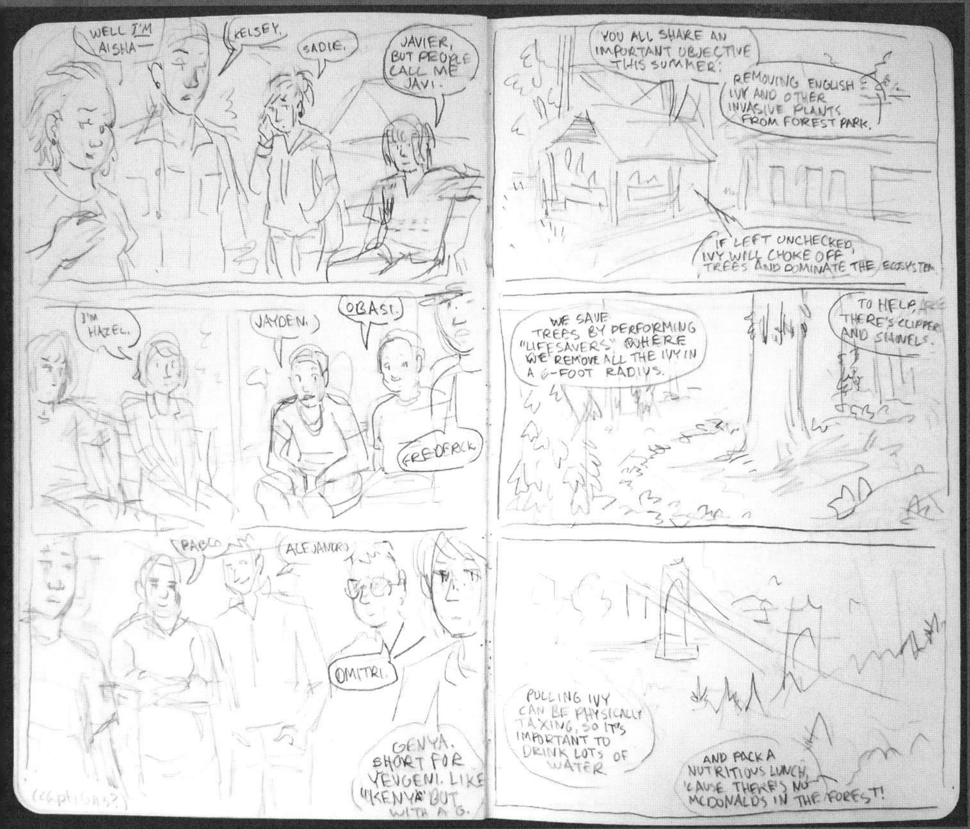

WELL I'M AISHA—
KELSEY.
SADIE.
JAVIER, BUT PEOPLE CALL ME JAVI.
I'M HAZEL.
JAYDEN.
OBASI.
FREDERICK.
PABLO.
ALEJANDRO.
DMITRI.
GENYA. SHORT FOR YEVGENI. LIKE "KENYA" BUT WITH A G.
YOU ALL SHARE AN IMPORTANT OBJECTIVE THIS SUMMER:
REMOVING ENGLISH IVY AND OTHER INVASIVE PLANTS FROM FOREST PARK.
IF LEFT UNCHECKED, IVY WILL CHOKE OFF TREES AND DOMINATE THE ECOSYSTEM.
WE SAVE TREES BY PERFORMING "LIFESAVERS" WHERE WE REMOVE ALL THE IVY IN A 6-FOOT RADIUS.
TO HELP, THERE'S CLIPPERS AND SHOVELS.
PULLING IVY CAN BE PHYSICALLY TAXING, SO IT'S IMPORTANT TO DRINK LOTS OF WATER.
AND PACK A NUTRITIOUS LUNCH, 'CAUSE THERE'S NO MCDONALDS IN THE FOREST!

My goal was to include enough detail in the thumbnails for them to be comprehensible to others. This was the stage at which I shared the work with friends and editors to get their feedback. I often ended up adding new scenes between existing ones, rewriting dialogue, replacing panels, and occasionally re-thumbnailing pages entirely.

Then, I made enlarged photocopies of my thumbnails and used an LED light box to transfer them onto watercolor paper, refining the pencils as I did.

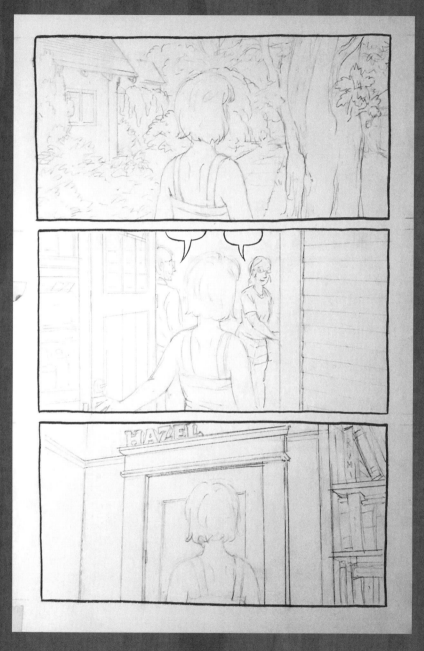

I inked the panel borders and word balloons with a brush and waterproof India ink, inked any lettering with a Micron pen, and erased the pencils underneath.

Next, I started applying broad areas of tone with black watercolor paint. (This book reproduces my grayscale original art with a dark green Pantone ink.)

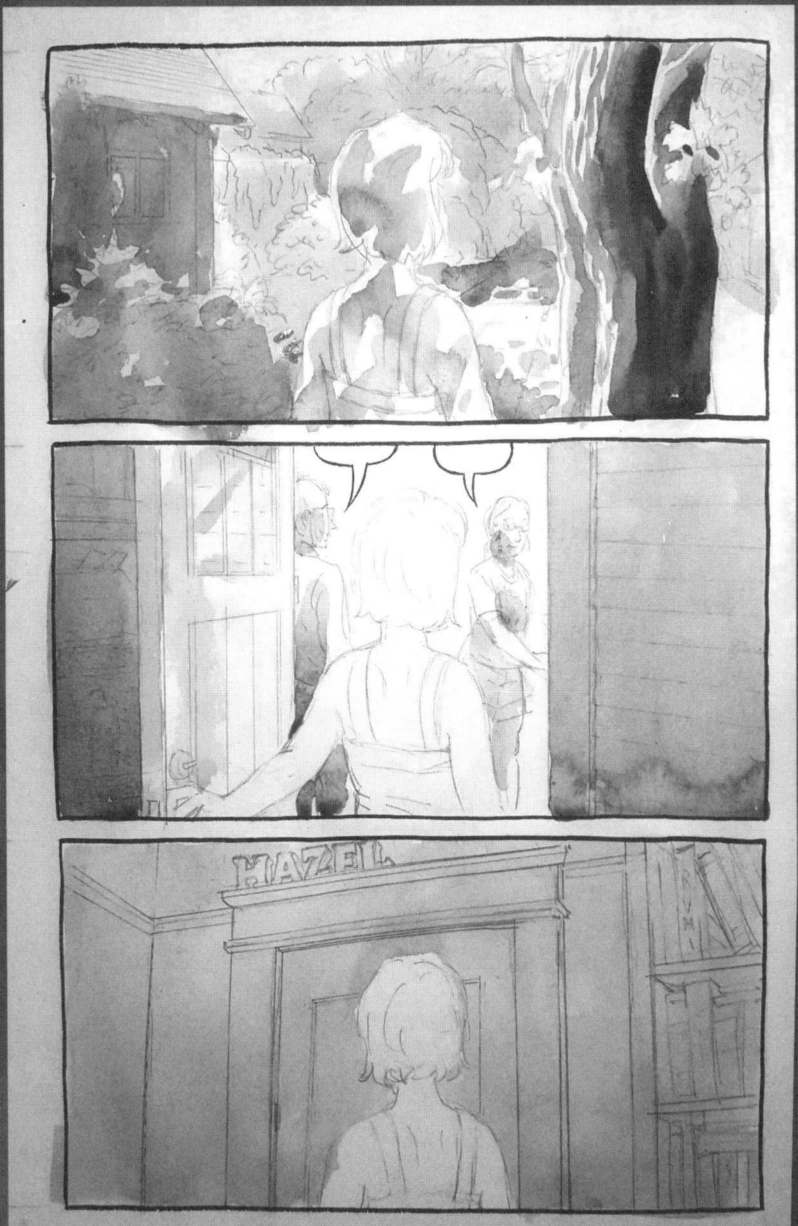
HAZEL

I tried (and usually failed) to use as few layers of watercolor as possible. The texture of a single layer of watercolor wash looks really nice, and it's easy to muck it up by overworking it.

Nearly completed watercolors!

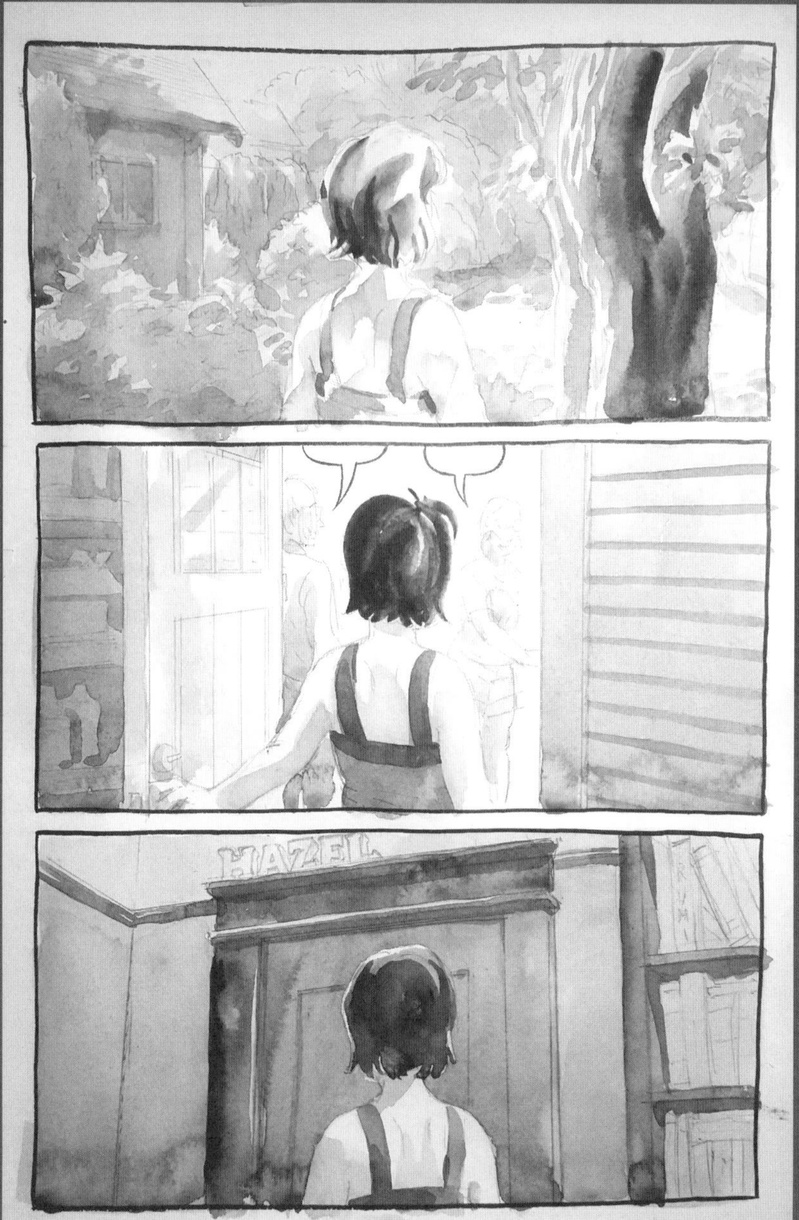
HAZEL

After finishing the watercolors, I inked a few things with a brush: characters, objects in the foreground, and anything that needed a bit more definition.

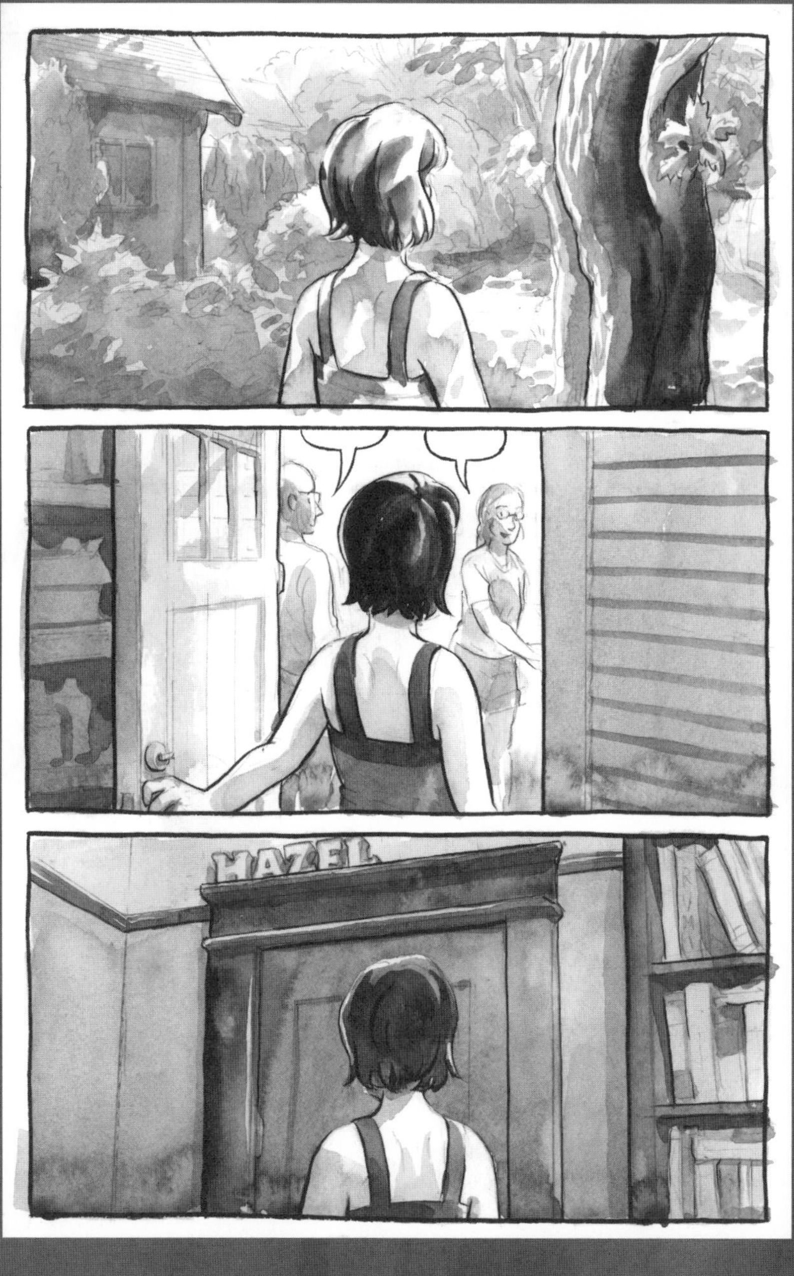
HAZEL

Lastly, I scanned the pages, used Photoshop to perfect the brightness and contrast, and cleaned up the panel borders and lettering, and that's it!

ROAR™

Quoted material on page 172: From *Hidden History of Portland, Oregon* by JD Chandler, copyright (c) 2013. Reprinted by permission of Arcadia Publishing and The History Press.

Quoted material on page 173: From *Why Are All the Black Kids Sitting Together in the Cafeteria?: And Other Conversations About Race* by Beverly Daniel Tatum, copyright © 1997, 1999, 2003, 2017. Reprinted by permission of Basic Books, an imprint of Hachette Book Group, Inc.

ISBN: 978-1-5493-0305-0
Library of Congress Control Number: 2018941127